REVIEWS FOR *BEYOND THE REFLECTION'S EDGE*

Action, intrigue, and take-home value—the very essence of a powerful story.

—Wayne Thomas Batson, Author of
The Door Within Trilogy, Isle of Swords, and Isle of Fire

... a sci-fi thriller, packed with action & adventure, that hurtles along at top speed from beginning to end.

—L.B. Graham, Author of *The Binding of the Blade* series

Davis so starkly contrasts good and evil amid a unique inter-dimensional mystery, the readers are left feeling that they received a glimpse of the pure love of Christ.

—Scott Appleton, Author & Editor for *MindFlights Magazine*

... a tale of families and friends bound by love and faith in the midst of scientific discoveries that could change creation for the better ... or the worse. A great read.

—Jason Waguespack,
The World of Rigel Chase: Legend of the Shaper

A true masterpiece worthy to be played before the Great Composer himself.

—C. Schlamp, Age 15

This is one book where even before you read the first page you'll need to buckle your seat belt and hang on for dear life!

—L. A. Clark, Age 17

... this latest story is not only Bryan Davis' best yet, it is by far the best novel that I have read to date.

—S. Baird, Age 19

Full of high adventure and spiritual truth, *Beyond the Reflection's Edge* had me spellbound from the first page to the last.

—T. Sasse, Age 17

... a beautiful, captivating story of genuine love, blended with plenty of action, adventure, and suspense. An absolute must read!

—M. Puckett, Age 22

Filled with unforgettable characters, intense action, and heart-wrenching moments, this book is a must read.

—T. Bowers, Age 15

... an amazing story of fantasy, adventure, and an unparalleled exploration that will keep you turning pages until you're done.

—C. Rochester, Age 16

The detail and complexity are amazing! Everything fits together like a puzzle just waiting to be solved.

—R. Hagan, Age 15

... just as powerful, action-packed, and deep as Dragons in Our Midst and Oracles of Fire. I can't wait to read the next one!

—C. Wolters, Age 26

A stunning tale, alternately chilling and tender ... a must read!

—J. Fulcher, Age 15

... an action-packed, fast-moving plot that both held me captive and challenged his characters. I can't wait to see what happens in Book Two.

—C. Shupe, Age 27

... a heartwarming and action-filled adventure that will keep you reading and asking for more when you are finished.

—J. De Reus, Age 16

On a scale of 1–10, this book is a definite 20!

—L. Lee, Age 11

ECHOES FROM THE EDGE

BEYOND THE REFLECTION'S EDGE

Pronunciation Guide:
Mictar — Mis-tawr'
Patar — Paw-tar'

ECHOES FROM THE EDGE

BEYOND THE REFLECTION'S EDGE

BRYAN DAVIS

ZONDERVAN®

ZONDERVAN.com/
AUTHORTRACKER
follow your favorite authors

ZONDERVAN®

Beyond the Reflection's Edge
Copyright © 2008 by Bryan Davis

Requests for information should be addressed to:

Zondervan, *Grand Rapids, Michigan 49530*

Library of Congress Cataloging-in-Publication Data: Applied for
ISBN 978-0-310-71554-2

Interior design by Christine Orejuela-Winkelman

Art direction by Michelle Lenger

Printed in the United States of America

08 09 10 11 12 • 23 22 21 20 19 18 17 16 15 14 13 12 11 10 9 8 7 6 5 4 3 2 1

ECHOES FROM THE EDGE

BEYOND THE REFLECTION'S EDGE

When images of the mind stretch beyond what we can see with our eyes, then the portals open, allowing us to view the face of God. As I searched for portals in my dreams, my son dreamed with me and found a golden key within a mirror. Thank you, Josiah, for being a reflection of God's image and helping me unlock another door to the beyond.

1

THE FIRST SIGN

Nathan watched his tutor peer out the window. She was being paranoid again. That guy following them in the Mustang had really spooked her. "Chill out, Clara. He doesn't know what room we're in."

She slid the curtains together, casting a blanket of darkness across the motel room. "He parked near the lobby entrance. We'd better pack up and leave another way." She clicked on a corner table lamp. The pale light seemed to deepen the wrinkles on her face and hands. "How much more time do you need?"

Nathan sat on the bed nearer the window, a stack of pillows between his back and the wall, and tapped away at his laptop. "Just a couple of minutes." He looked up at her and winked. "Dad's slide rule must've been broken. It took almost an hour to balance the books."

Clara slid her sweater sleeve up an inch and glared at her wristwatch. Nathan knew that look all too well. His tutor's steely eyes and furrowed brow meant the Queen of Punctuality was counting the minutes. They were cutting it close, and they still had to get the reports bound at Kinko's before they could meet his parents at the performance hall for the company's quarterly meeting. And who could tell what delays that goon in the prowling Mustang might cause? His father had noticed the guy this morning before he left, and he looked kind of worried, but that could've been from the bean and onion burrito he had eaten for breakfast.

Nathan frowned at the spreadsheet. "This formula doesn't make sense. Dad's trying to divide by zero."

"Can you call and ask him on the way? We have to hit the road."

Nathan pushed the laptop to the side. He knew how his father would respond. He'd just grin and say, "Dividing by zero reflects my creativity." Nathan laughed. Dad knew a lot more about math than he ever let on; he just concentrated on spying and research and let Nathan do the number crunching.

As Clara peered out again, he looked over her shoulder. The driver of the black Mustang was parked under a tree, sloppily eating a sandwich as he watched the front door of the motel. An intermittent shower of leaves, blown around by Chicago's never-ending breezes, danced about on the convertible's ragtop.

"Don't worry about him," Nathan said. "He's too obvious to be a pro."

"True enough. But you don't have to be a pro to frighten an old lady."

As she turned toward him, he gave her the goofiest clueless stare he could conjure. "I'm not an old lady!"

He waited for Clara's infectious laugh that had brightened a hundred mornings in dozens of strange and lonely cities all over the world. But it didn't come. A shadow of worry passed across her face, draining the color from her cheeks.

He squinted at her. "Something else is bugging you."

For a moment, she just stared, a faraway look in her eyes. Finally, she shook her head as if casting off a dream. "Did you pack the mirror your father gave you?"

"I think so." He jumped up and walked over both beds before bouncing to the floor in front of the shallow closet. A towel-wrapped bundle sat on top of his suitcase at the very peak of a haphazard pile of clothes. Carefully unfolding the towel, he revealed a square, six-by-six-inch mirror with an ornate silver frame. His father had entrusted this mirror to him just yesterday, calling it a "Quattro" viewer and warning him to keep it safe.

Nathan pondered the strange word that represented his father's latest assignment, something about retrieving stolen data for a company that used reflective technology. Dad had been tight-lipped about the details, but he had leaked enough clues to allow for guessing.

He gazed at his reflection in the mirror, the familiar portrait he expected, but something bright pulsed in his eyes, like the split-second flash of a camera. Clara's face appeared just above his blond cowlick, suddenly much closer.

He spun his head around. Strange. She was still near the window. When he turned back to the mirror, her image was no longer there.

As she walked up behind him, her face reappeared in the glass. Nathan glanced back and forth between the mirror and Clara. The inconsistent images were just too weird.

The opening notes of Beethoven's Fifth chimed from his computer—his custom sound for new email. Still holding the mirror, he leaped back to his computer and pulled up the message, a note from his father.

> Your mother is rehearsing with Nikolai, and that reminded me to remind you that she's going to call you to the stage to play your duet for the shareholders. She'll have your violin, all tuned and ready to sizzle. Since it's the Vivaldi piece, you shouldn't have any problem. Just don't mention your performance to Dr. Simon. Trust me. It will all work out.

Two words embedded in Nathan's mind, *Trust me*, the same words he had heard so many times before. With all the narrow escapes his father had engineered over the years, what else could he do but trust him?

Clara flung a pair of wadded gym socks that bounced off his chin. "Where is your tux?" she called as she searched through his crumpled clothes.

"I hung it on the shower rod." He patted a shiny motorcycle helmet sitting on his night table. He had hoped to ride their Harleys through town. With Clara in her new dress and him in a tux, they would've looked as cool as ice. But, no, they had to hitch a ride in the company limo. With their chauffeur, Mike, at the wheel, they'd be better off in a hearse. He wouldn't do more than thirty, even in a forty-five zone.

Clara disappeared into the bathroom and returned in a flash, brushing lint from his tux. "Aren't you going to help me?"

"Sure." He picked up his elastic exercise strap and karate belt and threw them into the suitcase. They were essential items. Since his dad was planning to rent an RV for a month-long trip out West, with all that driving, he had to do something to stay in shape. They'd have a whole month with no wild getaways, no running from crazed neo-Nazis, no dodging bullets from Colombian drug dealers. Sometimes those scrapes with death gave him a rush, and decking a thug or two with a well-placed karate chop was always a thrill, but ... He gazed at his motorcycle helmet and let out a sigh. It was probably better to avoid trouble than to dance with it. That's what his father always said.

Clara peeked out the window again. "The driver just got out, and I think he saw me."

"Here we go again." Nathan slapped the suitcase closed and zipped it up. "You got an escape plan?"

She snatched up her own suitcase. "There's an emergency exit down the hall. I'll call Mike and tell him where to pick us up when we find a place that's not so dangerous."

Nathan tucked the computer under his arm and grabbed the strap of his red backpack. "Yeah, like ground zero at a nuclear test site."

●

As the sweet tones of a divinely played violin faded, applause exploded from the audience. Two hundred exquisitely dressed ladies and gentlemen leaped to their feet, volleying a hailstorm of "Bravos" toward the stage. A beautiful, raven-haired woman tucked her violin under her arm and bowed gracefully.

Her ivory face slowly reddened as the cheers rose to a climax, the scarlet hue a stark contrast to her satiny black gown. Her smile broadening, she focused her eyes on a man in the crowd, the tall gentleman standing next to Nathan — his father, Solomon Shepherd, clapping madly. His old Nikon camera bounced against his chest, dangling from a long strap.

While his mother's strings still sang in his ears, Nathan clapped until his hands ached. Would anyone ever match such a virtuoso performance? She bowed again, now laughing joyfully at the adulation. Nathan clapped even harder, his heart leaping into his throat as he added a loud "Brava!" His own mother, Francesca Shepherd, the greatest violinist in the world!

When the applause finally settled and everyone took their seats, Nathan noticed a change in his mother's countenance. She glanced around the stage, two familiar worry lines now etching her brow as her cheeks paled.

Nathan looked at his father. On his opposite side, Dr. Simon, short and bald with owl-like eyeglasses, stared at a text message on his cell phone. Dr. Simon angled the tiny screen toward them, but it was too far away to read. He said with a hint of a British accent, "Mictar is on his way. There is no time to lose."

Tensing his jaw, Nathan's father lifted a hand and displayed four fingers. His mother nodded, then stepped forward, her long dress sweeping the platform. After pulling a microphone from its stand, she cleared her throat and spoke with a trembling voice. "Thank you, ladies and gentlemen. I'm overwhelmed by your response." She pointed her bow toward someone in Nathan's row about a dozen seats over. "I want to thank my first music teacher, Nikolai Malenkov, for being here today. Without him I would not be playing violin, nor would I even be alive. When my mother died, he took me into his home, and he and his dear wife gave every bit of love a grieving ten-year-old could ever want."

The crowd clapped again. His face beaming, Dr. Malenkov nodded, spilling his familiar unkempt gray hair over his signature large ears.

She turned toward Nathan. "I hope you have saved some warmth for our next performer, a young man who is on his way to stardom. I find no greater musical pleasure than to accompany him in our favorite duet."

His father leaned over and gave Nathan a one-armed hug. "Play your heart out, son, and never forget how much your mother and I love you."

As he returned the hug, Nathan peeked over his father's shoulder at Dr. Simon. The shorter man pursed his lips tightly but said nothing. Nathan whispered, "What's going on?"

"Please welcome," his mother continued, "my son, Nathan Shepherd."

Applause erupted again. His father pushed him back and gripped his shoulders firmly. A strange tremor rattled his voice. "Remember what I've taught you, and everything will be fine. If you ever get into big trouble, look in the mirror I gave you and focus on the point of danger. Nothing is more important."

Out of time to ask more, Nathan rose and headed toward the aisle on the right. As he squeezed past Clara's silk-covered knees, she patted his hand, her eyes glowing with pride. Her bright face, beautiful smile, and lovely white evening gown made her look half her age.

With his father's strange words echoing in his mind, Nathan felt as though he were floating outside his body, watching himself climb the four steps to his mother's level. The arched windows to his left cast filtered sunshine into his eyes as his shoes clicked along the hardwood stage.

When he drew near, his mother took his hand and pulled him close. She whispered in his ear and laid his violin and bow in the crook of his arm. "Just take a deep breath, my love, and follow my lead. Let your heart take over your hands, and your strings will sing with the angels." She kissed him on the cheek, then blew softly on his bow fingers, a ritual she began when he first took up the violin at the age of three. "To bless your playing," she had said. The warmth of her breath always calmed him down.

The audience quieted to a hush. Nathan raised the bow to the strings, his eyes locked on his mother's. He pressed his calloused fingers against the fingerboard, peeking out of the corner of his eye to catch his dad.

Strange. He was gone. And so was Dr. Simon.

Nathan shivered for a moment but refocused on his mother as she laid her own bow on her strings. With a long, lovely stroke, she began, her violin singing a sweet aria that begged for another voice to join it. As if playing unbidden, Nathan's hands flew into action, creating a river of musical ecstasy that flowed unhindered into the first stream of joy. The couplet of harmony joined in a celebration of life, part of Vivaldi's dream of four perfectly balanced seasons played as a sacred offering to their Creator.

His mother leaned close to him, as close as their vibrating bows would allow. As their strokes slowed, bending the music into a quiet refrain, she reached a rest in her part of the piece and whispered, "It is time for a very long solo, my love. Play it with all your heart." He glanced up at her, his fingers playing on their own. A tear inched down her cheek as she continued. "I will join you again when the composer commands me."

She backed away and lowered her bow. Nathan played on, closing his eyes as he reconstructed Vivaldi's theme, building measure upon measure until the composer sang spring into birth, new melodies sprouting forth from earth's womb in all their majesty.

His heart sang along. This was the best he had ever played

the piece, but he was glad it would soon be time for his mother to rejoin him, an arrangement they had created a dozen weeks ago to showcase his talents. But when the expected note from his mother didn't arrive, he flashed his eyes open, his bow scratching out a warped reflection of the notes.

Where was she? He laid his bow limply on the strings as he stared into the audience, scanning the dumbfounded faces row by row. His father's seat was still empty. Now Clara's was vacant as well. The auditorium seemed to swell in size, making him feel like a shrinking mouse, all alone up on stage with a toy violin and bow.

The onlookers buzzed with whispered words. Nikolai rose to his feet and pointed at a door to the side of the stage. "Your mother went that way, Nathan." He spoke in a kind, soothing voice. "Do you think she is ill?"

"I ... I don't think so." Nathan cleared his throat. Now he was even sounding like a mouse. "She didn't mention anything."

A muffled pop sounded. Nathan flinched. What could it have been? A blown circuit? But the lights were all still on.

The audience grew restless in the awkward silence. The side door opened, and Dr. Simon walked to center stage. After lowering a microphone stand to his level, he wrung his hands nervously. "Ladies and gentlemen," he called, his British accent now amplified, "please pardon the interruption. Nathan's parents had to leave unexpectedly. We will have a short break and then hear from our guest pianist." Shifting away from the microphone, he nodded toward Nathan. "Please come with me, and I will escort you home."

Nathan stayed put, staring blankly into the performance hall. As the audience filtered toward the back, a loud "Excuse me!" sounded from his left.

Clara stood at the side door Dr. Simon had just entered. "I will take Nathan home," she said.

Dr. Simon pushed his glasses higher on his nose, his eyes

darting all around. "Well . . . I suppose that will be suitable." His gaze locked on the room's main entrance behind the last row of seats. Two men stood near the doorway, their arms crossed as they stared at the stage; one, a tall white-haired man with a thin, pale face, and the other, a man of average height wearing a navy blue blazer and khaki pants.

Dr. Simon tugged on his collar. "Clara, please meet me in the main lobby in fifteen minutes. I have some important information to give you." His hands wringing again, he pattered off the stage and hurried toward the exit.

Nathan hustled to his tutor. "What's up?" he asked, glancing back at Simon. "Everyone's acting so weird!"

Clara yanked him through the doorway and into a dim hall. "Come with me!"

She led him briskly down the short corridor and flung open a door on the left. Inside, a steep staircase descended into darkness. Laying a finger on her lips, she set her foot on the top step and gestured for him to follow. Once inside, she closed the door and whispered so quietly he could barely hear. "While you were going up on stage, your father and Dr. Simon took off toward the exit in the back, so I followed."

A dim glow from somewhere on the lower level gave them just enough light to see each other's faces. Holding on to his elbow, she descended the creaking steps slowly and hurried through her words. "When I got into the foyer, I caught a glimpse of your father and Simon ducking into the hall, and I managed to stay close enough to watch them go down these stairs. I tried to listen from up here, but I could only hear violin music and a lot of whispering. Then I heard a gunshot."

"A gunshot? Are you sure?"

"Positive. Right after that, Dr. Simon ran back up the stairs, so I ducked behind the door. I don't think he saw me, so I just followed him back to the stage."

When they reached the bottom, they came upon two open

doors, one in front that led into darkness and one to the left, the source of the dim light. Carrying his violin by its neck, Nathan peered into the darker room in front. A glow from a hidden source revealed a system of large air ducts hanging from a low ceiling and a narrow wooden catwalk leading away from the door.

Nathan took a step through the door on the left. A bare bulb in an old lamp sat atop an antique desk, illuminating a hodge-podge of items in the eight-by-eight-foot chamber—hard-shell suitcases, sports equipment, wicker baskets, ancient typewriters, and two unvarnished coffins, each sitting on a low table in front of a head-high, tri-fold mirror. He blinked at the odd collection. Were the coffins stage props? Maybe they had recently put on a vampire skit.

He took another step. As he closed in, a body in each box came into view, barely visible in the lamp's weak glow. His legs suddenly weak, he stumbled into the gap between the two tables that held the coffins. Even in the dimness, their identities were unmistakable—Solomon and Francesca Shepherd.

Clara grasped his arm. Her mouth dropped open to speak, but she said nothing.

His heart racing wildly, Nathan could only clutch the coffins and stare at his parents. The bodies inside lay still, pale, and quiet. A dark blotch covered his father's breast pocket, and a hideous cut ripped open his mother's throat. Blood soaked her lovely gown, the same one she had so gracefully worn onstage only moments ago.

He shook his head and dug his nails into the wood, dizziness swirling his vision. "It ... it can't be ..."

Pain streaked Clara's voice. "It is." She pointed at an ornate gold band on his mother's finger. "Look at her ring. There's not another one like it in the world."

As a creaking stair sounded from above, a familiar British voice carried into the room. "Clara, I distinctly told you to meet me in the lobby. Coming down here was a big mistake."

She looked at Nathan and whispered, "Dr. Simon?"

Nathan didn't answer. He just bit his lip and drilled a stare right through the wall in the direction of the voice. If that creep had anything to do with this, he would—

"I intended to explain what happened here without exposing Nathan to this carnage." Simon reached the landing and aimed a flashlight beam into the room. "It is most unfortunate that events have played out this way."

Clara pointed a shaking finger at a coffin. "What do you know about this?"

"Everything. I arranged it. You see—"

"You *what?*"

"If you could understand the circumstances ..."

Nathan raised his stiffened arm and pointed at his mother's body. "They're fake, right?" He felt a trembling smile grow unbidden on his lips. "They have to be fake."

Dr. Simon let out a sigh. "I'm afraid they're quite real. Their deaths are a most unfortunate—"

"You monster!" Clara cried.

Raising a finger to his lips, Dr. Simon glanced at the doorway and lowered his voice to a whisper. "Now that my plan has gone awry, I need to make sure that your accidental discovery doesn't hinder our pursuits. I had planned for Nathan to join his parents, but if you continue shouting, we could all end up in coffins."

Nathan pointed at himself. "You planned for *me* to join them?"

"In order to protect our secrets, Dr. Gordon and I decided—"

"Who cares about your secrets?" Sucking in quick breaths, Nathan balled a fist so tight, his fingers throbbed. "Just back off. I'm walking out of here, and I'm taking my parents with me."

Clara picked up a baseball bat. "You'd better not try to stop us if you know what's good for you."

"I wouldn't dream of it," Dr. Simon said, "but you have far greater obstacles to overcome." With beads of sweat dotting his bare head, he nodded toward the tri-fold mirror standing behind the coffins. "We will soon have company, a man we must not rile. I insist that you remain silent and let me do all the talking."

Nathan gritted his teeth. "Why should I do what you say? I'll just—"

"Look in the mirror," Dr. Simon said, pointing at the reflection. "You will see."

Nathan stared at the crystal clear image—the three of them, standing in the dim props room, but two other figures had joined them, the two who had stood at the performance hall exit, the tall man and the guy in the blue blazer. Nathan swung his head back toward the door. The other men weren't there.

Grabbing his mother's coffin with one hand, Nathan wagged his head, trying to watch reality and the reflected image at the same time. Dr. Simon was just trying to distract him. The mirror couldn't show—

Footsteps clopped along the hall above their heads. Nathan glanced up. Could the men in the mirror really be coming? Tightening his fingers around the neck of his violin, he flexed his muscles. He was ready. One way or another, he and Clara were going to make a getaway.

Dr. Simon folded the mirror, hiding its reflective surface. As he slid it behind a bookshelf, the door at the top of the stairs swung open, singing a low creak. He waved frantically at Clara, whispering, "Hide your weapon!"

As she laid the bat at her feet, heavy footfalls rumbled down the steps, drawing closer. When a man entered the prop room, Dr. Simon's flashlight beam illuminated the emblem on the newcomer's blazer—three infinity symbols in a vertical stack, close to each other so that their lines intermeshed.

Nathan took a deep breath. Bad guy number two would be tougher than Simon.

"Dr. Gordon," Dr. Simon said, flashing a nervous grin. "You have come just in time. Where is Mictar?"

"He's nearby." Stroking his chin, Dr. Gordon scanned the room, first eyeing Nathan, then Clara before calling out, "It's safe."

More footsteps sounded from the stairs, slower this time, more like the tiptoe steps of a child rather than a man of any gravity. When Mictar finally entered, his thin pallid face seemed to hover over Dr. Gordon's shoulder. With his slick white hair pulled back into a collar-length ponytail, he looked like a lost hippie who forgot to die of old age.

As Mictar gazed across the room, a half smile turned one of his hollow cheeks upward. "What have we here, Dr. Simon? I hope you have not acted too hastily." His words echoed, though the room seemed to dampen everyone else's voice.

Nathan shuddered. This guy seemed more like a ghost than a man, a walking corpse fresh from the graveyard. He gripped his instrument once again. Now he had three guys to get past.

Dr. Simon laughed nervously. "I wanted to wait for you, but they were getting suspicious. I had to make sure they didn't run."

As if floating along the floor, Mictar padded up to the coffins and leaned his tall body over the lifeless forms, studying them from top to bottom. "A bullet in the heart and a slashed throat," he said, caressing Francesca's colorless cheek. "This is lovely work, Simon. Did you do the deeds yourself?"

Folding his hands behind him, Simon raised up on his toes, blinking rapidly. "Of course. No one else knows of your plan."

Nathan boiled inside. He watched for a good opening, maybe when at least two of the creeps had their backs turned.

"Is that so?" Mictar licked the end of the finger that had touched Francesca's cheek. "Show me your palms."

Dr. Simon lifted his hands. Mictar drew close and latched on to each of Dr. Simon's wrists with his spindly fingers. After taking a long sniff of Simon's palms, Mictar furrowed his brow. "I smell the blood of your victims as well as the gun's residue, but the sweet aroma of residual fear is missing."

Simon cleared his throat. "The Shepherds displayed no fear at all."

Mictar nodded slowly. "Ah! I see. But your fear is now so strong, I would wager that even the ungifted can detect its odor."

"Is that so unusual?" Dr. Simon jerked his hands away and wrung them more vigorously than ever. "Anyone who has seen your power would be frightened at your displeasure."

"That is true of my enemies. My loyal friends have no reason to fear me." Mictar reached into Nathan's mother's coffin and lifted her eyelid. "Her light is extinguished. They no longer have value."

"No value? I don't understand."

Mictar pulled away from the coffin. "You disappoint me, Simon. I wanted her eyes while they still breathed the light, her eyes above any others. And I was hoping to keep at least one of the Solomons alive long enough to learn their secrets."

Simon squirmed like a scolded schoolboy. "I didn't know. I mean, if I had known, I would have—"

"You have no need to explain." Mictar turned to Nathan and smiled, though his pointed yellow teeth revealed ravenous hunger rather than joy. "You have brought one of the offspring to replace what has been lost. An excellent gift, indeed, for he will likely possess what I wanted from her."

Mictar's gaze flooded Nathan's body with icy shivers. As weakness buckled his knees, he braced himself on the side of a coffin.

"Of course I brought him," Simon replied. "Never let it be said that Flavius Simon leaves any task undone."

Mictar's rapacious smile returned. "You have spoken well, for your tasks are now complete. With the four adult Shepherds dead, I no longer have need of your services. The fewer people who know, the better. The seeds of interdimensional disharmony are best sown by the hands of the ignorant."

Dr. Gordon grabbed Simon and twisted his arm behind his back, while Mictar glided closer and raised his splayed fingers. His cadaverous body seemed to become a shadow, darkening with each step.

Nathan heaved deep breaths, trying to keep from shaking uncontrollably. What was this ... this thing? He slid between Clara and the shadowy phantom. "Just stay cool," he whispered. "We'll get out of here somehow."

As Mictar drew within an arm's reach, Dr. Simon thrashed. "Just give me another assignment!" he cried. "I'll do anything you want!"

Dr. Gordon yanked Simon's arm up toward his neck, freezing him in place.

"Anything I want?" Mictar covered Dr. Simon's eyes with his dark hand and spoke softly. "I want you to die."

Dr. Simon's body stiffened, his mouth locked open in a voiceless scream. As Mictar kept his hand over his victim's eyes, sparks flew around his fingers, and the two men seemed to hover a few inches off the floor. Simon quaked violently, while Mictar's body gradually regained its light.

Nathan spread out his arms, shielding Clara. All he could do was try to protect his tutor. There seemed no way to stop whatever was happening to Dr. Simon.

After a few torturous seconds, Mictar pulled his hand back, revealing Dr. Simon's eye sockets, now blackened by emptiness; something had consumed his eyeballs and left behind nothing but gaping pits. With the sickening odor of charred flesh now permeating the room, Dr. Simon collapsed on the floor.

Mictar took in a deep breath and let it out slowly. "The combination of fear and death is an aroma surpassing all others." He turned to Dr. Gordon. "Collins and Mills stayed on guard in the hallway upstairs. Call them down. You will need help to dispose of all five bodies."

Nathan cringed. Five bodies?

Gordon pulled a cell phone from his pocket and pressed a button on the side. "Collins. Get down here."

Again tightening his fingers around the violin, Nathan whispered to Clara. "It's now or never."

Clara slowly crouched toward her bat. "You get the tall one."

Nathan lunged and swung wildly at Mictar's head. The wood smashed against his thin cheek with a loud crack, and the tightly wound strings sliced into his skin. The violin shattered into a dozen varnished shards, leaving only the fingerboard in Nathan's hands.

Mictar fell against the wall, covering his mouth as dark blood poured between his fingers and dripped onto the floor. Clara bashed Gordon in the groin. He collapsed to his knees and let out a loud groan, his eyes clenched shut.

Nathan latched on to Clara's arm and pulled. "Run!" They stormed out of the prop room, sidestepped a man with a gray beard as he neared the stairwell landing, and dashed through the other doorway into the dim air-duct room. Lowering their heads, they clattered along the narrow catwalk under a maze of interconnected duct work.

A muffled voice called behind them. "Don't worry about us. Get them!"

When they reached the end of the room, a single bulb attached to the low ceiling shone on a gray double door that rose no higher than Nathan's chest. He gave the door a hefty push with both hands. Although it bent outward a few inches, it snapped right back. He dropped to his bottom and thrust his feet against the latch. The wood cracked but didn't give way.

Behind them, footsteps rattled the catwalk. Nathan kicked again. The door splintered and banged open, revealing a four-foot drop to a hallway below. He sprang to his feet, ducked into the opening, and dropped to the ground. Clara followed. Her white evening gown poofed out like a parachute as she bent her knees to absorb the impact.

Nathan pointed at a sign over an alcove opening just a few paces away. "A fire escape!"

They dashed into the short corridor that ended abruptly at a tall window. Nathan threw the sash open, letting in a blast of cool air. After stepping out onto the wobbly fire escape landing, he helped Clara through. Just as he pushed the window closed, Mictar's henchmen turned into the alcove, the gray-bearded one drawing a pistol.

Nathan thrust his finger downward. "Go!"

Clara kicked off her high-heels and clambered down the steps. A bullet shattered the glass and zinged past Nathan's ear. He leaped halfway down the first flight, shaking the entire framework as he landed. "Faster!"

As his footfalls rang through the metal stairs, a shout sounded from above. "You follow. I'll get the car."

Scrambling across a landing, Nathan caught up with Clara as she turned down the next flight. Another gunshot cracked through the whistling wind. Nathan hopped up on the railing, slid past Clara, and dropped feet first to the landing. "Come on!" he shouted as Clara caught up. "He can't get a good shot through the steps!"

As they closed in on the ground level, they dropped below the top floor of the parking garage across the street. Nathan glanced up. Their pursuer was galloping down the steps two levels above.

Seconds later, Nathan halted at the final stretch, a long,

horizontal ladder that would swing them down to the sidewalk as they added their weight to the stairs. He leaped out, grabbed the railing, and rode the metal bridge to the ground. When the supports smacked against the concrete, Clara hopped on the rail and slid down, almost beating Nathan to the bottom.

They jumped from the stairs. As the rusty span sprang back up, Clara pointed down the road. "The limo's that way!" They broke into a mad sprint, Nathan intentionally staying one step behind, glancing back constantly. Suddenly, the black Mustang careened around a corner three blocks to their rear and thundered toward them.

"They have wheels now!" Nathan shouted.

"So do we!" Clara turned down an alley where the black stretch limo idled. A stubby man in a chauffeur's cap leaned against the front fender, tipping back a bottle of Mountain Dew.

"Mike!" Clara waved her hands as she slowed down. "I'll take the car!"

Mike spun around and opened the door for them. "In trouble again?" he asked.

"Big time!" Now puffing heavily, Clara slid behind the wheel. Nathan leaped on the hood and vaulted to the other side. Throwing open the passenger's door, he dove in and jerked upright in his seat.

The Mustang, its convertible top now folded down, skidded to a stop in front of them, blocking the alley's exit. Clara lowered the window and glanced between Mike and the Mustang, her eyes wide as she tried to catch her breath. "How do I get to the expressway?"

Mike pointed at the street in front of them. "That's Congress. Turn right, cross the bridge, and you're there."

As the window hummed back to the top, Clara smacked the floor stick into gear. "Get buckled!"

Nathan clicked the buckle and grabbed the hand rest. "Let's do it!"

She slammed down the accelerator. The limousine roared away, the tires squealing as she angled toward a narrow gap between the Mustang and a lamppost.

As they closed in, the bearded man stood on the seat, propped a foot on the window frame, and aimed his gun.

Clara ducked behind the wheel. "Get down!"

Nathan scrunched but kept his eye on the action. A bullet clanked into their limo as it clipped the Mustang's fender, shoving it to the side. The gunman toppled over and rolled onto the pavement.

Clara barged into traffic amid a hail of honking horns. "Maybe they learned their lesson and won't follow."

As he rocked upright, a tight lump squeezed into Nathan's throat. "Think we can somehow sneak back and get Mom and Dad?"

Clara grabbed his shoulder. "Nathan, they're—" She released him and spun the wheel, wedging the long car into the left lane between two yellow taxis. "Watch my back and tell me if you see them."

Nathan wheeled around. The black Mustang roared into view, weaving back and forth as it darted past car after car. Setting his fists on top of the windshield, the gray-bearded man aimed his pistol.

"He's going to shoot!" Nathan shouted. "Step on it!"

Clara jerked the car through traffic, zigzagging from lane to lane. They bumped a Mercedes on one side, then a pickup truck on the other. Tires squealed. Horns blared. A bullet ripped through the rear window and into the dashboard, shattering the radio.

Clara stomped the accelerator to pass a city bus, flattening Nathan against the passenger seat. He pushed back up and peered over the headrest. The Mustang careened around the bus but slowed as a car swerved in front of it.

Clara slowed the limo to a halt and pointed ahead. "The drawbridge!"

Nathan glanced between the shattered rear window and the windshield. Red-and-white crossbars lowered about four car lengths in front, while a pickup truck pulled behind them, preventing any escape to the rear. "Any ideas? We're sitting ducks!"

"Not if I can help it!" Clara jerked her thumb toward the rear. "Keep watching."

"What do you have up your sleeve this time?"

She clenched her fingers around the steering wheel. "Survival!"

He peered back again. The Mustang angled its front grill toward the left, inching back and forth to get enough room to go around the car that blocked it. Nathan lowered his head. "Looks like he's trying to push over the median!"

Clara scrunched down. "Perfect!"

"Perfect?" He spun around. "But they'll catch us for sure!"

"Only if we go back. We always go forward."

"But going forward puts us in the river."

"Tighten your strap, Kiddo! We're taking off!" She jerked the wheel to the left and floored the pedal, sending the limo lurching across the median and into the oncoming lanes.

Nathan grabbed his seat belt and pulled it tighter. "You can't jump the gap! There's no way this tank can make it!"

"And neither can that Mustang!" They crashed through the crossbars and zoomed up the steep metal incline. The limo launched over the edge and into the air, flying for a brief second before falling toward the river below.

2

REFLECTIONS OF MIND

The car splashed tires-first into the water. Nathan's head rammed against the ceiling, but his seat belt kept him from thrashing around. When the bouncing stopped, the car settled into a slowly sinking drift on the river's surface. He patted his torso. He was alive!

Clara lowered the two front windows. "Get your shoes off and be ready to swim." She squeezed through the opening and rolled into the river.

"My backpack!" Nathan reached over the seat and grabbed the strap. With water gushing in all around, he slipped off his dress shoes, took a deep breath, and dove out the window. He paddled furiously in the icy water, trying to keep his head above the wake of passing sailboats.

A splash erupted next to his shoulder, followed by a loud *Crack!* from up above. Nathan looked up at the bridge. The gray-bearded man had perched atop a supporting pylon, a pistol at the end of his outstretched arms.

Clara spat out a stream of water. "Dive!"

Nathan dove into the cloudy river. It would hide them, at least until they had to come back up for air. Weighed down by water, his backpack felt like concrete, but he couldn't let it go. Dad's mirror was inside.

A bullet splashed above and ricocheted off his shoulder, slowed by the watery cushion. Hiding helped, but they couldn't stay under forever. He popped back to the surface and shook the water from his hair. Clara appeared next to him. "Gotta get the mirror!" he called.

As the limo's roof sank below the rippling waves, Nathan unzipped the pack and grabbed the wrapped mirror, shivering so hard he could barely breathe. He finally let go of the strap and let the backpack sink to the bottom.

A bullet pierced the foaming surface, nicking a toe on Nathan's foot, again too slow to do any damage. He threw off the bundle's cloth wrappings, revealing the square mirror.

Clara flailed in the water, sputtering, "What are you doing?"

"Dad told me to look at it if I get in trouble." He angled the glass until he could see the bearded man standing on the pylon. With the bridge now beginning to close, the gunman lowered his weapon and jogged out onto the metal ramp.

From somewhere behind Nathan, music played over a raspy PA system. Nathan swiveled toward the sound. A tourist boat headed their way. Passengers leaned close to the edge taking pictures, their cameras flashing every half second.

Kicking madly to prop up his shivering body, he spun back to the mirror. He had to concentrate. His father never gave a warning without a good reason.

In the reflection, the man aimed his gun once again. Nathan cringed. Where was a cop when you needed one? A bullet ripped through the frame, shattering it in his grip. He juggled the mirror, finally grabbing the bare glass with both hands. Resisting the urge to glance up at the bridge, he pulled the glass closer. In the reflected image, the police arrived and nabbed the gunman.

Another bullet zinged into the river. Clara grabbed Nathan's elbow to help him stay above water. "Don't turn," she said. "Keep focused!"

Spitting oily water as the waves slapped against his lips, Nathan changed the mirror's angle slightly. The bridge had closed, and cars were crossing again.

"Okay." Clara let go of him. "It's safe now."

Nathan turned and looked up at the bridge. Two policemen cuffed the gunman as the span lowered to a close. He squinted at the scene. That had already happened. How did—?

A flotation ring splashed at his side. Another one bumped Clara's shoulder. They turned to the source, following the trail of two lifelines to the tourist boat. While a crowd of passengers looked on, two men held the ropes and waved, yelling something that the wind carried away.

Nathan grabbed his ring and made sure Clara had a good hold on hers. Still clinging to the mirror, he rode the swift tugs toward the boat. Whatever this Quattro viewer was, it held a lot more mystery than met the eye.

Nathan pulled a blanket around his body and tucked it in at the sides. It felt good—snug, cozy, warm. The car's vent blew a jet of heated air across his face, adding to the pleasure. Wearing a pair of mid-top boots borrowed from the tour boat captain, an oversized Chicago Bulls sweatshirt that one of the tourists stripped off as soon as Nathan climbed aboard, and jeans, gym socks, and underwear fished out of a police charity bin, he felt comfortable, almost strangely so, especially considering the calamities that had crashed down on his life just hours before.

Now able to rest and think, the ghastly image of his parents' lifeless forms pulsed in his brain. The police had found no coffins in the prop room, so the bodies had to be in Mictar's clutches. Why would that creep want them anyway? What else could he do that Dr. Simon hadn't already done? The thoughts sizzled through his brain like electric shockwaves. He had to concentrate on something else or he'd go crazy.

Leaning his head back, he cast a glance at Clara. Dressed in a purple jumper and matching shirt from the charity bin, she looked serene, far more peaceful than he expected. He couldn't resist grinning at her outfit. It reminded him of a

Voodoo priestess he had once seen as he passed by an alley in Port-au-Prince. She had fixed her dark eyes on him and chanted mysterious Creole verses into the midst of a boiling cauldron. Her brew suddenly spewed a plume of hot gasses and smoke. When it cleared, she was gone.

Nathan shuddered. Too many mysterious things had happened in his life, and the mirror's strange behavior seemed to top them all.

Clara gazed out the windshield of the Jeep Cherokee they had rented "on credit," as the sympathetic rental agent had termed their deal. After spending the night on a bench in the police station, she seemed wide awake, her eyes brimming with speculation. "Do you remember the field trip for our introduction to England class back when I first became your tutor?"

Nathan squirmed in his blanket and stared out the side window, but with dawn just beginning to break, it was too dark to see much, only the silhouette of the retreating Chicago skyline framed by a rising orange glow. "Yeah. At Scotland Yard."

"Do you remember what a safe house is?"

"I think so. A place where no one can find someone, like in a witness protection program."

"Exactly. I don't know what your father learned about Mictar and Dr. Simon, but it's obvious it led to his and your mother's deaths, and you're their next target."

"But I don't know anything. Dad never told me much about his assignments."

"He kept them to himself to protect you, but the murderers don't seem to care about that." Clara pushed a button, turning off the Jeep's global positioning system. "I'd better not leave any clues that might give away our destination."

Her last word throbbed in Nathan's ears. Destination. It sounded final, like perdition, a place to stay away from. How bad could it be? An old spinster's log cabin, squirreled away in a remote forest? There'd probably be nothing to do but play cribbage with her and listen to her complain about aching bunions while country music squawked on scratchy vinyl records. Or maybe it would be even worse.

He shook his head. It would be better not to ask. Clara would tell him soon enough. He thought about suggesting Dr. Malenkov's house, but that would be too obvious. Mom's stepfather's home would be the first place they would look.

"I'll have to leave you at the safe house," Clara continued, "and attend to some important details."

"Can I go with you? Nobody will be tailing you, will they?"

"We can't take any chances. Your father left me instructions in case something like this happened, and it's my duty to follow his directives to the letter. After we make one stop on the way, I'll get you settled at the house. But then I have to leave immediately to meet with your father's lawyer to receive your parents' estate for you. After that, I'll return with some clothes for you and a replacement violin."

As new warmth flowed into Nathan's cheeks, he pulled the blanket lower and dipped his chin close to his chest. He couldn't believe it. His parents were dead and now he had to hole up in some stranger's house. Not only that, his only real friend in the world was going to take off and leave him alone there. Could it possibly get any worse?

Clara reached over and rubbed his shoulder. "Going to the safe house is what your father wanted. You've always trusted him before, haven't you?"

He raised his chin just enough to nod. He had always trusted Dad, but he wasn't around anymore to make sure his promises were being kept.

She caressed the back of his head. "Oh, Nathan, I'm so sorry. There are a million things to do, and no one can expect you to do them. If I don't concentrate on my duties, I'll break down and cry."

A wave of sorrow swept through his mind, sending a hot flash through his body. "I know what you mean."

"I'll get everything you need to make you comfortable in your new home. You'll feel better in no time."

He squeezed his eyelids shut and whispered, "I don't want to feel better." Tears begged to get out. A new shaking sensation crawled through his insides, more like a cathartic convulsion than a shiver. Thoughts of his mother—her gentle touch, her kind words, her matchless talent—flashed in his mind. Then memories of his father—his strong embraces, his odd, yet direct way of teaching, his protective hands—seemed so real, almost as if he were whispering at this moment, touching his son's shoulder the way he always used to do when he wanted to share a philosophical gem.

Nathan trembled. It was too much. It was just too much. Finally, he wept. His head bobbed, and his nose began running. As Clara's fingers massaged his scalp, he swallowed down the pain. He couldn't let it boil over like that. If he kept it up, he'd be blubbering like a baby.

After a few seconds, he sniffed and looked at her through a blur of tears, trying hard to keep his voice steady. "I'll do whatever Dad said, but don't bother getting a violin. I don't want to play anymore."

"Don't go making promises you'll be sorry for later." She flipped on the Jeep's stereo.

Violin music streamed through the speakers. Vivaldi. At other times it would have made him feel better. Now? Not likely. He sniffed again and wiped his eyes with the blanket. He didn't really want to be comforted. He just wanted to go off and wander in the woods, feel sorry for himself for a while. He deserved it, didn't he? He'd lost everything and no one really seemed to care. It was time to mope and be miserable.

But Vivaldi had other ideas. As they drove on and on, the sweet violins bathed him in soothing majesty, stroking his aching heart with the very same four seasons of life he had so recently celebrated with his own violin.

After a Beethoven sonata, a Mozart symphony, and dozens of miles of dazzling cornfields waving their golden tassels in the brightening sunlight, Nathan slipped off his shoes and pulled his feet up under his body. He gazed at Clara, blinking through his diminishing tears. "Do you really think Mom and Dad are dead?"

Clara's lips wrinkled. "Yes, dear. You saw the bodies. That was no illusion."

Nathan gave a nod, then tightened his chin. He couldn't believe it. No ... he *wouldn't* believe it. No matter how many times his dad's investigations had exposed a nest of human rats, he had always managed to escape their plans for revenge. As a master illusionist, his collection of mirrors and lights would confuse his pursuers, allowing him to disappear like a phantom. Maybe even the bodies in the coffins were an illusion of some kind. And how could Dad ever be duped so easily by Dr. Simon? He was too smart for that. He was too ...

He shook his head slowly. Clara was right. This time everything was different. Dad was dead. So was Mom. Not only that, his father had said that Dr. Simon wasn't so bad, so maybe he really was fooled. And maybe this Mictar was just too powerful.

He breathed a deep sigh and pressed his teeth down on his bottom lip. He had lost this battle. Sure, he and Clara had escaped with their lives, but it was a retreat. He had tucked his tail between his legs and run away like a wailing puppy. But the war wasn't over yet.

Nathan gazed at the rearview mirror, imagining the scene of death back at the props room. Mictar's ghostly specter lurked there, a stalking shadow with deadly hands ready to suck the life out of him.

Nathan firmed his chin. It didn't matter. Soon enough he would fight back. For now, he had to wait for the right time to mount a counterattack. It was better to go along with Clara's plan ... his dad's plan. Maybe, even in the wake of this tragedy, there was still a glimmer of hope ... somehow.

"Wake up! We're here."

Nathan jerked his head toward Clara and rubbed his bleary eyes. Riding through miles and miles of farmland must have lulled him to sleep. He read the clock on the dashboard—11:20. Still morning.

He looked out the window. Rays of sunlight streaked through puffy clouds, highlighting a tall Ferris wheel and at least a half-dozen spires acting as center supports for striped tents of various sizes and colors. Stretching his arms, he spoke through a wide yawn. "Where are we? Some kind of carnival?"

"It's a county fair in central Iowa. This is the stop I told you about." Clara parked in front of a chain-link gate near a square sign that said, *Hand Stamp Required for Re-entry.*

Nathan scanned the grounds. Only a few people strolled along the flat grass, most lugging tools, ladders, or buckets. One high-school-aged girl, clad in denim overalls and a gray T-shirt, carried a claw hammer, tossing them a glance as she passed close to the gate.

"Looks like it's closed," he said.

"All the better." She opened the door and stepped out. "Let's go."

As soon as Nathan joined her, Clara flipped up the latch and pushed the gate open. "Excuse me, young lady," she said to the girl. "Where may I find the house of mirrors?"

The dirty-faced blonde stopped and set the hammer against her hip, smacking her gum as she cocked her head. "We open at one."

Nathan rolled his eyes. This girl was treading dangerous ground. She shouldn't mess with Clara.

Clara's voice changed to a formal, firm tone. "Had I asked

for your hours of operation, my dear, that would have been an adequate answer. Shall I repeat my question?"

"I heard you, Granny." The girl flicked her head back. "That way. Behind the merry-go-round. But the mirrors won't help you look any younger."

Clara gave her an icy glare. "Thank you." She stalked toward the tented attractions, muttering, "Impertinent, inconsiderate ... If I were her mother, I'd ..."

Nathan kept pace, breathing a sigh of relief. The girl got off easy. He remembered the last time he smarted off at Clara. It had been a few years, but the echo of the tongue lashing still reverberated in his mind. Sure, he deserved it, but he didn't wish it on anyone else.

As they passed the carousel, the operator gave them a nod and turned on the motor, apparently testing the ride in preparation for their opening. The bright-colored horses sprang to life and rode up and down their poles as if dancing to the merry-go-round's lively tune, an accordion rendition of "Hello Dolly!" that blared far and wide.

Just ahead, a sign on a blue-and-white striped tent said, *House of Mirrors*. Clara stopped in front of it and unfolded a sheet of paper. Raising her voice to compete with the music, she handed him the sheet. "Here are your father's instructions."

Nathan read:

Go alone to the center of the house of mirrors and stare at the only mirror that doesn't distort your image. In the reflection you will see a container I have left for you. Guide your image so that it picks up the container. Look straight ahead and exit the hall. It will be in your arms.

"You have to go alone," Clara said, "so I'll see you in a few minutes."

"What are you going to do?"

She glanced around at the various tents. "There's a sign that says, 'Watch a teenager make his own bed.' That's something I just have to see."

He stared at the only sign in view. "It doesn't say that. It says, 'See Dog Boy, the Only Living Canine Kid.'"

"Your sense of humor must be on life support," she said, nudging his ribs. "Better get going before Hammer Girl comes around with a security guard."

Nathan pulled open a flap and ducked into the tent. Sunshine filtered through the canopy, allowing him to see well enough to walk. After passing through an unmanned turnstile, he entered a wide hallway lined with mirrors on both sides and old-fashioned lanterns that colored the reflections with an eerie yellow glow. The first mirror widened his middle into a football shape. Another stretched him vertically into a wavy ribbon. A third shortened his body into that of a squashed midget.

Ignoring the rest of the mirrors, he hurried to the end of the hall and entered a large, circular room. A pole at the center reached to the apex of the tent, supporting the tent's canvas structure. Temporary partitions encircled the chamber, hinged between each fabric-covered section. A mirror hung on every partition, some circular, some square, and some full-length vertical rectangles.

He jogged around the room, glancing at the reflections, each one warped in some fashion. It seemed like a lame attraction, fun maybe for five-year-olds but not really exciting enough for today's kids who yawn at the special effects in *Star Wars*.

In one of the full-length mirrors, a squatting man appeared. The moment Nathan stopped and stared, the man vanished. Now everything in the reflection seemed normal, the central pole behind him, the other mirrors all around, and his own image. This had to be the mirror his father mentioned in his note.

The accordion theme drifted in, not loud, yet quite audible. Nothing else unusual appeared in the mirror, but the dimness under the canopy made it hard to tell for sure. He scanned the perimeter wall and spotted a switch near the entry corridor. After hustling over, he flipped it up.

Instantly a barrage of lights beamed down from a ring of high-powered bulbs at the midsection of the center pole. Flashing every fraction of a second, they transformed the chamber into a surreal digital video with half the frames removed. As he walked back to the normal mirror, everything seemed jerky, out-of-sync, hypnotic. Now the other mirrors took on a more dazzling aspect. The warped shapes looked like grotesque monsters, mutant images of himself on an alien planet. This was definitely cool.

As he stood several paces away from the undistorted mirror, he stared at the ground in front of his reflection. How could something show up that wasn't really there? That would be crazy.

The accordion music played on. The lights continued to flash, making Nathan feel like he was blinking his eyes rapidly. After almost a minute, something appeared during one of the flashes, but it vanished in the next. What was it? Something brown and solid, maybe knee high?

The object appeared again, this time remaining for two flashes before disappearing, then for three flashes, then four. Soon, it stayed put, a rectangular box about the size of a small trunk, like a treasure chest from a pirates' movie.

Keeping his eyes on the mirror, he leaned over and guided his reflection's hands around each side of the trunk so that his fingers could support it underneath. As he straightened, the Nathan in the mirror lifted the trunk. With lights blinking at a mind-numbing rate, the scene felt like a nightmare—disjointed and unearthly.

Although he couldn't feel the panels or the weight, he pretended the trunk was there, imagining it in his mind as he turned toward the entry hall and strode out, his gaze fixed on the lantern light straight ahead.

As soon as he entered the hall, a sudden weight burdened his arms. He looked down. The trunk was there, weathered and brown with a fine wood grain that bore little if any varnish. It seemed too light to be holding anything of significant weight. Could it be empty? If it was, why would his father want him to get it?

Nathan pushed the tent flap to the side, set the trunk on the ground, and looked back at the house of mirrors, his vision still coming in flashing frames. What in the world just happened in there?

A hand patted him on the back. Nathan turned slowly toward Clara, trying to blink away the strobe lights. She pulled on his elbow. "Let's get going. I ran into Hammer Girl again. She took off to call security."

He picked up the trunk and hustled behind her, trying to watch where he was going while checking out the trunk at the same time. It seemed so weird, no latches or lock, not even hinges or a lid. Never mind the impossible way he found the trunk; how was he going to get it open?

Clara turned onto a narrow street and eased the car between fields of corn. Although the tall, browning stalks barely allowed a view over their tops, a solitary house was visible in a clearing in the distance. "That's the place," she said.

Nathan gazed at the landscape, a thousand acres of rolling cornfields surrounding a beautiful old mansion framed by a dozen or more majestic shade trees. "What town are we in?"

"No town, really. We're between Iowa City and Des Moines, closer to Newton, Iowa, than anywhere else. This is the home of Tony Clark, a man your father and I knew years ago, but neither of us has had contact with him recently. Mictar will not likely track you here. We're pretty far out in the country. I even lost cell service a few miles back."

He pressed the window switch and lowered the glass enough to stick his head out. The air still carried the morning's chill. "I hope this guy doesn't mind me showing up out of the blue."

"He knows you're coming. I called just before we left Chicago."

"Anyone else live here?"

"His wife, a lawyer, I think, and a daughter named Kelly. I believe she's sixteen years old." Clara pulled into the long concrete driveway and stopped under the boughs of a mammoth cottonwood tree. An open garage revealed a pair of matching motorcycles but no car. "Tony said he's honored that you're coming. In fact, because your father's will so stipulates, he'll be your legal guardian, your new father, so to speak."

Nathan grimaced. "Don't say that." He closed his eyes again and shook his head. "Just ... don't say that."

"Okay, okay. Take your time." She opened the door and stepped out onto the driveway. "Just let me know when you're ready to go in."

Nathan grabbed the mirror and threw open the door. He walked to the front of the Jeep, leaned against the hood, and glared at the house. Except for the satellite dish on the roof, the massive residence was a perfect setting for a movie about a rich land owner back in the days before combine harvesters. Maybe Mr. Clark was a crotchety farming hermit who amassed a corn empire and sat on it, fat and happy, while his migrant workers hauled in the harvest and sold it at market, bringing him bags of cash for his amusement. Still, with its brick front and splendid marble columns, the house seemed friendly enough, almost inviting, in spite of the old miser who probably lived inside.

The cool autumn breeze swirled a menagerie of red and yellow leaves around his ankles, some of them funneling down from the cottonwood tree. Its deeply fissured bark and thick, serpentine limbs reached down at him like the long, gnarled arms of a giant.

He grabbed a triangular leaf out of the air and rubbed a finger along its coarsely toothed edge. The color of life had drained away, leaving only a pale yellow hue that reflected the sadness of its dying state. As dozens of other yellow leaves brushed by him, he released the one in his hand into the wind, letting it join the parade of death.

"I guess I'm ready."

"Then let's go." Clara marched toward the door, her purple sleeves flapping in the stiffening breeze. "Once you sound the call, you might as well be ready to charge."

Nathan pushed away from the Jeep and followed, the mirror tucked under his arm. He hopped up one step to a tiled porch and bumped the edge of a welcome mat with his heavy boots. Red-twine letters woven into the scratchy material spelled out, *If You Have to Duck to Enter, I'm Your Coach.*

Clara found a doorbell embedded in the brick wall and pressed it lightly. A loud bong sounded from inside, a sweet bass, like the lowest note on a marimba.

A female voice sang through a speaker at the side of the door. "Who is it?"

Clara nodded at the speaker and whispered. "Answer her, Nathan!"

He leaned toward the intercom. "Uh ... It's Nathan. Nathan Shepherd. Clara and I are here to—"

The voice pitched higher. "You're early!"

Nathan cleared his throat. "I ... I'm sorry. I didn't know what time we were supposed to—"

"But I'm not ready ... I mean, we're not ready. Your room is—" A loud thump sounded from the speaker. "Ouch! Now look at what you made me do! What a mess!"

"I made you?"

"Ooooh! ... Just wait right there. Don't move a muscle!"

Nathan glanced at Clara. She returned an *I have no idea* kind of expression and added a shrug. After a few seconds, loud, uneven footsteps stomped toward them. The door swung open, revealing a teenaged girl hopping on one bare foot. Her bouncing shoulder-length brown hair framed a pretty face with black smudges on each cheek.

She grabbed her toes and leaned against the jamb, scrunching her thin eyebrows toward her button nose, her cuffed jeans exposing her leg from midcalf downward. "That cabinet was heavy."

Nathan focused on her pink toenails, the shade of pink on Barbie doll boxes and inside Pepto-Bismol bottles. "Think you broke a bone?"

The girl set her foot down and tested her weight on it while pulling her dirty white T-shirt down to cover her midriff. "I don't think so. It's just—"

"You must be Kelly," Clara said, extending her hand. "I'm Clara Jackson, Nathan's tutor."

Kelly took Clara's hand and nodded. "Kelly Clark. Pleased to meet you." She reached her hand toward Nathan. "Pleased to meet you, too, Nathan. Are you a Bulls fan?"

Nathan shook her hand. "A Bulls fan?"

"Yeah." She pointed at his shirt. "You know. The basketball team. My dad loves them."

Nathan glanced down at the logo. "Oh, that. It's borrowed. I'm not really a basketball fan."

"Oh." A faint gleam appeared in Kelly's eyes, and she flashed a hint of a smile. "Good."

"Are your parents home?" Clara continued.

"No. Dad's leading practice with the team today, and then he's going out to get stuff for tonight's dinner, so it'll be a while." Kelly pulled in her bottom lip and drummed her fingers on her thigh. "And Mom's ... um ... in Des Moines for ... for personal reasons." As a pink flush tinted her face, she gestured with her head. "C'mon in. There're cold drinks in the fridge and—"

"I must leave immediately," Clara interrupted. "Our lawyer is meeting me in Davenport so I can settle Nathan's affairs. I'll collect some necessary items for him while I'm there. We had a mishap of sorts last night and lost our luggage."

"Oh, that's too bad. Nathan probably can't wear any of my father's clothes. They'd be too big."

Clara glanced at her wristwatch. "It's still early, so I should be able to come back this evening with some things." She placed a gentle hand on Nathan's shoulder and turned to Kelly. "Did your father tell you about Nathan's parents?"

Kelly's brow turned downward. "Yes ... he did."

"Then I'm sure you'll make him feel at home, won't you?"

A sympathetic smile spread across her face. "You can count on me, Ms. Jackson."

Clara kissed Nathan on the forehead. "I think you're in good hands." As a tear inched down her cheek, she whispered. "I'm sorry for leaving so abruptly, but I have a lot to do."

"It's okay. I understand." Nathan wrapped one arm around her shoulders and hugged her briefly.

"I'll see you tonight." Clara waved as she strode to the Jeep.

While it backed out and zoomed away, Kelly stepped up to Nathan's side. "So, you have a personal tutor? Must be fun."

"Yeah, it's pretty cool, I guess." He watched the Jeep as it turned onto the main road. His last attachment to the life he once knew was now gone. His throat sore and tight, he forced out a few words, hoping to end the questioning without hurting Kelly's feelings. "I don't have anything to compare it to."

She cupped her hand around his elbow and led him inside. "You tired?"

"Sort of." When the Jeep disappeared, the image of the trunk on the backseat flashed into his mind. He snapped his fingers. "I left the trunk in the car."

"A trunk? Is it important?"

"Maybe ... It's kind of hard to say." He stepped into the foyer, which opened up into a huge sitting room with a cream-colored leather sofa and loveseat on one side, a Steinway grand piano on the other, and a crystal chandelier suspended above. The dangling crystals sprinkled tiny shivering rainbows on the walls where they tickled the faces on a half-dozen framed portraits, mostly of pleasant-looking elderly folks who seemed to grin at the sudden attention.

Nathan resisted the urge to whistle at the rich décor. Kelly's mom must have been a pretty successful lawyer to afford all this stuff.

The breeze from the open doorway nudged the chandelier, making the crystals sway. The prismatic colors seemed to converge on the wall and spin, and the sparkles tumbled in a kaleidoscopic merry-go-round. He rubbed his eyes and looked again, but the rainbows had scattered into their former chaotic pattern.

Kelly closed the door and joined him in the piano room. "Are you okay?"

"Yeah. Sure." He took in a deep breath. The aroma of polished wood blending with a hint of peanut butter carried a warm welcome message that worked to ease his tortured voice. "This place looks great."

"Thanks. My mother really knew—I mean, really knows how to decorate."

He caressed the piano's glossy rosewood. "A Model B Victorian!" He glanced up at Kelly. "What is it? Seven foot two?"

"Good eye." She nodded at the matching bench. "Go ahead. My father told me you play."

"Well, I'm a lot better at the violin, but maybe I can remember something." He slid into place in front of the piano and set the mirror at his side. After reverently pushing up the keyboard cover, he draped his fingertips across the cool ivory keys. Then, with a gentle touch, he played the first measure of a Beethoven sonata. As he increased to forte, however, he fumbled through the piece, clumsily missing note after note. Heat surging through his cheeks, he stopped and cleared his throat.

Kelly's smile widened into an impish grin. "Yeah, this house is old, but it's completely renovated. When did you visit the Taj Mahal?"

"Taj Mahal?" he repeated while closing the keyboard cover. "Uh ... my mom had a performance in New Delhi in April." He squinted. "Why did you bring that up?"

"You brought it up first."

Nathan rose to his feet, sliding the bench back. "*I* brought it up? What are you talking about?"

"While you were playing the piano. You said you're glad you made it to the Taj Mahal."

"No, I didn't. I said I'm a lot better at the violin, but I'd try to play something."

Kelly closed one eye. "But after that, you said—"

"I didn't say anything after that."

As the chandelier's sparkles passed across her face, she tapped her chin with a finger. "I'll bet all the stress is getting to you. If you can't even remember saying something, you really need to get some rest."

"But I didn't say anything, I—"

"Your room's this way." Striding through the adjacent hall at a lively pace, she raised her voice. "C'mon. You'll get lost in this house if you don't keep up."

He grabbed the mirror and stepped in her direction, then halted, glancing around. "Did you say your parents aren't here?"

She shouted from a distant room. "Right. Dad'll probably get back in about three hours after he gets stuff for your welcome party. I'm making a special dinner tonight." She leaned out a doorway at the end of the corridor. "Why?"

"Then we're alone?" He edged toward the front door and reached for the knob. "I think I'd better wait outside."

"Wait!" Kelly hurried back to the foyer, her feet slapping against the tile. "My father told me you'd have a lot of old-fashioned ideas," she said as she grabbed his hand.

"Old-fashioned?"

She pointed at herself, her brown eyes gleaming. "Don't think of me as a girl. Think of me as your sister."

"But I never had a sister."

She pulled him toward the bedroom. "And I've never had a brother before. You could come in handy."

Nathan slid his hand away from Kelly's but followed close behind as she turned through the doorway. He stopped under the lintel and stared. The room was enormous! With high ceilings and soft beige carpet that seemed to run on endlessly, his new bedroom was even bigger than the piano room! He blinked and looked again. No. The size was an illusion. A huge mirror covered the entire back wall and reflected the room's interior, exaggerating its spaciousness. Still, it was bigger than most of the rooms he had slept in during his mother's latest world tour, especially the closet-sized hovel he had shared with his parents while in Warsaw.

Kelly knelt and began collecting books from the floor. "Sorry about the mess. I was trying to adjust the cabinet shelves, and while I was talking to you on the intercom, the screwdriver slipped, and the whole thing fell over."

After setting his mirror on the floor, Nathan lifted the cabinet and pushed it upright. "Don't worry about it." He scooped an armload of books and heaved them up to the shelves. Bending down to grab another load, he glanced back at the room's mirror and caught the image of two teenagers collecting books from the floor.

Although the room was brightly lit by a tri-domed ceiling fixture and a lamp on a desk near the only window in the room, the reflection darkened. In the image, looming shadows stretched across their heads and backs. The books, the cabinet, and the carpet disappeared, replaced by an endless layer of dead autumn leaves. Lightning flashed, and a breeze blew the leaves into a swirl, enveloping Nathan and Kelly, along with a little girl he didn't recognize, in a tornadic funnel.

He looked back at Kelly. There were no strange shadows in the room. No leaves. No storm. No little girl. He spun his head toward the mirror again. Everything was back to normal.

Kelly grunted as she lifted an unabridged dictionary to the top shelf. "That's where Dad wants it. 'Got to keep Webster handy,' he always says. 'You never know when you'll need a paperweight.'"

Smiling, Nathan set a hefty world atlas next to the dictionary. "Or maybe two paperweights."

She snatched a dusty rag from a dresser and stuffed it into her jeans pocket, then spread out her hands. "So, what do you think? Pretty cool, huh?"

"Yeah. It's nice. Roomy and ... well ..." He slid his hands into his pockets and shrugged his shoulders, nodding toward the desk. "I like having a desk. I read a lot."

She stepped toward a queen-size poster bed and pulled back the comforter. "I think you'd better lie down. You're as white as a ghost."

He let out a sigh and nodded. Those phantom images in the mirror proved she was right. He was so tired he was seeing things.

She fluffed up the pillow and patted it invitingly. "Take a nap. I'll wake you up when dinner's ready."

Nathan tried to talk through a long yawn. "Get me up right away if Clara comes back, okay?"

"I will." Kelly's eyes softened as she laid a hand on his shoulder.

"It may not be any help or comfort, but my dad says our home is your home. He and your dad were real close a long time ago."

He glanced at her hand out of the corner of his eye. Her touch felt warm and good. "It helps. When Clara told me about your family, it was the first time I ever heard of you, so I was kind of nervous."

"Don't be. I'm harmless . . . well, to my friends, anyway. And my dad's excited. He always wanted a son to play basketball with." She spread out her arms and posed like a pixie. "But all Mom and Dad could come up with was little old, five-foot-four me."

Nathan laughed. Kelly's comical grin, combined with her grimy cheeks and sparkling eyes, chased away his sorrows, at least for the moment. Having her as a sister promised brighter days ahead.

Kelly turned a dial on the intercom speaker next to the door. Classical music flowed into the room, a string quartet, but Nathan didn't recognize the piece. She scooted out on tiptoes, turned off the lights, and closed the door with a quiet click. The draped window on the adjacent wall allowed the sun's afternoon rays to filter in and wash the room with muted light, creating a host of new shadows on the floor. A fresh blotter covered the center of the desk, bordered by a fancy pen and three pencils on one side and a pencil sharpener on the other. Propped on a back corner, an eight-by-ten frame held a computer-printed message, *Welcome, Nathan*, in bold blue letters.

Nathan pressed his lips together. Kelly was really trying to make him feel at home . . . but it wasn't home. At least not yet.

He pulled his wallet from his back pocket, slid his fingers into a slot inside, and withdrew a photo: his mom and dad, each with an elbow leaning against a snowman, a funny pose they had struck during a hike on Mount Shasta in California. The vibrant smile on Mom's face both soothed and stabbed him at the same time. Dad's silly grin made him laugh inside. A tear pushed into each eye. He pinched the bridge of his nose, briefly closed his eyes, and laid the wallet and photo gently on the night table at his side.

Lowering his head to the pillow, he stared at the huge mirror through the space between the bedposts. In the deathly still air, the music seemed to grow in volume. A new piece began, Mozart's Requiem Mass in D Minor—lovely, yet haunting.

The window at his side hovered in the mirror's image as if suspended in thick liquid, gently swimming in a tight circle. As the room grew darker, his mind slumbered in a dreamlike haze. Mozart's Latin phrases streamed in. Nathan instinctively translated the familiar lyrics, imagining the words and notes on a musical staff floating above his head.

Grant them eternal rest, Lord,
And may everlasting light shine on them.
You are praised, God, in Zion,
And prayer will be returned to you in Jerusalem.
Hear my speech,
To you all flesh will come.
Grant them eternal rest, Lord,
And let everlasting light shine on them.

Darkness pushed deeper into the room. Lightning flashed. A soft rumbling sound passed over the ceiling, while raindrops pecked at the glass.

There will be great trembling
When the judge comes
To closely examine all!

The trumpet will send its wondrous sound
Throughout the region's tombs
He will gather all before the throne.

The hypnotic window, a soft light in the midst of deep grays and purples, stretched in all directions. As it filled the mirror, Nathan tried to focus on the image. Was this a dream?

Death and nature will be astounded,
When all creation rises again,
To answer to the judgment.
A written book will be brought forth,
In which all will be contained,
By which the world will be judged.

The drapes covering the reflected window slowly parted. Bright light seeped through, illuminating a hand as it emerged through a gap at the window's base. As the sash lifted, long, pointed fingernails bit into the varnish. The frame groaned, wood dragging on wood, and the gap expanded inch by inch. Soon, a face appeared, the thin, sallow face that had so recently burned an image in his mind with its hungry, greedy eyes.

Mictar was trying to enter.

King of tremendous majesty,
Who freely saves those worthy ones,
Save me, spring of mercy.

Remember, kind Jesus,
Because I am the cause of your suffering;
Lest you should forsake me on that day.

Nathan fought against sleep. His mind screamed at his body to wake up. This was too real. That mirror had somehow pierced his dream, warning him of an approaching murderer. He gritted his teeth and wagged his head on the pillow, but he couldn't seem to awaken.

The specter climbed into the room, showing his thin frame in full profile. Nathan strained his eyes to find Mictar's white ponytail, but it was no longer there. The ghostly creature turned toward him, but his face showed no bruise at all, no sign that a violin had crashed across his cheek. He approached the reflection's foreground, his expression void. Nathan cringed.

My prayers are unworthy,
But, you, good Lord, are kind,
Lest I should burn in eternal fire.

His eyes glowing red, the creature pointed straight at Nathan, as if he could see him through the barrier. "Beware, son of Solomon, lest you use your gifts unwisely and thereby come to calamity. If you allow grief to sway your purpose, you will perish. If you pursue vengeance, your light will drain away. If you fear, you will fail, for the power of Quattro is not to be trifled with."

The scene near the back of the reflection transformed. The room's surroundings faded away, replaced by the two coffins, still carrying his parents' bodies. Mictar reached into a coffin and withdrew a small sphere. As Nathan focused on the object, its identity clarified. An eyeball!

Spare us by your mercy, God,
Gentle Lord Jesus,
Grant them eternal rest. Amen.

Mictar held the orb close to the front of the mirror. His voice lowered to a whisper, yet it still seemed to ring in Nathan's ears. "Learn the mystery of the light within. Only then will you vanquish the darkness and defeat your enemies."

Gasping for breath, Nathan sat up in bed and shouted, "You murderer! How dare you touch their bodies! Give them back to me!"

The coffins vanished. Mictar faded away. The mirror image warped and then clarified, showing Nathan's room and a dim image of himself sitting up in bed. Lightning flashed again, illuminating his tear-streaked face, gaunt and pale.

He shivered hard. Pulling his blanket around his body, he

flopped back down in bed. It had to be a dream, the worst nightmare in history. As he turned to the side and curled into a fetal position, cold fingers seemed to stroke his skin, sending new shivers that shook his body so hard, the bed shook with him.

Closing his eyes, he bit his blanket. The horrible images impaled his brain—Mictar, the coffins, the eyeball. Would they ever go away? Would Mom and Dad ever find peace? Would he ever see them again?

> *Let eternal light shine on them, Lord,*
> *With your saints in eternity,*
> *Because you are merciful.*
> *Grant them eternal rest, Lord,*
> *And let everlasting light shine on them,*
> *With your saints in eternity,*
> *Because you are merciful.*

The cold fingers lifted. His shivers settled. Yet, a new spasm began to rock his body. Nathan wept. Biting his blanket even harder, he sobbed on and on until darkness finally overtook his mind.

3

THE MIRROR PUZZLE

"Wake up, Nathan." Radiance poured into the room. "It's dinner time!"

Nathan shot up in bed, blinking at the hallway light framing Kelly's dim shadow.

"Oh!" She flipped on the bedroom light. "Sorry to startle you."

He jumped out of bed, raced to the window, and tried to open it. Locked. Leaning close, he peered at the varnished sill. No scratches. Windblown raindrops pelted the glass, painting tear streaks on his ghostly image.

"What's wrong?" Kelly asked from the door.

He wiped his hand across his brow. "I don't get it."

"A nightmare?" She walked in. Now wearing clean blue jeans and a long-sleeved pink tunic, she set her hands on her hips and gazed at the window. "It's no wonder. Add a thunderstorm to all you've gone through and that'd give anyone nightmares."

Nathan stepped up to the mirror. "I could've sworn it was real." He stared at his reflection. Not only was his hair standing on end, his pupils had shrunk to the size of BBs, barely visible in the center of his blue irises. "There's something strange about this mirror."

"What do you mean?"

He touched a vertical line on the glassy surface, leaving a fingerprint over the image of his nose. "Is it divided into sections?"

"Yep. Three hundred and ninety-nine, to be exact." She wiped the print clean with the cuff of her sleeve. "Dad saw it for sale at a castle in Scotland and shipped it home. Some creepy museum curator convinced him that it could reflect what people were thinking." She pointed at the lower left corner. "One piece is missing. My dad said that your dad took it years ago for some sort of experiment. He never gave it back."

Nathan bent over and lifted his mirror, slowly unwrapping it as he watched Kelly's image in the reflective matrix. "I think I know where the piece is." Dropping the towel, he knelt at the corner space and slid his piece into the square vacancy. It fit perfectly.

A sudden burst of radiance erupted from the corner and spread across the entire mirror. Seconds later, it evaporated, like luminescent steam dispersing in the room.

Kelly slapped her hand on her chest. "Wow! What was that?"

"Too weird." He pulled on the square, but it held fast. "It's stuck."

Stooping low, she touched the reflective mosaic's newest piece. "The glue on the wall couldn't be wet after all these years."

Nathan pulled again, grunting. *Something* was making it hang on.

A loud voice pounded Nathan's eardrums. "Welcome!" A burly hand grasped his upper arm and pulled him to his feet. "I'm Tony Clark."

Nathan angled his head upward. A bug-eyed man with a boot-camp crew cut stared down at him from what seemed like two feet above his head. "Hi, Mr. Clark."

He spread out his huge palm and grabbed Nathan's hand, his long fingers wrapping around with a friendly, but painful grasp. "Call me Tony." Nathan squeezed him back with his violin-strengthened grip, more to relieve the pain than to show off.

"Now that's a manly handshake!" Tony said, glancing at Kelly. She sighed and folded her hands behind her back.

Tony nodded toward the hall. "C'mon out to the dining room. Kelly really cooked up a storm."

She rolled her eyes and whispered to Nathan, a look of disgust crossing her face. "A storm. Get it?"

As the three walked down the hall, Tony laughed. "A storm. Get it? It's raining outside." His deep voice resonated through the corridor as his long legs swept hurriedly past the grand piano. "Do you like Chinese?"

Nathan quickened his pace to keep up. "Sure."

"Too bad," Kelly whispered, following close behind. "We're having Italian."

Tony stopped at the dining room and extended his arm toward the table. "Too bad. We're having Italian."

The aroma of garlic-soaked tomato sauce flooded Nathan's senses. A huge rectangular dish of lasagna graced the middle of the table, and a salad marked each of four place settings, knives and forks aligned perfectly over folded napkins and a pristine white tablecloth. With five high-backed chairs on each side and one on each end, the table seemed more suited for a football team than for an only child and her parents.

Kelly touched his shoulder and whispered. "Daddy kind of rushed you in here. He's not exactly Mr. Sensitive. If you don't feel up to eating with us, I'll make an excuse for you."

"It's okay. I'll be all right." He nodded at each place setting, silently counting. "Four?"

"Clara called while you were sleeping. She'll be here any minute."

Tony sat down at the head of the table. "Sol and I called her 'Medusa' back in Poly-Sci class at Iowa. Her class was so hard we turned to stone. It'll be fun to see what she's like now."

Nathan pulled out a chair and motioned for Kelly to sit. She smiled, her gaze locked on her dad's face as she slid into the chair and pulled it up to the table. Nathan seated himself on the opposite side.

Tony grabbed a knife, cut out a quarter of the lasagna, and heaped it onto his plate. "Dive on in," he said, handing the knife to Nathan.

Nathan glanced up at Kelly. She gave him a quick nod, a sign that it was okay to serve himself before she could get hers. Just as he sliced into the lasagna, the doorbell chimed its low-pitched tone.

Kelly yanked her napkin from her lap. "That must be Clara." But before she could get up, an authoritative voice sang from the piano room. "Tony, Tony, Tony. You left the door unlocked. I thought I taught you about home security in class." Clara appeared at the dining room entryway. "You never know when a strange old woman might barge right in!" She unbuttoned a rain-dampened overcoat. "And a wet one at that!"

Nathan slid back his chair and stood up. Clara seemed much bubblier than she had been earlier in the day. That meant she had news.

Tony rose to his feet, stuffing his hands in his pockets while shifting his weight. "Don't worry. This house is plenty secure. We're out in the middle of nowhere."

"I met your daughter this morning," Clara said as she cast her gaze on Kelly. "I was delighted to see what a beautiful young lady she is!"

Kelly folded her hands in her lap, her face turning as pink as her shirt. "Thank you."

Tony gave Clara an uneasy grin. "Of course she's beautiful. Is that such a surprise?"

"Well, not to me, of course, but didn't the other students unanimously vote you the 'Most Likely to Produce a Troll' award? At the time, I said it was ridiculous, and you have proven me correct." She mussed Nathan's hair. "And I like being proven correct, don't I, Nathan?"

Nathan combed his fingers through his hair and smiled. "Rule number one: Clara is always right. Rule number two: If Clara is wrong—"

"See rule number one," Tony finished. "I heard that in her class more times than I can count." He gestured toward a vacant chair. "Are you hungry?"

"Yes, indeed," Clara replied, "but first things first. There's a trunk in the back of my Jeep. Would you or Nathan bring it in? It's not so heavy that an old lady like me couldn't carry it, but with the rain—"

"I can get it." Tony waved his hand at Nathan. "You three go ahead and eat." He disappeared into the piano room and, seconds later, the front door slammed.

Clara grimaced at the sound. "I hope I didn't upset him with the troll award comment. He really isn't nearly as ugly as his classmates said. He's just … unusual."

Clapping her hand over a widening grin, Kelly spoke through her fingers. "Don't worry about it. He'll be over it by the time he gets back."

Nathan helped Clara take off her trench coat and hung it on a coat tree near the doorway. "Any news?" he asked.

Clara allowed him to seat her at the table. "Some news. Our lawyer gave me an envelope from your father's safety deposit box. It contained money for your needs, so you won't be destitute for a while."

"Here it is!" Tony lumbered into the dining room and set the knee-high trunk on the floor, his face dripping.

Kelly jumped up and swabbed her dad's forehead with a napkin. "I guess it was pretty heavy, after all."

"It's not heavy," Tony said, pushing her hand away. "That's rain, not sweat."

Nathan laid his palm on the trunk's damp wooden top and looked at Clara, who was still seated at the table. "So, have you figured out how to open it yet?"

"Heaven's sakes, no!" Clara replied. "You and you alone should open it."

Kelly caressed the ancient wood with two fingers. "I don't see any seam; it's like it doesn't even have a lid."

Nathan grasped the top edge and lifted. It didn't budge.

Tony bumped him out of the way. "Let me try." He rubbed his hands together, then, squatting for leverage, he grabbed the top and jerked upward. The entire trunk lifted into the air, and Tony fell backwards, still hanging on and cradling it against his chest.

Kelly stifled a laugh. "Are you okay, Daddy?"

"Yeah," he said, gasping under the weight. "I think the only thing I injured was my pride." He scooted the trunk to the floor and vaulted to his feet. Breathing heavily, he grabbed Nathan's shoulder, his eyes bugging out more than ever. "I've got an idea. Be right back." He marched out of the room.

Nathan looked at Kelly, but she just shrugged her shoulders.

Tony strode back in, a cordless circular saw in hand. He pulled the trigger, making the motor whine and the jagged blade spin. "This'll cut through anything."

"But that'll ruin it," Nathan said, laying his hand on top of the trunk.

Tony spun the blade again. "You want it open, don't you?"

He glanced at Clara, but she just offered a shrug. "Okay," he said. "But be careful."

"I got you covered," Tony shouted as he gunned the motor. "I'll just cut off the very top." He set the blade next to an upper corner and pushed it against the dark wood. The teeth squealed, but they couldn't seem to bite into the grain. Smoke began rising from the saw. Tony's face reddened. As he pushed harder, his muscles flexed, and sweat trickled down his cheeks. Finally, he pulled back and let the saw wind down. "Whew!" He wiped his face with his sleeve. "I don't know what that trunk's made of, but I've cut steel with this blade before."

"So no one could open it to put anything inside," Nathan said. "It's probably empty."

"It felt empty when I picked it up and fell over. Nothing rattled around."

Clara clapped her hands. "Well, we have quite a mystery to solve, don't we? I have another suitcase to bring in, but for now I suggest that we all eat and rest. Perhaps tomorrow will provide new ideas."

Nathan reseated himself at the table. "Another suitcase? Are you staying here tonight?"

"I'm afraid not. The suitcase is filled with new clothes for you." Her eyebrows shot up. "Oh! I almost forgot your new violin. We should bring it in right away. After supper we'll test it out, and then I will be off to Davenport again where your trust fund is being set up. As executor of your father's will, I must be present to sign the paperwork."

Tony sat in his chair and propped his elbows. "Do you know how much moolah he's getting?"

"Daddy!" Kelly shouted. "What are you thinking? His parents were just murdered!"

"Oh ... yeah." Tony's head drooped an inch. "Sorry."

Nathan smiled weakly. "It's okay. Don't worry about it." Even as the words slipped out of his mouth, he regretted them. It really wasn't okay. Tony's remark was crass and stupid. Kelly was right. He wasn't Mr. Sensitive.

Clara patted Nathan's hand. "We're all probably curious about the money situation, but I'm afraid it's another mystery. The financial instructions were sealed with a directive to open them two days after your father's passing, which is a Saturday, so we had to make special arrangements to make sure all parties were available. I'll call Nathan as soon as everything is settled, but even if his money is locked in a trust fund, he'll likely have a stipend for his living expenses."

After Nathan retrieved the violin, everyone slid up to the table and began the meal. Tony dominated the conversation, talking about basketball games in college with "Flash," Nathan's father, and how he wasn't given that nickname because of his speed, but because of his love of photography. That's what led him into photojournalism, then into investigative reporting, and finally into technology security. And, Tony lamented, what probably got him into trouble with whoever killed him and his wife. "Flash was far too trusting. He refused to believe what I learned the hard way. You can't trust anyone. Everyone's in the game for themselves."

Nathan turned his head away and bit his lip hard. This new "father" was worse than insensitive. He was Captain Clueless, an ape in human clothing. He needed to be set straight.

Just as Nathan opened his mouth to object, he caught Kelly's gaze. Her sad eyes glistening, she mouthed the words "I'm sorry."

Breathing a silent sigh, Nathan gave her a little nod. It was okay. And this time, it really was. As long as Kelly cared about his grief, nothing else really mattered. But would she understand his nonverbal cues that he wasn't angry anymore?

As her trembling lips turned upward, Nathan smiled with her. She understood. Somehow his new sister was able to see a lot more than met the eye. If she could communicate that well without making a sound, maybe there was a lot more to her than a pretty face and pink toenails.

During the meal, he glanced at the trunk every couple of minutes. The lasagna, now barely warmer than room temperature, tasted good enough, but it was nothing more than a stomach-filler. Wondering what might be in his father's trunk consumed his thoughts. Since his father made sure he retrieved it, it couldn't really be empty. Maybe the inside was lined with instructions on how to defeat Mictar, or how to understand the technological secrets behind the strange mirror. Who could tell?

He caught Kelly's gaze again. Her eyes seemed melancholy, yet when she joined him in furtive glances at the trunk, her countenance carried a glimmer of hope that something new and exciting was about to happen. For years he had traveled with his parents all over the world, exploring strange, exotic lands and meeting hundreds of friendly people, yet he always felt alone, no real friends, no one his age to talk to. Now he had a sister. What would it be like living with this lonely, yet hopeful girl?

The mysteries of the evening sparkled in her eyes. They were definitely on the same wavelength. With two almost imperceptible nods, they silently agreed that they would figure out everything together, no matter what.

Nathan slid the trunk against the wall next to his bed and sat on its sturdy wooden top. Breathing a long sigh, he rested his chin on his hands and stared at his reflection in the mirror on the opposite side of the room. The house lay quiet. Clara had rushed away, hoping to get to Davenport and catch a few hours of sleep before her meetings. With his help, Kelly had washed the dishes, then retired to her room, complaining of a headache—something about food allergies. Tony left the house, spinning a basketball on his fingers. "Got a pickup game with the boys," he had said.

Nathan checked his new wristwatch, one of the many items Clara had brought in a hefty suitcase. The analog face read 11:15, matching the digits on the radio clock on his desk. A Haydn quartet played from the radio's little speaker, soft enough to blend into the background.

He looked at the mirror and raised a finger as if having a silent conversation with his reflection. Basketball, so late at night? He shrugged. Maybe Tony was telling the truth. Maybe it was one of those midnight basketball leagues. Lots of guys would want to go out and play basketball late on a Friday, right? His reflection shook its head, copying his own doubtful shake. Then again ... maybe not.

He stood and began unbuttoning a new shirt he had just tried on, walking close to the mirror as he reached the bottom button. With only a desk lamp to light the room, his slender, yet toned frame cast a long, narrow shadow across the floor. The image in the mirror mimicked his moves as he threw off his shirt and tossed it behind him, leaving him bare chested except for a small wooden cross attached to a thin leather strap that looped around his neck.

Something bright glinted in his eyes, like a laser beam passing just below his brow. The light in the room dimmed, as if the power were sagging, making his shadow darken. He spun to the side and shook his head scornfully. Like a clumsy oaf, he had draped his shirt over the lamp shade. He jerked it away and tossed it onto the trunk, allowing the lamp to flash to life.

He turned back to the mirror. In the reflection, his shadow grew, lengthening and widening until it shrouded the entire image in a dark gray cloud. The lamp's glow pierced the darkness and cast thin beams onto the mysterious trunk. His shirt had vanished.

Nathan turned completely around. His shirt still lay on the trunk. The light and his shadow remained normal.

A cold shiver sent goose bumps crawling across his skin. Slowly he turned to face the mirror again. Still cloaked in a gray fog, the trunk, the lamp, and the window were the only visible objects.

Creeeak!

That sound! The window! Nathan froze in place, slowly inching his head around toward the real window. Drapes still covered the glass, motionless. He edged toward them. One step.

Another. With a wild swipe, he threw them open. Nothing. Just a dark, rainy night.

A peal of thunder rumbled, sending a new shiver up Nathan's spine. He released the drapes and stood in front of the mirror again. A hand emerged under the window's image, pulling it up. No sharp nails this time, just a normal human hand.

He glanced back and forth, watching the action unfold in the mirror and keeping an eye on the real window, still in full light, still undisturbed. A man in a trench coat crawled through the window image, then a woman, the man with a finger to his lips while helping the woman climb in.

Nathan's whole body shook. He pinched himself, but this couldn't be a dream. Was the mirror showing a reflection of his thoughts like the museum guy had told Kelly's father?

The man in the mirror, unrecognizable in the shadows, skulked to the trunk and opened it. Nathan tried to peer inside, but he was too far away to see anything. The woman, also in a trench coat, tiptoed straight up to Nathan, her face becoming clear as she approached, beautiful and serene.

Nathan gasped. "M-Mom?"

He glanced to each side. The room was empty. The woman in the mirror leaned over his shoulder and kissed his reflection on the cheek. A hint of wetness brushed his skin. She then grasped his right hand and kissed it tenderly, finishing with a gentle blow on his knuckles as her distinctive raven tresses spilled across his wrist.

Nathan lowered his gaze to his real hand. His mother's lips were nowhere to be seen, yet somehow he could feel her breath, warm and gentle.

In the mirror, a sad smile crossed her face as she slowly turned away. She joined the man in front of the trunk, and their bodies blocked his view. They each pulled something from their trench coats, bent low, and placed the objects in the trunk.

They both turned, allowing a beam from the lamp to illuminate the man's face.

Nathan gulped. "Dad!"

His father crawled back out the window, then helped his mother through again. With a muffled thump, the window closed.

Nathan locked his eyes on the mirror. Only his own image, the lamp, and the trunk remained—the open trunk. He swung around. The trunk in the room was closed, his shirt still draping it. He spun back toward the mirror and took a step in reverse. His reflection stepped backwards. He took another step. His reflection took another step. As he continued to edge back, the Nathan in the mirror closed in on the trunk behind him until his heels collided with its base.

Slowly bending his knees, Nathan reached behind his body. Would his image lower its hands into the open trunk? It did! And he could feel his own hands go inside, moving farther down than the top of the trunk should have allowed.

Were his hands really inside the trunk now? He didn't dare turn to look. The trunk might slam shut and chop his hands off at the wrists. He pushed down, feeling carefully with his fingers. Each hand latched onto an object, familiar objects, but he couldn't quite figure out what they were. As though carrying downy chicks, he coaxed the objects slowly upward.

Still watching his reflection, now at a distance twice the length of the room, he pulled the objects out of the trunk and laid them carefully on the floor. Leaping to his feet, he spun around. The trunk was still closed, his shirt on top, but a camera and a violin lay in front of it.

He dropped to his knees and snatched up the camera. It was Dad's Nikon! He laid it down and picked up the violin, lovingly caressing its polished wood. Mom's Guaneri!

His throat caught. Tears welled in his eyes. He scrambled for his new violin case, snapped it open, and grabbed his bow.

Pushing his mother's violin under his chin, he rested the bow across the D string, then, with a gentle, reverent stroke, played a long, sweet note.

The sound penetrated his body, sending gentle vibrations along his skin. He played another note, then a melody, measures from the Vivaldi duet. Closing his eyes, breathless and crying, his soul drank in the beautiful music. His heart sang, and in his mind, his mother sang with him. Her voice soothed his grieving soul. He wept for her, for his father, for the tragedy that had left his life in a shambles.

After finishing a crescendo, he let his arms droop and laid the violin gently on the floor. He picked up the camera again and checked the counter. Six pictures left.

He slid the violin in front of his knees and focused the lens, then, with a flick of his finger, he turned on the flash. His father had never upgraded to a modern digital camera. That wasn't his way. He preferred the quality of film and the nuances of craftsmanship he could add to his photo creations by developing them himself. Nathan had spent dozens of hours in dark rooms watching him bring negatives to life, even helping him at times and learning the basics of the art.

He caressed the surface, marred by dozens of bumps and dings it had earned through its years of service. As he smiled at its familiar touch, his skin tingled. Now the camera was his. More valuable than gold, this treasure would be with him forever. Yet, it would also be an eternal reminder, flashing again and again the image in the coffins, his dead parents mutilated by a brutal traitor. A wave of sadness drew his lips downward. This camera would be a bittersweet token, carrying both a burning acid and a healing salve.

Aiming the camera at the violin, he pushed the shutter button and listened to the auto-advance zip the film ahead. He stood again and turned toward the mirror. It was back to normal—no open window, no weird shadows. The trunk was closed, and his shirt covered the top.

He strode halfway across the room and raised the camera. What would a picture of his reflection look like? He pressed the button. The flash of light bounced off the mirror and radiated back to the lens, sending an electric jolt through his hands. The camera flew from his grip, but, just before it hit the ground, he snagged the strap and swung it back up.

Looking the casing over, he checked the meters. The film had advanced, and the flash indicator showed a charge. Everything seemed fine. He draped the strap around his neck and let the camera dangle at his chest. Taking a picture of the mirror wasn't a great idea.

Echoes of laughter filtered through the hall, male and female, then a shushing sound. Grabbing his shirt and throwing it on, he tiptoed to the bedroom door and paused there, fastening his buttons under the swaying camera. A light knock sounded from the other side, then a whispered call. "Nathan!"

Kelly's voice! He turned the knob and cracked the door open. "What's up?"

"Shhh! . . . Are you decent?"

"Yeah, I—"

She pushed the door and squeezed through. "Good." Dressed in a long bathrobe and wool socks, she glanced around the room, her voice barely audible. "Who else is in here?"

"Who else?" he whispered back. "What are you talking about?"

"I was on my way to the bathroom. I heard voices."

He peeked out the door. "I heard a woman laughing. Could that be it?"

"No." She pushed the door closed with her back and held the knob. "That's my dad. He's . . . uh . . . playing cards, I think."

"Oh . . . Cards." Nathan furrowed his brow. He finally realized what Kelly's father was up to. "Is he playing solitaire?"

She tilted her head downward and shook it slowly. "He's not really playing cards at all." After a few seconds, she lifted her head again and gazed at him. Her brown eyes glistened. "I guess your dad never did stuff like that, did he?"

"No." He crossed his arms over his chest. "He had a lot of old-fashioned ideas."

Kelly's lips curled downward. She spun to the side and bit one of her knuckles.

Nathan's heart sank. How could he be such a pig? What her father was doing was breaking her heart. He reached for her shoulder, but pulled back. "I'm sorry. I ... I didn't really mean it that way."

Her voice cracked. "Yes, you did, and I deserved it."

He reached again. This time he let his hand settle gently on her shoulder. She flinched, but only for a second. "How long has your mother been gone?"

"Maybe three months, but they've been sleeping apart for years." Wiping her eyes, she shrugged and forced a trembling smile. "She just found another guy and took off, like trading in an old car for a new model."

He pulled his hand away. "And you got left in the backseat?"

"Yeah. Something like that. She said I was more like a son than a daughter, so I'd be better off with Daddy."

Nathan winced. "Oh, man! That's gotta hurt!"

"Don't worry," she said with a sigh. "I'm used to it." Shaking her hair out of her eyes, she turned toward him again, wiping a tear. Her voice still trembled. "Anyway, I heard other voices. They came from your room."

"There's no one else here." He gestured toward the mirror. "Just me and my reflection."

"I know what I heard, and it wasn't your voice. Someone said, 'Buckingham is as opulent as I imagined,' but I couldn't make out the rest."

"Buckingham? Like Buckingham Palace?"

"I guess so. I'm not the one who said it."

"Well, I didn't say anything about Buckingham Palace." He turned toward the mirror—still normal. "But lots of weird stuff has been going on."

She slid her finger behind the camera strap. "Like taking pictures of your room at midnight?"

"That's part of it." He held the camera up for her to see. "This is ... I mean, was, my dad's camera. It was in the trunk."

Her eyes lit up. "The trunk? How'd you get it open?"

He shifted his weight from one foot to the other. "That's kind of hard to explain."

"Was anything else in there?"

"Yeah." He pointed at the violin on the floor. "That was my mom's."

She scooted to the trunk and knelt, squinting at its weathered wood. "I still don't see any seam."

Nathan squatted next to her, picked up the violin, and nervously plucked a string.

She rose and sat on the trunk. "Did you say something?"

"I don't think so." He laid the violin back down. "Maybe I was thinking out loud."

"About what?"

"I'm trying to figure out if I should tell you how I got into the trunk."

Two lines dug into her brow. "Why wouldn't you tell me?"

"Because it was so weird. You'll think I'm crazy."

"Maybe I will." A wide grin crossed her face. "Maybe I already do."

Nathan plopped onto the bed, making the mattress coils squeak. He gazed at the mirror for a moment, hoping it would try some of its tricks so Kelly wouldn't be tempted to haul him away in a straightjacket, but its images and shadows reflected the room with perfect precision.

She leaned forward, her red socks tickling the flat, beige carpet as she cupped her hands around her mouth. "Earth to Nathan. This is mission control. I'm waiting for transmission." She stretched her arms and yawned. "Report your extra-terrestrial findings, please, before I fall asleep."

"I'll do better than that." He lifted the camera to his eye and took Kelly's picture. "I'll transmit a photo of a female Martian to go along with my report."

4

ECHOES FROM THE PAST

Nathan paid for the photo pack and stuffed it into his jacket without opening it, keeping his promise to Kelly not to peek until he got home. The jacket, a leather one borrowed from Tony, complete with a soft inner lining and a Newton High School "Cardinals" logo, was a bit warm for the late summer morning, but the extra protection seemed appropriate, considering his mode of transportation. Besides, it looked great.

Alternately running and jogging, he hurried out to the Wal-Mart parking lot where he had left the motorcycle. Finding the store hadn't been too hard—near the interstate, just as Kelly had said. She had wanted to come along, but since her allergies were acting up, he set out on his own.

Tony had left before dawn on this early autumn Saturday, taking the only car, so Nathan borrowed Kelly's motorcycle right after breakfast. Snapping three quick photographs of her in front of the house, he had finished the roll, anxious to reveal the secrets that lay hidden in his father's camera.

Now, after sliding his helmet over his head, he started the engine and wheeled around toward the parking lot exit, riding in the shopping center's outer perimeter road, a two-lane access that ran parallel to the storefront on his right and the highway on his left.

When he reached the intersection with the entrance lanes, he stopped and waited for a long line of incoming cars, giving him a moment to gaze at the miles of pavement on the main road. Although he couldn't see them from here, he remembered the endless stretch of pregnant cornfields begging to be harvested. It had been a pleasant ride to the only one-hour film-developing lab around, a good chance to get away and think—about Mom, about Dad, and about mornings just like this one: Saturday breakfasts at a pancake restaurant and playing cards on a long flight from who-knows-where to some other nameless place across the ocean.

He flipped down the helmet's glass shield. Yes, the ride home should be just as pleasant, another chance to reminisce in private. Through the visor, nobody could see him crying.

One of the cars in the line, a blue Mustang convertible, turned right on the perimeter road and drove slowly past, then stopped suddenly, while the cars behind him all turned left or headed straight into the store's central parking lane.

Nathan gulped. It was Mictar's gunman from Chicago. The car was a little different—royal blue and not a scratch on it—yet there was no disguising the gray-bearded man behind the wheel. But how did he get out of jail? And how could he have known to come all the way out here?

As he waited for the last car to pass, Nathan angled his face away. Would the helmet be enough to keep this guy from recognizing him?

The Mustang backed up and stopped again. Pulling off a pair of sunglasses, the driver stared at Nathan. "Hey, kid! What's your name?"

Nathan squeezed the bike's handlebars and lowered his voice. "Who wants to know?"

"Don't get smart with me. I'm looking for my nephew, a boy about your age. He's a runaway from my brother's home, so I'm helping him search around town. His name's Nathan. Seen any strangers lately?"

"What's he look like?"

The man squinted, apparently trying to get a closer look at

Nathan's face. "About five-foot-nine, short blonde hair, a square jaw, kind of like you, only shorter."

Nathan sat up straight and crossed his arms, more confident now that the gunman hadn't recognized him. "Well, I haven't seen anyone who looks like me."

The driver's icy stare chilled his heart. Had he guessed the truth? Nathan glanced around the parking lot. Only two escape routes were in sight. One was the main exit, where someone was waiting at the red light to get out. That wouldn't work. The other lay straight behind him, the perimeter road that would eventually lead to the side entrance, but a Wal-Mart tractor-trailer approached from that way, taking up most of the access road.

"Gotta go!" Nathan restarted the engine and wheeled the bike around, yelling over the roar. "Sorry about your nephew!"

The man pulled a gun from under his seat. "Nathan!"

Nathan took off toward the oncoming Wal-Mart truck, hugging the left-hand side of the road. Cringing at the thought of a bullet in the back, he sped toward a gap between the truck and the curb, barely enough room for the bike but far from enough for the Mustang. Just as he roared past the front cab, he glanced back. The truck driver suddenly swerved to his left, cutting off Nathan's pursuer. A horn squawked, followed by skidding tires. As Nathan whirled around and idled his engine, a loud string of obscenities burned in the air.

With the truck nearly jackknifed between him and the gray-bearded man, Nathan could only see the back of the truck driver's head up in the cab. Seconds later, the Mustang took off out of the main parking lot exit, roaring its engine as it peeled away.

Nathan rolled up to the driver's window. A burly man wearing a Chicago Bears cap stepped out of the cab and crossed his tree-trunk arms over his chest. "Everything all right?"

Nathan cut his engine and pulled off his helmet. "Yeah. What did you do to spook him? He had a gun."

The driver nodded toward his truck. "I had a bigger one."

"Good thing." Nathan took a deep breath and let it out slowly. "Thanks. I think you saved my life."

The man waved toward his truck, his muscled forearms a stark contrast to his fifty-something face. "Want me to call the cops?"

Nathan shook his head. "I'd better just get home. I need to kind of stay under the radar for a while."

He peeled off his cap and scratched through his graying hair. "Are you in a witness protection program or something?"

"I really shouldn't be talking about it." Nathan extended his hand. "Thanks again, Mister ... "

"Stoneman." He shook Nathan's hand firmly. "Glad to be of help." He pressed his cap back on and raised his eyebrows. "You got far to go?"

"A few miles. Not real far, why?"

"Just wondering."

As the trucker shuffled back toward his truck, Nathan set his hand on his stomach. A sick feeling churned inside. The Mustang driver might be gone for a while, but he probably wouldn't give up.

He revved the engine, squeezed between the truck and the curb, and cruised to the exit, looking every direction for any sign of the gunman, but he was nowhere to be found. Prickles stung the back of his neck. Somehow not knowing where the gray-bearded man lurked was worse than staring down the barrel of his gun.

A loud diesel engine sounded to his rear. The trucker pulled up behind him, flashing a thumbs up sign as Nathan glanced back. Obviously, Mr. Stoneman had the same concerns.

Nathan throttled up and cruised toward home. With the comforting sound of the Wal-Mart truck trailing him by a hundred feet or so, he savored the ride, wind whistling through his helmet and the musty aroma of damp earth filling his nostrils. He pressed his hand against his pocket, feeling the photo packet inside. Who could guess what might be on his father's last roll of film? Maybe a keepsake photo of his mom that he could frame and hang above the desk in his new bedroom. A clue to why Dr. Simon stole the lives of his parents. Or, better yet, some kind of message his father had intentionally left behind, something that would add to the mystery.

As he neared the narrow road leading to his house, Nathan peered over his shoulder. Cresting the hill behind him, the truck sent up a plume of black smoke from its vertical exhaust pipe, its diesel engine making a loud racket as it downshifted to coast the hill. Nathan waved and turned onto the side road. A horn tooted in reply, and the engine roared louder as the big rig accelerated and sped away.

Nathan skidded to a stop at the farmhouse's garage and closed the automatic door, watching the road through the gap as it lowered. Pulling off his helmet, he stopped at the inner door and poised his knuckles over it, ready to knock.

He laughed at himself. This was his home now. He could just walk right in. After passing through the laundry room, he found Kelly sitting on a stool at the kitchen bar, leaning over an open notebook, pen in hand.

He pulled the photo pack from his jacket. "I'm back!"

Kelly slapped her notebook shut and patted the space on the bar. "Let's have a look."

He opened the envelope and laid out the photos, following the indexed thumbnail guide to make sure they stayed in chronological order. "Okay," he said, pointing at the photo of his mother's violin, "here's my first picture, so all of these before the violin are my dad's, and all the ones after are ..." He squinted at the photos, picking up the one he had placed after the violin. "This should have been the mirror." He brought it close to his eyes, then handed it to Kelly. "What do you make of it?'

She held one corner and angled it toward the light. "Looks like two people in heavy fog. Almost like a pair of ghosts."

"What are those red things behind them? Brake lights, maybe?"

She held it with both hands, altering the angle several times as she studied it. "I see a dark form around them, a human form, maybe a young girl. Her eyes reflect the light, like a cat's eyes."

"I've never seen a cat with red eyes. An alligator, maybe, but not a cat." He pointed at the next photo. "And this one was supposed to be of you. Remember? The female Martian?"

"Yeah." She bent forward and studied the image, a girl sitting on the trunk, but she couldn't have been older than ten or eleven. "It's certainly not me." She slid it closer to Nathan. "Anyone you recognize?"

"She looks kind of familiar, but I don't think I know her." He tapped the countertop next to the last three photos. "And look at these. They're supposed to be of you in front of the house this morning."

She held the first of the final trio by its edges. "That's definitely our house," she said, hovering her finger over it. "Look. There's our cottonwood tree, but it's smaller, and the leaves are green like in summertime. And that's not me in front of it. She looks like ..." She picked up the "Martian" photo and held the two side by side. "Like this girl. And she's holding a violin."

"A violin?" Nathan snatched the photo and studied the little black-haired girl. "I think I know who she looks like."

"Who?"

"My mother." His hands trembled slightly as he gave the photo back. "I haven't seen many pictures of her when she was little, but this could definitely be her."

Kelly held the pair of photos together again. "You're scaring me, Nathan."

"Yeah. Me, too."

She laid both down and pointed at the last two. "And these buildings aren't anything like my house at all. They're enormous." She looked up at him. "Do you recognize them?"

"Yeah." Trying to keep his hand from shaking, he pointed at them in order. "That's the Taj Mahal, and that's Buckingham Palace."

Holding his mother's violin in his lap, Nathan sat on the trunk and stared at the mirror. Two faces stared back at him—his own, darkened by his somber countenance and the closed drapes, and Kelly's, wide-eyed and expectant. They had spent their Saturday taking pictures, a few action shots of birds flitting around the cottonwood tree, several portraits of Kelly standing in front of the house, and, with Kelly as photographer, three animated poses of Nathan trying to stand on his head with his body leaning against the wall while playing his violin. Now, with the evening advancing toward the hour of the previous night's reflective miracles, he hoped for a repeat performance, this time with a witness present.

Kelly, wearing loose-fitting jeans and a navy sweatshirt, fidgeted, first leaning on one hand, then on the other. "Nothing weird yet."

"Nope. Can't get much more normal."

She glanced around the room. "Are you sure everything's the same?"

He stood up, pointing out objects as he did a slow, three-sixty turn. "The desk lamp's on, the curtains are closed, and my bed covers are pulled back."

"Dad'll be back soon with the new pics, and Clara should be here any minute."

"Maybe she'll have some news that'll help."

"Maybe." She pushed a curtain to the side and peeked out the window. "I'd better put the coffee on. It could be a long night."

"Think we should let your father in on what's going on?"

Kelly waved both hands. "No way! Bad idea! Only you, me, and Clara should look at the photos. If what you're saying is true, my dad'll go nuts!"

Nathan tightened his grip on the violin. "*If* it's true? Don't you believe me?"

"Look," she said, placing a hand on his arm. "I know you're my brother now, but I just met you yesterday." She let her hand slide down as she averted her eyes. "No offense, but for all I know, you might hallucinate on a regular basis. Or maybe you're so upset about losing your parents, you're seeing things. All I've seen so far is some pics from your dad's camera. He could've easily taken photos of Buckingham Palace and the Taj Mahal, and you could've been muttering about them because you visited them recently."

He tightened his jaw but tried to keep his voice calm. "I wasn't muttering about them."

She set her fists on her hips. "I know what I heard."

With a swipe of his hand, he grabbed the picture pack. "But those buildings were the last pictures on the roll! Dad couldn't have taken them."

"The lab could've gotten everything out of order, or maybe they mixed in someone else's stuff." She shrugged. "Who knows?"

Nathan waved his arm toward the window. "But what about the tree in front of your house? How do you explain its size and color?"

She let her arms droop at her side. "Okay," she said, her tone now apologetic. "You got me there." With a quick spin, she began pacing in front of the mirror, making it appear that twin Kellys were marching in stride. "But if my dad even gets a hint that something spooky is going on, he'll set up a media circus. He's dying to, as he says, 'liven up this one-horse town.' He's said a thousand times that he'd like to be on one of those reality TV shows."

She stopped and faced Nathan. "Remember *Field of Dreams*, that movie about ghosts coming out of a cornfield to play baseball? He'd probably want to make a real *Field of Dreams* reality show right in your bedroom."

Nathan tucked the opening flap into the picture pack. "Think he'll look at the new batch of photos before he brings them home?"

"No," she replied, shaking her head. "If anything, he'll be looking through all the sports magazines he probably bought. He likes to do that while he drives. Scares me to death."

"Try jumping over an open drawbridge in a limo. That was the most scared I've been in a long time."

Kelly narrowed her eyes. "You don't have to top my story, Nathan. I know you've been through more scary stuff than I have."

"I wasn't trying to top your—"

"Save it," she said, holding up her hand. "I'm having enough trouble believing you already."

He lowered his head, feeling a scowl forming in his brow. "At least Clara will believe me."

Kelly's lips turned downward as she walked slowly to the door. "Whatever." She opened it just enough to squeeze through. "I'm gonna put the coffee on." The door closed with a louder than usual click.

Nathan stared at the knob, mumbling a mimicry of Kelly's voice. "I'm having enough trouble believing you already." He sighed and moved his gaze back to the mirror. The reflection wasn't going to perform on demand and prove to Kelly that he wasn't going crazy. He had to stop dwelling on it. But what could he do while waiting for the new photos to arrive? Obviously there was no homework. He wasn't supposed to start at Kelly's school until Monday.

Her words echoed in his mind. "Maybe you're so upset about losing your parents, you're seeing things." Could she be right? Could he be hallucinating? Maybe he really was going crazy.

He tucked his mother's violin under his chin. If only Dad were here, then he would have someone who would listen. Or Mom. She'd play something soft while he talked, closing her eyes and nodding her head. She'd believe every word, then, with her eyes open and her bow at her side, she'd whisper poetic wisdom, coating him with comfort whether he understood her counsel or not.

He raised the bow to the strings and began playing "Brahms' Lullaby," holding some of the high notes a bit, just as his mother used to do when her strings sang him to sleep as a young child. Tears welled up again, spilling over his lids and trickling down his cheeks, but he didn't bother to brush them aside. He played on and on, closing his eyes and pretending to nestle in his own bed, in those rare times between Mom's world concert tours and Dad's spy missions.

A vision of that bedroom entered his mind. As the mental portrait of his younger self pretended to sleep, the imagined child peeked through his eyelids and watched his mother's flawless strokes, an angel from heaven sitting in a rocking chair, playing for the King of kings, and he had a front row seat.

Nathan played the final note, stretching it out and softening his touch to make it fade away, but when he lifted the bow, the song began again, more vibrant, more beautiful than ever. He popped open his eyes. In the mirror, his mother sat in the old rocker in his bedroom back home, playing the lullaby. He saw himself, a child of about five, lying in bed with the covers pulled up to his chin.

A knock sounded at the door. "Nathan! What's going on? I hear voices again!"

His throat tightened into a knot. He couldn't move or speak.

Kelly pushed the door open, then closed it quickly. When she saw the mirror, she gasped, pointing. "Nathan! It's ..." She ran to him and grabbed his arm. "What is it?"

His voice shook as he laid the violin on his mattress. "That's my mom. And that's me in bed. This is exactly what I was thinking a minute ago, and it suddenly appeared."

Just as the sweet music eased to a quiet hum, the door swung open again. Clara barged into the room, her purse in one hand and a laptop computer case in the other. "Nathan, your practice is really paying off. You sound—" She raised her hand over her mouth. "Oh, my heavens!"

In the mirror, Nathan's mother approached the foreground of the reflection, her eyes seeming to focus directly on him. She reached up and began pulling down a shade. "Good night, sweetheart," she said. "I'll see you in the morning." The shade slowly covered the entire image and faded it to black. Seconds later, the mirror returned to normal, reflecting the pale faces of everyone in the room.

Tony's voice echoed in the hall. "Where is everybody?" He appeared at the door, his big eyes scanning the room. "Oh. Here you are."

As Kelly turned toward him, her voice shook. "Uh ... hi, Daddy."

"Got your prints." He tossed a photo package on the bed and crossed his arms. "You all look like you've seen a headless ghost."

Nathan tried to catch Kelly's eye. He had no idea what to say. And would Clara spill the beans?

Kelly sprang to her father's side and pushed him out the door. "Nathan was playing a sad song on his violin. It made us all feel kind of blue, you know, with his parents dying and all." Her voice faded down the hall. "Coffee's ready. You want some?"

Nathan scrambled for the package, tore it open, and dumped out the photos. He leaned over and quickly arranged them on the bedspread. "Clara, take a look. Recognize anything in these pictures?"

Clara set the computer case down and hobbled over to the bed, her voice trembling. "Nathan, what did I just see? Was that really your mother?"

"I'll explain later, or at least I'll try to. Just look at these before Tony gets back."

"Very well." She pulled a pair of glasses from her purse and peered at the first photo while Nathan looked on. It showed three laptop computers on a curved desk that abutted an equally curved wall. The room appeared dimly lit, and a Microsoft logo floated randomly across each screen. "No," she said, pulling back, "that place is unfamiliar to me."

Nathan held up the second photo. This one was even darker than the first, some kind of large room with a tall cylindrically shaped bulge in the middle of the floor. "What do you make of this one?"

"Is that a telescope?"

Kelly breezed back into the room. "Okay. I got him interested in a rebroadcast of an old Lakers game." She hustled to the bed and wrapped her arms around Nathan. "I'm so sorry!" she said, looking into his eyes. "I should've believed you."

He patted her on the back and managed a smile. "It's all right. I wasn't sure I believed it myself."

She released him and turned toward Clara. "I heard voices coming from this room. I know I heard them."

"Voices?" Clara repeated. "What did they say?'

Kelly sat down next to Clara. "I couldn't catch it all. A man said, 'The computers decode,' then a woman said something about a telescope."

"Maybe it *is* a telescope."

"What do you mean?" Kelly asked.

Clara picked up the second photo and handed it to her. "Does that look like a telescope to you?"

Nathan stared again at the dim room. He tried to twist the central shadow into a telescope sitting on a pedestal. It worked. Sort of.

"I'm not sure," Kelly said. "Maybe."

"What else did the voices say?" Clara asked.

"I was out in the hall. I couldn't understand them." She laid the picture back on the bedspread. "The voices were pretty loud, Nathan. You must've heard them."

"I didn't hear anything but Brahms." He lifted the violin to his shoulder. "When it's right next to my ear, I can't hear much else." He played several quick notes, ending with a high C.

Kelly's face turned ashen. Her lips parted as her jaw began dropping open.

Clara placed a palm on Kelly's forehead. "Are you feeling sick?"

"No. I heard it again. Just now." She pulled Clara's arm down and looked at her and Nathan imploringly. "Didn't you hear it? It was a woman's voice, loud and clear."

"No," Nathan replied with a slight shake of his head.

Clara locked her hand with Kelly's. "I didn't hear a word. What did she say?"

Kelly's face fell slack. Her eyes opened wide, and she spoke in an eerie monotone as if trying to mimic a ghostly voice echoing in her mind. "Hurry, Nathan, before it's too late."

"Play some more!" Clara said, pointing at the violin.

Nathan laid the bow across the strings. "Brahms again?"

"Anything. Let's see what happens."

Nathan restarted the lullaby, trying to play softly enough to hear the voices. He and Clara looked at Kelly expectantly.

Kelly closed her eyes and concentrated. After a few seconds, she spoke softly. "I hear something. Quiet voices, like people

85

whispering to each other." She opened her eyes. "But I can't understand them."

Nathan switched to his part of the Vivaldi duet, increasing the volume slightly.

"How about now?" Clara asked.

She concentrated again. "No. Still just whispers."

After trying several different compositions and getting the same response from Kelly, he finally lowered the violin with an exasperated sigh. "Are you sure you heard words before?"

She set her hands on her hips. "As sure as you were when you saw that weird stuff in the mirror."

Nathan pointed the bow at her. "Good call."

"How strange," Clara said. "The voice seemed to be speaking directly to us."

"But hurry and do what? What happens when it's 'too late'?"

Clara snatched up a photo. "Look, Nathan. Interfinity."

"Interfinity?" He peered over her shoulder at the picture of his father standing next to a man wearing a white laboratory smock. "Is that a company name?"

"That's what they're called now. They're a research and development company that observes strange astronomical features. At first they were associated with alien hunters, looking for signs of life out in the great beyond, but later they moved into serious science, like figuring out all that stuff about dark matter and axions."

Kelly scrunched her eyebrows. "What are axions?"

"I don't know enough about them to explain." Clara wiggled her fingers as if typing on a keyboard. "I just typed out Solomon's notes when he took a case for them. Someone had stolen Interfinity's technology, so he had to get it back, some kind of device that creates what they called an interfinity corridor. I have no idea what that is, but I do remember that they used a special kind of mirror."

Nathan pointed at her. "And that's the connection. A mirror."

"And that's probably why your father gave it to you for safe-keeping." Clara walked over to the wall mirror and stared at her reflection, but the tall gray-haired lady on the other side just stared back at her with the same skeptical aspect. "Obviously there is much more here than meets the eye."

"So what do we do?" Kelly asked. "Go to Interfinity and see what's going on?"

"That's one option, but I'm thinking we should go straight to the horse's mouth." As Clara stroked her chin, her glasses slid down her nose. "Nathan, you can access your father's webmail account, can't you? Perhaps we can find out more about his latest project there."

"Yeah. I think I remember his password." Nathan kept his gaze locked on the mirror. The lamp in the reflection had dimmed, but everything else looked normal ... at least for now. He pointed at the computer case Clara had brought in. "Is that a new laptop?"

"Since yours is sitting at the bottom of the river, I bought you a new one," Clara said, backing toward the lamp on Nathan's desk.

Clara's shadow drew Nathan's eye to the mirror. The lamp's light dimmed further, and the walls in the reflection darkened, but nothing really alarming appeared. Shadows always made things darker, though this one somehow seemed denser than most.

Kelly's eyes darted to the mirror and back. Obviously, she had seen it, too.

He refocused on Clara. "If I can't remember it, I'll try some passwords I know he's used before."

"Go for it, but if we can't figure it out soon, we can get the ISP to let us in. I have your father's Social Security number."

He turned on the computer and laid it on the bed. "I'll hack into it tonight."

"Anyone hungry?" Tony swept into the room with a mobile phone in his hand. As soon as he entered, the lamp in the mirror cast a reddish glow over his reflection. Hunching over and wearing nothing but an animal skin, his image looked like a caveman carrying a slingshot.

Kelly stepped between her father and the reflection, blocking his view.

"It's halftime," he continued, "and my stomach's begging for a liver and anchovy pizza. I could order an extra large if anyone's got the munchies."

Nathan edged away from the mirror, hoping Tony's gaze would follow. He had to do something to keep his attention diverted. "Liver and anchovies? You really put that on a pizza?"

"I guess your dad never fed you a real man's food." Tony flexed his bicep. "Stick with me, and you'll have a set of these in no time." Now his reflected image grew long hair all over his body and looked like a chimpanzee showing off his muscles.

"Dad," Kelly said, sliding her arm around her father's elbow and turning him toward the door, "why don't you go to the Pizza Ranch and get an extra large with half liver and anchovies and the other half with ..." She raised her eyebrows at Nathan.

"Uh ... pepperoni?" Nathan offered.

"Yeah. Pepperoni."

"Pepperoni's okay," Tony said, nodding. "It has protein." He dug a set of keys out of his jeans pocket. "Anything else?"

Nathan suppressed a grin. Seeing a chimpanzee in the mirror holding a set of keys almost made him burst out laughing.

"Sure. Can you pick up some of those fruit drinks at Wal-Mart? They're Nathan's favorite."

Nathan lifted his eyebrows at her, but she shot a keep-your-mouth-shut glare at him. He complied. This was no time to protest.

"But that's the opposite direction from the Pizza Ranch,"

Tony said. "I don't have time to do both before the second half."

Kelly pushed him toward the door. "I'll record it for you, and we can all watch it together when you get back."

Setting his feet, he paused and eyed the photos on the bed. "What's up with the pictures? Did you get something cool?"

"They're some old ones that belonged to Nathan's father." She pushed harder and guided him out the door and down the hall, her voice fading. "You'd better get going. I heard Nathan's stomach growling."

As soon as the door closed, Clara's shadow dimmed, and the reflection returned to normal.

Nathan ran his hand through his hair. "Whew! That was close!"

"I know." Clara laid a hand on her abdomen. "When I saw that chimpanzee, I strained so hard to keep from laughing, I think I reopened my hernia."

He touched her shoulder. "Are you okay?"

"It's a joke," she said, patting him on the shoulder. "I hope you get your sense of humor back soon."

"Yeah." He dipped his head low. "Me, too."

She slid the photos together into a pile next to the laptop, careful to keep them in order.

She pointed at his laptop bag. "By the way, I put a new cell phone in there and a debit card for any immediate expenses, so make sure you find them and put them away."

"I will. Thanks."

Clara turned the laptop on the bed and tapped a few keys. "Better get started on your father's email as soon as possible. We need to figure everything out before your parents' funeral on Tuesday."

"Tuesday? Did the police find them?"

"An anonymous person sent a photograph of their bodies and

said he would reveal their location by Monday. If that tip pans out, I want to be ready."

Nathan swallowed a painful lump. "Do I have to go?"

"Of course you have to. You will be a pallbearer, and I was hoping you'd play something. Dr. Malenkov suggested that you and he should play your favorite duet."

"No." Pressing his lips together, he lowered his head. "I don't think I could handle that." As he stared at the bedspread, he sensed her sympathetic gaze, the teary-eyed one she always got when something tragic happened.

"I understand," she said. "I'll arrange something else." She reached down and took his hand. "Do you want to be a pallbearer?"

Keeping his head low, he nodded. "I guess I can do that."

Kelly barged in and leaned back on the door, slamming it shut. "Whew! That was close!"

"That's exactly what I said." Nathan laid a palm on his abdomen. "But I didn't know I liked Wal-Mart fruit drinks."

Kelly flashed an injured expression. "I had to get him out of here, didn't I?"

"I guess so." Nathan turned to the computer screen but kept his eye on her. "But you didn't have to lie."

She set her hands on her hips and scowled. "Get real, Nathan. Don't tell me you never lie."

Clara forked her fingers at them. "Both of you hush! This is no time for a spitting match." She handed the stack of photos to Kelly. "If you two can't work together, we'll never figure this out."

Kelly's frown lifted, but only a fraction. "If he keeps looking down on me, we can't work together."

Clara pointed a finger that almost touched Kelly's nose. "Listen, little lady; condescension isn't a one-way street. Maybe you both need to come down off your high horses and trust each other." She jerked open the door and stalked away.

As soon as Clara's heavy footsteps faded, Kelly crossed her arms and glared at the mirror, her socked foot tapping the carpet. With her back turned, Nathan couldn't see her face directly, but the mirror clearly reflected every drooping line from her forehead to her lips.

His heart sank. Maybe he had judged her too harshly. She was really the first girl he knew outside his parents' circle of friends, and Dad had often whispered subtle warnings about the allure of pretty females who didn't adhere to his family's beliefs, that they would be willing to deceive to get what they wanted.

Like wispy phantoms from the past, his father's words filtered into his mind. *"The key is to discern between the truly deceptive girl and one who is simply unaware of the dangers of spinning webs of lies. The former knows full well what she is doing and seeks to fill her treasure chest with whatever jewels you possess, while the latter needs you to give your pearls of wisdom to her freely so that she may learn the surpassing joy of the children of light, those who love and honor the truth. The secret is to plumb the depths of her soul. Question her heart. It won't take long to learn if light dwells within or if darkness alone colors her soul."*

Nathan took a deep breath and spoke as gently as he could. "Are you mad at me or your father?"

"Both." Her foot's rhythm quickened. "He's a clueless buffoon. What's your excuse?"

He gritted his teeth. A dozen witty comebacks flew through his mind, like, I guess it runs in the family, and I hear buffoonery is genetic, but any crass statement would probably make her head explode.

He gazed at her reflection again. She seemed so hurt, so sad and vulnerable. How could he possibly inflict another emotional wound? In the midst of the turmoil within her tragically fractured family, she had probably suffered from her father's nonverbal cues, unintentional signals that she was unable to live up to the vision of the son he had always wanted. Her mother had abandoned her, tossing her away with a casually blown kiss. Now Kelly trudged along the only path she knew, one of compromised values and disloyal loved ones. She was a lost angel searching for home.

Finally, he just sighed and strode up behind her, looking at the mirror over her shoulder, close enough to hear her stifled sobs, yet not quite close enough to feel any warmth.

Pulling her lips in, Kelly swung her head to the side, avoiding Nathan's stare. Her foot continued its frantic tapping.

As he studied their reflections, a strange sensation poured over his body, a tingle that radiated across his skin. In his reflected image, an almost imperceptible light coated his face, microscopic particles that attached to his skin. Then, although he didn't move a muscle, his reflected head shifted, leaving the aura of light behind. Somehow the boy in the mirror had detached and moved on his own, first laying his hands on the shoulders of Kelly's reflection, then turning her around. "I didn't mean to hurt your feelings," his mirror image said. "You're my sister now, and I'll do anything to make sure you're my friend, too."

The real Kelly focused on the mirror again, trembling. Her reflection wrapped her arms around Nathan's reflection and laid her head on his chest.

"I'm sorry for being such a jerk," her reflection said. "We just need to get to know each other better."

As the two reflections embraced, Kelly slowly turned and faced Nathan. "Is ..." She swallowed hard. "Is that what you're thinking?"

Nathan licked his lips. "Yeah. I think it is."

She slid her arms around his waist and laid her head against his chest. "Then say it."

Her trembling arms sent shivers up his back. He reached around to return the embrace but kept his touch gentle. Clearing his throat, he whispered into her ear. "You're my sister now, and I'll do anything to make sure you're my friend, too."

"And I'm sorry for being such a jerk." She looked up at him. "We really do need to get to know each other better."

He patted her lightly on the back. "Like Clara said, we need to trust each other."

"Do you trust me?" she asked, her teary eyes sparkling.

Giving her a light clasp on the shoulder, he nodded. "Yes, I trust you."

She pulled away and lowered her head, silent for a few seconds before whispering, "I hope you'll keep trusting me, no matter what."

Nathan glanced at the mirror. It had returned to normal, including Kelly's sad profile as she kept her eyes averted. What could she have meant? Did she have some dark secret that would challenge his trust? Swallowing back a surge of compassion, he reached for her hand and interlocked their thumbs. "Trust is a two-way street. As long as we trust each other, we'll be fine."

She lifted her head and tightened her grip on his hand, a hint of a smile brightening her face. "I can live with that."

He nodded at the mirror. "I think my reflection has been quite the troublemaker, hasn't it?"

She turned toward it and leaned her head against his shoulder. "I'd say it's more like a truth serum. I feel like it kind of probes your brain."

"I know what you mean. It's embarrassing when my thoughts are on a theatre screen."

Her face brightened. "Whatta ya know? Nathan's a movie star!" Laughing, she let go of his hand and headed for the door. "I'll see you in a few minutes."

"Where you going?"

"To record the game, like I promised, but if anything happens on *The Nathan Show*, I want to hear all about it."

5

PIERCING THE VEIL

Nathan awoke to the sound of chirping birds. With the morning sun filtering through the drapes, the room carried an eerie dimness. The mirror reflected the gloom accurately, including his bare feet protruding from the disheveled bedcovers, proof of the fitful night he had suffered—dreams of walking through remnants of shattered violins, every fragment covered with blood, a trail that led to the twin coffins he had seen back in Chicago. In the dream, however, each coffin held only a human-sized black stone with strange symbols etched in white on its surface.

"Rosetta!" Nathan sat upright in bed. That was the key to the password! Throwing off the bedspread, he scrambled out from under the sheets and plopped down in his desk chair. After punching the laptop's power button, he turned on the lamp and the digital clock's FM radio. As the classical station played a Tchaikovsky piano concerto, he squirmed in his seat, waiting for the boot-up process to finish. Now he could start reading his father's emails and look for clues. He had been so tired last night, he couldn't remember the password.

A light tap sounded on the door. "Nathan? Are you up?"

He smiled. It was Kelly's voice. He glanced down at his clothes. Gym shorts and T-shirt. That would do. "Sure. Come on in."

The door pushed open, and Kelly walked in. Wearing a pink knee-length nightshirt that said, *Sanity Is Overrated*, and combing through her tangled hair with her fingers, she shuffled her purple bunny slippers across the carpet and peered at the computer.

Nathan grinned at her. "You look ... uh ... relaxed."

"I hardly slept a wink." She poked his forearm. "But I'm your sister now, so you'd better get used to my casual look."

"I didn't sleep much, either." He checked the digital clock on his desk. 8:15. "What time is your church service?"

"Church? Uh ... we haven't been ... I mean ..."

He waved his hand at her. "Don't worry about it. When Clara wakes up, we'll figure out where to go." He opened the Internet browser and brought up his father's email provider. "I should have thought of this password last night." As he typed in "Rosetta Speaks," he recit each letter out loud.

Kelly bent over behind him and rested her chin on his shoulder. "Rosetta? Like the Rosetta Stone?"

"Yep." He scanned the long list of folders. "Dad wasn't much for email organization. Looks like I've got over five hundred to go through."

Kelly muttered a curse word, then quickly covered her lips. "Sorry. Too many hours around Dad's basketball team."

Nathan suppressed a grimace. Another apology for cursing. That's what people always did around his father, too. He resurrected his smile. "Do you actually play basketball with the guys, or just watch?"

"Dad makes me play." She thumped her chest with her fist and deepened her voice. "To toughen me up."

"I guess it works. You're pretty tough."

"Hey!" Kelly punched him sharply on the arm. "Aren't I feminine enough for you?"

Nathan rubbed the sore spot. "Punching me isn't exactly the best way to prove it."

"Oh really?" She leaned close and nuzzled his ear, whispering, "Is this better?"

As heat rushed into his cheeks, he leaned away from her touch. "Uh ... well ... I don't think we should ..."

She flicked his head with her finger. "I was just kidding. Get a grip."

Nathan shook off an attack of goose bumps. Her breathy tickle didn't feel like she was kidding. Maybe she had no clue what that kind of touch did to a guy. Sure, he was old-fashioned, but he wasn't a corpse.

He set his hands back on the keyboard. "Let's just concentrate on the emails."

"Sure." She perched over his shoulder again, this time not so close. "Look at all those with 'Rosetta' in the title. It must be important."

"Probably. I even had a dream about it. That's how I remembered the password." He pulled a tablet from the desk drawer and scribbled a picture as he described his dream. "The stone was split in half, and the pieces were lying in two coffins. There was a trail of bloody violins leading up to them."

"Bloody violins?" Kelly shuddered. "That's creepy."

He set the pad down and spelled out "Rosetta" in block letters. "I think the dream was sort of like a puzzle. Dad loves ..." He paused. That wasn't right. Not anymore. Pushing down a new surge of sadness, he breathed a sigh. "Dad used to love puzzles."

Kelly rubbed his back. "Say it however you want. I'll know what you mean."

Keeping his focus on the drawing, he nodded. "Thanks."

She gave him a playful rap on the head with her knuckles. "You know, I don't think your father put that dream in your head. It was probably just the pizza. You shouldn't have let my dad talk you into a slice of liver and anchovies."

He looked up at her silly grin. She was trying to shake him out of his funk. "Actually, I kind of liked it." He thumped his chest, mimicking her earlier move. "I felt like a real man."

"Oh, no!" Clutching her throat, she stuck out her tongue and staggered with dramatic flair. "I ate an anchovy! I'm growing hair on my chest, and I left the toilet seat up! Don't ask me to stop for directions; I'm turning into a man!"

As Nathan laughed, he caught a glimpse of Kelly's comical display in the mirror. The two Kellys seemed to be performing a weird tribal dance, completely out of sync with the classical music playing on the radio. The girl in the mirror turned fuzzy for a moment, then sharpened again, now dressed in loose-fitting khaki pants and a short-sleeved safari shirt. When the real Kelly turned toward the mirror, she released her throat and stared.

Nathan shot up from his chair. He, too, was dressed in khakis in his mirror image. Their reflected surroundings morphed into a dim chamber with a faint glow seeping in through arched windows near the high ceiling. Shards of varnished wood littered the smooth floor, making a trail through a maze of music stands toward two coffins that sat on a long table in the gloomy distance.

"This is my dream!" Nathan took two uneasy steps closer. "It's the performance hall, the same place my parents were killed, but now the coffins are on stage."

Kelly sat on the bed, still staring. "The mirror's reflecting what you're thinking again. You put us both into your dream."

He pointed at his image as it crept side by side next to hers. "Where did I come up with the safari outfits? I've never owned anything like that."

"I have. My dad wanted to take me hunting, so—" She stopped abruptly. "That's exactly how those baggy old pants fit me. How could you know?"

In the image, a man in a navy blue blazer rose from behind the coffins. "How did you cross the barrier?" he asked.

The real Nathan stepped closer to the mirror and whispered, "I can hear him."

"Same here." Kelly, shivering hard, pressed close to his side. "Your imagination is going nuts!"

"He's one of Mictar's men. I think his name's Dr. Gordon."

The Nathan in the mirror halted. "I crossed the same way as before. I had a dream, it showed up in the mirror, then music, a flash of light, and zap, I'm here. Why?"

"You're not carrying it," Dr. Gordon said. "How could you transport without it?"

"I have my ways."

Dr. Gordon walked to the front of the coffins, a pronounced limp in his gait. "I asked you to bring it. I wanted to teach you how it works."

Nathan retreated a step. "It's too dangerous. I'm having it locked up forever."

"How will you return to Blue?"

"You seem to know how. I'll just follow you."

Dr. Gordon eyed Nathan suspiciously. "Very well. Come over here. I'll show you why I called you."

"You have their bodies?" Glancing all around, the Nathan in the mirror skulked forward, Kelly's reflection at his heels. He peered into one of the coffins. Clutching the side with tight fingers, he growled at Dr. Gordon. "How did they get here?"

"I suppose Mictar thought Earth Yellow would be a safe place to hide them."

His jaw shaking, Nathan reached into the coffin and lifted a feminine hand. "How did you find them?"

Suddenly, a tall, dark figure in the mirror grabbed Nathan from behind, covering his eyes with his thin hand. As the boy struggled, the real Nathan clenched his fist. "Mictar!"

Kelly yelled at the mirror. "Don't just stand there, Kelly! Help him!"

In the mirror, Kelly leaped onto Mictar from behind and gouged his face with her fingernails. As Nathan's double slumped to the stage floor, Mictar reached around and tore

Kelly from his back. Now with an aura of light surrounding him, he covered her eyes with his hand. Sparks flew from beneath his palm. She stiffened, and her mouth dropped open, but only a timid squeak came out. A few seconds later, she, too, collapsed.

Straightening his pulsating body, Mictar heaved in a deep breath and looked up toward the ceiling. "Ah! The ecstasy of youthful vigor!"

Dr. Gordon hobbled forward and frisked Nathan's clothes. "He didn't bring it!" He jumped over to Kelly and searched her body, running his hands along every curve.

The real Kelly shivered again. "I think I'm going to be sick!"

Gordon grabbed a shock of Nathan's hair and jerked his head high enough to speak to him face-to-face. As the wounded boy's features stretched out, his eyelids opened. Empty eye sockets encircled by black sooty scorch marks were all that remained.

A purplish vein on the side of Gordon's forehead pulsed. "I'll find it eventually. With you and your daddy dead, that doesn't leave very many who could be hiding it." He dropped Nathan, letting his face thump hard against the floor.

Gordon moved back to Kelly and pushed open one of her eyelids, revealing a gaping hole. He looked up at Mictar. "A thorough excision, as usual."

"To get to the reservoirs," Mictar replied, "one must open the spillways."

Leaving the bodies on the stage, Gordon and Mictar slowly descended the stairs to the audience level, passing so close to the front of the mirror, every facial detail clarified. Mictar touched a scratch wound on his cheek. As if responding to his touch, the scratch faded and vanished.

A fresh cut also marred Gordon's face. Nathan leaned closer to get a good view. It looked like he had been in a fight.

"We have to get to the girl's house," Gordon said as he limped along. "The burglar is due to arrive in the morning. My leg should be okay by then." As the two men headed for the exit door, Dr. Gordon's voice faded. "That old fiddler didn't do too much damage."

The sound of a car motor shook Nathan's attention away from the mirror. He peeked outside and saw the blue Mustang pulling into the driveway with the gray-bearded man behind the wheel. He stepped out of the car, holding a gun at his side.

"We've got big trouble."

Kelly spun toward the door. "I'll wake my dad!"

"No time!" Nathan grabbed her wrist. "Is there a place to hide?"

The front door banged open.

"Daddy!" Kelly screamed. "Daddy! Help!"

The gunman burst into the room. As he aimed his pistol at Nathan, he pushed the door closed with his foot. "The locals aren't exactly tight-lipped around here."

Holding up a trembling hand, Nathan stepped in front of Kelly. "Leave her alone, all right? Do whatever you want to me. Just let her go."

"Easy enough to put a hole right through both of you." When he pulled the trigger, the gunpowder flashed, its sparks flying away from the gun in slow motion. Nathan reached for his chest, expecting a sharp pain, but as he refocused, the brass-colored bullet came into view, maybe three feet away, floating toward him at a barely perceptible rate.

He gasped for breath, but his lungs froze. He wanted to grab Kelly and duck, but as he tried to turn, his limbs and torso locked in place. Only his eyes and brain seemed able to function at all.

As the bullet continued its unyielding advance, he glanced at the two dead bodies in the mirror. Had the reflection predicted their murder somehow? The other Nathan and Kelly were in a faraway place and wearing strange clothes. It wasn't the same at all. Somehow theirs was a different world.

The mirror began to darken and expand in every direction. The dead bodies pushed out from the glass, creating a hologram that blended with reality. The lifeless Nathan and Kelly floated inches off the bedroom floor, lying still, with gaping holes in their eyes, as the two rooms merged into one.

Nathan glanced at the space between him and the gunman. The bullet moved within a foot of his chest, spinning slowly as it inched along. He screamed at his body to jump, to duck, to collapse, to do anything—even to trade places with his dead twin on the floor. At least then he wouldn't suffer the slow torture of a sizzling missile drilling into his heart.

Just as the bullet touched his clothes, darkness spilled over the room, like jet-black paint flowing down the walls. Now without sight, a falling sensation overtook his mind, a plunge into a dark void. He cringed. Any second his body would crash against the floor and thrust out his final earthly breath.

The painful thud never came. He pushed his hands forward, but they wouldn't budge. The surface at his fingertips felt hard and cool. Had he fallen? Had the bullet struck? Why didn't he feel the agony of a mortal wound?

Another popping noise throttled his eardrum. When his eyes adjusted, he tried to look around, but his cheek was pressed against a wood floor. The room slowly brightened from blackness to a gray gloom. Someone lay next to him, a female form, but her face pointed the other way.

Nathan waited, trying not to breathe. Maybe the gunman would think he was dead and take off, if he was still there at all. After a few seconds of silence, he whispered, "Kelly?"

The body curled up at his side whispered back, "Is he gone?"

"I think so." Nathan pushed against the floor, still checking for pain, but everything seemed fine.

Kelly rose and knelt next to him. "Where are we?"

"I'm not sure." He got up and helped her to her feet. "I'm not hurt. Are you?"

"I don't think so." She wiped her hands on her safari shirt. "When did I put this hideous hunting outfit on?"

"You got me." He nudged a violin fragment with his laced boot and sniffed the air. The odor of fresh paint permeated the cool chamber. "This is just like my dream."

"I hope it's a dream. Either that or we're in the dark tunnel people talk about when they're on their way to heaven." She closed her eyes and wrung her hands. "Somebody please wake me up. I'll never shout at my alarm clock again if it will just wake me—"

The sound of laughter made them turn. A rectangular image floated behind them, a pondlike reflection that showed a skewed picture of Nathan's bedroom. In the image, he and Kelly, still dressed in their sleep attire, lay on the carpet, the gunman standing over them.

The safari-clad Kelly clutched a handful of Nathan's sleeve and jerked him close, whisper-shouting. "Are those our dead bodies back in your bedroom?"

Nathan tried to calm his quick breaths. "I don't know ... Everything's going crazy."

In the image, Tony burst through the doorway. He grabbed the gunman from behind in a headlock and wrestled him to the floor. But the gunman was too slippery. He smashed Tony's head with the butt of the pistol. As Tony fell limp, the man stood up and hobbled out of the room.

Before the image faded, they could hear the roar of the Mustang as it spit gravel from underneath its tires. The image slowly reshaped into a tri-fold, floor-standing mirror, reflecting their dumbstruck faces, khaki clothes, and gloomy surroundings.

Kelly bent over, clutching her stomach. "I think I'm really going to be sick this time!"

While she heaved, Nathan patted her back, his own stomach boiling with nausea. "It's going to be okay," he said in a soothing tone, as much to settle himself as to calm her down. After shaking off a skin-tingling chill, he took a deep breath. "We'll figure it all out."

Straightening, Kelly pushed her hair back, her eyes flush with tears. "We're dead!" she shouted. Her cry echoed in the empty chamber, calling out, "We're dead," over and over.

"We're not dead. Maybe we just got transported into the mirror. This place is exactly what we saw from my bedroom."

She set her fists on her hips. "Oh, well, like *that's* a lot better! We're either dead or nothing but reflections in a mirror world."

"But we're still in physical bodies." Nathan stooped and picked up a piece of a violin. With two curling strings still attached, the tawny wood carried a splattering of reddish stain. "And this place is too real to be just a reflection."

Rubbing her upper arms, she turned toward the coffins. "So, if this is the same as your dream, do you think the Rosetta pieces are over there?"

"I don't think so. Didn't you see the lady's hand?" He rose and strode toward the boxes, Kelly following, their shoes crunching violin pieces as they weaved around the music stands. As his eyes adjusted to the dim light, the chamber slowly took on its familiar surroundings. "I was right," he said, suddenly stopping.

"Right about what?"

"This is the performance hall where my parents died. But it looks different, like it's been remodeled."

"In just a couple of days?"

"Fast workers, I guess." He pointed at the floor. "But the coffins were downstairs in a prop room, not up on stage."

Kelly crept closer to the coffins. "If your parents' bodies are still in there ..."

"They can't be," Nathan said confidently, but his tone proved stronger than his legs. They trembled as he stayed close to Kelly's heels.

A siren wailed from somewhere outside. The front entrance door burst open, and Gordon limped in, reaching into his jacket. "Stay where you are!" he ordered.

Nathan grabbed Kelly's hand and pulled her toward the side exit. "This way!" Running through the dark hallway and down the darker stairs, their shoes stomped over the creaking wood. Not bothering to look for a light, he dashed into the maintenance area and clattered along the familiar catwalk, darkness cloaking their escape.

Finding the low exit door, already repaired since his previous visit, he dropped down, pounded it open with his shoes, and leaped to the hallway below. Kelly followed, step by step, only her heavy breathing giving away her presence.

He dashed into the fire escape alcove and threw open the window. A cool rush of air breezed in. This time, in the fullness of night, the black stairwell seemed invisible against the dark background. It would be like stepping out into nothingness.

Watching the street below, Nathan pushed his body through the window and felt for the metal grating under his feet. When it caught his weight, he straightened and helped Kelly out. Striding confidently now, he hustled down flight after flight of stairs, listening to Kelly's footsteps clanging in the rear.

He glanced up at the dark window. No sign of Gordon following. Slowing his pace as he walked out onto the swinging bridge, he looked back at Kelly, talking as he hung on to the railing. "Watch for him. The front door's around the corner, so he might show up there and try to catch us from below."

When the stairway hit the sidewalk, they clambered down

and leaped off. The bridge lifted slowly back to the sky, whining as it rose.

Kelly pointed. "There he is!"

Slowly jogging toward them, Dr. Gordon held a gun close to his side but said nothing.

Nathan took Kelly's hand and spun in the opposite direction. "Run!" He hustled into the alley where he and Clara had found the limo and pulled Kelly against a brick wall, pinning his own body near the corner.

"What are we going to do?" she asked, panting.

He raised a tight fist, held his breath, and listened. Heavy footsteps drew closer. Kelly pressed a hand against her chest and closed her eyes. When the pounding reached a climax, Nathan leaped out and swung his fist, nailing Gordon square on the cheek and knocking him flat on his back.

Crouching over his body, Nathan searched for the gun, but Gordon's hands were shrouded in darkness.

"Let's just run!" Kelly shouted, pulling Nathan's shirt.

Gordon latched on to Nathan's pant leg. "Without me, you'll never get home. You have no idea where you are."

"We'll take our chances." Nathan jerked away and ran down the sidewalk with Kelly. The city of Chicago rose up before them, towers everywhere ascending to dizzying heights. They turned right on Wabash and sprinted alongside the busy street. He listened for their pursuer, but the rumble of an approaching 'L' train on the overhead track buried every other sound.

Halting at the first intersection, Nathan wheeled around. Nobody following ... yet. They waited for the light to change and tried to blend in with the dozen or so pedestrians as they crossed the street.

A man in a lime green leisure suit and platform shoes approached them. Something gold flashed on his chest, drawing Nathan's gaze to his open shirt where a gold chain suspended a silver-dollar-sized medallion in the midst of a dense nest of hair. A movie poster on a building across the street advertised the film *Animal House* opening July 28.

When he and Kelly reached the other side, he looked back again. Gordon jogged toward them, grimacing and favoring a leg.

The light changed. A bus lumbered between them and Gordon, pausing to allow a late-arriving pedestrian on board. A Ford Pinto stopped behind the bus, beeping its shrill horn. Nathan stared at the car. It looked brand new. Spinning back, he pointed at a stairway leading to the train platform. "Let's catch it while he can't see us!" They sprinted up the stairs, not daring to look behind them.

When they reached the turnstile, he skidded to a halt and eyed the uniformed attendant leaning against a column and staring off into space. Digging into his pockets, Nathan glanced all around. "What do we need? A ticket? A token?"

Kelly leaped onto the turnstile's cross bar and vaulted over. The attendant jerked his head toward them and raised a hand. "Hey! You need a—"

"Sorry!" Nathan said, setting his hand on the turnstile. "It's an emergency!"

He jumped to the other side and dashed up another flight of stairs. After running out onto the passenger platform, he jogged along the line of cars, peering into each window. Where was Kelly? She couldn't have just disappeared!

A signal chimed. The train was about to leave. At the last car, Kelly pushed out from the inside and wedged her body between the closing doors. "Hurry!" she called, straining against the two panels.

The doors popped open again. Kelly lurched back and fell to her bottom. Just as the panels began to close, Nathan leaped inside and grabbed a support pole to stop his momentum. As he straightened, he kept a grip on the pole, panting. "I think we lost him."

"Maybe." With a nod of her head, she gestured toward the front of the train. "I saw a couple of people get on while you were running this way, but I couldn't tell if he was one of them. It was too dark."

He scanned the nearly empty train. One old man sat in the seat closest to the front access door. As a light snore passed through his nostrils, his chin dropped to his chest and nestled in a coffee stain on his white button-down shirt. A sign above his head warned passengers not to pass between the cars.

Rising to her feet, Kelly smiled. "Good job back there. Did it hurt?"

Nathan lifted his fist and looked at his knuckles, red but not bleeding. "It does now. I didn't feel a thing when I decked him."

As the car swayed back and forth, she braced herself against the back of a seat and peered out the window. "If he didn't get on this train, he's sure to follow on the next one."

"Let's get off pretty soon. He won't be able to guess where we stopped."

Sliding into a window seat, she fanned her face with her hand. "Give me a few minutes to catch my breath. I'm not an experienced spy like you."

He pushed a section of a newspaper off the seat next to her and sat down, gazing at the darkened skyline. "What do you mean? You did great."

"No, I didn't." She crossed her arms and shivered. "I was scared to death!"

"So? You don't think I was scared?"

"You didn't act like it."

"That doesn't mean I wasn't. I just did what I had to do. There wasn't much choice."

"I guess that's true." Yawning, she rested her head against the window and closed her eyes. "I feel a little better knowing you were scared, too."

"Glad I could help." He looked at the newspaper on the floor at his feet, and his gaze fell across the bold type above an article—"Nightmare Epidemic Continues." He tried to read the smaller type but couldn't make it out.

Just as he reached for it, a whisper buzzed through Kelly's barely parted lips. "Do you think your parents were in those coffins?"

He straightened. "I don't see how. When that reflection of myself looked into the coffin, he never said a word about the bodies belonging to my parents."

"You're right." Her voice trailed away. Seconds later, her breathing turned heavy and rhythmic.

Nathan gazed at her pale skin and let out a quiet sigh. No wonder she was tired. Anybody would be worn out after that chase. His own first narrow escape pumped so much adrenaline through his body, he slept for half a day when he got home. And, not being purposefully trained as he had been, Kelly's fear was even more understandable. Facing death wasn't for the fainthearted, and even now he couldn't avoid a rash of jitters when his life was on the line.

He settled back and gazed at the tall, boxy skyscrapers outside, each one filled with hundreds of square lights aligned in perfect rows and columns. With fear still lurking somewhere in his mind, one of those odd training sessions seeped in from his memories. The orderly matrix of lights morphed into one of the many spreadsheets he had worked on for his father, countless numbers in precise arrays. As the moon cast shadows across the rumbling train, his father's voice pierced the veil of long-lost recollections.

His father leaned one hand against Nathan's desk. "It's almost midnight. Everything's ready for your jump."

Nathan kept his fingers on his computer's keyboard. "But I haven't finished the financial statement yet."

"That can wait. Numbers aren't as important as this step in your training."

"But this'll take me at least—"

"Nathan." His voice deepened but stayed calm. "Are you really worried about getting the report done?"

Nathan shook his head, still watching the screen. "No. Not really."

His father's shadow glided to the other side of his desk. "It's no shame to admit that you're scared."

"Okay." He looked up at him, firming his chin. "I admit it. I'm scared."

"Good." His father's bushy eyebrows pressed toward his nose. "Measured fear is healthy, even vital."

"Why aren't you ever scared of anything?"

"Who says I'm not? I've been scared lots of times."

"When? I've never seen it."

"Last month. Remember the snipers on the rooftops?"

"How could I forget? I about had a heart attack!"

"Me, too." His father laid a hand on his chest. "My heart pounded louder than bongo drums."

"You didn't show it. You stayed as cool as ice."

"You're right. I didn't show it. But staying cool, as you call it, doesn't mean I wasn't scared."

"What do *you* call it?"

"I would say it's a combination of faith and courage. If you really believe you have an immovable foundation, even if you plunge through a thousand evils, you know you will eventually land in a place of safety."

"But you're scared while you're falling, right?"

"Many times, yes." His father rolled his hand into a fist and tapped lightly on his breast. "Courage isn't the absence of fear. It's the ability to control fear and do what you have to do in spite of it. If you have faith in the one who calls you to a task, you just do it and trust that he'll get you out of a jam."

Nathan grinned. "Is this speech supposed to talk me into jumping without shaking in my boots?"

He gave Nathan's shoe a gentle kick. "Shake in your boots all you want. I told you it's voluntary. You can back out if you think you're not ready."

After taking a deep breath and letting it out slowly, Nathan turned off the computer monitor. "I'm ready."

A few minutes later, Nathan climbed through the darkness and reached the top rung of a ladder that leaned against his two-story house. After stepping carefully onto the nearly invisible roof, he walked up to the top of the angled shingles and slid close enough to the edge to peek at the driveway below. He cringed at the sight. Shrouded in darkness, it had to be at least twenty-five feet down.

At ground level, his father waved a flashlight, guiding it along the cracks in the driveway. "Remember," he called. "Although it looks like certain injury or death awaits you if you jump, it is an illusion, as are all things you see with your eyes that violate the sacred truths you have learned."

His father laid a hand over his heart. "I make you a solemn promise that your fall will be softened enough to prevent all injury. If you trust me, you will put aside your fears and take a step in the progress of your faith. If not, you are free to turn around and come down. I won't be angry if you decide not to jump. It would just mean that you're not quite ready for this step." He raised a clenched fist. "But I believe in you. I think you're ready."

Scuffing his shoes against the gritty surface, Nathan edged to the precipice and looked down. Only bare concrete lay at the bottom, no sign of a trampoline, mattresses, or a net of any kind. Anyone else would think he was crazy for even considering such a feat. And besides that, what father in his right mind would ask his son to do anything so crazy?

He nodded. Solomon Shepherd would. Although his father's

training methods were unique, no one could say that Nathan was unprepared for the dangerous adventures that often faced him. And this next step would be yet another preparation. If he could overcome fear, the next death-defying leap would be much easier. His father had never failed him before. It didn't make sense to doubt him now.

Taking a deep breath and holding it, Nathan jumped, keeping his eyes open as he plunged. The dark concrete seemed to transform, changing rapidly to something with more depth. His feet struck a soft, rubbery surface, like dense gray foam. It bent downward, slowing his momentum until he touched the ground as gently as if he had been placed there by a loving hand.

As the material began to bounce back, he leaped to the side and landed on the grass bordering the driveway. Waving his arms to keep his balance, he groped for something to catch. A strong hand clutched his wrist, steadying him. Nathan swung toward the grip and caught sight of his father.

His eyes glistening with tears, his father wrapped Nathan in a powerful hug. "Never forget two things," he said, his voice shaking. "One, you are a courageous young man. And, two, as God gives me strength, I will always keep my promises."

A scratchy voice broke Nathan out of his reverie. The driver announced the next stop from a hidden speaker, but it was too garbled to understand. As the train rounded a curve, the front half bent into sight, every car slowing as it approached a well-lit platform. A dark-suited man passed from car number two to three and limped toward the back of the train.

Nathan shook Kelly. "Time to go!"

"What?" She jerked away from the window and wagged her head sleepily. "I had this horrible dream, I—"

"Later." He crouched and pulled her into the aisle. "Gordon's found us."

6

THE ROAD HOME

Staying low, Nathan and Kelly scuffled behind a partition next to the side exit door. As the train slowed to a crawl, Nathan peeked past the rows of seats to the car directly in front of theirs. No sign of him yet.

"Ready to jump?" he asked.

Kelly took in a breath and rocked back and forth on her toes. "As ready as I'll ever be."

The train finally came to a halt. Gordon burst through the door between the two cars and limped toward them, aiming a handgun. "Don't move or you're dead!"

Nathan froze. Kelly grabbed his arm, her hot breaths puffing against his neck as the side door slid open.

Gordon pressed the gun barrel against Kelly's brow, the purple vein on his forehead again pulsing. "Give it up, or I'll blow her brains right out of her skull. Just come with me. Mictar wants to see you."

With a quick slap under Gordon's wrist, Nathan pushed his weapon arm straight up, then kicked him in the groin. Gordon bent over, and as he tried to aim the gun again, Nathan kicked him in the face, sending him in a backwards somersault through the aisle.

Nathan grabbed Kelly's hand, lunged for the loading platform, and hit the ground running. They scrambled down the stairway and sprinted along a sidewalk in a construction zone, leaping over broken concrete and dodging orange barricades as a few streetlights guided their way.

He spotted a dark alley across the street. "That way!" he said, pointing. While waiting for several cars to pass, he looked back toward the 'L' station. Gordon limped down the stairs and gazed at the sidewalk in the other direction.

"I don't think he's seen us yet." Bending as low as he could, Nathan pulled Kelly along as he crept across the street and into the alley. In front of them and on both sides, brick buildings stretched to four stories high. A fire escape rode up the wall to the left, similar to the metal stairway they had used for their earlier getaway.

He eyed the horizontal bridge that would serve as the first flight of stairs ... if only he could grab it and pull it down. Hovering at least a dozen feet off the ground, it might as well have been a mile in the sky.

Scanning the dark alley, he spotted a trash dumpster several feet away from the fire escape. "Think we can push the dumpster under it?" he asked as he strode toward it.

Kelly stood under the ladder and looked up. "If we do, he can use it to follow us."

"Maybe. Maybe not. He was limping, so he might not be able to jump." Setting his hands on the side of the dumpster, Nathan gave it a hefty shove. It budged an inch or two.

Kelly hurried over and leaned her shoulder against the worn-away lettering on the back. Looking up at him, she said, "On three. Ready?"

Setting his feet, Nathan gave her a nod. "Ready."

"One ... two ... three!"

Nathan pushed with all his might. As the dumpster slid, the metal bottom screeched against the pavement. He pulled Kelly back, stopping its progress. "With all that noise, we might as well send up a flare and shout, 'We're over here!'"

"Think it's close enough for us to jump?"

"We have to try." Nathan climbed the dumpster and perched on the edge closest to the fire escape, still a few feet away from being directly underneath the ladder's bottom step. Bending his knees, he jumped and latched on to one of the rungs, but the rusted stairway wouldn't come down. Grunting as he swayed, he looked back at Kelly as she moved into position on top of the bin. "It's stuck!"

She jumped and wrapped her arms around his waist. With a squeal, the ladder eased down a half inch, but stopped. Swinging her legs back and forth, she forced their bodies into a sway.

Nathan tightened his fingers over the rung. They ached, slipping a fraction of an inch with every swing. As the hinges continued to whine, the stairway eased down in rhythmic pulses until Kelly's feet touched the ground. Now loosened, the bridge descended the rest of the way.

They dashed up to the staircase level, waiting for a moment as the bridge elevated again, its hinges still squawking a rusty complaint. Careful to keep their footfalls soft on the metal steps, they hurried up to the top of the building and ducked behind a parapet, a three-foot-high wall that bordered the entire roof.

Stretching out his numbed fingers, Nathan peeked down at the street. Dr. Gordon, keeping a hand in his jacket pocket and swinging his head from side to side, skulked into the alley.

Nathan jerked back and whispered, "He's down there!"

"Did he see us?"

"Hard to tell." He crouched and duck-walked toward an access hatch at the center of the roof, rising to his feet as he drew near. He tried the latch. "Locked."

Kelly bent low and joined him. "If he thinks we're up here, he's bound to find us. He'll just come up the stairs on the inside."

Nathan pointed toward the far side of the building. "Not if we can get to the next roof." They hustled to the opposite parapet and scanned the gap between the buildings. "It's gotta be fifteen feet across!" he said. "Maybe more!"

"So we'll get a running start." She backed up to the access hatch and sprinted toward the edge. Leaping up to the parapet, she launched her body across the gap and touched down on the border wall on the other roof, but her foot slipped, sending her tumbling forward. She disappeared behind the wall.

Nathan gritted his teeth. Now he had to go for it. Kelly was probably hurt, and there was no other way to help her. Besides, she had shorter legs. If she could do it, he could do it.

Copying her approach, he ran from the roof access and vaulted over the gap. As he sailed in a high arc, time seemed to slow to a crawl. He glanced below. The alley floor had to be forty feet down! Ahead, the border wall drew closer, but he was already past his peak and descending.

Stretching his leg forward as far as he could, the toes of his boot landed on the outer edge of the wall. As his momentum carried him forward, he bent his knee and jumped again, propelling him over Kelly's crumpled body. When he came to a stop on the gravelly roof, he ran back to her and stooped at her side. "Kelly! Are you okay?"

Turning her body face up, he cradled her in his arms and brushed gravel out of her hair. Blood streamed from a scalp wound, forking into three rivulets that traced across both cheeks and over her nose. She blinked her eyes open and dabbed the wound with her finger. "I must have landed wrong."

He shifted her to a sitting position. "Can you get up?"

"I think so." She lurched forward, and, with Nathan's help, rose to her feet. As she swept more gravel from her pants, she turned back to the other building. "I guess we'd better lay low for a while in case he shows up over there."

With their backs to the parapet, they sat side-by-side on the roof, low enough to keep their heads out of sight. A pair of sirens wailed in the distance, one somewhere in front and another, farther away, behind them. Now high above the street-lights, only the glow of a half moon and a single exposed bulb next to this roof's access door illuminated their surroundings. Still, it was enough to reveal the damage. Blood oozed into Kelly's ear and dripped from her lobe, falling into her hair and clotting before it could reach her shirt.

"Are you sure you're all right?" Nathan asked. "That's a nasty cut."

"I've had worse." She touched her scalp and winced. "One of Dad's basketball buddies plays like a gorilla with razor blades for elbows. He caught me square in the nose once. I bled like a stuck pig for almost an hour."

Nathan grinned. "So that's why you jump like a kangaroo. All that basketball."

"Yeah. At least it's good for something." After staring straight ahead for a few seconds, she nudged him with her elbow. "Hey, you were awesome again. Nice kick."

"Thanks." He squirmed, trying to get comfortable on the rough surface. "I thought you might be mad at me. It was a pretty risky move. He could've shot you."

"I *was* mad. For a second, I thought you were nuts. But you really showed your stuff." She scooted a bit closer and folded her fingers into a fist. "Was that karate?"

"An ugly form of karate. I'm not much good unless I catch someone off guard, and he kind of left himself open."

She smirked and nudged him again. "Left his jewels un-guarded, huh?"

"Um ... yeah." Nathan let out a nervous laugh. "I guess that's one way to put it."

Her smile melted into a frown. But what could he say? He wasn't used to hearing a girl talk like that. The other girls he knew would've blushed if anyone talked about male anatomy in mixed company, but Kelly acted like she wouldn't flinch walk-ing through the guys' locker room during shower time.

He settled back and folded his hands on his stomach. "Okay, so we're back in Chicago, but it looks different."

She glanced at him, arching her brow. "Different? How?"

"Didn't you notice how people are dressed? One guy looked like a disco hall reject. And the cars ... I even saw a Pinto. The only place I've seen one of those before was in a junkyard."

"I saw the disco guy. Did we ... travel in time?" She seemed to have a hard time even saying the words.

Nathan shrugged. "Maybe it's some kind of parallel universe or something."

"You say that like it happens all the time." She altered her voice to a deep southern drawl. "Hey, Buford, what did you do today? Same old stuff, Bubba. Went through a mirror and visited another universe. How 'bout you?"

He laughed and let his gaze drift toward her. As blood continued to trickle between her gleaming eyes, she seemed the picture of startling contrasts—humor and femininity packaged in toughened leather. She was right. He was pretty calm about the whole thing. She didn't seem too flustered, either, though she had good reason to be. She didn't share his advantage. Hanging around his dad got him used to crazy stuff happening, though his confidence took a big hit when he saw him lying in that coffin. Still, that dash through the city seemed to get his juices flowing again. Maybe he was getting his moxie back. "I guess I felt pretty confident, but more like the guy whistling while he's walking through a graveyard. Maybe I'm just pretending I'm not afraid of ghosts."

"Speaking of graveyards, I didn't tell you about the dream I had on the train. I was standing in front of the coffins, but not on that stage. It was a funeral with flowers and music, and that Mictar guy came up behind me and put his hand over my eyes. It burned like fire, and I fell. Then I floated above my body and could see myself on the ground. My eyes were completely burned out of my skull." She shuddered. "It was awful."

"I hate nightmares. I've been having them, too." The article headline flashed in his mind: "Nightmare Epidemic Continues." What could it have meant? Should he mention it, or would it just scare her more? He looked up at the night sky. With lights streaming from a hundred directions, the haze seemed to glow, as if emanating a light of its own. It seemed heavy ... close. Too close.

"Well," Kelly said, giving him a slight nudge, "we can't just sit here."

He angled his head toward the building on the other side of the alley. "We have to be sure Gordon's gone, then we should try to get back home, maybe through the mirror on the stage."

Her eyebrows shot up. "Nathan! Remember the picture of my house? The cottonwood tree was smaller."

"And greener, too." He drew up his knees and draped his arms over them. "I know what you're thinking. It feels like a summer night, so the tree's bound to be exactly like it was in the picture."

"Right. I say we should go to my house and see if the girl in the picture is there. She's probably the key to the mystery."

He interlocked his fingers. "The answer has to be linked to the coffins somehow. We have to figure out that part of the puzzle."

"I'll bet they were murdered by Gordon and that Mictar guy. Remember what they said about the burglar and the girl?"

"Think it's the same girl?"

"Only one way to find out."

"Okay, so we head for Iowa." Nathan reached for his back pocket. "No wallet. We don't even have bus fare."

She set her arm in a hitchhiker's pose. "We have thumbs. We can bum a ride."

Nathan looked over the side of the building and saw a bank

clock. Five past midnight. "Who's going to give us a ride this time of night, especially with you bleeding like that?"

"I guess we'll see who's brave enough."

She started to rise, but Nathan pulled her back down. "Let's stay put a little while longer. At least until we're sure Gordon gave up."

For the next half hour, Nathan and Kelly chatted quietly. She prodded him for stories about his adventures, and after each tale, she asked for another. His final story involved his and Clara's escape from a terrorist in Saudi Arabia. They zoomed on motorcycles down rough stone staircases and through filthy alleys teeming with rats until they vaulted over a deep channel their pursuer couldn't cross. When he finished the story, Kelly's mouth hung open for five full seconds. Finally, she swallowed and said, "Take me with you next time. I want to go for a ride like that."

Nathan rose to his feet and dusted off the seat of his pants. "Maybe you'll get a chance sooner than you think." He walked to the roof access, a wooden door in a small dormer that rose about eight feet above the gravel. Although it was locked, a hard kick from his boot splintered the jamb and banged it open, revealing a steep flight of dimly lit stairs.

He tiptoed down. Kelly followed close behind, clutching his hand. After the narrow first flight, the stairwell widened and brightened, finally coming to a dead end at a metal door. He pushed it open, revealing the seating area of a delicatessen, now closed for the night and illuminated only by the streetlamps outside.

Looking at her bloodstained fingers, Kelly nodded toward the restrooms. "Let's get cleaned up before we hit the road."

After washing, the two met at the front door. "Easy enough to get out," Nathan said, turning the deadbolt, "but we can't lock it up again."

"So the manager loses a little pastrami from his fridge. He'll survive." She pushed the door open. "You worry too mu—"

A loud siren blared, pulsing a horn that vibrated the windows.

"A burglar alarm!" Nathan yelled. "Run!"

They rushed out to the sidewalk and headed for a crowd of people streaming from a corner pub about a block and a half away. Just before they reached the next street, Nathan pulled Kelly to a halt. "Just play it cool. We didn't steal anything."

Slowing her breathing, she looked up at him. "I'm not worried about the cops. I'm worried about Gordon. That alarm would wake the dead."

As they ambled toward the pub, a police siren whined in the distance. Nathan pointed at the customers who were still filing out, some laughing, most staggering. "Let's just blend in with them. No one will know."

"Except that we're underage, not acting drunk, and don't smell like booze." Kelly wrinkled her nose. "We don't smell like it, but we could fake being drunk."

He pulled her into the doorway of a closed bail bond office. "I wouldn't know how to fake it. I've never been drunk."

She rolled her eyes. "That's not exactly a shock, Nathan."

"Have you?"

She nudged a dark bottle on the doorstep with her shoe, then leaned over and picked up the bottle. "Tipsy enough to know what it feels like."

"I guess that's not exactly a shock, either."

"Listen," she said sharply, raising a finger near his face. "I used to do a lot of things I don't do anymore. My life changed drastically this summer, and that's all I'm going to say about it right now."

"Fair enough." He leaned against the brick building. "Show me how to act drunk."

"Just do like I do, and don't exaggerate." Kelly stepped out from the doorway and walked back onto the sidewalk, her body angling slightly and her feet misaligned in a sporadic gait. She seemed to be using the bottle as a counterweight to keep from falling.

Nathan shook his head at the pitiful sight. There was no way he could do that. It just wouldn't be right. He ran to catch up and grabbed her arm. "Kelly. Stop."

She halted and pointed at a man across the street. In his early twenties and wearing a muscle shirt, he was unloading a string-bound stack of newspapers from the back of an old over-sized van marked, *Stoneman Enterprises.*

"Look!" she said. "Let's ask him where he's delivering."

Glad for a chance to stop Kelly's antics, Nathan strode up to the muscular young man. "You heading out west at all?"

"Yep." With his collar-length brown hair falling into his eyes as he worked, he dropped the stack and cut the string with a flick of a pocketknife. "I take the early edition as far as Des Moines. I'm heading out as soon as I deliver these."

"That's perfect." When Kelly joined them, Nathan took her hand. "Do you have room for a couple of hitchhikers hoping to go a little farther than Iowa City? We ... uh ... kind of lost our transportation home."

"It'll take till morning to get there." He eyed them suspiciously. "You look kind of young to be out drinking this late, especially in this part of town."

Kelly held up the bottle. "Oh, you mean this stage prop. We're brother and sister. We were acting in a play at a theatre and lost our way on the 'L' train." Setting the bottle down, she pinched her pant leg with one hand and touched her still-bleeding cut with the other. "See? Our costumes, the cool makeup job they did on my machete wound ... "

The young man gave them a smirk that didn't reveal whether he believed her or not. "With all my papers, there won't be any room in the back, but you can squeeze in up front."

Nathan extended his hand. "I'm Nathan Shepherd, and this is Kelly."

The man wrapped Nathan's fingers in his powerful grip. "Gunther Stoneman."

"Pleasure to meet you." Nathan read the lettering on his van again. Could he be related to the Stoneman who helped him at the Wal-Mart? "Your name sounds familiar. Have we met?"

"Not that I can remember. I know some Shepherds, but none that look like you."

Nathan gave a little shrug. "Okay ... well, thanks for the ride."

"Sure thing. Let me load this paper box, and I'll be right back."

After Kelly boarded the van through the front passenger door, Nathan slid in next to her, hip to hip. He pulled a newspaper from the bundle behind him and checked the date, stealthily showing it to Kelly. "Get a load of this!"

She whispered, "Nineteen-seventy-eight?"

"Yeah. And it's summer, just like we thought. July the twenty-ninth." He flipped to another section. "Look at that! Four thousand bucks for a new car!"

"That's fresh off the press," Gunther said through the open window on the driver's side. He opened the door and climbed into his seat. "There's supposed to be a blurb about the double murder at Ganz Hall."

"A double murder?" Nathan repeated.

"Yeah." After starting the engine, he raised his eyebrows at Nathan. "What's it say?"

As the van pulled away from the curb, Nathan fanned out the front page over Kelly's lap and began reading the short article. "Police report that two musicians were murdered backstage shortly after their quartet's performance. Their bodies were found in twin coffins surrounded by broken instruments but later mysteriously disappeared. A woman who found the bodies claimed that their eyes had been burned out. Although police refused to comment about the victims' identities and possible suspects, bystanders report that two teenaged—" He stopped and cleared his throat.

"Tired, Nathan?" Kelly set her finger on the article. "Bystanders report that two teenaged African-American girls left the scene, both wearing straw hats and purple miniskirts."

Gunther whistled into the fresh breeze blowing in through the windows. "African girls in straw hats? They should be easy to find."

Leaning close to Kelly's ear, Nathan whispered, "They didn't call black people that in nineteen-seventy-eight. Your lies are going to get us in trouble."

She turned his way, also whispering. "My lies are keeping us in this van. If he thought we did it, he'd dump us at the police station for sure."

"If we told him the whole truth, maybe not."

"The *whole* truth? You gotta be kidding—"

"Is something wrong?" Gunther asked.

"No," Kelly said, straightening quickly. "Nothing at all."

Nathan folded the paper and set it in his lap. "Actually, Gunther, there is something wrong. We're the two teenagers the witnesses saw, but we're actually running from the murderer ourselves. We were going to be his next victims, but we escaped on the 'L' and got off at the station up the street. The police would never believe us, so we have to get home as soon as possible."

Gunther turned sharply onto a new road. "I already read the article, so I thought you might be the fugitives."

Nathan tightened his grip on the newspaper. "Are you going to take us to the police?"

"I was, until you came clean. You two don't look like murderers to me. Your sister's a bad liar but not a murderer."

Nathan sneaked a peek at Kelly. She clenched her fingers tightly on her lap, her head bowed in silence.

After driving the van up a ramp and merging into the traffic on a major highway, Gunther settled back in his seat. "Why don't you tell me your story while we head west?"

As the breeze stiffened and swirled through the van, rattling the newspapers in the back, Nathan explained how he had found his parents dead in the prop room at the same performance hall, and how tonight, he and Kelly were searching for clues, trying to figure out how they had died. Although he left out the strange time shift and the visions in the mirror, every word he spoke was true. Finishing with enough details about their harrowing escape over the rooftops to make his story believable, he finally let out a long sigh. "I guess that sounds pretty crazy, huh?"

"Not really. You know what they say. Truth is stranger than fiction." At that point, Gunther took over the conversation, rattling on and on about his favorite books, his evening classes at college, his beloved Chicago Bears, and his life in general. Although his night job kept him up until dawn, he caught three short naps a day and subsisted on turkey-and-tomato sandwiches and Hawaiian Punch. And so the chatter continued as the van tunneled into the dark outskirts of the city.

Soon, Kelly's head listed to the side. She leaned on Nathan's shoulder, and her breathing deepened to a rhythmic rumble. He tried to keep as still as possible. She had mentioned not getting any sleep the night before. Not only that, the crazy chase and her loss of blood gave her every reason to be exhausted. Even Gunther's frequent stops and door-slamming didn't faze her.

After a few hours, Nathan caught himself dozing, the van door awakening him as Gunther battened down the hatches after another delivery. The sun's early-morning rays stretched across the horizon and painted the sky and clouds in a wash of orange and blue.

"We're just past Iowa City," Gunther announced as he slid behind the steering wheel. "I can take you straight to your house if you want."

"Sure." Nathan nudged Kelly. "Can you give Gunther directions?"

"Directions?" She jerked her head up and glanced around, blinking rapidly. "Where are we?"

Gunther pointed at a wrinkled map attached by a rubber band to his sun visor. "Ten miles west of Iowa City."

Kelly yawned and rubbed her eyes. "Do you know where the Wal-Mart is in Newton?"

"Wal-Mart? There's no Wal-Mart in Newton."

"Right," Kelly said, laughing nervously. "I must have been dreaming."

"I wouldn't mind having one there." Gunther shifted the van into gear. "That would be a great delivery job. They say Wal-Mart's a good company to work for."

As they pulled back onto the interstate, Kelly leaned forward and squinted at the map. "Do you know where the exit for Highway 14 is?"

"Sure do." Using his finger, he traced a line on Interstate 80 from Des Moines to Newton. "About seventy miles. I have a stop there."

"Good." She nodded toward the windshield. "I'll guide you from the exit."

Gunther narrowed his eyes at Nathan. "Why couldn't you give directions?"

"Oh, he'd get us lost," Kelly said. "He knows he's terrible at—" She halted, squirmed for a second, and cleared her throat. "Nathan's not as familiar with the area as I am. He's been traveling overseas a lot, and you know how fast things change around here."

"If you say so," Gunther said, shrugging.

Nathan focused on the road ahead, not wanting to give

Gunther a chance to read his eyes. He was suspicious enough already.

After about an hour of quiet travel, they turned off the main highway. Kelly seemed lost, frequently shifting forward and swinging her head back and forth. Finally, after several miles, she pointed at a street sign. "There it is! Turn right here!"

Gunther pulled the van onto a narrow dirt road, even narrower than the familiar road to their house. As they passed between the cornfields, the van's draft brushed the stalks, shorter and greener than the stalks they had so recently seen.

Kelly bounced in her seat, extending her finger. "There! There's our house!"

Gunther rolled alongside the huge estate and whistled as he came to a stop. "Nice place. Looks brand new."

"We just moved here. That's why I had a hard time finding it." Kelly set a hand on Nathan's shoulder. "Let's get out."

Nathan pushed the door open and jumped to the dirt road, then helped Kelly down. "Thanks," he said, nodding at Gunther. He held up the section of newspaper he had read earlier. "Can I keep this?"

"Not a problem." Smiling, he winked at Nathan. "Keep your sister out of trouble."

"I will!" Nathan tore off the front page and folded it into his back pocket. As he and Kelly walked slowly toward the house, Gunther wheeled the van a few feet into the yard to make his U-turn before driving away.

Kelly reached for a leaf on the cottonwood tree. "Green. Just like in the picture."

"This whole scene is exactly like it."

"Yeah. It's spooky." She angled her body to look around the side of the house. "I wonder where the little girl is."

"Let's check." He marched straight toward the door.

"Nathan! Wait!"

He spun around. "What?"

"We need a story." She caught up with him and touched the wound on her scalp. "It's so early in the morning, and no one's going to want to talk to a stranger who looks like this."

"Another lie?"

She flashed an angry glare. "Get off your soapbox. If you have a better idea, then let's hear it."

"Just be casual." He hopped up to the porch. "If we pretend not to notice, maybe whoever lives here will pretend, too."

She joined him, raising her shoulder to wipe the still-oozing blood onto her short sleeve. "That's like pretending there's no elephant in the room when he's sitting on your lap."

Nathan shrugged, then knocked. "Scratch him on the back and maybe he'll go to sleep."

After a few seconds, the door swung open, revealing a thirty-something redheaded woman wearing a blue smock. A graceful smile decorated her lovely, slender face, but her bloodshot eyes gave away an inner weariness, and the cane she leaned on revealed some kind of crippling handicap. "May I help you?"

Nathan gawked at her. Except for the red hair and hazel eyes, she looked exactly like his mother. "Uh ... I ..."

A young raven-haired girl stepped into the foyer, clutching a three-quarter-size violin and bow. "Who is it, Mommy? I heard someone mention an elephant."

Nathan's gaze riveted on her. Wearing a blue and white pinafore and purple and pink canvas shoes over white lacy socks, she defined cuteness. This was definitely the girl in the photo. "We're kind of lost," he finally said. "Can we use your phone?"

She stifled a yawn. "Maybe when my neighbor gets off. We don't have a private line yet."

As the girl wrapped her arm around her mother's waist, Kelly spoke to her in a sweet tone. "Is your name Francesca?"

A broad smile crossed her face. "Yes."

"How old are you?"

"I just turned ten."

Kelly pointed at her nose. "How did you get that nasty scratch?"

"My cat, Leopold. I was giving him a bath." She furrowed her brow. "How did you know my name?"

Her mother's brow knitted in exactly the same way. "Yes. How *did* you know?"

Kelly pushed Nathan's shoulder. "We found the right place after all." Reaching for Francesca's hand, Kelly looked at the girl's mother. "I know it's kind of early, but we're here from the music school to interview your little prodigy. We heard she has the potential to become one of the greatest."

A smile emerged on her mother's face, proud, but still suspicious. "Well ... she *is* good. At least I think so." She gave them a curious squint. "How did you hear about her?"

"From her teacher, of course." Kelly glanced at Nathan and began snapping her fingers. "What was the name again?"

"Nikolai. Nikolai Malenkov." He extended his hand. "And you must be Mrs. Romano."

She shook it with a firm grip. "Pleased to meet you." As soon as she released his hand, she again covered up a yawn. "I'm sorry. I slept terribly. Bad dreams all night."

"It's okay. We're tired, too." Nudged by memories of the nightmare article, he lowered his voice. "Were you worried about something?"

She copied his quieter tone. "Ever since my husband died, I worry about ..." She glanced at Francesca. "Well, about security, you know, being alone way out in the middle of nowhere, and since I have lupus, I can't defend myself. I'm thinking about getting a German shepherd."

He gave her a nod. "Not a bad idea."

"What happened to your shirt?" Francesca asked, pointing at Kelly's bloodstained sleeve.

Kelly quickly re-tucked the hem. "Sorry. It must have come loose on the way."

"I didn't mean that. I meant the bl—"

"Where do you normally practice?" Kelly interrupted. "That would be the best place to do the interview and maybe get some pictures."

"In my room."

Kelly took Francesca's hand. "Can you show me?"

"This way." As the little girl led Kelly toward the hall, Kelly looked back, gesturing for Nathan to follow.

When Nathan stepped in that direction, Mrs. Romano grabbed his arm with an iron grip. "Wait. I can't let you go in there without me."

"Oh ... yeah. I understand."

She began a slow hobble toward the bedroom, her cane leading the way. "I'm not saying you're one of them, but with all the crazy people out there, I can't take any chances with my daughter."

"Of course. I'd be the same way." Nathan placed a hand under her elbow and walked slowly next to her. How could he blame her for being suspicious? Two strangers with matching khakis showing up early in the morning claiming to be from a music school wasn't exactly normal, especially since one of them had a nasty cut.

With the thumping cane accentuating her words, she looked up at him with teary eyes. "You remind me of my dear husband. Whenever my lupus acted up, he would walk at my side, until leukemia took him away from me. He was such a gentleman." She stopped and patted his hand. "Thank you for raising that lovely memory."

Nathan shook his head. "Don't thank me. Thank my father. He told me I should always treat women as treasures, especially mothers. Without them, where would we be?"

As a tear made its way to her cheek, she smiled. "You're a lucky boy to have such a wise father."

"Lucky?" Nathan kept his voice steady. "I *was* lucky, I guess. My father died a couple of days ago. The funeral's tomorrow."

She looked him in the eye, her hand trembling on her cane. After a few seconds of silence, she nodded down the hall. "Go ahead to Francesca's room. Your friend is probably wondering what happened to you."

Nathan pulled back. "Are you sure?"

"I'm sure." She scanned his body. "Where's your camera?"

He tried to hide his nervous swallow. "Camera?"

"Aren't you going to take pictures?"

He patted his shirt. "I forgot to bring it."

"I have one you can borrow. I'll get it and meet you there."

As Mrs. Romano shuffled away in the other direction, Nathan strode ahead and turned into the bedroom, his bedroom, at least what had been his bedroom ... or would become his bedroom. He shook his head hard. Everything was so confusing!

When he entered, he quickly scanned the room. Instead of a huge mirror on the wall, a pastel-colored mural decorated the smooth plaster—a painting of a serpentine musical staff with happy-faced notes climbing on the lines like mischievous spider monkeys. He deciphered the notes and nodded. The first measures of "Brahms' Lullaby."

Against the wall opposite the mural, a trunk sat on the floor, its lid open. He wanted to shout to Kelly, "That's the same trunk!" but decided to wait. No use startling Francesca. He stepped closer to see the inside. Sheets of handwritten music covered the bottom, maybe an inch or so thick.

"Where have you been?" Kelly asked.

"Just talking with Mrs. Romano. Sorry to keep you waiting."

"We've been having a nice little interview." Kelly bent toward Francesca and twirled the little girl's dark locks. "How long have you played violin?"

"Six years."

"Six years?" Nathan repeated. "Do you remember why you started playing?"

"Why does anybody play?" She looked up at him, her eyes filled with mystery. "Are you a musician?"

"Yes." He glanced at Kelly, then returned his gaze to Francesca. "Yes, I am."

Her serious aspect deepened. "Then you know why I play."

Lowering himself to one knee, he looked into her beautiful, innocent brown eyes. "Because your spirit has to sing. Every musician's heart bears a song from the Creator, and he spends his life trying to duplicate it as an act of worship. His ultimate dream is to play it flawlessly for an audience of one at the great throne in heaven."

"That's what my teacher says." Francesca touched his lips with two fingers. "But there are two songs in your heart, one for God and one for the woman who will be your wife."

Nathan resisted the urge to look at Kelly again. "My wife?"

"My teacher says if a musician marries another musician, they harmonize their songs into one, but when he marries a nonmusician, he creates a new song for her and teaches it to her heart."

"I have heard that before from a very wise woman." He reached for her violin. "May I?"

She laid the violin and bow in his hands, her expression solemn. "Only if your spirit teaches me its song." As she released her instrument, she blew on his bow hand. Her breath tickled his skin, sending shivers all the way up his arm. She then looked at him with sparkling irises. "My teacher always does that. He says music is the breath of God."

Nathan's entire body flushed with warmth. Tears welled in his eyes. As hot prickles covered his skin, he tried to shake off the emotional surge. He couldn't break down. Not now.

He closed his eyes and raised the violin to his chin, reliving his childhood as he adjusted to the instrument's smaller size.

Then, playing long, gentle strokes, he interpreted the mural on the wall, giving life to the lullaby. The violin sang like a nightingale, whispering a melody of comfort, security, even sadness, and his mind repainted the lovely portrait of his mother playing the same hymn as he lay nuzzled in bed.

Barely opening one eye, he peered at Francesca. Now his mother played the part of the captivated child as she gave her own interpretation, swaying on her toes like an enchanted ballerina, every movement capturing the heart of his spirit's song.

"You're very good!"

Mrs. Romano's voice jerked him back to reality. He lowered the bow and nodded. "Thank you."

She leaned her cane against the wall and hobbled in. "I guess you really are music students. I tried to call Nikolai to check you two out, but his secretary said he never returned from his quartet's performance last night."

"Where did he perform?" Nathan asked.

"At Ganz Hall in Chicago. Maybe he fell ill and stayed an extra day. He has been rather sickly lately."

Concealing a shudder, Nathan felt his back pocket for the newspaper. Should he tell her about the murder? Could Nikolai have been one of the victims? If only he'd had a chance to get a look in the coffins.

She extended her arm. A camera dangled from her hand by a strap. "It's a Nikon F2. Do you want me to show you how to use it?"

Nathan recognized the camera immediately—his father's. As he stared at it, he felt his jaw drop. Could it have been a gift from his mother? He traded glances with Kelly, but her furrowed brow told him she had no more answers than he did.

"It's really not hard," Mrs. Romano continued, pointing at the camera body. "All you do is focus and press the button. The flash is electronic."

"Are you a photographer?" Kelly asked.

"It was my husband's hobby before he died." She gestured for them to gather together. "Squeeze in, and I'll take one of the three of you."

Keeping the violin and bow pinned under his arm, Nathan set a hand on Francesca's shoulder as she stood just inches in front of them. When Mrs. Romano raised the camera to her eye, the sound of wood on wood banged from the house's main entry way.

Nathan jerked his head around.

"That happens a lot when it's windy," Mrs. Romano said as her finger reached for the shutter button. "Must be a storm coming."

Nathan glanced at Kelly. Was she thinking what he was thinking? It wasn't windy when they arrived.

"I hear footsteps," she whispered.

He clutched her hand. "We'd better—"

The camera flashed, bright and blinding, far brighter than any normal camera. Kelly strangled Nathan's fingers. "What's that?"

A dark human-shaped shadow appeared at the bedroom doorway. A new flash exploded from its hand, and a loud popping noise echoed all around. Mrs. Romano seemed to twist and bend, her body warping like a reflection in a circus mirror. The entire room contorted, becoming a kaleidoscope of colorful swirls.

Seconds later, the swirls spread out again, repainting the room with new details—the wall mirror, Nathan's desk and poster bed, and the sprawled bodies of their dead twins. As each detail crystallized, the bands of color thinned out. But just before they disappeared, they swept over the two younger corpses, pixelizing every square inch of their bodies until their multihued dots blended into the flow. The swirls, now reenergized, orbited the room twice and flowed into the mirror, creating a splash of color that spread across the surface and slowly faded.

When the movement settled, Nathan rocked back and forth on his feet, dizzied by the chaos. Setting his hand on the wall to keep his balance, he felt a glassy surface—the mirror. He glanced down at his body, still clothed in khaki, and Francesca's violin still tucked under his arm.

Kelly clutched the front of her safari shirt. "We're back!"

"What happened to my room?" Francesca asked. "It's so different!"

Kelly set her hand at the side of her mouth and called, "Daddy!"

"Clara!" Nathan shouted.

Francesca joined in. "Mommy!"

Tony stormed into the room, his eyes bulging. "Kelly! Nathan! But you were—" He staggered backwards. "I mean, I saw you—"

Clara careened around the doorway. She stopped and stared. "You were dead! Your eyes were burned out! How?"

"Who are you?" Francesca asked Clara. "Where's my mother?"

Clara rushed forward and embraced Nathan. "Thank God you're alive! We thought you both were dead!"

Nathan embraced her warmly for a moment, then pulled back. He touched the top of Francesca's head. "This is Francesca Romano."

Clara gave Nathan a quizzical look but said nothing.

"Romano?" Tony repeated. "My father bought this house from the Romano estate when the old lady got plugged by a burglar back in—"

"Daddy!" Kelly barked. "Hush!"

Clara bent over and reached for Francesca's hand. "I'm pleased to meet you, young lady."

A tear trickled down Francesca's cheek as she took Clara's hand. "Do you know where my mommy is?"

Clara looked up at Nathan. "Do I?"

Nathan sighed. "I guess I'd better start from the beginning and tell you everything."

Kelly shuffled close to Nathan and whispered. "Do you really want to tell my dad the truth? He's bound to make this place a media circus."

"I have to. He's already seen too much."

Nathan pulled out the desk chair for Kelly and gestured toward the bed for the others. "Have a seat. This could take a while."

7

A VOICE FROM BEYOND

"So," Nathan concluded as he paced in front of the mirror, "we don't know what happened to Mrs. Romano. We don't know how we got into that alternate universe or how we got back. We don't know how several hours could pass there and only a few minutes here, and we don't know how we took over the clothes of the other Nathan and Kelly or where they went, but Francesca is proof that it all really happened." He glanced at the little girl. Had he disguised the details of the story enough? Or had she figured out that she was actually his mother in another world and that her own mother seemed to be in great danger?

Seated in the desk chair, Kelly twisted a rubber band between her finger and thumb. "We don't even know the whole point of it all. Why did that stage show up in the mirror in the first place? And who could've been in the coffins?"

With an arm draped over Francesca, Clara drummed her fingers on the bed. "All this alternate universe talk makes me dizzy, but if you and Kelly had dead bodies in this dimension, and you're still alive, maybe there's hope for your parents."

"You mean maybe they switched places like we did?" Nathan slowly clenched his fingers together. It was just a theory — too early to get excited. "If only I could figure out how to look for them."

"Can you use the mirror again?" Francesca asked.

Nathan swiveled toward her. "What do you mean?"

She touched the surface with her finger, creating the image of two Francescas making friendly contact. "Does it just show places in your mind, like in your dream, or does it come up with the places by itself?"

"I'm not sure. I think everything came from my head, but I don't know how the thoughts got there. I couldn't have dreamed about the broken violins by accident." Nathan watched the little girl's reflection. Her eyes seemed to shine with insight beyond her years, and her presence gave him a sense of peace, as if his real mother were there offering him seeds of wisdom he could use to solve this puzzle. And what a puzzle it was! Time warps, coffins on a dark stage, broken and bloodstained violins. It would take a genius to figure it all out.

He imagined the coffins on the stage again and replayed the other Nathan's words in his mind. *"I crossed the same way as before. I had a dream, it showed up in the mirror, then music, a flash of light, and zap, I'm here."* That had to be a clue, a big clue.

As he scratched his head, Nathan scanned the four sets of eyes staring at him. "Hang on," he said. "I'm thinking."

"I know," Kelly said with a smirk. "I feel the heat rising."

Nathan gave her a quick wink and returned his gaze to the mirror. So, the image showed up before any music played, and then music allowed the other Nathan to enter. And it worked the same way when he showed up himself. He had the dream, music was playing ... but was there a flash of light? Even if there was, the biggest part of the puzzle was still missing. How does the whole process start? Why do the images show up in the mirror in the first place? Could it really paint a picture of what was in his mind? Could he learn how to control what it showed?

He glanced down at Francesca again. Still staring at her reflection, she seemed mesmerized. Her eyes sparkled with light as she murmured, "Something's happening."

The image in the glass wrinkled, changing the surface to a jigsaw pattern. As it smoothed over again, the room in the reflection altered. The walls changed to the feminine pastels they had so recently seen. In the mirror, Francesca withdrew a sheet of paper from her trunk and set it on a music stand. Then, lifting her violin and bow, she concentrated on the sheet and played. After a few strokes, she picked up a pencil from the stand and made a mark on the handwritten score. She then lifted her bow again and played on.

"That's me in the mirror," Francesca said, pointing. "I'm playing my birdsong piece."

"Birdsong piece?" Nathan squinted at the music, but it was too far away to read. "Can you hear it?"

She nodded. "Can't you?"

"I can watch her fingers and imagine it, but I can't hear anything."

Tony rose slowly to his feet. "So that crazy museum guy was right after all! This mirror shows your thoughts."

"Who was thinking about Francesca's room?" Nathan asked.

"I was." Francesca picked up her own violin. "I was thinking about going home."

Nathan glanced between the two Francescas. Was the mirror now reflecting her thoughts? Maybe there was a way to make her wish come true, take her home and check on her mother's safety. "Can you play the same piece?"

"I don't have it memorized," she said, raising her bow, "so I'll be a step behind." While watching her twin in the mirror, she played a series of short high notes, making her violin chirp like a songbird. The lovely melody filled the room with the bright sounds of an early spring morning.

Nathan marched to the lamp on his desk, ready to make the bulb flash on and off, but the music suddenly stopped. He swung back to Francesca. "What happened?"

She touched the mirror with a finger. "I heard a door slam and a loud popping sound. Then I hid under my bed, like I was scared of something."

Nathan eyed his bed's dust ruffle. What would happen if ... No. It couldn't happen ... Could it? ... He reached for the lamp's switch. It was worth a try. With a few twists of his wrist, he turned the lamp on and off three times.

"What are you doing?" Kelly asked.

"An experiment." He rushed to the bed, dropped to his knees, and looked underneath. Nothing. Nothing but his mother's violin in its case and a few dust bunnies.

Rising to his feet, he looked back at the mirror. Once again it had reverted to a reflection of his room and everyone in it. Francesca stood next to Kelly, who was still seated in the desk chair. Tony sat beside Clara on the bed, both staring at Nathan.

In the mirror, Tony propped his foot against the side of the trunk ... the open trunk. "Well, if you ask me—"

"Everyone freeze!" Nathan raised his hand. "Don't move a muscle!"

"Why?" Kelly asked. "What's going on?"

Nathan stepped slowly backwards, keeping his eyes straight ahead. "Just look at the mirror. Watch me in the reflection."

When he backed all the way to the trunk, his heels tapped the wood. Out of the corner of his eye he saw Tony swing his head back toward the trunk. "Don't look!" Nathan ordered. "It won't stay open if you do!"

"But it's not open," he said. "How can it stay open?"

Kelly growled but kept her gaze locked on the mirror. "Just do what he says, Daddy!"

"Okay! Okay!" Tony crossed his arms and stared at the reflection. "Satisfied?"

"Perfect." Nathan reached behind him and bent his knees, lowering his hands until they descended into the trunk. This time, he had to stretch farther. If the sheets of music were still there, they would be flat at the bottom.

"Hey!" Tony bellowed, pointing at the mirror. "It's open!"

Clara laid a palm on Tony's cheek. "Don't turn yet! Stay focused!"

Now almost completely squatting, Nathan sensed paper at his fingertips. He searched for the edges and gathered up the sheets before straightening his body. "Okay. It's safe to look."

As everyone turned toward him, Tony touched the top of the trunk. He quickly swiveled back to the mirror. The trunk in the reflection was now also closed. "How'd you do that?"

"I wish I knew." Nathan leafed through the handwritten music compositions, pausing at a fairly complex piece several pages down. He played the notes in his mind through the first few measures. Humming them quietly, he aimed his gaze at Francesca. "This is really pretty. Did you write this, too?"

She pushed aside her dark locks, revealing flushed cheeks. "I wrote all of them, but I never showed them to anyone who knew how to read music."

Nathan scanned the sheet again, now more analytically. Could the combinations of notes mean something? The letters, the key signature, the arrangement on the staff? What could it be? Could it all relate to Rosetta or Quattro somehow?

Nathan reached under the bed and pulled out his mother's violin.

"An impromptu concert?" Clara asked.

"Sort of." Standing again with bow to string, he smiled at Francesca. "Mind if I play one of your pieces?"

Holding up the thin stack of music, Francesca grinned. "Which one?"

"Choose your favorite."

She paged through her collection and pulled out a sheet. "Can you read it?" she asked, holding it high enough for him to see. "It's pretty messy."

"I think so." He leaned closer to the page. "I just want to test a theory."

As he played, he glanced between the music and the mirror, watching for a change, but nothing obvious showed up. The melody, though simple and sweet at the beginning, grew in complexity, calling for difficult fingering.

Clara strolled slowly toward the mirror, crossing her arms as she gazed into the room's reflection. "Everything's normal so far. The trunk's still closed."

Nathan kept his focus on the music. When he neared the end of the page, Francesca held up another, waiting for him to begin playing it before lowering the first sheet. "This is the end," she said. "I'm still working on it."

Following the girl's scribbled notes, Nathan increased his volume from *piano* to *forte* and shifted through a series of arpeggios. As he stroked the strings, he tried to concentrate on the notes and, at the same time, on thoughts of his parents. Were they still alive? If so, where were they?

The lamp in the mirror dimmed, and the walls darkened. As he watched the new drama in the mirror, his legs shook. The music was doing its part. Now it was time for a flash of light, but maybe this time it should be something different. He used his foot to point at the desk drawer. Sight reading new, hand-written music was hard enough. Trying to talk at the same time was almost impossible. "Get the camera," he grunted.

Clara rushed to the desk, pulled out the camera, and draped the strap around her neck. "What should I take a picture of?"

"Wait." As the music reached a crescendo near the end of the page, the reflection undulated, like ripples on a pond. The bedroom faded to black. New dark images formed deep within—ghostly shadows in a haze.

In the mirror, a ray of light from somewhere to the side cast a glow over the scene, bringing clarity to the dim room. This time a spacious chamber materialized. The outer walls seemed curved, as if cordoning off a circular floor. Two people skulked across polished tiles toward the source of light, a lamp on a desk in the far background. They passed a shadowed object at the center of the circle, something that looked like a bulky cylinder on a pedestal aimed toward the ceiling at an angle.

Returning to the beginning of the page and playing with all the passion he could muster, Nathan gawked at the image. It was exactly the same as one of the photos from Dad's camera!

Wearing long trench coats with pulled-up collars and walking away from the front of the mirror, the two forms gave away few details, though the more curvaceous shape of the smaller person revealed her gender as she carried a violin case in her feminine hand. Near the top edge of the scene, copies of their hunched forms echoed their moves, but the copies walked upside-down, as if projected on the ceiling like an inverted movie.

When they reached the desk, they each took a seat in rolling swivel chairs. As they turned toward one another, their profiles came into view.

Clara raised a hand to her mouth. "Your parents!"

Nathan pulled the bow across the D string to play the final note and nodded at her, his voice rattling. "Take a shot of the mirror. Let's see if we can go there."

"Or bring them here," she added as she sidestepped to the center of the room and focused the camera. When the ready light came on, she pressed the shutter button. The camera flashed. The mirror reflected the light and shot back a radiant bolt that sizzled into the flash attachment, ripping the entire unit from Clara's hands. It fell to her chest and bounced back and forth at the end of the strap.

Nathan grabbed the camera, leaving it on Clara's neck as he examined the casing. Everything looked okay. When he turned to the mirror, the image seemed to zoom in on his parents, sharply clarifying as it filled the glass with the upper half of their bodies. At the desk, his father pecked at a laptop keyboard while his mother looked on.

Tucking the violin under his arm, Nathan laid his hand on the mirror. It remained hard, impenetrable. As he caressed the surface near his mother's cheek, she turned toward him and sighed, her voice tired and plaintive. "I'll try again, but it seems hopeless. I just don't have enough power."

Solomon made a final tap on the keyboard and swiveled her way. "We have to keep trying. We have to stop interfinity."

"But if Nathan figures out how to use the Quattro camera and my violin, together we might—"

"It's too late for that. We have to push forward." He stood and reached for her hand. "The scope is in position. Give it all you've got. This might be our last chance."

As a frenzied mix of sounds began to play from somewhere in the background, she took his hand and rose from her chair, still clutching the violin case. Hand in hand they walked to the middle of the chamber, and the mirror's eye followed them, panning back as if held by a cameraman. When they stopped near the center of the circle, she withdrew the violin from its case and set it under her chin. As she hovered the bow over the strings, she looked up, but the mirror focused on her entranced eyes, not revealing what had engaged her attention above. Her pupils danced with chaotic colors that intermeshed with her brown irises, and a gentle smile graced her lips as if a long-loved memory had found its way home.

Then, with a sudden burst of strokes, she played a series of high eighth notes that seemed void of melody, but, with her gaze still trained on something high above, she soon transformed the musical chaos into consonance, creating a glorious rendition of her birdsong piece, much fuller and more vibrant than her younger self had so recently played.

After several seconds, the colors in her eyes dispersed, and the black pigment in her pupils transformed into brilliant white.

The whiteness expanded and emerged from her eyes, like twin lasers shooting into the twilight. As she played on, the lasers strengthened, becoming so bright, they washed her skin into a ghostly pallor.

Solomon circled behind her. "Do you see, Francesca? Have you found it?"

Nodding and breathing heavily, she increased to fortissimo, sending the loudest, most lovely notes yet into the upper reaches of the chamber. A bow hair broke away and flew wildly. Her fingers blurred. Her eyes blazed so bright, Solomon backed away and gasped, "Shekhinah!"

As a loud cracking sound blended into the musical flow, Nathan's fingers began to sink into the image. The glass felt like cool jelly, becoming thinner every second.

Solomon's voice again rose above the din. "Hang in there, Francesca! My darling, you can do it!"

Nathan pushed through up to his shoulder. "I'm going in," he said, extending the violin toward Kelly. But just as she took it, his mother heaved a groan and crumpled to the floor. With a loud pop, her eyes flashed a ring of sizzling fire in all directions. The ring crashed against the mirror, sending Nathan flying backwards into a pair of strong arms.

Tony lifted him upright. "You okay?"

"I'm fine." Nathan shook the mental cobwebs away and leaped back toward the mirror. He laid his hand on the surface, now rigid once again. Leaning his forehead against the glass, he bit his lip, trying not to lose control, but a tear forced its way out of each eye.

In the reflection, his father sat on the floor cradling his mother. "What did you see?"

With her eyes still emanating a faint glow, she replied in a dreamlike whisper. "I stood at the edge of the chasm and gazed down into an endless void. A shimmering golden rope was fastened around a rocky projection at my feet. As taut as the strings on my violin, it seemed to span the celestial wound, but I couldn't be sure since it disappeared in the darkness. I plucked it. It produced a perfect tone, an E, loud and lovely, and shook the ground upon which I stood, so much so, that I could no longer bear to stand. As I lowered my body to sit, I noticed three other golden ropes, so when the shaking ceased, I plucked the others and found that they played the A, D, and G notes. I tried to play the song, running as quickly as I could between the strings, but after only two measures, I became too weary to keep the timing." She blew out a long breath and shook her head. "I don't think I can try again, not without Nathan to help me."

He joined her sigh. "Then I guess there's no hope."

Shifting upward in his arms, she gazed at him hopefully. "He'll find the email—"

"It won't be enough. I thought he'd come with us, so I didn't put much information in it. He won't figure out the best way to find us."

"There's still the girl, the interpreter." She turned her gaze back to the ceiling. "And there's always his supplicant."

He tilted his head upward. "And Patar, but will he help or hinder? We'd be better off shoving that vision stalker and his brother back through the hole they came from and plugging it with a cosmic cork. Patar would tell Nathan the right thing to do, but he's likely to scare him away."

She took his chin in her hand and turned his head, setting his eyes directly in front of hers. "Our son will not be frightened. He will choose wisely. He has the same warrior spirit I saw in you when you were his age."

His countenance turned grim. "If Mictar gets wind that Nathan is punching through dimensional walls, he'll follow the trail and find us. Even a portal view might expose our whereabouts."

Nathan pulled back from the mirror. "A portal view!" As

soon as his skin left the surface, his mother swiveled her head to the side.

"I hear footsteps!" she said.

His father lifted her to her feet. "Let's go!" The scene darkened, then slowly illuminated again, growing brighter and brighter as the objects in the bedroom reappeared.

Nathan slapped the mirror. "We almost did it! We were so close!"

Jumping to his side, Kelly displayed the violin in her hands. "Can you try again?"

Clara pointed at the mirror. "You heard your father. It sounds like all this dimensional travel and poking around and whatnot is putting them in danger."

Tony crossed his arms over his chest. "It looked like he was already in trouble, like someone was coming."

"I know!" Nathan backpedaled and flopped into his desk chair. What else could he do? Without another clue to go on, every option seemed like it ended at a brick wall with no fire escape ladder in sight. But at least now there was hope. At least his parents were alive.

He glanced at the digital clock on his desk. Still before noon. They spent maybe twelve hours in that other world and came back only a few minutes later than when they left. After shaking his head wearily, he looked up at Kelly. "You got any ideas?"

"Not a clue." She smoothed out her safari shirt and drew closer. "With the whole clothes-swapping thing and clones of us getting murdered, there's some serious sh—" She winced but continued with barely a pause. "Some serious stuff going on. Maybe we really did travel through time."

Nathan shook his head. It couldn't have been time travel, but he was too tired to argue the point. After all, how could they have made drastic changes in the past without affecting the present? He shifted his gaze toward Francesca. Not only that, now they had his ten-year-old mother in his bedroom. If she stayed with him, then he couldn't have been born. Time travel just didn't make sense, but, then again, neither did anything else. What other options were there? She couldn't have come back to life and then aged backwards.

Taking the violin from Kelly, Nathan got up and put it away. "It looks like our only plan is to find the email Dad mentioned."

"But was that your father?" Kelly asked. "There was more than one Nathan. Maybe that was the other Nathan's father. Maybe he's the Nathan they were talking about."

Nathan sagged his shoulders. She was right. How could he know who they were for certain? If there was another Nathan, there had to be another set of parents, and they probably experienced the same events in their lives, even the stuff about Quattro.

He thinned out his lips. "Thanks for the uplifting theory."

"Sorry. I'm just looking at all the angles."

Francesca pulled on Nathan's sleeve. "Can we find my mother now?"

Bending over, he lifted her fingers to his lips and kissed her knuckles. "We'll do our best. I promise."

"Is there anything else we might have missed?" Clara asked. "A puzzle piece you might have overlooked?"

He pulled the newspaper from his back pocket. "There is one clue ..." Unfolding it, he showed the article to Clara. "Do you know anything about this murder back in nineteen-seventy-eight?"

Clara's eyes darted back and forth across the page. "No. Nothing like this ever happened."

"How can you be sure?"

"I attended this concert. Your mother's teacher, Dr. Malenkov, and his wife were the violinists in one of the quartets, so I remember it well. Since my dear husband was a percussionist, I was quite involved in the orchestra social circle. Eventually that's how I first met your mother, when she joined the CSO as its concertmaster at the age of twenty-one."

Nathan creased the newspaper and laid it on the bed. He stared at the article as it lay open, searching for more than the scant information in the wrinkled type. Since Dr. Malenkov never returned from the concert, maybe he really *was* one of the victims. Could he and his wife have replaced the pieces of Rosetta from his dream? He tapped Kelly's shoulder. "Let's see if Dad has any emails from Dr. Malenkov."

Kelly scooted the mouse pointer and pressed the button. A list of messages appeared. There were several from Nikolai Malenkov.

He joined Kelly's hand with Francesca's. "Kelly, can you and your father get some lunch for Francesca while Clara and I look at these emails?"

"Sure." She looked at Tony, who was still glaring at the mirror. "Daddy, what can we whip up for lunch?"

Half closing one eye, he gazed at the ceiling. "We have a lot of tuna-banana salad left over and buffalo wings marinated in ketchup and mayonnaise."

Taking Francesca along, she reached for her father's hand. "C'mon. We're going on a safari hunt in the freezer."

As they walked down the hall, Tony's voice echoed, "I think we have some eels still frozen from the fishing trip. What do you think? Serve the eels with some of my special rattlesnake sauce?"

"No! Don't you dare!"

After bringing in a chair from another bedroom, Nathan and Clara sat together at his desk, studying his father's inbox. The messages from Dr. Malenkov focused on his visit to Chicago, expressing his concern about attending the shareholders' meeting even though he had no interest in the company. Since he hadn't seen Francesca in so long, he just wanted to hear her play. Another email asked if her favorite flowers were still white roses, but there seemed to be no hidden messages, at least nothing Nathan could spot.

Clara pointed at an icon on the screen. "Looks like there's something in the draft folder."

He clicked on it. "One message. It's addressed to Dr. Malenkov. It was never sent."

They both leaned close and read it silently.

Nathan, in case you happen to find this and read it: The mirrors lead to alternate dimensions. Dr. Simon maintains a steady state. Must find the hole and seal it, or interfinity will result. We will need your help to produce the musical key. Tell no one that we have discovered how to heal the wounds.

Nathan clenched his fist. This had to be the email they were supposed to find, locked away in the draft folder where it couldn't be intercepted during transmission.

Clara's eyes darted back and forth as she read the message again. "Very interesting. Alternate realities that are out of phase with each other on the timeline."

Nathan propped a pencil eraser on his chin. "Just like I thought. We didn't travel through time. We went to another dimension."

"That's what pure logic demands, but it doesn't explain your dead bodies."

"Maybe it does. Maybe there are exact copies of everyone in the other world. Our copies died over there and somehow got transported over here." He pointed his pencil at the mirror and shrugged. "When we came back, they got zapped into their world again. Two corpses, special delivery."

Clara jerked off her glasses. "Nathan!"

He squinted at her. "What?"

"You're acting like it's no big deal. A couple of dead kids, who happen to look just like you and Kelly, are getting thrown back and forth like an old pair of shoes, and you're as cool as a cod." She set her fingers against her neck. "I put my hand on their lifeless pulses. I mopped their hair back from their ashen faces and stared at the scorched pits where their eyes used to be." Pointing her glasses at him, she gave him a stern glare. "You need a dose of reality, Nathan Shepherd, and a heaping bowl of compassion."

Nathan lowered his head, shaking it slowly. What could he say? Clara had nailed him to the wall. Letting out a long breath, he looked up at her. "You're right . . . as usual. I guess I never felt like the other Nathan and Kelly were real. I only saw them in the mirror, like it was a movie or something."

"And let's not forget this." She tugged on the sleeve of his safari shirt. "These aren't your clothes. Or, then again, maybe they *are* yours. Maybe you're really the Nathan from the other dimension."

"That's impossible." He nodded toward his reflection. "I remember being here before I went over there. That place didn't even have the mirror, and I never saw this shirt before this morning."

"Fair enough. You're the Nathan I know. But there are still mysteries aplenty. I don't understand what your mother was doing. How did the light appear in her eyes? And what was that dark chamber she was in? With all the reflections and colors, it looked almost like the house of mirrors."

"You're right. That was too weird." He tapped the pencil on his knee. Should he tell her about sometimes seeing light in his own eyes when he looked in the mirror? But how could that help? She couldn't possibly know why it happened. And the bigger mystery was all that stuff Mom said about playing a huge violin. She was great at storytelling, but she sounded dead serious.

"So," Nathan continued, "Dad says Dr. Simon maintains a steady state. Any idea what that means?"

"Maybe. Here's how I would piece the puzzle together."

She set a finger on the screen. "The part about sealing the hole makes me think someone figured out a way to open passages between the dimensions. Somehow this hole threatens to bring about some kind of catastrophic state called interfinity, and Dr. Simon was keeping that from happening."

"But he killed them! Why would he be on Dad's side, keeping a steady state?"

"Your guess is as good as mine."

"And now Simon's dead, so interfinity is probably on its way." He kept his eyes on the message, reading it absentmindedly. "Didn't you say Dad did an assignment for a company called Interfinity?"

"Yes. And that reminds me. With all the excitement, I forgot to tell you that the police called this morning. They found your parents' bodies, so I have to go to Chicago early tomorrow morning to finalize the funeral arrangements. I'll pay Interfinity a visit after everything's settled."

Nathan sank in his seat. "Now I'm more confused than ever. I don't know if I'm an orphan, if I'm trying to rescue my parents or someone else's, or if I'm just chasing after ghosts." He glanced at the suitcase on the floor of his closet, still not quite unpacked. "What time do we leave?"

"We?" She patted his leg. "You have to stay here."

"What? Why?"

She rose to her feet and stretched, speaking through an extended yawn. "You have to register for school Monday."

"Can't school wait till we get back?"

"Not a chance. We set up your secret identity and filed your transcript, and they already know you'll be out on Tuesday for family matters, or so we told them. When you and Kelly come to Chicago, we'll talk about what I find at Interfinity. Since your father says it's dangerous for you to be peeking through dimensional peepholes, you might as well stay here."

Nathan slumped his shoulders. "Is Kelly's father coming to the funeral?"

"I asked him to, but he says he has to stay here. Kelly will have to drive."

"Why? I have my license."

"Because it's their car." She planted a finger on his chest. "And you'd better get used to the idea. Tony rides his motorcycle to his morning shift at a machine shop, so he doesn't get to the school for coaching until the afternoon. That means Kelly will be driving every day."

Nathan sank another inch in his chair. "I guess I can deal with that."

"Of course you can. She's a sweetheart. She even volunteered to help you through the registration process, and she'll probably want to introduce you to her friends."

Nathan tightened his grip on the pencil but said nothing. Was the prospect of meeting Kelly's friends supposed to cheer him up?

The clatter of a metal pan rang from the hallway, making him swing his head around. "That reminds me. What are we going to do with Francesca?"

"What choice do we have? I should take her with me. She can't stay here by herself, and we can't very well send her home."

"Yeah. With Gordon and Mictar stalking her, it won't be safe for her here or there." As he replayed their escape from Francesca's house, he shook his head sadly. It looked like the burglar killed her mother just like in his own dimension, but now he knew his mom escaped thirty years ago by hiding under the bed. Obviously, Gordon and Mictar had planned to kill this new Francesca and make sure the burglar got the blame.

So that meant he had at least done something right. Even though he had altered the events in Francesca's dimension, he had saved her from Mictar. As goose bumps rose all along his skin, he shuddered and looked up at Clara. "I don't want to think about what would happen if that creep got hold of her."

Clara clapped her hands lightly. "But he didn't, and we'll make sure we keep her safe. I'll take her with me to Chicago. I'm sure she won't be any trouble at all."

He rose from his seat and gave Clara a serious stare. "She's my mother. Take good care of her."

"I'm going to warn her about the crazy son she might have some day." Giving him a sly wink, she turned toward the bedroom door. "Let's go and see what Kelly's cooking up."

"Wait." Nathan picked up a screwdriver from the top of his cabinet and took it to the mirror. Kneeling at the bottom left corner, he inserted the blade end behind the square he had placed in the matrix.

Clara walked closer. "What are you doing?"

"This is the piece Dad gave me, but it won't come loose." Sliding the blade in as far as he could, he pushed against the handle. "If I'm supposed to look in the mirror whenever I get into trouble, I'm taking it to school with me, and I don't want it creating any of those portal views by itself."

The square popped loose into his free hand. "Got it!"

A burst of light flashed from the mirror, making a hollow popping sound. Like a splash in a pond, ripples of radiance emanated from the center, fading as they approached the edges. After a few seconds, the light disappeared.

"Well," Clara said, setting her hands on her hips, "I think the big mirror's back to normal."

"Yeah, it's weird." He balanced the extricated piece on his palm, eyeing it as he turned it slowly. "I feel like I'm holding another world in my hand, like there's billions of people in there who have no idea that someone's got them all teetering in his grasp."

She shook her head. "That's too deep for me to think about, especially on an empty stomach."

"Then let's get some grub." Tucking the mirror under his arm, Nathan climbed to his feet and headed for the hall. "But I hope we're not having eel pie for dinner."

8

THE KEY TO THE MIRROR

Sitting in the front passenger's seat of Kelly's Camry, Nathan glared at his watch, trying to read the numbers in the dimness of the garage. If she didn't hurry up, they'd be late for sure, and that wouldn't be a great way to make a first impression at a new school.

He pulled down the sun visor and stared at his eyes in the mirror. Yep. Red streaks. Nightmares again. This time about driving Kelly's car in a crazy highway chase. He unzipped a red backpack sitting on the floorboard between his sneakers. The mirror was still fairly secure, wrapped in a Gatorade towel and a sweater. Without any books yet for padding, he'd have to be careful to keep it from knocking against anything. At least the sweater would help. Although it was kind of muggy this morning, the radio had mentioned the possibility of a cold front coming through, maybe before school let out in the afternoon. Apparently the weather was going crazy. The temperature was supposed to drop below freezing that night.

Opening the backpack's external pocket he checked for his cell phone and ATM card. Everything was exactly where it was supposed to be. Now if only they could get going.

He shifted his gaze to the door between the garage and the house, hoping every second it would swing open and reveal Kelly's familiar form. He narrowed his eyes. What would she be wearing on this warm morning? Something tight and revealing like most girls nowadays? He hoped not. Sure, with her athletic body she'd look great, but ... He squirmed in his seat. He'd just have to stay cool. He could handle it.

The door slammed. Fishing in her purse for her keys, Kelly scooted toward the car. The legs of her loose-fitting beige slacks swiped together as she hustled, but her hair, pinned back neatly with a pair of silvery barrettes, stayed in place. Finding her keys, she stopped at the car door and brushed her short-sleeve navy polo shirt, smoothing out a wrinkle where it overlapped her waistband.

She slid behind the wheel, threw her purse into the back next to his violin case, and pressed a button on the car's sun visor, triggering the automatic door opener. As the door rumbled upward, she thrust in the keys and cranked the engine. "Good," she said, patting the dashboard. "It's behaving today."

As she gave the car plenty of gas, Nathan listened to the engine roar. "Starter troubles?" he asked.

"Sometimes." The idle speed died down to a slow, rattling hum. "Sorry I took so long. I couldn't decide what to wear."

Nathan locked his gaze on her, trying not to get flustered. "You look ... uh ... nice."

As she zoomed out of the garage and down the driveway, she smiled. "You think so?"

"Yeah. I thought—" Nathan bit his tongue and faced the front. How could he possibly tell her that he expected something more revealing? "Never mind."

When the car straightened on the road, Kelly stepped on the gas, giving the tires a slight squeal. Her smile vanished. "You thought what?"

Fingering his backpack zipper, Nathan shifted closer to the door. "I'm not going to say. It was stupid."

She turned onto the main highway and accelerated, her lips thin and taut. After a few seconds of silence, she shook her head, speaking barely above a whisper. "It wasn't stupid."

He pulled the zipper back and forth along its track but said nothing. Had she really figured it out? If she had, would she think he actually wanted her to dress that way? A surge of warmth flooded his cheeks. This was going to be a long day.

She glanced at him for a half second before turning back to the road. "No offense, Nathan, but I'm not looking forward to this at all."

"Are you worried about what I'll think of your friends?"

She breathed a nervous chuckle. "Not exactly."

He checked out his own clothes. He didn't have much to choose from this morning, only what Clara had bought after their luggage went for a swim in the river, but no one would think jeans and a black polo shirt were geeky, would they? The white lettering on the front of the shirt spelled out Hebrew words from the Bible, but what high school student could figure out what the message said? He sighed. "This isn't going to be easy for me, either."

She kept her eyes on the road. "Why is that?"

"I've never been to a real school before. I'm sure to do something that'll make me look like an idiot."

"You'll be fine. Just relax and be yourself." Kelly flipped on the radio. The wail of an electric guitar screamed from the speakers, scratching out note after note in a cacophonous frenzy. She changed the station and scanned through the frequencies. "You like classical, right?"

"Sure. Classical, baroque, romantic. It's all good."

"The classical station isn't one of my presets, but I'll find it."

"Don't worry about me. I like almost anything with a melody."

"Okay." She punched a button. "Country music always has a melody."

He was about to repeat his statement, emphasizing "almost anything," but changed his mind. He closed his eyes, leaned against the window, and lost himself in the wash of warbling steel guitar riffs and lamenting lyrics about a cheating wife. Every few seconds, he partially opened one eye and sneaked a look at Kelly. With her stare trained on the road and both hands firmly gripping the wheel, she displayed the perfect portrait of a careful driver. Yet, with her fingers clenched so tightly, something more had to be going on. He let his gaze wander up to her face where a tear began to trickle toward her cheek.

She punched the radio power button and swiped at the tear. "Did you hear something strange?"

"You mean besides the singing?"

"It's kind of a moaning sound ... sort of muffled. It didn't come from the speakers."

"Nope. Nothing like that." He reached into the backseat and pulled his violin case into his lap. "Could this be talking again?"

She angled her head and listened. "I don't hear it now."

He flipped up the latch but left the lid closed as he caressed its cool black surface.

"Whose violin is that?" Kelly asked. "Yours, Francesca's, or your mother's?"

"Francesca took hers to Chicago. I wanted to make a good impression with the orchestra, so I brought my mother's."

"The way you play?" She gave a gentle laugh and rolled her eyes. "I don't think you have anything to worry about. They'll think you're the second coming of Mozart."

"I didn't want to take any chances."

She pointed forward. "School's right around this corner."

He straightened in his seat. As she turned onto an oak-lined road, the building came into view, a modern, two-story brick structure—L-shaped with a tall flagpole just outside the elbow. A long white banner stretched across the front of the pole with *Cardinals* spelled out in red letters.

Nathan leaned forward. "It's bigger than I thought."

"Not huge. About a thousand kids." With the parking lot

nearly full, she rolled into a space in the back row. "Let's get moving. First period's in five minutes, and we have to get you registered."

Pulling his backpack and violin, Nathan ducked out of the car. Kelly had already charged ahead, not bothering to lock the door. He balanced his load and followed her, trying not to look like a fool as he trotted in her wake. As he passed between two parked cars, a driver flung open his door. With a deft twist, Nathan lifted his load high and squeezed through the narrow gap. He accelerated again, glancing back. The driver in a dark blazer got out of his Lincoln Town Car and crossed his arms, watching him run. Although Nathan had swept past the man quickly, he saw enough of the driver's face to give him the feeling that they had met before.

Now jogging more slowly, Kelly made a wide circle around a clique of girls and breezed past the flagpole before waiting at the main entrance's double doors. With a brisk wind kicking up, the pole's empty ropes snapped against the metal, tapping out a rhythmless jangle.

Nathan raced across the patio and joined her as she held one of the doors open for him. He brushed past and pulled open the closest of a second set of doors only a few feet in front of the first, returning the favor as he propped it with his knee.

After striding to the middle of the circular lobby, Kelly paused. She pointed at a hole in the ceiling, a smaller circle that created an opening to the second floor. "We call this the rotunda." From the floor up above, two girls leaned against a railing and looked down at them with blank stares.

"Let's go." She led him to the office, a large room adjacent to the rotunda. A girl, somewhat close to Kelly's height and build and wearing jeans and a red Abercrombie T-shirt, bustled through the open office doorway. "Hey, Kelly girl," she said. "You're looking ..." Her gaze drifted up and down Kelly's body for a moment, then, flashing a nervous smile, she continued. "Well ... prim today."

"Thanks." Pinching the girl's cheek, Kelly pursed her lips. "And you look positively conformist."

As the girl walked away, she aimed a finger at Kelly. "I'll get you for that, my pretty!" With a wide grin, she added, "And your little dog, too!"

Nathan pointed at himself. "Am I supposed to be your little dog?"

"Oh, don't mind Daryl," Kelly said with a wave of her hand. "That's a *Wizard of* Oz quote. She's a genius and a movie geek."

He watched Daryl jog down the hall, her long red hair flapping behind her back. If not for her hair and freckles, she could be Kelly's clone. She seemed nice enough, maybe a bit airheaded, but nice.

"Is she your friend?" he asked.

"Practically my best friend. Why?"

"Just wondering." Smiling, he closed the door to the hallway. It was kind of cool to see best friends poking fun at each other like that. Some of the girls he knew would get all bent out of shape if anyone kidded about how they were dressed.

Inside the office anteroom, two ladies stood behind a counter looking at a clipboard together, obviously preoccupied for the moment. The soft buzz of rock music played somewhere nearby, strangely muffled and tinny. A boy in a black T-shirt and untied sneakers sat in one of the waiting area chairs at the back, his head lolling to the side. With one of his iPod earbuds dangling and his mouth wide open, he seemed either sick or asleep.

Nathan traced the sounds of classical guitar, a well-blended drumbeat, and vibrant vocals to the loose earpiece. An old Fleetwood Mac song? Apparently this kid enjoyed seventies rock.

One of the women stepped up to the counter. "May I help you, Kelly?"

Kelly smiled at the friendly face. "Hi, Mrs. Washington! I brought the new student my dad told you about."

The silver-haired lady pushed her half-lens glasses down her nose and peered over the frame. "Oh, is this Kyle Simmons?"

"Uh-huh. He's staying with us for a while."

Nathan extended his hand over the counter. "I'm pleased to meet you, Mrs. Washington."

After shaking hands, Mrs. Washington searched through a stack of file folders on her workspace. "Daryl had your paperwork out on Friday. I'll have to find it."

A new voice breezed in from the side. "He's good looking and polite, Kelly. Nice catch." A tall, shapely girl sashayed along the office's inner hallway. She propped three books against her diaphragm, her fingers interlaced underneath. "Or should I say, 'nice rebound'?"

Kelly spoke in a condescending tone. "Better stick to makeup and hairspray, Brittany. Basketball terms are a bit out of your league."

Nathan stared at the two girls. Obviously this wasn't playful banter, and Brittany was about as genuine as press-on nails. But what could he do? This was their territory, not his.

Apparently unfazed, Brittany strutted closer in her low-neck ribbed tunic. "Kelly and Kyle has a nice ring to it," she said. Then, giving Kelly a wink, she added, "I guess living together gives you a lot of . . . opportunities."

Kelly arched her brow at the taller girl and spoke in an innocent tone. "I'm sure I don't know what you're talking about."

Brittany let out a mock gasp. "You don't? Even after going out with Steven for two whole months?"

Speaking through clenched teeth, Kelly sharpened her voice. "No. I don't."

Brittany touched a bejeweled heart pendant dangling from

a necklace. "Well, I must say that I'm amazed. From what I understand, your mother took a few opportunities while your father was at away games. You could have learned a lot from her."

Her cheeks ablaze, Kelly raised a tightened fist. "Listen, Brittany, you might be taller than me, but I swear, if you—"

"Swear?" Brittany covered her mouth. "Nuns don't swear, do they?"

Kelly drew her head back. "Nuns? What are you talking about?"

"I heard from Daryl that you changed." Brittany's eyes moved up and down, scanning Kelly's clothes. "But I didn't know you went Catholic school on us."

"Miss Tyler!" Mrs. Washington said, glaring at Brittany. "You may leave now. You've already caused enough trouble for one morning."

A book slid from Brittany's pile. She chirped a girlish "Oops" and kicked it toward Nathan's shoes. As he squatted to pick it up, she bent way over to receive it, obviously flashing as much skin as she could.

Averting his eyes, Nathan handed her the book. "Here you go."

"Thank you, Kyle." She blew him a kiss and continued her strut toward the door. "I'll have to tell Steven about your change, Kelly. He might want a new picture of you to add to the gallery of Kelly photos in his locker."

When she closed the door, Kelly balled up both fists. "Acid-tongued—"

Biting her lip, she swung around toward Mrs. Washington, who slid a piece of paper toward Nathan and nodded firmly at Kelly. "Say whatever you want, girl. My lips are sealed." Kelly loosened her fingers. "If I said what I was thinking, the paint would peel."

Mrs. Washington stood and tapped on the sheet. "You and

Kyle are in every class together except for last period. Kyle has orchestra during your PE class." She laid two pink memo slips on the counter. "Here are your tardy passes."

"Let's go," Kelly said, snatching her pass. "Chemistry's already started."

Nathan picked up his schedule and pink slip and grabbed his pack and case. "Thank you, Mrs. Washington."

They quick-stepped through the empty halls, passing vertical banks of blue lockers on each side. She halted at one and spun the combination dial. "No time to dump your stuff at your locker. We'll find it after chemistry." She opened the door and, leaning over, grabbed a textbook and yellow legal pad, but suddenly straightened, her eyes growing wider. "Are you sure you don't hear anything?"

Nathan glanced around. "Just the fluorescent lights humming."

"That's not it." Her voice lowered to a ghostly whisper. "It's a man ... like he's in pain."

He lifted his violin case. "Check it carefully this time."

She bent over and set her ear close to the case. After a few seconds, she shook her head. "I'm sure that's not it."

As he let the case down again, he scuffed his shoe against the floor. "Look. It's not that I'm doubting you, but if I can't hear it, I can't help you find it."

"I know." She closed her locker door. "Let's get going."

After marching halfway down another hall, they stopped at a classroom where a nameplate read, "Marshall Scott."

Kelly reached for the doorknob and looked back at Nathan, her face reddening as she whispered. "I should have told you this earlier. Brittany mentioned Steven. He's my old boyfriend from last school year, and he wants me back. He might not be too happy when he sees us together."

"Maybe he already knows," he said, shrugging. "Wouldn't Brittany have told him about me by now?"

Kelly shook her head. "Brittany's in 'math for morons' first period. She couldn't pass chemistry if her life depended on it." After taking a deep breath, she opened the door. As they walked inside, Nathan scanned the classroom from the teacher's space on the left to the three rows of two-person worktables on the right. A couple of girls smiled at him, but most students kept their gazes aimed at their desks, some with closed eyes, apparently asleep.

Kelly extended her pink slip to a bespectacled, gray-haired man up front. "This is Kyle," she said, gesturing toward Nathan. "He's new, and I've been assigned to show him the ropes around here."

Nathan handed him his tardy slip and schedule. Using long, bony fingers, Mr. Scott opened a class roll book and scribbled down the information. "Welcome, Mr. Simmons." His voice was nasally but not unfriendly. "I hope your previous school has introduced you to stoichiometry. Otherwise, you will find it difficult to catch up."

Nathan took back his schedule and smiled as graciously as he could. "Thanks. I think I'll be okay."

"Very well." Mr. Scott pointed his pencil at a boy at the front table near a window on the far end. "Steven, please be kind enough to move to the empty spot next to Daryl so Kyle can sit with Kelly. They'll have to share her textbook until I locate another one."

"Sure thing." A shaggy-haired boy with a dark goatee rose to a staggering height, glaring at Nathan as he shuffled past. "Cute violin case," he mumbled.

Kelly whispered out of the side of her mouth. "I forgot to tell you. He plays football and basketball."

"Great," he whispered back. "He'll crunch me into a little ball and shoot me through a hoop."

After Nathan pushed his backpack and case under Steven's old space on the left side of the table, he sat in a red metal chair. Kelly opened the chemistry book and slid it to the middle of their workspace. "I still hear it," she whispered. She then cleared her throat to mask her comment.

Mr. Scott poised a marker over a transparency sheet on an overhead projector. After rambling for several minutes about the importance of laboratory safety, he stopped and scanned the classroom. "Who can tell me the chemical formula for silver nitrate?"

Nathan glanced at Kelly, but she was busily writing something on her pad and covering it with her hand. Why would she be taking notes? The teacher hadn't even said anything important yet.

"Come now," Mr. Scott continued. "This is review. We just did this equation on Friday."

Nathan glanced around the room. One boy yawned, a girl filed her nails, and most of the others just stared straight ahead. Finally, Nathan slid his hand up.

"Yes, Kyle."

"Uh ... A G N O three."

"Excellent." He wrote the symbols on the overhead. "Leave it to the student who wasn't even here on Friday to know the answer."

Nathan firmed his chin. The note of sarcasm in Mr. Scott's voice was more than a little irritating. Besides, it wasn't fair to level that charge against the whole class, especially Kelly. He lifted his hand again. "Excuse me, Mr. Scott, but Kelly wasn't here either. She was helping me settle in at her house."

A deep voice piped up from behind him. "Yeah. I'll *bet* she was."

As muffled snickers erupted around the room, Kelly ducked her head and covered her flaming ears.

"Quiet!" Mr. Scott aimed a menacing glare at his students. When the murmuring subsided, he pointed his marker at Steven. "See me after class." He then shifted the marker toward Nathan.

"Kyle, I realize you're new here, but I must ask you to abide by my rules. You will not speak unless called upon."

Nathan straightened in his seat. "Yessir."

"In any case, there is no need to defend Kelly. Her test scores will speak for themselves."

A few more snickers flittered about but faded quickly.

Kelly's hand shot up. Her face had again turned red as a beet.

Mr. Scott raised his eyebrows. "Yes, Kelly?"

"I'm feeling sick," she said, laying a hand on her stomach. "I have to go."

"I understand. Embarrassment likely incited an unusual gastric discharge." He nodded toward the door. "Go ahead."

Bending forward and keeping her gaze away from Nathan, Kelly tapped her yellow pad as she passed in front of her desk. He angled his head to read it silently. *It's coming from your backpack. Make an excuse to go to the restroom. Lie if you have to!*

While everyone watched Kelly shuffle toward the door, Nathan quietly tore the top page away from the pad and folded it in half. He then slid out the backpack and unzipped it in one motion.

As the classroom door clapped shut, Nathan withdrew the mirror, removed the towel, and looked into its reflective side. A man hung suspended by chains against a stone wall, while another man, veiled in shadows, held a knife to a woman's throat. The woman, seated on the floor, faced the wall, preventing Nathan from seeing her clearly, but the dark locks streaming down her back gave away her identity. His mother.

"Now," Mr. Scott continued, "when we combined the silver with the nitric acid we created a reaction that produced a gas called what?"

While the shadow of one of his classmates rose behind him, Nathan, his hands now shaking, pulled the mirror closer and studied the hanging man, turning the mirrored surface away from the window to avoid the glare. Although his face was dirty and appeared older than usual, there was no doubt about who the man was.

"Anyone?" Mr. Scott prodded.

Nathan almost blurted, It's Dad!

The image faded away, leaving only Nathan's worried face along with the wide eyes of a girl staring over his shoulder—Daryl.

Although Mr. Scott had not risen from his seat, he appeared in the mirror, stumbling and falling hard to the floor between the front desk and Nathan. He lay motionless, blood oozing from his nose.

The teacher got up and walked toward him. "Kyle, is there something I can help you with?"

Nathan laid the mirror on the desk. With a desperate lunge, he pushed his body in front of Mr. Scott just as he tripped over a power cord. The teacher fell on top of Nathan, softening his landing.

Someone laid a hand behind Nathan's head. "Are you all right?" she asked.

In a daze, it took Nathan a second or two to recognize her. "Yeah, Daryl. I'm fine."

As Mr. Scott got up and brushed off his pants, Daryl helped Nathan to his feet. "I saw it in the mirror before it happened!" she said.

"Nonsense, Daryl," Mr. Scott said, putting his glasses back on. "Kyle obviously saw that the tape on the cord was loose and couldn't warn me in time." He patted Nathan on the back. "I'm grateful for your quick action."

Nathan stuffed the mirror and towel into his pack and pulled his violin case out from under the desk. "I ... uh ... better go to the restroom and get cleaned up." He slung the pack over his shoulder and backed toward the door. "That is, of course, if you don't mind."

Mr. Scott nodded. "Go ahead. But keep that mirror out of sight. It's too much of a distraction."

"Sure. No problem." When he reached the door, he set his hand on the knob. "Uh ... which way to the restrooms?"

"I'll show him!" Daryl ran to the door. "Back in a minute!"

She led Nathan down the hall, chattering rapid fire. "That mirror thing is so cool! What is it, anyway? Sort of like a scenario predictor? The microprocessors they put in there must really be fast to analyze all the probabilities and display the most likely outcome in such high resolution. It was perfect video quality! I'll bet the military would love to get their hands on it, or maybe stock brokers and gamblers. Yeah, that's it. Sports bookies would kill for a device like that."

She took a breath and turned a corner. "I want to learn virtual reality programming and apply it to holographic imaging. The video gaming industry would go nuts over it. Can you imagine physically walking through a shooter game where you can see your targets all around you without having to wear a bulky helmet? It would be *Battlestar Galactica* come to life."

"Wait." Nathan halted.

"What?"

He pointed at a recessed area in the wall. "The restrooms, right?"

"Oh, yeah. Right." Daryl blushed. "I got carried away." She pointed to the left side. "Men's that way."

"Yeah. I saw the sign." He stepped into the alcove and paused in front of a two-tiered set of water fountains. "Thanks."

She crossed her arms and leaned against a locker on the other side of the hall.

"Uh ... " Nathan said as he stepped toward the men's side. "I can make it from here."

"Oh. Right again." She spun and hurried down the tiled floor, looking back once before turning into the adjacent hallway.

Taking two long, quiet steps, Nathan shifted over to the

ladies' side of the alcove and paused. There was no door to knock on. Should he call her name? Just go in? There wouldn't be anyone else in there, right? He gave the tiles at the side of the doorway a light rap with his knuckles, but it hardly made any sound at all. He leaned in and whispered, "Kelly?"

No answer.

He breathed a deep sigh. Maybe he had taken too long to leave the classroom. Maybe she had gone to the car. He spun back to the men's room and breezed inside. Might as well take care of business before he searched for her.

As he approached a urinal, a loud "Pssst" made him halt.

"Nathan! Over here!"

He leaned toward the bank of toilet stalls. "Kelly?"

"Yes. Last stall."

He hustled to the back of the restroom and faced the closed door of the handicapped-access stall. "What are you doing here?"

Her reply came in a sharp whisper. "Waiting for you."

"In the men's room?"

She pushed open the stall door. With her Nike's on the toilet seat, she squatted low. "I knew you wouldn't set foot in the ladies' room, and we need to talk privately."

"I was thinking you might have gone to the car. How'd you know I'd come in here?"

"I saw how much orange juice you drank this morning."

He glanced at the entry door. "What if someone walks in?"

She grabbed his sleeve and pulled him into the spacious stall, closing the door behind them. "If someone comes in, the only shoes they'll see will be yours."

Nathan set the violin case down and pulled the mirror from the backpack. "I saw who was moaning."

"Your father," she replied. "I heard someone say his name, like he was being taunted."

"But was it my real father, or my father in the other dimension?

I mean, if my real father's dead, then the guy in the mirror isn't *my* father over there, he's the father of—".

"Stop!" She set her fingers on her temples. "Don't explain it. You'll give me a headache."

"I guess right after my mother heard footsteps, someone captured them, so trying to see them again can't do any harm now." He handed her the mirror. "Let's see if I can open a viewer on this one."

"Go for it."

He unlatched the case and set the violin under his chin. "I feel like an idiot playing in a bathroom stall."

"Maybe, but the echo effect will be awesome."

He raised the bow to the strings. "I think *pianissimo* is called for here."

"The softer the better," she whispered.

He raised his eyebrows. "You knew what I meant?"

"I took piano for five years. My mother taught me."

While he played the first measures of "Brahms' Lullaby," they stared at the mirror. At first their widened eyes stared back at them, but within seconds, his eyes gleamed once again, and the reflection's background darkened, framing their faces with blackness. Soon, even they disappeared, and the darkness faded, giving rise to a dim stone wall, the same wall his father had been hanging from, but now only four loose chains dangled from their attachment points.

"He's gone," Nathan whispered.

"Shhh! I hear voices. Very quiet voices."

"I'll play louder."

Nathan increased the volume to *mezzo piano*, now loud enough to create an echo in the porcelain-coated room. Kelly's head bobbed, her lips moving as she mentally recited every syllable she heard.

A nasally voice blended in with the violin's sweet tones. "Kyle? Are you in here?"

Nathan stopped playing. The voice, Mr. Scott's voice, had come from the entry door.

"Yes?" he replied.

Kelly scooted back on the toilet while Nathan slid his feet into position in front of it and sat down.

"The fall bloodied my nose, so I thought I'd clean up and check on you at the same time. Now I see why you're delayed."

Nathan cleared his throat. "Thanks. I'll be done soon."

The sound of a stream splashing a urinal reverberated quietly in the room as Mr. Scott continued. "You must really be enamored with your violin to be practicing even in there. I usually read a magazine, but to each his own, I suppose."

"I guess so. Violin music really moves me." Nathan grimaced. What a stupid thing to say!

Mr. Scott laughed out loud. "That's a good one."

Water splashed from the sink directly in front of him. Through the gap between the door and the stall's frame, Nathan could see the teacher washing his hands.

"Kelly never came back to class," Mr. Scott continued. "I called into the ladies' room, but no one answered."

Nathan squirmed. Sitting on the toes of Kelly's shoes had grown painfully uncomfortable. "I did, too. I don't think she's in there."

"I'll send Daryl to look for her." He grabbed a paper towel from the dispenser and walked out of Nathan's view. "I'll see you back in class." A few seconds later, all was quiet.

Kelly pushed Nathan out of the way. "We have to get home!" she whispered. "Now!"

"What did you hear?" Nathan asked as he repacked the violin.

With the mirror still in her grip, she stepped off the toilet lid. "I'll tell you when we get out. The less talking we do, the better."

Nudging the stall door with his elbow, Nathan slid through the opening and skulked to the entryway. Then, peering around the corner, he motioned for Kelly. "It's clear."

"Wait!" She pushed the mirror into his backpack. "Okay. Let's go."

They stepped out just as Daryl came into view in the hallway.

Kelly mumbled a curse word and ducked her head to take a drink from the water fountain.

Daryl stopped. Her eyes darted back and forth between Nathan and Kelly. "Well," she said, a deep furrow in her brow, "this puts me in an awkward situation. I could simply tell Mr. Scott that I found Kelly coming out of the restroom, which would be truthful, but it wouldn't be a complete report. And this story would be the most delicious lunchtime gossip since Brittany and the band director."

Rising from the fountain, Kelly swallowed and hooked her arm around Daryl's. "Listen, brainiac. Here's your complete report. We have a mirror that sees into alternate dimensions, and it gets activated by music. Nathan was playing the violin in the bathroom while we watched for another dimension to appear. While he plays, I hear voices that tell me what's going on. We experimented in there so we could do it in private and not scare the entire school." She released Daryl's arm and looked her in the eye. "Tell that to your gossip girls at lunchtime."

Daryl's mouth dropped open. She took in a deep breath and let it out, stuttering, "I ... I believe you."

"Good!" Kelly stalked down the hall, dragging Nathan behind her.

Daryl called to them. "Aren't you coming back to class?"

Kelly turned and walked backwards. "We have to travel to another dimension to rescue his father."

"That is so Narnia!" Daryl folded her hands, begging. "Can I come? I've never been on any kind of adventure!"

Nathan halted and spun around. "You have no idea how dangerous this is."

"But I can help. I've studied stuff like this all my life!"

"How could you study dimensional travel?"

Daryl bit her lip. "I ... uh ... well ..."

A deep voice entered the hallway. "You can tell them, Daryl." A tall man wearing a dark blazer rounded the corner, his eyes trained on the three teenagers. "They already know about Interfinity."

Nathan stared at the newcomer. As he drew closer, his piercing eyes and a pulsing vein on his forehead clarified. *Dr. Gordon.*

9

A NEW ALLY

"Dr. Gordon!" Daryl pushed past Nathan and extended her hand. "Why are you here?"

He took Daryl's hand and shook it politely. "Because you told me about the new student. He fit the profile."

Nathan scanned Dr. Gordon's cheek. His skin was smooth, no sign of the cut he had suffered only a day earlier. "What profile?"

"I know who you are, Nathan. Daryl alerted me to your presence on Friday when you registered under a false name."

Kelly stared at Daryl, her expression hardening.

Dr. Gordon waved his hand at Kelly. "No need to pour wrath on your friend. I am the head of research and development at Interfinity Labs. We handpick the brightest students in the country to come to my seminars. When Nathan's father was murdered, I knew Nathan would go into hiding, so I asked my seminar graduates to be on the lookout for a new arrival in their schools. I told them that finding Nathan was a life or death emergency, so Daryl's actions were not treacherous in the least."

Kelly bent toward Daryl. While the two girls chattered in buzzing whispers too quiet to be heard, Nathan eyed the breast pocket on Dr. Gordon's blazer. It carried an emblem embroidered in gold, three infinity symbols, just like the one he wore when he was with Mictar. "You're right about life and death,"

Nathan said, glancing around for escape routes. "One of the people looking for me tried to kill me."

Dr. Gordon sighed. "Yes, my competition is quite aggressive."

Balling his fist, Nathan squared his shoulders. "Why is it that one member of your 'competition' looks very familiar to me?"

"I know why you are guarding your words. All I can say is that I am not who you think me to be. We can discuss the particulars at my office near Chicago, but it's important that we go there immediately. There is much to be done and very little time to do it."

"I can't go with you. My parents' funeral is tomorrow."

"Yes, I know. I will arrange for overnight accommodations at my expense, and I will get you to the funeral service on time."

Nathan peeked at Kelly. She and Daryl had finally stopped their whispering. As he looked back at Gordon, he tried to put on a casual front. "I have to go home first and pack some stuff."

"Very well. I will give you a ride home."

Kelly set her hands on her hips. "Now, wait just a minute. I'm not about to let a stranger come to my house. You talk a good talk, and you have a cute emblem on your bellhop blazer, but that doesn't mean you're anyone we can trust." She nudged Daryl with her elbow.

Standing straight, Daryl cleared her throat. "I'll go home with them, and I'll make sure they come back here."

Dr. Gordon shook his head. "That won't be good enough, Daryl. At this point, I'm afraid I'll have to insist on both of them coming with me. I have to make sure—"

Kelly pointed at Daryl, raising her voice to a shout. "I know you, you little vamp! You just want to hone in on my new boyfriend!"

Daryl pushed Kelly's chest, shoving her back into Nathan's

arms. "You don't have the brains to compete with me, you dumb jock!"

Nathan helped Kelly regain her balance. "Let's just go and—"

She twirled and shook a finger at him, now screaming right in his face. "Stay out of this!" She then whispered. "Play along."

A bell sounded, signaling the end of the period. Students began pouring out of their classrooms. As Nathan stepped in front of Dr. Gordon, Kelly spun back to Daryl, shouting again. "Don't call me a jock, you cyberspace geek. I'll—"

"Cat fight!" a lanky boy yelled. Within seconds, kids of all shapes and sizes surrounded the battling females, who now stood glaring at each other with their fists clenched.

A muscular male teacher pushed through the crowd, shouting, "What's going on here?"

Kelly thrust her finger toward Dr. Gordon. "Mr. Ryan, this pervert tried to kidnap me!"

As excited chatter buzzed through the corridor, Kelly continued, her voice now meek and trembling. "When I came out of the bathroom, he was there! He said I had to go with him."

Mr. Ryan grabbed Dr. Gordon's forearm. "Let's take a walk to the office."

Dr. Gordon tried to shake free, but the teacher's grip tightened.

"This is absurd. I assure you—"

"Just shut up and come with me." As he pushed Dr. Gordon along, the crowd of students funneled behind them. "Kelly," Mr. Ryan called, looking back. "Meet us in the office. We'll need your statement."

Kelly grabbed Daryl's hand and squeezed against a row of lockers, waiting for the students to disperse.

Daryl touched a button on Kelly's shirt. "I didn't hurt you, did I?"

"No. You did great."

Daryl folded her hands and renewed her begging stance. "Now you're taking me with you to the other dimension, right? I mean, I'm not sure what to believe about Dr. Gordon, but I did what you wanted. Don't leave me here to face him when they let him go."

"Yeah. I guess I promised, didn't I?" Kelly tugged Nathan's sleeve. "We'd better hustle before they figure out what happened."

A new voice sounded from the restroom alcove. "What did happen, Kelly Clark?" Steven emerged. "I know when you're putting on a show, and that was one of your better performances."

"Buzz off, Steven." She turned toward the exit. "We're in a hurry."

Grabbing Kelly's arm, Steven jerked her toward him. "Not so fast. I want to know what's going on."

Nathan pulled Kelly free and stepped between her and Steven. "You heard the lady," he said, looking up at the taller boy. "Buzz off!"

Steven wrapped his long fingers around Nathan's throat and pushed him against the lockers. "A lady?" he repeated, laughing. "She's got you fooled."

"Steven!" Kelly pushed him, but he didn't budge. "Just stop it."

Nathan squeezed out a choked, "Get in the car. I'll meet you outside."

"But—"

He slowly curled his fingers into a fist. "Just do it!"

While Daryl collected Nathan's violin, Kelly picked up his backpack, and the two ran down the hall. "Don't hurt him too badly!" Kelly called as she turned the corner.

Steven laughed. "Don't worry. I won't." When they were out of sight, his grip loosened. "I could hurt you real bad, but I'm going to give you a break ... this time. I don't want Kelly mad at me."

Nathan glared at him. "When she said not to hurt him, she wasn't talking to you."

Steven released Nathan and backed away, laughing. "That's pretty funny. Like you could hurt me."

"Look," Nathan said, his throat aching. "I'm not trying to steal anyone's girlfriend. We just live—"

"Yeah, I know the story. I'm not stupid. She's like your sister now, right? You gotta stand up for her, right?" He poked Nathan in the chest with his finger. "You got guts."

"Thanks." Nathan massaged his throat and sidestepped away. "Well, I have to go."

As he jogged down the hall, Steven called, "Hey, that Daryl's not a bad-looking girl. She's a real brainy type, but she's cool. You might want to check her out."

Nathan rushed toward the main entrance. He would have to pass by the office, a dangerous gauntlet, since Mr. Ryan and Dr. Gordon would be there, but the student drop-off site was the only place he knew to go. Gordon was sure to be raising a ruckus, so he had to get by in a hurry.

As he approached the throng of students gathered in the rotunda, Nathan slouched and tried to blend into the crowd. Just as he passed the office door and quick-stepped toward the exit, Dr. Gordon shouted, "There he is! That's Nathan Shepherd!"

Nathan burst outside and sprinted past the flagpole. He stopped at the curb and spotted Kelly's Toyota idling in the parking lot. Squealing its tires, the Camry zoomed toward him. He looked back at the school. Mr. Ryan had just opened the door and spied him. Raising his hand, the athletic teacher leaped into a rapid jog. "Hold it right there!"

Kelly skidded to a stop. The passenger door flung open, and Nathan dove headlong across the front seats. His stomach landed on the console's glove box, his legs stretched across Daryl's, and his head flopped face down into Kelly's lap. Jerking his body, he twisted around until his face pointed upward and his bottom slid in between the glove and gear boxes. Heat scorched his ears. "Sorry about that."

Kelly pinned him with an elbow and set her hand on the gear shift. "Just cool it! You're fine!"

Mr. Ryan grabbed the door handle. "Don't you dare take off—"

"Gotta run!" Kelly stomped the gas pedal. The Camry shot away like a rocket, ripping the handle out of Mr. Ryan's grip. Daryl pulled the door closed and began laughing, shaking Nathan's legs as her spasms pulsed so hard she could barely breathe.

Kelly tried not to laugh, but as she held her breath, her stomach contractions jiggled Nathan's head.

"What's so funny?" he asked, now looking straight up at Kelly through the gap between her arms.

A wide grin spread across her face. "Oh ... nothing."

"You are!" Daryl cried. As she tried to stifle her laughs, her cheeks turned redder than her hair. "You're so embarrassed!"

The heat spread to Nathan's cheeks. "Well, I'm not used to being in that position."

"That's perfect!" Daryl clapped her hands. "That's so perfect!"

Kelly lifted his shoulder. "You can get up now. I didn't want you in my way when I peeled out."

He sat upright and slid over the glove box toward the backseat, trying to keep his balance as the car swept around a curve. "What's so perfect?"

"You are," Daryl said. "I didn't think such old-fashioned guys existed anymore!"

"Old-fashioned?" Nathan seated himself in the rear between his backpack and violin case but kept a shoe on the glove box. "I've been called that before."

"You had it right the first time," Kelly said, tugging on one of his laces. "Perfect is the best word. He's a perfect gentleman."

"Thanks ... I guess."

"No problem." She glanced back at him. "I see you got away from Steven. You didn't hurt him, did you? I mean, the way he was standing you could've easily—"

"Let's just say we came to an understanding." He looked out the windshield, trying to recognize the surroundings, but everything zipped by too fast. "So, where are we heading?"

"My house real quick, then I thought Chicago would be best—catch up with Clara and see what's going on at Interfinity. It won't take long for Dr. Gordon to figure out where we live, so we'd better grab some stuff and hit the road."

"What about Daryl? Won't she need some clothes?"

"I'll pack extra for her. She's borrowed my clothes before."

Daryl touched Kelly's shoulder. "You got a fresh toothbrush I can borrow? I'll share jeans, underwear, and soda straws, but I gotta have my own toothbrush."

"Not a problem."

Nathan leaned forward, trying to catch Kelly's attention in her rearview mirror. "What did you hear when we were in the stall?"

"I'll tell you later." Their gazes locked in the narrow mirror. Her eyes seemed warm and sympathetic. "It's kind of ... personal. It won't change anything if we wait a little while."

He reached into the front pocket of his backpack and pulled out his cell phone. "I'll call Clara and get her up to speed."

"Be sure to tell her about Dr. Gordon. He'll probably head back to Interfinity."

He punched in her number and waited through the trill. After the third ring, her familiar voice buzzed through the earpiece. "Yes, Nathan?"

"Where are you? At Interfinity?"

Her voice dropped to a whisper. "We are. Francesca and I are playing tourist. We blended into a school group's guided tour.

I'm looking for a chance to sneak away, maybe get into the offices when they close."

"Make sure you look for Dr. Gordon's office. He's the head of R&D, and he was at the high school looking for me, so he can't possibly get back there in time to walk in on you. I'll tell you more later, but we need to stay away from him no matter what."

"Great information. Why was he looking for you?"

"Not just looking. He was going to make me come back with him to his office, but Kelly and I got away." As they approached a sharp curve, Nathan checked the speedometer. Kelly showed no sign of dropping under fifty-five. "We're getting ready to come to Chicago," he continued, clutching the seat in front of him, "because Gordon's sure to find out where we live, and we have to come to the funeral anyway."

"We'll figure out a place to meet. You have your ATM card, right?"

As the Toyota careened around the bend, he lurched to the side and draped his arm over his backpack. "I got it right here," he grunted.

"Then you have plenty of money. Be sure to take care of all the expenses."

"Gotcha."

"Don't call again," Clara warned. "I'll estimate the time of your arrival and call you. I'm sure you can find Interfinity's address on the Internet. The observatory is northwest of the city."

"No problem. We'll see you in a few hours." He slapped the phone closed.

As the Camry roared down the country highway, Kelly explained their story to Daryl, cutting out enough details to keep it short. Nathan added what happened to him when he first saw his parents in the coffins and the subsequent pursuit by the gunman in the Mustang. He finished with his suspicions about Dr. Gordon. "The guy who chased us looked exactly like him, except, when he showed up at school, he didn't have a cut on his cheek. So until I know otherwise, he's a murderer in my book."

Daryl interlaced her fingers behind her head. "Well, it's a good thing I'm coming along. Let me tell you what I know."

"Cool your jets." Kelly pressed the brakes and skidded into a turn down their cornfield-bordered road. "Let's get our stuff. You can tell us the rest on the way to Chicago."

After pushing the garage opener, Kelly zoomed inside, barely fitting the car under the rising door. Screeching to a halt, she jumped out and ran into the house. Nathan slid on his backpack and followed Daryl through the laundry area, across the kitchen, and into the formal living room.

Kelly pointed down the hall. "Daryl, you first in the bathroom. No potty breaks if we can help it."

When Daryl trotted away, Kelly pulled Nathan close. "When you played in the stall, I heard your mother and father talking." She breathed a gentle sigh. "Nathan, I've never heard anything like it. They were so sweet."

Nathan dipped his head. "Yeah ... I know."

"Anyway, your father said he was being tortured to draw you to their dimension. They think someone called Simon is behind it, but they're not sure."

"But Dr. Simon is dead. How could that be?"

"Your parents are dead, too, but they still seem to be talking."

The sound of a toilet flushing came from down the hall, followed by a closing door. Kelly glanced that way and sped through her words. "They're worried about you. Something's gone wrong in their plan, and if you follow the clues they've left behind, you could be in big trouble. Apparently, Simon set some kind of trap for you. He thinks you'll respond to your father's suffering and come to help him."

Daryl peeked around the corner. "That sounds like *The Empire Strikes Back*. Darth Vader tortured Han Solo to get Luke to show up. That was a trap, too."

"I remember," Nathan said. "Luke went anyway."

Daryl flashed a thumbs up. "He had to go no matter what. That's what heroes do." Angling her thumb toward the hall, she grinned. "Speaking of having to go, who's next in the bathroom?"

Kelly pushed Nathan's backpack. "You go. I already went."

"In the guys' bathroom at school?"

"Why not? They all work the same." She pushed him again. "Hurry! I'll get my stuff packed."

Nathan rushed through his bathroom stop, picking up his toothbrush on the way out. When he got back to his bedroom, he flipped on his desk lamp and laptop computer, threw his suitcase on the bed, and hurriedly packed it. He glanced at the mirror on the wall. Everything seemed normal. The trunk was closed. The lights stayed constant.

He pulled open a desk drawer and lifted out his father's camera by its strap. No sense in leaving it behind for Gordon to steal. He laid it gently among his clothes, and, after zipping his suitcase, he slid into his chair and opened the browser. Interfinity was easy to find. He pulled the observatory's address up on a map. Just as he clicked on the print button, Kelly bustled into the room, a duffle bag strap over her shoulder.

"You ready?" she asked.

He nodded at the suitcase on the bed. "Yeah. I just sent a map to the printer."

She set her bag down. "I'll get it. Daryl's already in the garage."

Nathan packed his laptop and grabbed his suitcase, but he couldn't resist another look at the mirror. Still normal—a perfect reflection. This would be his last chance to see the big mirror for quite a while. Might it be able to show images his little corner section couldn't?

Moving quickly, he slid off his backpack, fished out the mirror, and reapplied it in the blank corner section. It stuck in place and once again sent a shimmer of light across the glass. He pulled his new violin from under the bed and took it out of its case. Then, with a few quick strokes, he played part of a Sibelius piece that had been running through his head, "Finlandia."

As he watched the mirror, his eyes glowed yet again, becoming brighter than ever before. Soon, the glass surface flickered and transformed into a close-up of a man's profile—Dr. Simon's. As Nathan played on, the portrait clarified. Simon clutched a steering wheel, bouncing up and down as if driving over a bumpy road. The scenery through the window behind him passed by quickly, farmland of some kind. Several black-and-white cows grazed in fenced, grassy fields, and, in another lot, a big-wheeled tractor dragged a plow through rich black earth.

Simon's lips moved. Soon, his voice became audible, a slow, careful speech seemingly designed for recording.

"Nathan Shepherd, if you can hear me, you have learned by now that music is the key to opening a video and audio portal between dimensions. You might have also learned that flashes of light allow you to move between the dimensions once the portal is open."

Kelly walked into the room, her eyes widening. "Holy—"

"Shhh!" Nathan warned.

Dr. Simon continued. "You can use a flashlight, a flickering lamp, almost anything that surpasses a certain lumens minimum, but that is far too technical for this message. I need you to come here to help me stop a madman who is trying to manipulate these dimensions for his own purposes. I know you have lost your mother and father, but there is still hope. Come to this place so that we can prevent interfinity. The entire cosmos is at stake."

The message began again. Nathan lowered his bow and re-packed his violin. Within seconds, Dr. Simon's image faded, and the mirror returned to normal. Leaving his violin case on the bed, he grabbed the screwdriver from the shelf and pried his mirror loose again.

Kelly shivered. "I don't like how he said that."

"I didn't like anything he said." He stuffed his mirror into his backpack. "What part bugged you?"

She picked up her bag and mimicked his voice. "The entire cosmos is at stake."

"Maybe that's part of the bait." After sliding the backpack on, he picked up his suitcase. "He probably doesn't know that you heard my parents talking about him, so he's luring me every way he can."

"So what are you going to do?"

He took Kelly's bag and slung the strap over his shoulder. "Be a hero."

"Don't overload yourself, hero." She smiled and pointed at the laptop case on the floor. "I'll get that."

They hurried out to the Camry. With the garage door rumbling open, Daryl lifted a bag into the trunk and tossed the keys toward Kelly, who snatched them deftly out of the air. While Kelly started the car, Nathan shoved the other bags on top of Daryl's. When he opened the back door to get in, Daryl was already sitting there.

"Ride up front," she said, reaching for his backpack. "When I get done with my story, I'm gonna lie down and snooze."

As soon as Nathan hopped in and slammed the door, Kelly screeched out of the driveway and zoomed onto the main road. Now driving at a safer speed, she angled her head toward Daryl. "Okay. Time to spill it. Tell us everything you know about Interfinity."

Daryl closed her eyes and leaned back in her seat, a proud smile spreading across her face. "Interfinity used to be called 'StarCast.' They got a lot of press about their project to send radio signals into space, you know, hoping to contact any intelligent life out there." She opened her eyes. "Remember the movie *ET*? This was bigger, like souped-up, extraterrestrial phone tag. Crazy, right? But, guess what? They got an answer!"

Kelly's eyes shot wide open. "Not from an alien!"

"No! That's the weirdest part of all. They got an answer from themselves!"

"From themselves?"

"Yeah. And a whole lot quicker than they thought possible!"

"Did the signal bounce off something?" Nathan asked. "Maybe it went in a circle?"

"Nope!" Daryl gave him a mischievous smirk. "You of all people should be able to figure it out. Keep guessing."

"Keep guessing? That could take hours!" Nathan thumped his head back against the seat. As the countryside zoomed by, scenes of approaching autumn—a hint of color in the maple trees, withering corn tassels, and a flock of birds beginning a migratory journey—the theme from Vivaldi's "Autumn" played in his mind. As the sweet violins eased his tensions, he closed his eyes and imagined the notes' arrangement on the staff, each one sprouting in its proper position as it played. When the pages filled, a breeze picked them up and carried them into the sky, page after page joining in a musical chain reaching toward heaven. Finally, when the last page drifted away, he opened his eyes. "They sent music into outer space, didn't they?"

Daryl pointed at him. "Smart boy!"

"What made them decide to play music?" Kelly asked.

Daryl restarted her rapid-fire chatter. "They tried everything, but when they sent music, they finally got an answer, and it was the same music they sent out. So they started experimenting with different varieties. They recorded about a hundred songs, mostly classical, but some rock and country, even some polka, and they started broadcasting them in order. But do you know what happened? They started getting back song number five on the list while they were still sending song number three!"

"So it couldn't have been bouncing back at them," Nathan said.

"Brilliant deduction, Holmes!" Daryl grinned and pushed Nathan's elbow with her foot. "So after all their experiments, they came up with a wild theory. When Dr. Gordon presented his paper on it during a seminar at a fancy scientists' convention, he got laughed out of the building, and he lost his grant from the National Science Foundation."

"I'll bet that really ticked him off," Kelly said.

"Oh, yeah! He went out and got what you might call"—Daryl drew quotation marks in the air—"alternative funding from some kind of fringe group."

"How do you know they're fringe?"

"Are you kidding me? Anyone who would throw money at this crazy project has got to be fringe."

Kelly glanced at her in the rearview mirror. "But you don't think it's crazy, right?"

"Normal people think it is, but, as you know"—Daryl pressed her thumb against her chest—"I'm far from normal."

"No argument here," Kelly said, rolling her eyes. "Go on."

"Anyway, Dr. Gordon sponsored this seminar for students who were interested in learning about radio telescopes and broadcasting into space, which sounded reasonable enough to a lot of teachers, so he had about four or five hundred kids show up. But as he got to know the group, he pulled some of us aside into a special workshop and explained his newest theories."

She lowered her voice to a dramatic whisper. "He believes there are multiple dimensions exactly like ours, only they're slightly off time-wise." She set her palms close together. "While something happens here," she said, wiggling the fingers on one hand, "it happens a little while later in one of the other dimensions." She wiggled her other fingers to match. "But it might have already happened in a third one."

"So that's why they got the music before they sent it," Nathan said. "They were sending it to themselves from another dimension, only they were farther ahead in time."

"Exactly!" Daryl leaned back and sighed. "It's fun talking to smart people. I don't have to spell everything out."

"How many dimensions are there?" Kelly asked.

"No clue. Dr. Gordon identified at least three, but he thinks there might be more. We tried to pry more information out of him, but he went all Gandalf on us. You know ..." Daryl leaned between the front seats and glanced at Kelly and Nathan in turn. "*Keep it secret. Keep it safe.*"

Kelly pushed her back with her elbow. "You and your movies."

"Dr. Gordon seemed to be a good guy," Daryl continued, "so when he emailed me about Nathan's parents and said he could help find the killer, I decided to keep a lookout and tell him if Nathan showed up at our school. I heard he did the same for a lot of kids at other schools." Flashing a grin, she winked at Nathan. "I guess I got lucky."

Nathan plopped back against the headrest. "I need a witness protection program. If they broadcast my address on the news, only a couple more people will know where I live."

"Want some music?" Kelly asked, reaching for the radio. "It'll help you relax."

"And risk hearing another moaning call from a different world? Not really. My head's about to explode."

Watching her side mirror, Kelly merged onto the interstate. "Then settle back and chill. We have about five hours to go."

He closed his eyes. "What about your dad? You gonna call him?"

"Later. I'll just tell him we're out on a date. He'll get a kick out of that."

He opened one eye. "Really?"

"Well ..." Kelly let a smile break through. "He likes you."

"Yeah," Daryl piped up. "And after Kelly decided to give up guys because of her mom—"

"Daryl!" Kelly tightened her grip on the wheel. "Hush!"

"What's the big deal? Everyone knows about your parents. Anyway, Steven decided, with parents like that, she'd be kind of loose, too, so one night she had to put him in his place."

Kelly's cheeks turned bright red. "Daryl, cut it out!"

"Why? I'm complimenting you. He deserved that kick in the groin."

"Daryl! If you don't stop it, I'll—"

"So she said she wouldn't ever date anyone again unless the perfect gentleman came along, and that worried her dad. I guess he thought she'd turn butch or something, but since she just called you a perfect gentleman, everyone will be happy."

Kelly lowered her head and growled. "You won't be happy when I kick you out of the car and make you walk home."

"You can't. I know all your secrets." Daryl closed her eyes and yawned. "Wake me when we get to Illinois. I like to blow kisses at state welcome signs."

Kelly gripped the wheel with stiffened fingers, her biceps flexed and her gaze fixed straight ahead.

Nathan pulled his lips in. No way was he going to breathe a word right now. If Kelly got any hotter, steam would spew out her ears.

After a few minutes, a light snore sounded from the backseat. Kelly let out a long sigh and relaxed her grip. With a glistening tear in her eye, she spoke softly. "I guess I don't have anything left to hide, do I?"

He replied with a light shrug. "I didn't hear anything so terrible."

"Daryl made it sound a lot better than it was." As she turned toward him, the tear meandered down her cheek. "I'm not the kind of girl you'd be interested in."

"Don't you mean ..." Leaning toward her, he lowered his voice. "... you *weren't* that kind of girl?"

She wiped the tear, but a new one streamed from her other eye. "Does it make any difference? What's done is done."

"Yeah. It makes a difference." He rubbed his finger along the seatbelt strap, swallowing to keep his voice from quaking. "It makes a big difference, at least to me."

Her lips formed a trembling smile. "Why should it make a difference?"

"Like you said. What's done is done." He raised his shoulders in another casual shrug. "I love you for who you are now."

Kelly's eyes slowly narrowed, and a hint of anger spiced her voice. "Don't use that word on me."

He drew his head back. "What are you talking about? What word?"

"I've heard it too many times. My mom used it. My dad used it. Steven used it. And none of them ever meant it. They just *used* it."

"You mean *love*?"

She rubbed a new tear away from each eye. "You can't possibly love me yet. Don't say it unless you really mean it!"

"Okay, sorry." He folded his arms over his chest and slid closer to the window. Who would've thought he could get into trouble by using *that* word? He *did* love his new sister, so didn't it make sense to let her know?

Her lips trembled again, but she said nothing. As new tears streamed, she kept her eyes focused ahead.

Nathan let out a quiet sigh. Kelly didn't need to hear the word; she needed to see love acted out. He popped open the glove box. "You got any tissue in here?"

"In my purse."

He fished out a pack of tissues and handed her one. "Want me to drive a while?"

Wiping her eyes, she nodded again. "Thank you. We need gas anyway."

Nathan turned and yanked on the cuff of Daryl's jeans. "Wake up, O keeper of the dimensional secrets. It's time to dock the Millennium Falcon."

Blinking her eyes, Daryl yawned. "You know, you shouldn't talk about movies so much. It gets kind of annoying after a while."

After stopping at a convenience store, filling up with gas, and grabbing some snacks, Nathan set his Dr Pepper bottle in the cup holder and started the car. "Everyone ready?"

"I'm ready," Daryl called from the backseat. She pulled a Hershey's Kiss from her bag of candy and unwrapped the foil. "Anyone want a Kiss?"

Kelly smirked. "Not from you." As she leaned against a pillow she had squished between her head and the window, she closed her eyes and pushed Nathan's leg with her sock-covered toe. "Ask him. Guys always want a kiss."

He reached back. "Sure. I'll have one." After popping it in his mouth, he found a classical station on the radio and kept the volume low, hoping it wouldn't activate the mirror in the back. During a soothing Chopin sonata, Daryl fell asleep, again snoring quietly, while Kelly eased into a restless nap. Her eyelids twitched from time to time, and her brow furrowed. Once, she even let out a low groan and whispered something imperceptible.

Nathan squeezed the steering wheel. Bad dreams. But it would be such a shame to wake her up. With her lips slightly pursed, her eyes closed, and her hands spread softly on her lap, she looked more like a child than a young woman. Still, she had probably experienced far more pain than any child should have to suffer.

Thinking back on her recent tirade, Nathan shook his head. It was tragic. She didn't know the true meaning of love. She couldn't even stand hearing the word. Yet, she needed love. She deserved to *be* loved. Oh, so desperately.

Edging his hand toward her, he watched her out of the corner of his eye. He slid his hand under hers and held it, barely touching her skin. Her fingers twitched and returned the light grasp, and a gentle smile spread across her face. He caressed her knuckles with his thumb. Maybe now her bad dreams had finally ended.

A cell phone rang. Nathan jerked back his hand and scanned the seats. "Where did I put it?"

Kelly sat upright, her eyes blinking. Daryl's heavy breathing ended with a snort.

The chime sounded again, leading Kelly to the floorboard. "Right here." She picked it up and laid it in Nathan's palm.

Opening the flap with one hand, he raised it to his ear. "Hello?"

"Nathan, are you almost here?"

"Hi, Clara. We've got about three hours to go. Why?"

"Tell Kelly to floor it. I need you to—"

Silence.

"Clara?" Nathan looked at the phone's screen. The call had dropped.

Kelly leaned toward him, her brow lowering. "What's wrong?"

He closed the phone. "It sounds like Clara's in trouble."

10

WARP SPEED

As the speedometer pushed past eighty, Kelly set a hand on the dashboard. "This isn't a back road, Nathan. If a state trooper clocks you, it'll take a lot longer than three hours to get there."

"Good point." Easing up on the accelerator, he glanced at the mirror again. "Someone's following us. As soon as I took off, he did, too, and now he's slowing down again."

Kelly swung around and stared out the back. "Could it be Dr. Gordon?"

"Looks like his Town Car. I saw it at the school."

She swiveled back and tightened her seatbelt. "Then floor it. Now we *want* a cop to catch us."

Daryl flopped back in her seat. "All right!" she said, slapping her thighs. "It's adventure time!"

When the digits read ninety-one, Nathan reached toward the back. "Can you find my mirror? It's in my backpack."

Daryl pushed his hand away. "Keep your eyes on the road. I'll get it." After jerking it out, she held it on her lap. "What do you want me to do with it?"

"Just look into it. Use it like a rearview mirror and tell me what you see."

She held the mirror in front of her face. "Ew! I'm a mess!"

As the speedometer passed one hundred, the engine whined and rattled loudly. Nathan turned up the radio and glanced at her through his own rearview mirror. "Watch the road. Not your face."

"I can do both." Daryl pushed her hair back and primped her curly red bangs. "Nothing yet."

Kelly looked at the speedometer, her grip on her armrest tensing along with her voice. "I can't believe you're going this fast."

"Once in Israel, Clara and I did a hundred and ten on motorcycles, running from six guys with Uzis in the back of a pickup. She told me, 'When a life's in danger, there is no speed limit.'"

Nathan weaved around cars, alternately braking and accelerating again as he changed lanes. After a few minutes, Daryl called out, her voice calm. "What am I supposed to be looking for?"

Keeping his focus ahead, he reached back. "Give it to me!" He jerked it forward and propped it on the dashboard.

"I'll hold it for you," Kelly said, reaching to secure it.

Constantly glancing around—from the road ahead, to the normal rearview, to his father's mirror—he continued his mad dash, banking left, then right, then back again. A memory flashed. This was his nightmare! How could that be?

The Lincoln closed in, following in his wake like a skier behind a boat, matching swerve after swerve.

"Kick it, Nathan!" Daryl shouted. "You have the smaller car. Take it somewhere he can't follow!"

Up ahead, a conversion van and a gasoline tanker drove side by side, blocking the way. Nathan pressed the brake and cut the wheel hard to the right. Now riding the shoulder, he floored it again. As the driver's side mirror barely brushed by the tanker's running board, two of the Camry's tires rumbled on the grass, shaking the three passengers.

"Nathan!" Kelly thrust out her finger. "A bridge!"

He jerked to the left, missing the bridge abutment but clipping the tanker's front fender with the Camry's rear. With a loud squeal, the driver slammed on his brakes, swinging the trailer wildly. It slapped the conversion van into the median and then swung back toward the Lincoln, which had squeezed between the trailer and the side of the bridge.

The Lincoln zoomed forward. As the trailer fishtailed, it spanked the Lincoln in the rear, sending it lurching ahead.

The tanker tipped to its side and skidded, sending up a shower of sparks as metal scraped metal.

"Oh, my God!" Daryl shouted. "It's going to blow!"

Keeping one hand on Nathan's mirror, Kelly hunkered low in her seat. "Tell me when it's over!"

Clenching the wheel, Nathan floored the pedal again.

"Did it explode?" Kelly asked, peeking over the seat.

"No. It might have been empty." He eyed the mirrors. Now the car's rearview mirror showed a jackknifed tanker on its side, a van slipping through the grass in the median, and a black Lincoln closing in, while his father's mirror reflected a deserted country road winding through a tree-spotted meadow. "I need a light! What do we have?"

Daryl searched around her seat. "Where's your camera?"

"In the trunk!"

Kelly pointed at the keys in the ignition. "There's a little flashlight on the ring, but it's not very bright."

"You got anything bigger?"

"My father sometimes keeps ..." She reached under her seat and withdrew a foot-long camper's flashlight. "Here it is."

"I got the mirror," he said, grabbing its edge. "Get ready to turn it on."

"Here he comes!" Daryl bounced on her knees, staring out the back. "Think he'll push us off the road?"

Nathan shook his head. "Or worse. He might have a gun. I'd keep my head down if I were you."

"Gotcha." Daryl ducked low. "Avoid lead poisoning."

Kelly held the flashlight close to the reflection. "Let me know when you're ready."

He checked the image again—still just a country road. "One second. I want to see if something happens."

The Lincoln cut into the left lane and gave the Camry a little shove on its left rear fender, jostling everyone inside. Nathan grimaced. Exactly like the dream. But he woke up at this point. What would happen next?

Kelly grabbed her armrest. "Can't you go faster?"

"It's floored!" Nathan shot back. "I can't compete with that eight-cylinder road hog!"

Kelly waved the light. "What are you waiting for?"

"Go ahead and flash it!"

She aimed her flashlight at the mirror and pressed the button. As soon as it blinked on, the light surrounding the car dimmed.

"That's weird," Daryl said, rising from her crouch. "I don't see him anymore."

Kelly squinted out the side window. Rolling pastures whisked by, some dotted with trees. "I don't even see the highway. Where are we?"

"Perfect." Nathan slowed the car to a normal speed. The engine's whine lowered, but the rattle continued. "Exactly what I hoped for."

After putting the flashlight away, she took the mirror and set it on her lap. "Was this road in the reflection?"

"Yep. But I wasn't thinking about it at all. It's like the mirror chose the place."

Sporting a wide grin, Daryl leaned forward between the front seats. "You gotta love it. We cause a highway pileup, vanish in a puff of smoke, and reappear in the middle of nowhere."

"This isn't a movie," Kelly said. "Those people might have been hurt."

"She's right about one thing. We're in the middle of nowhere." Nathan searched the side of the road. "Do you see any signs?"

"There!" Kelly said, pointing. "That intersection up ahead has a sign."

Nathan stopped and angled his head to read the numbers. "Two fifty-one."

"Did you read the top?" Kelly spiked her voice. "It's *Illinois* 251!"

Daryl pushed farther into the front to get a look. "You mean I missed the welcome sign?"

"We all did," Nathan said. "We made some kind of quantum leap into another state."

Kelly opened her window and looked up at the sky. "Brrr! It's cold!"

Nathan pointed at the windshield. "Snowflakes."

Daryl leaned forward, squinting at the tiny crystals landing on the glass. "Did you guys see *The Day after Tomorrow*? It was so cool! Weather disasters all over the world. Global warming on steroids."

"I doubt this is from global warming." Nathan resisted the urge to say more. No use scaring anyone. But could the approach of interfinity have anything to do with the weather?

"So where do we go from here?" Kelly asked as she rolled up her window. "We don't have a GPS, and I can't even tell which way north is."

Nathan turned on the heater. "Find a gas station, tell them we're lost, and buy a map."

"You're a guy," Daryl said. "Isn't it against one of the rules of manliness to stop and ask directions?"

"Staying lost when you don't have to isn't my idea of manly."

Daryl reached forward and felt Nathan's bicep. "Oooh, Kelly. Strong and sensible in the same package. Can we clone him? One for you and one for me?"

Kelly pulled Daryl's arm away and pointed a finger at her. "As long as I get the original model."

"Hey! I won't quibble. His clone would be better than the clowns I've been out with."

Nathan groaned. "How many more hours of this do I have to put up with?"

After a few minutes, they found a Shell gas station. Nathan pulled in and glanced around. With a stack of bald tires in front of an empty mechanic's garage, a dirty window advertising several brands of beer, and no protective canopy over two older-style pumps in front, it didn't hold promise of carrying a great inventory. Still, they might have a map.

"Better pull out our sweatshirts," Nathan said as he opened the door. "I'll see what they've got."

Daryl held out her hand. "Fork over the credit card, dearie, and I'll fill the tank."

"It doesn't look like it takes cards. Just start pumping. It shouldn't need much, so I'll use cash. Stop it at twenty dollars if it goes that high."

When Nathan walked in, a bell jangled over his head. In the background of the dim store, a radio played, a news broadcast blending with an annoying buzz. He spotted the source, a little portable sitting on a snack display in the corner.

A portly bald man with a three-day beard sat on a stool behind the counter, surrounded by a shelf full of cigarettes and snuff on each side, a tall jar filled with red licorice in front, and a rack of hunting magazines in back.

"Help you find something?" the man asked.

Keeping his eye on the radio, Nathan gave him a nod. "Do you have a map?" He tried to listen to the news report. The word *nightmares* had caught his attention.

"Sure."

As the man waddled to the back of the store, the radio announcer broke through the static. "One expert claimed that media hype rather than paranormal sources has incited most of the outbreak, but he admits his theory doesn't explain how the first of these dreams began in Chicago before the phenomena became well-known." After a brief pause, the announcer continued. "Now to the weather. The unusual winterlike storm continues to spread throughout the Midwest, bringing heavy snow to—"

"Buck twenty-five, tax included," the man said as he returned to the counter. He plopped the map down and slid it toward Nathan.

Nathan reached into his pocket. "Is that all? I thought it'd be more." He laid a crumpled dollar bill and a quarter on the counter. "I guess there's not much demand for maps now that they're available on the Internet."

"The Internet?" The man slid the money into his register. "What are you talking about?"

Nathan stared at him for a moment. He seemed sincere. Not a hint of a wink or a smile.

He pulled a twenty from his wallet and laid it on the counter. "If we don't pump that much, I'll come back for the change."

"What are you filling? A Sherman tank?"

"No. A Toyota." Nathan pushed open the door and looked at the map. On the back, the price read $2.95. As the door swung closed, he glanced back at the store. Could the map have been on sale?

Now wearing a black sweatshirt, Daryl twisted the lid on the gas tank. "I topped it off at fifteen even."

Nathan eyed the price-per-gallon on the pump. A little higher than normal, but not much. Daryl tossed him his sweatshirt. He caught it and pulled it over his head, still clutching the map as he pushed his arms through the sleeves.

"You going back for the change?" she asked.

"I'd better not. Something strange is going on." As the snowfall thickened, he strode to the driver's door and got in. He laid the map on Kelly's thigh and shoved the key in the ignition. "We'd better get going."

Kelly unfolded the map and compared it to the one they printed out from the computer. "Believe it or not, we're only about a mile off the main highway that we would have been on anyway, and we're about a hundred miles ahead of pace."

"I'm ready to believe anything." He turned the key. The engine churned but wouldn't turn over.

Kelly groaned. "Not now!"

He pumped the accelerator, but the Camry kept grinding without firing. "How do you get it to start when it's being stubborn?"

"Dad cleans the spark plugs and lubricates the cylinders, but it might be the weather. I'm not sure if it'll do any good."

Nathan turned back the key. "Do you know how to do all that?"

"Sure. Just some carburetor cleaner and WD-40."

He eyed the window ads, searching for automotive supplies. "Maybe the store has some."

"Probably. And see if they have duct tape. Dad uses that, too."

"I'll check!" Daryl reached out her hand. "Grease my palm, moneybags."

Nathan pulled a five from his wallet. She snatched it from his fingers, jumped out of the car, and jogged into the station's mini-market, her red hair bouncing freely in the snowy breeze.

Kelly pulled her feet up into the seat and set her chin on a knee, gazing at Nathan. As the outside air seeped into the car, bringing a chill, he settled back and focused on her searching eyes. "What's up?" he asked.

"Just trying to figure out how to say I'm sorry."

"Sorry for what?"

"I'm not sure." She gave a hint of a shrug. "Everything, I guess. You're so different, I can't figure you out. Neither can

Daryl. But she just acts natural around you, so I guess I should, too."

"I'll try to do the same, but ever since my parents ..." A wave of sorrow flooded his mind, clamping his throat shut. He pressed his lips together. He couldn't possibly say another word without losing it completely.

She laid a gentle hand on his shoulder. "Don't worry about it. Just take your time."

"Thanks." A tear trickled down his cheek. "Sorry I'm not as easygoing as your friends."

"Daryl and I will help you. And besides ..." Leaning over the glove box, she wiped the tear away and kissed his cheek. "I'd rather be with a kindhearted mourner than a celebrating fool."

Daryl flung open the rear door. "Leave you two alone for one minute and look what happens!"

Kelly fell back into her seat. "Just a kiss of comfort, Miss Bigmouth."

"I only report what I see." Daryl bounced into her seat and closed the door. "A big yes-sir-ee on the cleaner and the WD-40." She held up a blue and yellow can. "This was the last one. And the man said, 'No charge.' He owed you five bucks." She slid Nathan's five dollars into the glove box.

"Good. Now we can—"

"But there's a problem. The store guy says the snow's backing up the highway. No one was prepared, so it's a mess. Lots of delays."

Nathan slapped the steering wheel.

"Nathan ..." Kelly smiled as she sang his name. "When you can't change the weather, you have to learn to chill."

Closing his eyes, he nodded slowly. She was right. No use banging his head against a wall. "Okay. Let's get the car started and see what happens."

"The store guy said we could borrow his tools," Daryl said. "Do you need them?"

Kelly nodded. "If it's something other than the spark plugs, I'm not sure what I'll need."

"Back in a flash!" Daryl opened her door, scurried to the market, and returned seconds later with a toolbox and a clean white rag. "Pop the hood, hot rod!"

As Nathan reached for the lever, Kelly got out and circled around to the front of the car. When she raised the hood, he and Daryl followed to help, but they became no more than shivering observers as Kelly expertly removed, cleaned, and re-installed the spark plugs. She wiped her hands on the cloth and smiled at Nathan. "Give it a try."

He jogged back to his seat and turned the key. The Camry roared to life and purred, sounding better than when they had started.

Kelly slammed the hood. "Gotta wash up!" she called as she dashed with the toolbox into the curtain of snowflakes.

When she disappeared into the store, Daryl climbed into the backseat and shut the door. "My turn to give you a kiss," she said.

Nathan kept his gaze locked forward. "That's okay. You don't—" A foil-wrapped piece of candy fell into his lap.

Daryl covered her mouth, giggling. "Sorry. Couldn't resist."

Snatching up the candy, Nathan turned and looked at her. As her carefree eyes gazed back at him, she smiled and blew him a kiss. "I'll get you to chill out eventually."

He relaxed his shoulders and allowed a smile to break through. "Thanks. I appreciate it."

Kelly ran back and jumped into the car, the can of WD-40 still in her grip. "Let's make tracks!"

"Not long, skidding ones, I hope," Nathan said as he backed out.

She unfolded the map and, peering through the steady snow-fall, guided him through a series of turns that led to the main highway. As forecasted, cars lined up on the four-lane road, bumper-to-bumper.

Nathan glanced at the map. "Any other routes?"

"Sure. But it'll take forever."

"It'll take longer than forever if we use the interstate."

Following Kelly's new instructions, Nathan turned around and traveled narrow, snow-covered roads, slipping and sliding on occasion. Traffic proved to be much lighter, but the slow going ate away at their time. Radio reports didn't help. Weather forecasts seemed to change by the minute, as did road and traffic conditions. No one seemed to know what was going on.

After a couple of hours, the clouds raced to the east, giving way to warm sunshine that quickly cleared the roads of snow and ice. Nathan rolled down his window and let the warm breeze circulate through the car. As his hair flapped in the wind, he looked over at Kelly. "This is getting out of control."

She pulled off her sweatshirt and tossed it into Daryl's lap. "It's either the most realistic nightmare I've ever had, or I'm ready for the loony bin. Take your pick."

He stopped at an intersection and stripped off his own sweatshirt. "No way. I'm not touching that one." He tried to keep his mood lively and "chill," but her mention of nightmares again reminded him of the radio report. Too much weird stuff was going on, and questions without answers kept piling up.

An hour or so later, they pulled in front of a semicircle driveway that led to a long, two-story building with a high turret at one end. The cylindrical turret was capped by a white dome with a narrow telescope opening from the apex to the base—Interfinity's observatory.

Nathan stopped well away from the building and lowered his window. "We'd better go in on foot."

"Good thinking." Kelly folded the map and tucked it under her seat. "I don't see Gordon's car anywhere, but we'd better hide ours. He might've called ahead and told them what we're driving."

After glancing around for any onlookers, Nathan ran the Toyota up on the curb and into a wooded area, where he parked under an evergreen tree. He gestured for Kelly and Daryl to lean close. "Listen. I've done this kind of thing a couple of times before, so just follow me and don't be shouting stuff like, 'Nathan, be careful!' because 'careful' isn't going to get the job done. Who knows? They might be holding Clara hostage, so we can't just cruise in through the front door." He pointed at the mirror. "Daryl, I'm going to trust you with that. Guard it with your life."

She saluted. "Aye-aye, sir!"

"Kelly, you take the violin. Leave everything else here. We need to travel as light as possible."

She reached for the black case on the rear floorboard. "I got it."

With Nathan leading the way, they skulked through the woods toward the observatory, eventually finding a narrow stone path that led to a back door in the two-story section of the complex.

He grabbed the door's metal handle and pulled. "Locked," he whispered.

Kelly pointed at a numeric pad on the wall. "Want to make a guess?"

"Waste of time." He looked through a square, head-high window in the door. Inside, a short, empty hallway ended at what looked like another hallway. Standing at the intersection, a tall man in a short-sleeved, blue security-guard uniform yawned and looked at his watch. The logo on his sleeve matched the one Dr. Gordon wore on his blazer—the triple infinity sign.

Backing away, Nathan scanned the gray cinder block walls. "Look for an open window, even just a crack."

Daryl pointed up. "I see one on the second floor."

"I guess whoever left it open thought it was secure," Kelly said. "There's no way to climb."

Nathan strode up to the wall and pushed his fingers into a gap between two blocks. "I see a narrow ledge between the floors. If I can get up there, I might be able to stand on it and reach the sill."

Daryl shook her head. "That's a big 'if,' Spider-Man. And the ledge isn't any wider than half a foot."

Nathan backed off a step. "There's got to be a way to get up there." He looked out over the lush grassy field surrounding the building. "The lawn's well kept, isn't it?"

Kelly followed his gaze. "Yeah. So?"

"If they keep the landscaping equipment on site, maybe there's an outbuilding we can search."

"If we split up," Kelly said, "I'm sure we can find—"

"No." He pointed at a thin trail of pulverized leaves leading away from the building. "Looks like their mower bag has a leak. We'll just follow the path."

Ducking low, they ran across the lawn and stopped behind a thick clump of trees. A small metal storage shed stood between two saplings, its door open, exposing a lawn tractor parked within.

Nathan rushed inside and looked around. A stepladder leaned against one wall. That would help. A rope lay coiled on the ground. Perfect. Now he just needed something that would . . . a towing hook!

Marching quickly, Nathan hauled the ladder. Daryl carried the rope while Kelly trotted alongside fastening one end of the rope to the hook while keeping the violin case tucked under her arm. When they arrived back at the observatory, he grasped the rope near the fastening point and began swinging the hook back and forth.

"Wait!" Kelly set the violin case down. "Let me."

"Just like shooting hoops?" he asked, passing the rope to her.

She let the hook dangle under her hand. "Not quite. But I have a good feel for throwing things." She swung the hook back and heaved it upward. It flew into the opening and landed with a dull clank inside.

The three rushed to the wall and flattened themselves against it, gawking at the window to see if anyone would look out. Nathan shifted his stare to his violin case, out in the open where Kelly had left it. Anyone peeking out the window would see it for sure. Five seconds passed. Ten seconds. No one appeared up above.

Nathan grasped the rope and pulled hard. It held fast. "Quick! The stepladder. Then get my violin."

After setting it up, the girls steadied the legs while he scrambled to the top. Taking hold of the rope again, he began scaling the wall, pulling fist over fist and scraping his shoes against the concrete until he could brace his feet against the ledge. Now standing with his toes on the narrow projection and hanging on to the rope for balance, he leaped and snagged hold of the window sill, letting go of the rope to grab with both hands.

Twin gasps arose from the girls below. He could almost feel their anxiety as he muscled up to the window. Straining quietly, he pulled with his arms and pushed his knees and shoes against the wall. Finally, he managed to get his chest up to the sill, allowing him to slide the rest of the way in.

He stood and looked around. A long oval conference table, surrounded by plush swivel chairs, sat in the center of the dim room. A folder had been placed on the table in front of each chair, as well as a pencil and glass of water. He took a closer look. Ice floated in the glasses. A meeting was about to start.

He found the hook wedged under the window's interior apron and jerked it free. Leaning out the opening, he reeled the line through his hands, lowering the hook toward the ground.

He whisper-shouted to the girls. "I'll try to open another window somewhere lower."

When the hook touched down, he released the rope. As soon as the end snaked its way to the bottom, the back door on ground level creaked open. The girls quickly swung their heads toward the sound.

The security guard stepped out. Holding the door open, he nodded at Kelly and Daryl. "May I help you ladies?"

Kelly walked up to him, so close she had to angle her head upward to look him in the eye. "Could you tell us where the tour group is?" She twirled her hair around her finger, giving him a sweet, innocent smile as she swung the violin case back and forth.

"Sure. It's almost over, though." He glanced at Daryl. Holding the mirror against her side, she copied Kelly's hair-twirling act, but she looked more clumsy than innocent. "How did you two get back here?" he asked.

Kelly pointed toward the side of the building and switched to a little girl voice. "We walked from that way."

The guard squinted at the ladder. "I wonder what that's doing there."

Nathan pulled his head back. Now he could only listen.

"Some guy was using it a minute ago," Kelly replied, "but he's gone now."

Sounds of conversation drifted in from the hallway. Nathan stiffened. People would be coming in at any second. He glanced around. A closed door at each end of the room represented his only ways of escape. But which one?

He spied a table on the right hand side of the room. A coffee pot sat near one edge next to a tray of doughnuts stacked like a pyramid. Apparently the door on that side would be the entry point. He sprang up and headed toward the opposite end of the room, picking up one of the folders on the table as he passed by. Just as the other door swung in, he quietly opened his door and slid into the hallway.

Not bothering to look back, he strode confidently down the carpeted hall. Tingles spread across his neck as he imagined a dozen eyes staring at him, but no one called for him to stop. He found a stairway door to his left and pushed it open. Once inside the stairwell, he leaned against the wall and let out the breath he had been holding for who knows how long. Now all he had to do was find the tour group without being noticed.

He crept down the stairs, stepping lightly on each one. He had to avoid Dr. Gordon's people at all costs. Of course, Gordon was probably looking for Daryl and Kelly, too, so they had to watch their steps. Were they thinking about that? If they got caught, he'd get the mirror and violin. That would be a disaster! Would Kelly be smart enough to hide them just in case?

When he reached the lower level, he opened the door leading to the hall and looked both ways. The guard was now gone, probably still helping the girls find the tour group. He padded along the carpet toward the observation turret and found a door at the end, as well as another corridor to his right. A sign on the door's window said, *Security Level A Required*. A keypad hung on the wall next to the door. He tried the knob. Locked. No surprise.

Conversation buzzed at the end of the right-hand corridor, moving closer. He ducked back into the first hall and glanced around. Ah! Restrooms! As he hustled toward the men's room, he kicked a crumpled foil wrapper lying on the carpet just outside the ladies' room door. He snatched it up. A Hershey's Kiss! And another wrapper had been wedged at the corner of the Ladies nameplate. He laid a palm on the door. Should he knock or just barge in?

Chattering noises grew; no time to decide. He jerked open the door and tiptoed into the small room, listening for the slightest sound, but it seemed to be unoccupied. Hurrying to the farther of two stalls, he pushed the door open. Yes. There they were. His violin and mirror. Kelly had guessed right again.

Just as he stepped inside to pick them up, the restroom door swung open. He closed the stall and sat down, his limbs stiffening as he strained his ears.

A gruff voice called from the hallway. "Hurry it up!"

Soft footsteps padded his way. Two shoes came into view in the adjacent stall, purple and pink canvas running shoes.

Nathan tightened his throat, trying to sound like a woman. "Francesca?"

A tiny gasp echoed in the room. "Who's there?" she whispered.

He lowered his voice to its normal tone. "It's Nathan."

"Am I in the wrong bathroom?"

"No. I am." He leaned closer to the partition. "Where's Clara?"

"In the big telescope building. Some men won't let us go, and I heard one of them say they're looking for you. He's the one who's waiting for me out in the hall."

"Yeah. I thought they'd be looking for me."

Her voice changed to a pleading tone. "Are you going to rescue us?"

"I hope so, but you're going to have to help."

"What do I do?"

"When that guy takes you back to Clara, make sure he pays attention to you. I'll be following, so you can't let him look back."

"Okay, but I have to go now."

"Don't worry. I'll be right behind you."

"No. I mean I have to *go*."

Francesca's guard rapped on the door. "Hurry up!"

"Go ahead." Nathan waited. As trickling sounds entered his stall, his cheeks grew warm. Never having a sister had its disadvantages.

He opened his case, creating a sharp draft that lifted a scrap of paper from the violin strings and sent it floating to the floor. He quickly folded the conference room report into a pocket inside the lid, snatched up the paper, and read the scribbled note—"Nathan, we'll try to get into the telescope room. Meet us near the door."

Pressing his lips tightly together, he stuffed the paper back into the case and latched it. How in the world could he possibly find them? At least he knew he had to find a door to the telescope room, but where could it be?

Francesca whispered, "I'm done."

He set his hand on the partition as if trying to give her a pat of comfort. "I'll give you a head start. Remember to keep him occupied."

"Okay."

Her pink and purple shoes shuffled out of the stall and, after a quick splash sounded from the sink, she disappeared from sight. Nathan picked up his violin and mirror and hurried to follow. Pushing the door open an inch or two, he peeked out. A heavyset man walked alongside Francesca, but the rest of the hall was empty.

Francesca suddenly crouched, holding her hands over her stomach and moaning. The guard squatted next to her. "What's wrong? Are you sick?"

She moaned even louder. The guard scooped her into his arms and carried her toward the high-security door at the end of the hall.

Nathan bolted from the restroom, marching as fast as quiet steps would allow. When the guard reached the end of the hall, he set Francesca down, but when she let out another loud groan, he picked her back up.

Nathan stopped and pressed himself against the wall, now within ten feet of the door.

The man set a thick finger over the numeric pad and punched

in four digits. When the door buzzed, he pulled it open and carried Francesca inside.

Nathan leaped for the door and jammed his foot in the gap just before it closed. Still using his foot, he opened the door slightly and peeked in. The guard carried Francesca down a curved hallway and, seconds later, walked out of sight.

After squeezing in, Nathan let the door close silently and followed. As the walls ahead bent gradually to his right, he used his mirror to watch the area behind him, glancing between it and the corridor as his violin case swung at his side. He slowed his pace, thinking about the possibilities that lay ahead ... and behind. At least the mirror might give him some warning, but if someone showed up in the reflection, what would he do? With no doors in the hallway, there seemed to be no escape route.

The click of a door latch sounded from somewhere in front of him. He turned around and paced slowly backwards, watching the mirror again to guide his painstaking steps. When the guard appeared in the reflection, he stopped. Glancing back, he saw just walls and carpet, but the mirror still showed the guard, now closing a door and walking in his direction.

11

ECHOES FROM THE EDGE OF THE UNIVERSE

Nathan backed up against the wall. Time to think fast. Could he take this guy by surprise? He was pretty big, and, being a guard, he might have a gun. He set the violin case down and clenched a fist. What should he use? A leg sweep? A groin kick and a chop to the neck? He took in a deep breath. If only there was an easier way out!

After whispering a quick prayer, he let out a quiet sigh. As he settled his mind, the last words his father spoke flowed through his thoughts. *If you ever get into big trouble, look in the mirror I gave you and focus on the point of danger. Nothing is more important.*

He turned the mirror back toward the sounds. As the guard drew closer in the reflection, Nathan's hands began to sweat. Biting his lip, he scolded himself. The guard wasn't that close yet. The mirror was showing a future time dimension, right? Still, the guard's thick biceps and thicker neck seemed more impressive than the mirror's track record for accuracy, at least for the moment.

The guard suddenly spun an about-face and walked in the opposite direction. After a few seconds, he disappeared. The door latch sounded again, not from the mirror—for real. Would the guard head his way now?

Clumping footsteps drew closer, but the mirror showed only empty carpet.

"Arnie! C'mere."

The voice came from somewhere beyond the guard. The footsteps halted for a moment, then returned, but now their sound diminished.

Nathan picked up his violin and resumed his backwards walking. As he approached the door the guard had closed, nothing appeared in the reflection. Pinning the mirror to his side, he wiggled the knob gently. Locked, of course. He tapped lightly with his knuckles. "Clara? Francesca?"

"Nathan?" Clara's breathless voice drew near. "Is that you?"

"Yes. How long have you been in there?"

"Too long."

He wiggled the knob again. "I don't think I can overpower the guard, so—"

"Hush and listen. Do you see a keypad by the door?"

He glanced up at the wall. "Yeah. But I didn't see him punch in a code. I couldn't get close enough."

"Francesca says he covered it with his hand, so she couldn't watch, but she heard the tones."

He studied the telephone-style buttons. "Each number has a different tone? That's not very secure."

"The difference is so minute, only Francesca can detect it."

Nathan poised his index finger over the pad. "Okay. What do I push?"

"Punch zero through nine slowly. Francesca is listening."

His heart pounding as he watched for the guard, Nathan pressed the numbers, pausing between each one. A few seconds after he finished, Francesca called out, "Eight, four, seven, one."

He entered the numbers. When the lock clicked, the door opened, pushed from the inside by Clara.

"Where's Kelly?" she whispered.

"We got separated. I have to find her and another girl, a friend of hers who came with us."

"We don't have time to look for anyone. We have to figure out what Mictar is up to."

He picked up his violin case. "Mictar is here? At Interfinity?"

"Follow me. It's not safe to stand around here." Taking Francesca's hand, Clara bustled down the hall in the direction the guard had gone. Clara ducked into a recessed area in the wall, an alcove for an elevator, and pressed a series of numbers into the keypad by the door. "I found this code in Dr. Gordon's office — six, six, five, three. Memorize it."

When the door opened, the three squeezed into the one-man elevator car, making it bounce slightly. In order to fit, Nathan had to tuck his mirror at his side again and hold the violin case in front of him. Francesca, now wearing a long-sleeved red tunic with a hemline that fell past her hips, snuggled in between him and Clara.

The door closed again, leaving them with only a dim glow from a low-wattage bulb in one corner of the ceiling. "Push the button for the third floor," Clara said. "I can't reach it."

Unable to see any numbers on the darkened buttons, Nathan shuffled forward and felt with his pinky for the third button from the bottom. As soon as he pushed it, the car jerked. Then, as the motor whined softly, they crept upward.

Clasping Nathan's shoulder, Clara spoke into his ear. "From the conversation I overheard, they should all be gone."

"Who are 'they'?" he whispered.

"Mictar and his scientists."

The car halted. "Turn around," Clara ordered.

The three twisted in place, rubbing shoulders and elbows as a door on the opposite side slid open. They stepped out into an enormous, dome-covered chamber. Up above, shining pinpoints speckled a purplish curved ceiling, creating an evening-sky canopy that enfolded the room in twilight. A few desk lamps at workstations near the outer walls provided an adequate amount of light for exploring.

Nathan turned back to the elevator door. Since they were on the top floor, the lift ended at their level, inside a tall closet-like room that abutted the wall. Just above the door frame, a red numeral three shone from a matchbook-sized LED screen. "Mictar is a part of Interfinity?" he asked.

"He's not on their organizational chart, but he acts like he runs the place." She headed straight for the lighted desks where three laptop computers lay open and turned on. "I'll tell you more in a minute. I have to figure out how the controls work before they get back. Prime sky-viewing time starts in about an hour."

"We also have to find Kelly." Nathan approached a large object at the center of the floor. Standing on an octagonal wooden platform, a cylindrical metal pedestal supported a huge telescope. Its wide lens pointed toward a breach in the dome—a skinny, rectangular hatch that opened to the evening sky. "I found a note from her that said she would try to be near the telescope room door." Still hanging on to his mirror, he set down his violin case and felt the pedestal's smooth surface. "Does this place remind you of where my parents were in the mirror?"

"I noticed that as soon as I saw this room with the tour group." Clara pointed at a cordoned off area near a wooden door. "We were allowed to get that close, and after one of the scientists gave a talk, they cleared us out. When Francesca and I sneaked back in, they caught us and threw us in that room where you found us. If Kelly's hanging around out there, it won't be safe for her."

"I'll be right back." Nathan hurried toward a series of thick ropes that sagged between metal support poles. After stepping over one of the ropes, he bent low, straining to see something shiny on the floor, crumpled foil wrappers. "More Kisses?"

"Kisses?" Clara walked closer, leading Francesca by the hand.

He picked up two pieces of foil and showed them to her. "Wrappings from Hershey Kisses were stuffed under the door."

"So?"

Tucking the mirror under his arm again, he turned the doorknob. The door suddenly jerked open, and Kelly and Daryl burst through. Spinning around, Kelly grabbed the knob and closed it gently. "Whew!" she said in a hoarse whisper. "That was close!"

"How long have you two been waiting there?"

"Just a minute or so, this go 'round." She pointed at a watch on Daryl's wrist. "We timed the guard's circuit. When he came by to check this door, we ducked into a janitor's closet. When he left, we knelt here and stuffed a couple of candy wrappers through the crack."

"How'd you know I'd find them and figure out it was you?"

"We went by the bathroom where we left your mirror and violin. The wrappers and your stuff were gone, so—"

"No more time for chitchat," Clara said as she led Francesca toward the computer desks. "You can compare notes later."

Nathan followed, gesturing for Daryl and Kelly to come along. "Clara, this is Daryl, a friend of ours. She's a computer genius, so she should be a big help."

"Nice to meet you, Daryl." After sliding into a desk chair, Clara scanned the laptop. "Let's see if we can figure this thing out."

Daryl pointed at a control icon on the screen. "That one says, *Dome Mirror Magnitude*. Sounds pretty harmless."

"Let's try it." Clara clicked a mouse pad button and slid her finger down the surface. The pinpoints of light on the ceiling faded away. Seconds later, an aerial image appeared, all five of them looking up at the dome.

"It really *is* a mirror," Kelly said, tilting her head upward.

"That explains why Nathan's parents looked upside down on the ceiling."

Clara's eyes moved all around as if checking the reflection for flaws. "The tour guide told us the entire ceiling is a curved mirror. I suppose it's similar to the one on Nathan's wall back in Iowa. They both seem able to show scenes that aren't reflected images."

Daryl sat in front of one of the other laptops. "I'll try to figure out if this station does anything."

Setting his mirror on the desk, Nathan leaned close to Clara's computer. A three-dimensional rendering of the room's telescope filled most of the display area. "Which control did you use to switch to mirror mode?"

Clara pointed at the slider bar widget on the screen. "I dragged it all the way down to the bottom."

"Let's turn it back on for a minute." Nathan moved the slider to near the top. The ceiling faded to purple, a darker purple than before, and the pinpoints reappeared. He set his fingers on the keyboard. "I'll bet we can adjust the telescope's position by changing the coordinates in those three text boxes." He entered new numbers, changing each by a single unit. The telescope in the middle of the room hummed and shifted slightly, as did the entire dome above, moving the opening in the ceiling to match the telescope's new direction. As if in concert, the stars on the ceiling shifted as well.

Clara aimed her gaze at the ceiling again. "I'll wager that the mirror's showing what the telescope sees. It's just the evening sky."

Kelly pointed upward. "So that mirror isn't a dimensional window?"

A tapping noise turned everyone toward Daryl as she clicked her fingernail on the other computer's desk. "I think the key to the dimensions is on this laptop."

Nathan scooted over and tried to make sense of what

he saw on the screen. "How do you know? It looks pretty complicated."

"This laptop is Dr. Gordon's. I remember it from the seminar." Daryl set her finger over a screen icon. "Look. Three windows labeled Earth Red, Earth Blue, and Earth Yellow. Earth Red is highlighted, so I'm guessing the mirror is showing the stars in the Earth Red dimension."

She glided the mouse pointer across the screen. A line connected Earth Red and Earth Blue, and when Daryl let the mouse hover over the line, a message popped up saying, "Network Active."

Nathan let out a low whistle. "A multidimensional computer network!"

The three windows had captions underneath that showed the date and time for each dimension. Nathan glanced at his watch. Earth Red's time matched his, so that settled which dimension was theirs. Earth Yellow showed December of 1978, and Earth Blue showed September of this year; five days in the future.

Kelly slid in between Nathan and Daryl, crossing her arms as she studied the screen. "How can they know the date and time in the other dimensions?"

"Sun, moon, and star positions." Daryl looked up at the ceiling. "If they can precisely monitor the heavens in each dimension, they can know exactly what time it is there."

Nathan bent closer. "Watch how the seconds change on Earth Blue. Sometimes they go slow, and sometimes they go fast. And on Earth Yellow, they're going a lot faster. What's up with that?"

"Like I told you before," Daryl explained, "the dimensions are in parallel, but they aren't anchored to each other in time. It's sort of like three boats on a river that catch different currents. Sometimes one will go faster than the other, then it might slow down again."

Kelly leaned in. "It looks like Earth Yellow is trying to catch up with the others."

Daryl set her finger on the mouse pad. "Let's switch it and see what happens. I want to get a look at the future." She clicked on the Earth Blue icon. Less than a second later, the mirror flickered, and the stars shifted slightly.

"That didn't do much," Nathan said, backing away from the desk as he looked up. "But I guess we shouldn't expect it to. It's only five days, and it's about the same time of night."

Daryl squinted at the screen. "Here's a selector in the corner that's set to 'Optical Telescope.' The other option is 'Radio Telescope.'"

Clara flicked her thumb behind her. "Interfinity has a hookup to a radio telescope about ten miles away. That selector probably allows them to control it from here."

"Let's check it out." Daryl clicked on the radio telescope option. The mirror on the ceiling flashed, and the starry canopy changed to a frenzied jumble of tiny multicolored shapes—polygons, ribbons, ovals, and indistinct globules—each one morphing from one shape to another. "Looks like I hit the jackpot."

Nathan and Kelly stared upward. It was mesmerizing, almost hypnotic.

Daryl leaned back in her chair to get a look. "It's probably a computer rendering of the radio noise from space. Some programmer translated it into a visual array."

Shaking her head, Clara turned to Nathan. "But what good is it? It looks like a chimpanzee's finger painting."

"Maybe all the information is there," Nathan offered. "It just has to be decoded."

Francesca tugged on Nathan's shirt. "Aren't the sounds amazing?"

Lowering himself to a crouch, Nathan gazed into her eyes. "What sounds are you talking about?"

"Can't you hear them? It's like every shape up there is sing-ing a note, but they aren't in harmony."

Nathan looked at Daryl. "Is there a volume control?"

"Maybe this is it." As Daryl adjusted a slider bar, thousands of dissonant musical notes poured from speakers embedded somewhere in the walls.

Nathan covered his ears. "It's like the worst orchestra in the world. Every musician's on a different page, and Clara's chimp is conducting."

"I hear a melody," Francesca said. "It's all mixed up inside the noise, but I hear it."

"Do you recognize it?"

Francesca shook her head. "But I think I could play it."

Nathan looked at her eyes. Her pupils reflected the cacoph-ony of colors up above, just as his mother's eyes had done. He hustled over to his case, flipped it open, and handed her his violin. As she settled it under her chin and curled her fingers around the neck, her brow furrowed. "Yours is bigger than mine, but I'll see what I can do."

"Just do your best, sweetheart," Clara said. "I'm sure it will be fine."

She hovered the bow just above the strings, her eyes closed as she concentrated. Then, setting the bow hairs lightly on the A string, she played a long, quiet note, moving her fingers along the string to adjust the sound. She then shifted to the E string and did the same. Blinking for a second, she said, "This is hard. The melody is fast and intertwined with the noise."

"Maybe the violin's too big after all," Nathan said.

"That's not the problem. I love how it sounds. It's way better than my own."

Nathan's throat tightened as her words rebounded in his mind. *Better than her own.* That *was* her own violin, or at least it would be in a different dimension. He patted her gently on the back. "Just keep trying."

Francesca continued playing notes, sometimes several in succession that kept to a reasonably melodic scheme. As the minutes ticked by, her connected phrases lengthened, creating several measures that began to prod Nathan's memory. "That's starting to sound like something familiar, but it's a little off."

"I missed some of the notes." She set the bow on the strings again. "This should be how it goes."

The notes sang out, now blending together beautifully. Nathan stared at the colors on the ceiling as she played and whispered to himself, "It's Dvořák, from the *New World Symphony.*"

The shapes broke apart and seemed to bleed their pigments into each other, creating new forms, indistinct and miscolored—humanoids with knobby blue hands and spaghetti-thin green torsos. As they blended, Francesca's eyes brightened with the same white light that shone from the eyes of her adult namesake, yet not quite as brilliant and without the expanding beams.

He touched Francesca's shoulder. "Can you play it louder?"

She moved away from him and, dipping her head and arms, began stroking her instrument with passion. Her fingers danced along the neck like charmed ballerinas, while her bow flew back and forth in a hypnotic sway. Heavenly music filled the room, rising like angelic prayers to the mirrored roof. Her eyes began to blaze. The colors sharpened, as if called to order by the musician's bow. The shapes molded into real human forms, two men standing in some kind of dimly lit room.

Nathan let his mouth drop open. He tried to keep an eye on the scene above while, at the same time, watching his mother, in the guise of a youthful prodigy, play her part of this strange New World performance. She was a miniature model of the lovely woman he once knew, now a bright-eyed china doll slowly turning on a music box. But there was something more. She had become a generator of musical energy, a pint-sized dynamo who could somehow feed on the sounds of the ages and pour out their vitality in a visible spectrum. Her eyes had become a conduit for her magical gift of perfect interpretation.

Up above, the men in the mirror image sharpened to photo-realistic quality, moving about their scene in apparent real time. Daryl pointed skyward. "That's Dr. Gordon!"

As if drawn by the music, Clara walked with a swaying rhythm to the center of the room. Nathan joined her, mesmerized by the scene above, an exact copy of their own chamber, yet populated by a different set of characters. Gordon was there, all right, standing next to the telescope in the middle of the room. Mictar stood next to him, looking as pale as ever. They seemed to be talking to each other in the Earth Blue dimension.

Nathan strained his eyes, trying to pick up an important detail, a bandage on Dr. Gordon's cheek. So there had to be two Dr. Gordons, one on Earth Blue who tried to kill him and Kelly, and one on Earth Red who showed up at the high school.

As the scene continued to brighten, a third person, a woman, came into view in the background. With her hands tied behind her back, she sat in one of the rolling swivel chairs, her head up and her chin firm. Although her dark locks fell haphazardly over her face and across her shoulders, there was no mistaking her identity.

His tongue suddenly dry, Nathan could barely speak. "That's my mother."

The figures in the image began to change their shapes, becoming muddled and indistinct. Nathan swung his head toward the younger Francesca. Her bow elbow sagged, and her fingers slowed on the violin's neck. Although her eyes still flashed like brilliant stars, she seemed worn out, far more fatigued than normal playing would cause. Whatever this amazing display of musical decryption and light emanation was, it obviously took its toll on her.

"Do you want to stop?" he asked.

Francesca shook her head. After taking a breath, she increased her volume again, reaching for a second wind as she whipped her bow across the strings. One of the hairs snapped and flew above her bow like a spider thread caught in a breeze.

The reflection clarified. Mictar's thin, pale lips moved, but no voice came out. Leaning toward the older Francesca, he set his long fingers around her throat. His voice broke through the chaotic noise. "If you don't tell me the secret of Quattro, I will feed on your eyes."

Balling his fists, Nathan spoke through clenched teeth. "Leave her alone!"

Mictar shoved her backwards. She tipped in her chair and, unable to brace herself because of her bonds, toppled over. As she looked up at him, her expression defiant, he pointed a long, skeletonlike finger. "Take her to her room!"

Mictar stalked away in one direction while Dr. Gordon helped their prisoner up and led her in the other. Seconds later, the room in the reflection lay vacant.

"We've got to get there!" Nathan yelled.

"But how?" Kelly spun around to Daryl. "Is there a button on the computer that'll send us?"

As the younger Francesca played on, her chest heaved, and her brow furrowed tightly.

"A flash of light!" Nathan dug into his pocket and yanked out the keys. He aimed the flashlight at the ceiling, but the enormous room swallowed its tiny glow.

Clara hurried toward the wall. "I'll look for switches."

"Quick!" Nathan called. "Before Francesca gets too tired!"

Daryl sprinted to the other side of the room. "They have to be around here somewhere."

While Nathan rushed back to the desk to grab his mirror, Kelly stooped in front of Francesca, speaking a mile a minute.

"You can do it! You play like an angel! I wish I had talent like yours. Just hang in there and keep making beautiful music!"

Francesca let out the slightest whimper but played on, her intonation staying true. Nathan rejoined her, breathing heavily. "Just a few more notes! Just a few more!"

"I found the switches!" Daryl called.

Lights blinked on from all around the base of the perimeter. Trumpet-shaped track lights aimed their white beams toward the ceiling. The flashes gathered at the top of the dome, each one splitting into a hundred thin shafts of light that rebounded toward the floor, some piercing Nathan, Kelly, and Francesca, while other shafts surrounded them in a laser-beam cage.

The ceiling reflection slowly filtered toward them, sliding down the laser pathways and along the entire perimeter wall. Within seconds, the scene from the other dimension spread over the trumpetlike fixtures, blocking out their glow. Clara and Daryl faded away along with the failing lights.

Francesca stopped playing. Kelly clutched Nathan's arm, her nails digging into his skin. Tensing his muscles, he ducked his head, unable to tell if the reflection was descending and enveloping them or if they were rising into its enfolding arms.

Soon, their surroundings clarified. They remained inside the observatory dome, but the telescope was turned in a different direction, only two laptop computers rested on the workstation table, and the tour group door stood wide open. The mirror above displayed the starry sky, a darker purple now, with more yellowish-white pinpoints.

Nathan swung his head toward the light switches. Clara and Daryl were nowhere in sight. A motor hummed. He spun back toward the elevator entrance just as the red numeral switched from a two to a one. "He must be taking Mom to a room downstairs. We have to follow him."

Kelly stepped up near the elevator call button. "Think it's safe to wait for it to come back?"

"Can't risk it. It might show up with Dr. Gordon or Mictar in it."

Pivoting on her heel, she nodded toward the tour door. "We could go that way, but if this dimension is the same as ours, we'd need a code to get into the secure area."

"I don't know that code. I just caught the door before it closed."

Francesca raised her violin bow. "I know the numbers. The guard couldn't cover the pad with his hand, because he was carrying me."

"The code might not be the same in this dimension," Nathan said, "but it's worth a shot."

The elevator motor kicked in with a low thud and began humming. The number above the door changed to "two."

Kelly sucked in a quick breath. "They're coming back!"

Nathan gave Kelly the mirror, repacked the violin and bow, and took Francesca's hand. "Come on!"

They raced through the open door and down the carpeted hall. Kelly turned into another corridor, whispering, "This way." After hustling to the end of the hall, she jerked open a door leading to a stairwell. Once they all filed inside and the door swung closed, Nathan pulled Kelly and Francesca into a corner. "Let's think for a minute."

Leaning against a wall, Kelly held a hand against her chest. "Thinking's good. I think my heart's kicking my lungs."

After setting down the violin case, Nathan leaned over the metal rail and looked down the gap between the flights of stairs. "This looks like the one I used earlier."

"Right." Kelly took a deep breath and let it out slowly. "If you go down to the second floor, you'll be right next to where you climbed in the building."

"So on the first floor it'll come out near the secure area." He turned to Francesca. "What's the code?"

She closed her eyes tightly. "Nine, three, eight, zero."

Nathan tilted his head. That was strange. The code on the door where they kept her and Clara was eight, four, seven, one. They followed a definite pattern. "When we get to the first floor, I'll sneak out by myself and try the code, while you watch from the stairwell. If it works, you two follow."

After picking up the violin and descending the stairs, Nathan opened the hallway door a crack and peeked out, keeping his mirror tucked close to his side. No one was around. So far, so good. He slipped into the hall and headed for the door to the secure area, but when he passed the adjacent hallway that led to the rear door of the observatory, a strange light caught his attention.

He looked back toward the stairs. Kelly's eyes appeared through a tiny sliver in the doorway. Raising a finger, he mouthed, "Just a minute" and set the violin case down. Then, running on the balls of his feet, he hurried to the exit door and looked out the square window. The only light he could find shone from a fixture hanging on the curved wall of the domed building at his right. Since night had taken over the skies, not much else was visible.

Just as he was about to turn back, lights flashed—low-beam headlights. A small car drove into view, scuffing the sandy driveway as it skidded to a stop. The driver jumped out—a tall, muscular guy wearing a tight gray sweatshirt. With his oversized hood pulled up, shadows covered his face, though billows of white puffed from within. Obviously it was a cold evening on Earth Blue. Maybe the freakish weather had invaded this dimension as well.

As the driver moved to the back of the car, the trunk popped open. He withdrew a square white box, about the size of a small toaster oven. Pausing for a moment, he leaned over and peered into the car's window as if looking for something on the backseat.

He suddenly jerked his head around. Another set of headlights flashed into his face. He raised a forearm to shield his eyes, then, ducking his head low, rushed to the observatory.

A black Mustang convertible screeched into view and smacked into the side of the smaller car. The Mustang driver leaped out, carrying a double-barrel shotgun at his hip.

A HERO'S GIFT

Nathan crouched and squeezed his body against the corner next to the hinges. Since the hall was barely wider than the entryway, there was nowhere else to go.

The security pad beeped four times. As the lock disengaged, twin shotgun blasts ripped into the metallic entrance, sounding like a thousand pebbles thrashing an aluminum garbage can. Something thudded against the door, swinging it open. The sweatshirt-clad man fell into the hallway, still clutching the white box, now smeared with red. Lying facedown across the threshold, his buckshot-riddled body held the door open. Blood spread across the back of his sweatshirt, connecting the dozens of holes in a wash of muted scarlet.

Nathan leaped toward him and looked out the door. The attacker had broken the shotgun open and was reloading the barrels. Grabbing the victim's wrists, Nathan pulled, but something caught. He couldn't budge the hefty man.

Groaning, the man looked up at him. "Nathan? You really *are* alive!"

Nathan dropped to his knees. "Mr. Clark? Tony Clark?"

Tony slid the box into Nathan's hands. "Clara sent this to your father. She said it might be his only hope."

The gunman snapped the barrels back in place and stalked toward them. Tony pushed against the floor, and, with Nathan's help, was able to rise to his feet. Staggering in place, he pushed

Nathan to the side. "Go! I'll hold him off!" He pulled away from Nathan's grip, took a long stride out the door, and slammed it shut.

Tony's distinctive voice penetrated the metal barrier. "Back off, Jack!"

Like booming thunder, the shotgun replied with two volleys. More pellets rained on the door, followed by a thud and the scraping sound of Tony's body sliding down the outer side.

Nathan clutched his stomach but kept silent, not daring even to breathe. He slowly eased toward the door's window and peeked through the glass. His heart pounded. Tony lay motionless in front of the door, his chest now a ragged mess of bloody, shredded cotton. Not a hint of movement. He had to be dead.

The Mustang driver, his shotgun again at his hip, stalked toward him. Although he also wore a hooded sweatshirt, the light passed across his bearded face, making the details clear.

Nathan gulped. It was the same driver from Earth Red that broke into the Clarks' house! Or was this guy the Earth Blue version?

He ducked back into the corner and fixed his gaze on the bloodstained box in his hands. The doorknob rattled. Nathan scrunched lower and looked up. The man pressed his face against the window, making his nose look pink and bulbous. With a grunt, he thrust his shoulder against the door, but it wouldn't budge.

Inching forward in a painful crouch, Nathan held the box in one arm and kept the mirror in front of him with his other hand, allowing him to see the window while staying as low as possible. Suddenly, the butt of a shotgun smashed through the glass, sending a shower of sharp pellets over Nathan's back. The man stuck his long arm through and stretched for the doorknob, but it was just out of reach of his groping fingers.

When the man pulled his arm back outside, Nathan waited and listened. The mirror continued reflecting reality, nothing that would help him decide what to do. A cold draft descended from the shattered window, carrying with it the man's low voice, grumbles peppered with obscenities. Seconds later, a clacking noise cut into the sounds.

Nathan cringed. Was he reloading? Would he try to shoot through the door? Nathan eyed the box again. Tony's words echoed in his mind. *Clara sent this to your father. She said it might be his only hope.* Taking a deep breath, he nodded. It was now or never. He lunged forward and sprinted down the hall.

"Hey!" the man shouted. "Wait!"

Nathan shivered. Would a shotgun blast follow the killer's call? Just as he turned the corner toward the stairwell, a blast of pellets smashed the wall, ripping a wide hole at the intersection of the *T* where the two hallways met. The gun's echoing boom immediately followed.

Kelly and Francesca rushed from the stairwell. "What was that?" Kelly asked as she grabbed the violin case from the floor.

"Someone shot the guy who delivered this box." Nathan showed it to her. He couldn't tell her who the deliveryman was, at least not yet. He needed her to stay calm.

Tucking the box under his arm again, he edged toward the exit corridor, gesturing for the girls to stay close. "As soon as we hear another gunshot," he whispered, "we're running for the door to the secure area. No looking back. He's probably going to shoot out the lock and come after us, but he'll have to reload before he can shoot again."

"What if the code's different?"

"Then get ready for some unexpected ventilation!"

The shotgun boomed. They rushed across the exit hall and scrambled down the additional twenty feet or so of their own corridor.

"I'll watch the mirror," Nathan said, holding it up. "You punch in the code."

Kelly gave Francesca the violin and raised a trembling hand to the keypad. "What were the numbers again?"

"Nine, three, eight, zero." Bracing the mirror in one hand and pressing the box against his opposite side, he watched the area behind him in the reflection.

She pushed the numbers. "Nothing happened! He's going to get us!"

"Maybe not. I see two people way down the hall who aren't really there yet, so the mirror's working. And I don't see the shotgun guy anywhere."

"What should I try next?"

Nathan looked up at the ceiling, trying to invent a new string with the pattern he had noticed. "How about ... seven, five, six, two?"

She pressed through the digits, then balled up her fist and cursed. "I messed up!"

"Try again." He showed her the mirror. "We still have time. Maybe he didn't break the lock."

"I hear footsteps!" Francesca said.

"I don't see him yet, but the other two guys in the mirror are almost here!"

Francesca pointed down their hallway. "Do you mean them?"

Nathan spun around. Two guards carrying scoped rifles dashed toward them from the far end of the hallway.

Kelly grabbed Nathan's arm. "They must have heard the gunshots!"

The guards slowed to a trot and aimed their guns. "Put your hands up!" one of them ordered.

"What do we do?"

Nathan spoke in a calm tone. "Just press the buttons."

Another shotgun blast sounded from the exit hallway. The guards halted just before the intersection and dropped to their haunches.

Nathan clenched a fist. The guards' timing was perfect! "There's a guy breaking in!" he yelled. "He has a shotgun! We've been trying to get away!"

One of the guards touched the other on the shoulder. "Cover me, Dave!" Lowering his head, he charged toward the exit. The other guard stood and fired round after round toward the door, aiming high enough to miss his partner.

The shotgun sounded again, followed by the clanking racket of a door banging open. The second guard rushed toward the exit.

Nathan kept the mirror in place. "Now, Kelly! Now!"

Two more weapons fired, a rifle and a shotgun.

Kelly flinched. "What were the numbers again?"

A deep voice from the hallway cried, "Dave! Dave!"

"Seven, five, six, two!" The Mustang driver appeared in the mirror, but Nathan dared not tell Kelly.

Another shotgun blast. A man groaned. A single set of footsteps approached, slow and labored.

Kelly punched in the numbers. The lock buzzed. She flung the door open, and the three bustled through. Nathan jerked it closed and took the violin case from Francesca. "Flatten!" he whispered, pushing the girls down.

Kelly arched facedown over Francesca, bracing her weight on her elbows. Moving quickly, Nathan leaned the mirror and violin against the wall and shoved the box against the floor molding. He huddled over both girls and pushed them sideways against the bottom of the door. "Hold your breath," he whispered. Inwardly he cringed. If the guy thought they were inside, he could just blast through.

The sound of stomping feet drew nearer, out-of-rhythm footfalls that slowed as they approached. Kelly's body trembled. Francesca's fingers dug into Kelly's arms.

Something slapped against the door. A few seconds later, beeps sounded from the security keypad, but the lock stayed quiet. A deep groan filtered through the wall, then some muttered cursing and more uneven footfalls. Finally, there was silence.

Nathan let out his breath slowly, and the girls did the same. Still on his knees, he straightened his torso and angled his head to get a furtive glance at the window. A bloody handprint smeared the glass.

Picking up the mirror, he rose to his feet and looked out. Nobody was there. He reached a hand to each of the girls. "Coast is clear."

When they pulled up, Kelly threw her arms around Nathan's neck and held him close. "I'm sorry I lost my cool," she whispered.

Her body brought a surge of warmth to his damp skin. "You did great. We made it, didn't we?" He handed Kelly the mirror and picked up the violin and box.

"What's in it?" she asked, touching the box's blood-spattered top.

He looked it over, searching for a way to open it. "We'll figure it out later. Right now we have to check if my mother's in the same room where they kept Clara and Francesca prisoner."

With Nathan leading the way, the three marched quickly through the curving hallway. When they reached the door, Nathan paused, looked down the corridor both ways, and rapped lightly. Setting his ear close, he held his breath and listened. No answer.

Kelly put her mouth near the jamb and spoke into the gap. "Mrs. Shepherd? Are you in there?" Still no answer.

Nathan reached for the keypad, punching numbers: eight, four, seven, one. The lock clicked. He jerked the door open, revealing a dark room.

Kelly reached in and swiped her fingers across the wall. Dim lights on the ceiling flickered to life.

Nathan peered inside. The room, about twelve-by-twelve

feet, held only a short wooden stool, a green beanbag chair, and a few scattered sheets of paper. On one of the carved stone walls, four chains dangled from rings embedded at points spaced roughly where hands and feet could be locked in place. Obviously this was where his father had been hanging, causing him to send moans of pain across dimensional boundaries and into Kelly's ears.

While Nathan propped the door with his foot, Kelly walked in and touched one of the shiny chains. "If Mictar wants to kill your parents, why the torture?"

"He wants the secret of Quattro. At least that's what he said to Mom." He picked up one of the sheets of paper near the door and read the beautiful script, definitely his mother's handwriting. Maybe there would be a clue to where they had taken her. "Let's gather these up and get out of here."

As he kept watch down the hallway, Kelly and Francesca collected the sheets of paper and brought them back to him.

"Here's a stub of a pencil I found," Kelly said, holding it in her fingertips. "I'll bet one of your parents used it."

Francesca showed him the top page. "This looks a lot like my handwriting. Whoever wrote this puts little swirls on the ends of words just like I do."

Setting down the box and mirror, he took the rest of the pages and smiled at Francesca. "I guess your writing is a lot like my mom's." He thumbed through the pages until he found one with bolder strokes and darker, more hurried letters. "My dad wrote this one."

"What do they say?" Kelly asked.

He flipped to the next page and shook his head. "It looks like a bunch of rambling nonsense, so I'm guessing it's all in code. We have to find a safe, quiet place to decipher it."

"And get that open," she said, pointing at the box on the floor.

Nathan leaned farther into the hallway, but he couldn't see

around the curve. "I think we should stay in the secure area. With that murderer stomping around out there, I don't think anywhere else is safe."

Kelly winked at him. "Is there a ladies room in this hall?"

Holding the white box in his lap, Nathan sat on the floor next to Francesca, his back against the cool, tiled wall. Kelly, standing with her back to him, held a handful of paper towels under the running faucet until they were moist. After turning and giving them to Francesca, she pulled another towel from the dispenser. "Want to wash your face, Nathan?"

"In a minute." He gave the box a light shake, but nothing rattled inside. "Maybe I could open it like I did my trunk . . . you know, look at it in the mirror."

While dabbing her forehead with a moistened towel, Kelly sat on his other side with the violin case between them.

A low boom thundered from somewhere in the distance.

Kelly flinched. "It seems like we're just waiting for him to find us."

"At least the noise lets us know how far away he is."

"Oh, thanks. Now *that's* a comforting thought." Kelly wadded her towel and tossed it at the wastebasket across the room. It sailed right in and thudded at the bottom. "I wonder if Clara and Daryl got away in our dimension."

"Yeah, I was just wondering about that, too." He nodded at the bathroom exit. "We could try to go back, but who knows who might be there? And I don't want to leave without finding my parents."

Kelly laid a hand on his arm. "Don't forget. They might not be your real parents. They might be from this dimension."

"Yeah. I remember." He drooped his head. Did it matter which dimension they were from? They didn't look any different or act any different. What would Kelly think if she knew her Earth Blue father just got blasted by a shotgun? Would it make a difference to her? Probably not. No matter how much she didn't like what he did, she'd be devastated. It wasn't a good time to tell her. Not yet.

Francesca threw her wadded towel toward the wastebasket, but it hit the side and fell to the floor. She let out a sigh and gazed at Nathan. "When are you going to tell me what's going on?" she asked. "I figured out some of it, but I'm confused about a lot of things."

Nathan swiveled his head toward her. "You're not the only one who's confused, but if you ask some questions, maybe I can answer them."

She ran her finger along her tunic's embroidered hem. "I haven't said much, because I was too scared, and all this stuff you're saying about different dimensions makes it worse. Not only that, while I was playing, I saw some things I've seen before in my nightmares, but this time I felt like I was really there. I stood next to a huge violin and bow lying on the ground, big enough for a giant, and a normal-sized man walked up and told me I had to play it to live. When I reached for the bow, the ground collapsed. As I fell, the violin and bow fell with me. I caught the bow, and pushed it toward the strings, but just as I played the first note, I was back with you. That's when I always wake up from the dream."

She took a deep breath and continued. "Anyway, after listening to everyone talk, I figured out that there are three dimensions. Both of you are from one, I'm from another, and this is the third one."

"That's right," Nathan said. "Very good."

"But one thing doesn't make sense. You're looking for your mother, but you think I'm your mother."

Nathan slid his hand under hers. When she accepted his grasp, he cleared his throat and spoke slowly. "You're going to be the mother of my counterpart in your dimension, which happens to be behind mine in the flow of time. This one we're in now is ahead of mine by five days."

"But if there are only three dimensions, how do you see stuff in your mirror before it happens even when we're in this one?" Francesca lifted her hand again, now displaying four fingers. "Wouldn't that mean there has to be a fourth dimension?"

Nathan thought for a moment. "That's right ..."

Kelly rose to her knees. "The kid's a smart one."

"What do you expect?" Nathan said, grinning. "She's my mom."

Francesca blushed. "I'm not your mom, silly. I'm only ten."

Reaching across Nathan, Kelly patted Francesca's hand. "Don't you listen to him, sweetheart. Just have fun being a girl, and forget about being a mom."

Nathan raised four fingers of his own. "I wonder if Gordon and Mictar believe there's a fourth dimension."

"They already know about the three," Kelly said, "so, since *cuatro* means four in Spanish, they probably believe it."

"My father had a project he called Quattro, and he spelled it with a Q. He probably knows a lot more about it than they do, and they're trying to turn the screws on him." He looked at the mirror in his hands. It had come through for them at every dangerous turn. No wonder his father wanted him to look at it in times of trouble. It really worked. So was it the key to the secret of Quattro? Did his father want to keep it out of his own hands, knowing he might get captured?

Still, there were problems with the fourth dimension theory. After all they'd been through, whenever the mirror worked one of its miracles, instead of going to a fourth dimension, they always stayed in the dimension they were in already. And what about the blue and yellow dimensions? If they had Quattro mirrors, would they show fifth and sixth dimensions? He sighed. Too many questions. It was time to bounce it off another brain.

"Wouldn't my mirror also be in this dimension?" he asked Kelly. "If Gordon and Mictar knew about it, wouldn't they do anything to get it? And if they already killed us in this dimension, they should have been able to take it from me."

"Unless you didn't have it with you when you died. Remember what Gordon said when he searched our bodies ... I mean, the other Nathan and Kelly bodies? He was upset that the other Nathan didn't bring something with him. The other Nathan said something about it being locked up forever." She picked up the box. "Want to bet it's in here?"

"Could be." Nathan stared at the bloodstained surface, imagining the square of polished glass sitting inside. So Tony wanted Dad to have the mirror, but how could he open the box? Wouldn't he need a Quattro mirror to get to it in the first place? It was like having a treasure chest, and the key was locked inside. Still, maybe this box wasn't as impenetrable as his trunk. Whoever sealed it up must have thought Dad could figure out how to open it. Unless, somehow, Tony knew someone was already there with a mirror. But how could that be?

Kelly pulled a barrette from her hair, causing her locks to fall over her eyes. "I think I see something. If I can just get rid of a little of this blood." Biting her partially protruding tongue, she scraped the barrette against the surface. "I got it." She held the box close to the light fixture on the wall and squinted. "It says, 'To Flash, from Medusa.' Does that mean Clara sent it?"

"I guess that fits." Nathan brushed the dried blood away. "But how could she know where to take it?"

Another shotgun blast thundered in the distance, louder than before.

Kelly rubbed her goose-bump-covered arms. "Let's just try to get it open."

Rising to his knees, Nathan turned toward the wall and leaned his mirror against it. If it worked like last time, he would have to look in the mirror and watch the box. If it opened, then he could guide his mirror hands into it and take out whatever was inside.

He slid the box a couple of feet in front of the mirror, which reflected the blood-splotched container perfectly, including its unopened state.

"Nothing's happening yet." He picked up the stack of paper and sat down. While they were waiting, maybe he could decipher his parents' words. Good thing the pages were numbered. He rifled through the sheets until he found page one, then gave the rest to Kelly. "Can you sort these while I work on this one?"

"Sure." She divided the stack and handed half to Francesca. "Want to help?"

Francesca grinned. "Anything for my son."

He returned the grin. "Cool it, Mom." Settling back against the wall, he dug the pencil stub out of his pocket and underlined every three-syllable word on the page. He and his father had often used this quick algorithm for handwritten notes. The last letter in the first underlined word would be the first letter in the decrypted note. The second to last letter in the next word would follow, and so on. When he reached the beginning letter of a word, he would start again with the last letter of the next three-syllable word.

He pointed at the first word. *Royalty.* He jotted *Y* down in the margin. The next word was *pollution,* so the second letter was O. Next came *interrupt,* so the letter was *U.*

He continued the tedious process, penciling the letters neatly around the margin, adding hyphens where he thought the words might break. When Kelly handed him the second page, he copied his letter string on the back of the first sheet and used it for his decoded message from that point on.

From time to time, he glanced at the mirror, but the box was always closed. As he grew tired, he paused after every deciphered word, leaning his head back and closing his eyes for a few seconds. Two more shotgun blasts, each one louder than the others, brought new chills, but he stayed calm and worked slowly. He couldn't afford to make a mistake. One missed three-syllable word or a miscounted letter would ruin the entire decryption. He resisted the urge to read the message, forcing himself to move on letter by letter. Not knowing what it said would force him to work faster.

Kelly's yawns grew frequent, and Francesca fell asleep on the floor, but Nathan had to keep going. Finally, he took a deep breath and set down the last page. "Okay, let's see what we've got."

Kelly scooted over and looked on.

He read, barely whispering the words. "Your goal, stop Mictar from making interfinity, collision of dimensions. Trust Gordon Red, not Gordon Blue. Trust Simon Red. Unsure of Simon Blue. We are your parents from other dimension, not your real ones. Help us escape to stop Mictar, but get to the funeral on Earth Red."

Nathan let the page slip from his fingers. Taking a deep breath, he tried to speak, but his throat clamped shut. Mom and Dad really were dead.

Kelly rubbed his shoulder. "Oh, Nathan. I'm so sorry."

He leaned his head against the tiles and squeezed his eyelids closed. As tears seeped out, he bit his lip hard, fighting back a spasm. After taking a quick breath, he choked out, "I really thought ... I could find them ... I still hoped they were alive."

She slid her hand into his, interlocking their thumbs. "But we can still save the other Nathan's parents."

"I know," he said, blinking away the tears, "but the other Nathan is dead. I'd be an orphan, and they'd be childless."

She brushed her fingers across his knuckles. "I guess, if you want, you could trade places. You could be their son, and you'd have new parents."

"It wouldn't be the same, and you know it."

"Maybe I don't know it." She released his hand and folded

hers in her lap. "I'd take your parents from the other dimension any day."

He gazed into her sad eyes. "I guess I can't blame you for that. You have it pretty rough."

As a flush of red colored her cheeks, her voice sharpened. "You don't know the half of it! He makes me play basketball with guys more than a foot taller than me, and when I get punched in the face, he laughs and makes fun of me if I cry. Last year, when he wanted Steven on the team, he practically made me go out with him, and he even picked out this low-cut dress for me to wear." She laid her hands on her breasts. "I guess he notices I'm a girl only when it's convenient for him."

Nathan waved for her to lower her hands. "I get the picture. You don't have to do that."

She sighed and returned her hands to her lap. "And you already know he brings women home, even though he and Mom aren't divorced yet."

"Yeah." He lowered his head. "That's pretty bad. I'm sorry."

She touched his knee with her fingers. "Don't be. It's his fault, and nobody else's."

Nathan watched her fingers. Still slightly dirty from cleaning the spark plugs, her gentle caress spoke volumes. Again, this strange blending of femininity and toughness enchanted him. "I guess I always hope that people can change, you know, decide to reform. Maybe your father has a spark of ... chivalry, I guess you could say. We just have to find it and help it grow."

"My dad?" She rolled her eyes. "Get real. He's so stubborn, he makes mules look compliant. To him, chivalry means not belching quite so loud when women are around."

He closed his eyes. One comment she made attached itself to his brain and wouldn't let go. He just had to ask. After a few seconds, he looked at her again. "Can I ask you one question?"

"As long as I'm spilling my guts, you might as well."

He spoke softly, trying hard to convey a tone of sympathy. "That dress ... the low-cut one. Did you wear it?"

Kelly tightened her clasped hands. Her cheeks flushed again as she whispered, "I wore it."

"Because your dad made you wear it?"

Now focusing on her lap, she shook her head. "To be honest, I liked it. I knew it was wrong, and I knew my father shouldn't be using me that way, but I liked how I felt when I wore it. I liked the way Steven looked at me."

He tried to gain eye contact as he softened his tone even further. "Would you wear it now?"

As she looked up at him, a tear made its way toward her cheek. "During the summer, my father was playing an away game in his summer league, so I went out with some girlfriends to the mall in Des Moines, and I saw my mother in a restaurant with a guy I didn't recognize." She lowered her head again. Tears dripped to her jeans as her voice trembled and pitched higher. "She was wearing my dress, and the guy was staring at her, but not at her eyes. I wanted to scream, 'Mother! What are you doing? Are you some kind of hooker?'" Raising her head, she pointed at herself. "But then I realized that I was the hooker. I was the one trying to hook a guy into doing something by giving him a look at my ..." She glanced at Francesca, who was now stirring. "My body."

"So what did you do?"

"When my mother got home and went to bed, I sneaked into her room and took back my dress. I burned it the next morning."

Nathan couldn't stop a smile from breaking through. "You burned it?"

"It was kind of ceremonial. I went to the backyard and laid it over some dried cornstalks along with this skimpy tank top I had and set it all on fire. Then I buried the ashes and stomped on their grave." She, too, let a thin smile turn her lips. "I swore out loud that I wasn't going to be like my mother, so I started replacing my wardrobe bit by bit. And when I met you, it made me more determined than ever."

He set a finger on his chest. "*I* made you determined? How?"

"Nathan, don't make me get all sensitive and sappy. I've bared my soul enough for one day."

He took her hand and raised it to his lips. After giving her a soft peck on her knuckles, he said, "You gave me a great compliment. You don't have to explain it."

As he let go of her hand, her cheeks turned redder than ever, but she just stared at him and said nothing.

Pushing his hands behind his head, he peeked at Francesca, who snoozed without a care. "So I guess people *can* change," he said. "Even your father."

"You don't know him like I do."

"How can you be so sure? He might—"

"Nathan!" Kelly pointed at the mirror.

He spun around on his knees. "The box is open!"

NEW FRIENDS, OLD FRIENDS

Kelly laid her hand on top of the real box. In the mirror, her fingers passed right through the flipped-up lid and stopped at the opening. "That's creepy."

Sliding forward, Nathan pushed close enough to the mirror to get one knee on each side of the box while staying in view of the reflected image. "Okay. Just like with the trunk, don't look at the real box while I do this."

"Gotcha."

While staring at the reflection, he leaned forward, moving his field of vision until the real box was out of sight. He guided his mirror hands over the bloodstained top, which opened away from his body, blocking a view of what was inside. He reached in and felt something flat, smooth, and glassy, just like the mirror, but as he slid his fingers farther down, they came across something unexpected, something more tactile and bulky.

He grasped the bulky object and, lifting carefully, placed the contents on the floor. Then, he picked up the box and turned it over, hoping to dump out anything left inside. After closing his eyes for a brief moment, he set the box down and looked at it on the floor rather than in the mirror. As expected, it was closed.

He pushed the box, now much lighter, out of the way. A mirror identical to the other one leaned against his thigh. His father's camera was attached to the back, secured by at least three layers of duct tape. He picked up the package and showed it to Kelly.

As she touched the silvery tape, her lips twitched. "Who would attach a camera to a mirror with duct tape?"

"Kind of strange, isn't it?" He looked up at her. Had she figured out who really brought it? As he carefully peeled the tape and rubbed away the glue residue from the mirror, he focused on his work, not wanting to face Kelly's piercing stare. He didn't even want to think about the possibilities, just in case she could somehow read his mind. "So," he said, still rubbing away glue, "if someone wanted us to get this stuff to the other Nathan's parents, we'd better start looking for them again."

"What about the shotgun guy?"

"It's been quiet for a while. The way he was bleeding, he might be dead by now."

"So if your parents aren't in that room with the chains, where else could they be?"

Nathan searched her eyes, so inquisitive, so sincere. Since he had the benefit of knowing what happened to her Earth Blue father, shouldn't she have the same benefit? It would be tough, but she could handle it. He motioned toward the hall with his thumb. "Let's see what we can find out."

Less than a minute later, Nathan pushed open the door to the secure area, carrying the violin case and both mirrors, while Kelly, wearing the camera strap around her neck, led the bleary-eyed Francesca by the hand. After padding quietly through the hallways and stepping over the two dead guards, they approached the back door. A breeze poured through a basketball-sized hole that perforated the jamb and panel where the lock used to be. The door swung open an inch or so, making the hinges squeak a soft complaint, then thudded shut again. As it repeated the opening and closing cycle, the hallway appeared to be breathing.

Nathan set down his load and pulled the door open. Bloodstains smeared the threshold and the concrete pad on the outside, but Tony's body and his car were gone.

Suddenly, headlight beams swept across the lawn and aimed their way. Nathan hustled the girls back inside and pushed them into the same corner he had hidden in. As he eased the door closed, he kept watch through the shattered window. It looked like the same car Kelly's father drove, but it was too dark to tell.

Kelly bolted from the corner and peered through the hole in the jamb. "That's our Camry!"

As the car turned under the light that radiated from the fixture on the wall, the driver's face came into view. "Clara!" Nathan whispered. He swung the door open and ran outside.

The car stopped abruptly. Clara jumped out and embraced him. "Oh, Nathan! It's really you!" She laid her hand behind his head and pulled him close, her entire body shaking. "My dear boy! I thought I'd never see you again!"

The passenger door opened, and Daryl emerged, shivering in her gray hoodie. When she saw Kelly, her eyes shot open. "You're here!"

Kelly spread out her hands and smiled. "In the flesh."

Daryl ran around the car and wrapped her arms around Kelly. "I can't believe you're both alive!"

Nathan allowed Clara to enjoy the embrace, not wanting to remind her that he wasn't the Nathan she remembered. Still, there was too much to do. He pulled back slowly and looked into Clara's glistening eyes. Dried tear tracks stained her cheeks. "Are you all right?" he asked.

She brushed away a new tear. "Many terrible events have taken place, but as soon as I gather my wits, I will explain."

"Right. We all have to get our bearings." He nodded at Kelly. "We're from another dimension, and you're—"

"We're from Earth Blue," Daryl interrupted, "while you're from Earth Red. The other Daryl explained it all to me."

He narrowed his eyes at her. "The Earth Red Daryl contacted you? How?"

"Apparently Interfinity has a rudimentary network connection between the dimensions. It's not like they can browse the web from another dimension, but Daryl Red figured out how to send me an email." She grinned broadly. "I'm so proud of her!"

Kelly's stare riveted on the Camry. Her voice took on a slight tremble. "So did the other Daryl tell you to bring the mirror and the camera to us?"

"We were trying to get them to your parents ... or the other Nathan's parents, I guess." Daryl shook her head, making her red hair fly in the breeze. "It's all so confusing, but Daryl Red gave me the code for that door, so we thought we could get it done."

Kelly cleared her throat. Punctuated by suppressed sobs, her words broke into shattered pieces. "Who ... who brought ... the box ... to the door?"

While Daryl embraced Kelly again, Clara grasped Nathan's arm and led him to the Camry, whispering, "We put him in the backseat, but I wanted to show you first."

Nathan peered through the window. Tony's body lay face up on the blood-soaked fabric, his sweatshirt ripped and still dripping red. Even though he had already seen this carnage, a gut-wrenching pain stabbed his heart. He looked back at Kelly.

She turned his way, her bottom lip trembling. "Is it ... Is it him?"

Before he could answer, she tore away from Daryl's arms and rushed to the car, but he grabbed her before she could look. "Brace yourself. It's really horrible."

She jerked from his grip and pressed a palm against the window. As her hand smeared the glass, her voice squeaked, "Daddy?"

Clara laid her hands on Kelly's shoulders. "He's not—"

Her body stiffening, Kelly banged her fist on the glass and cried out, "Daddy!"

Clara slapped her palm over Kelly's mouth. "Quiet!" Pulling her away from the window, she turned Kelly toward her, grasping her upper arm firmly. "He's not your father," she said, keeping one hand over Kelly's lips. "He *is* Tony Clark, but he's the Tony Clark in this dimension, not yours."

As Kelly stared at Clara, her eyes grew big.

"Do you understand?" Clara asked.

With her mouth still covered, Kelly gave her a weak nod.

Clara slowly lifted her fingers and motioned for everyone to move close to the building where a dark shadow shrouded them. As they huddled, she spoke softly, her eyes constantly darting around. "Here is what we know, or at least, think we know. In this dimension, Nathan and Kelly are dead, and now Tony is, too, so it's clear that whoever wanted that box will murder any-one who stands in his way. From what we gathered from Daryl Red and Clara Red, Nathan Red's parents are also dead, but their counterparts are alive in this dimension, probably prison-ers somewhere in the observatory. We knew enough about the Quattro mirror to realize that if Solomon had it, he could use it to escape. The idea was to get it to Nathan Red so he could open it with his mirror, and he'd get it to Solomon somehow.

"Nathan Blue had hidden the mirror and camera in a bus depot locker in Chicago, so, since we were already in town for Nathan's funeral, we brought them to the observatory. Tony insisted on going to the door alone while Daryl and I hunkered down in the car, but, as you know, he didn't make it. When the murderer went in, we dragged Tony's body to the car and parked under the trees where no one could see us, but where we still had a view of the back door. Since Tony was already dead, there was no use rushing him to the hospital. We had caught a glimpse of you taking the box, so we decided to wait and see if you would come back out. When you did, we came out of hiding."

"Why did Nathan Blue hide them in the box?" Nathan asked. "And how did he get them in there?"

"He decided the risk of the camera and mirror falling into the wrong hands was too great, so he put them in a metal box, and Tony welded the lid shut. Then, if anyone saw the box, they wouldn't think anything was inside."

"And if you needed to," Nathan said, nodding slowly, "you could always break in again."

"Exactly. So, since you know how to get into the box, and Solomon knows how to use the camera and the mirror, we hoped you could get it to him so he could escape or transport himself and Francesca out of there."

"You mean the other me, right?" Francesca asked.

Clara gave Nathan a sharp stare. "Where are your manners, Nathan? You haven't introduced us to this young lady yet."

"Didn't Daryl Red tell you about her?"

"She mentioned a girl but not who she is. She looks quite familiar."

Nathan set a hand on Francesca's shoulder. "This is Francesca, my mother from Earth Yellow. You probably already know that dimension's quite a few years behind ours."

"Then she's not your mother," Clara said. "She's the future Nathan Yellow's mother."

"I know. It's just easier this way." He patted Francesca's head. "Right, Mom?"

Francesca grinned and looked up at him. "Right, Son."

Clara reached for Francesca's hand. "My name is Clara. I'm pleased to meet you."

Francesca smiled meekly. "Pleased to meet you, too."

"We'd better get going." Nathan slid his fingers around Kelly's arm and gave her a light pull, but she didn't budge. Her gaze was locked again on the car. "Kelly," he said softly. "Are you all right?"

Her lips barely moving, Kelly whispered, "I just realized something."

"What?"

She turned to him. "He's a hero, isn't he?"

"Definitely. He gave his life trying to help us. Even after he'd been shot once, he blocked the door to keep the shooter away from me."

Her jaw suddenly tightening, Kelly turned away and pulled in her bottom lip.

Nathan winced. She was hurt that he hadn't told her. He had kept an important secret from her, the very person he had promised to trust. "I'm sorry," he said. "I was just trying to protect you. I wasn't sure what to do."

She let out a deep sigh. "It's okay. I understand. I haven't exactly been Miss Calm and Collected." She glanced at the three other females. "Do you think all people in this dimension are exactly the same as in ours?"

Nathan slid his hand from Kelly's arm down to her fingers and interlaced them with his own. "I think they are. Clara and Daryl are just like they are at home, and it sounds like the other Nathan and Kelly were just like us."

Her fingers tightened. "So maybe my father ..." Her voice faded away.

"Really is a hero?" He gazed into her shadowed eyes. "I think your real father would have done exactly the same thing."

She tightened her grip on his hand once more before pulling away. "Thanks. I know you really mean that."

"Come on. We have to search the building without being seen by the nut job with the shotgun."

Daryl ran ahead and pushed open the door. "What are we waiting for? I want to see the cool telescope room my new best friend told me about."

Once inside, Kelly picked up the violin case while Nathan tucked both mirrors under his arm. "So on to the telescope room?" he asked.

Clara pointed toward the domed part of the building. "It's the best place to find clues."

"What if Mictar's gang is there?"

"They're not." Daryl held up a wide-screen cell phone. "Portable email. Daryl Red's keeping me up-to-date. She and Clara figured out how to monitor our dimension's telescope room from their dimension, and it looks clear."

Keeping a careful watch for the shotgun man, they skulked into the secure area and stopped to check the prisoner room again. Finding it still empty, they continued to the elevator.

"We'll have to go in shifts," Nathan said, as he punched six, six, five, three into the security pad and pushed the call button. Fortunately, the Earth Red code worked for this elevator, too. "Kelly and I will go first, then Clara, Daryl, and Francesca."

When the door opened, Nathan and Kelly stepped inside. Once in the car, he bent over and spoke to Francesca. "Mom, please make sure these two stay quiet and out of sight. Okay?"

A wide grin stretched across her lovely face. "You got it, kiddo!"

He pushed the button for the third floor. As the door began to slide shut again, Daryl raised her cell phone and looked at the screen but disappeared from sight before she could tell them what it said.

When the car lurched upward, the camera dangling from Kelly's neck swayed. Nathan turned to face the other door. "I wonder if she got a message from the other world."

"Maybe." Kelly turned with him and leaned her head against his shoulder. "It's so amazing," she whispered. "My father was a hero."

Nathan squeezed the mirrors against his side and smiled. As the elevator motor hummed along, a muffled call sounded from below. "He's up there!"

Nathan pressed his hand against the wall. There was no place to hide. And the man would hear the elevator, so he'd know someone was coming.

Kelly backed into a corner, holding on to the violin case with both hands. "What do we do?"

He pulled out his mirrors, pressed them together as one, and angled them toward the door. In the image, the door opened, revealing the murderer with the shotgun aimed directly into the elevator car. The reflected Nathan leaped at him with a high leg kick, deflecting the gun just at it fired. The force of the blow knocked their attacker to the floor.

Kelly eyed the scene. "How are you going to do that if you're watching the reflection?"

He extended the mirrors toward her. "You hold them."

She set the violin case down and held the mirrors with a firm grip. "Like this?" she asked, setting them slightly to the side.

"That should work." The car ground to a halt. "Get ready."

She cringed. "How?"

"Pray real hard."

"All I know is 'Our Father.'"

"That'll do." He pointed at the elevator's control panel, barely visible in the dim corner. The door slid to the side. Just as the man aimed the shotgun, Nathan leaped into a flying leg kick. His shoes struck the gun barrel, knocking its angle off kilter. A blast of orange erupted from the end, and a deafening crack ripped past Nathan's ears. The force of the kick threw the man onto his back.

Nathan lunged and draped himself over the shooter's body, grabbing the gun with both hands. The man offered little resistance as Nathan wrestled it away and leaped to his feet.

"Start talking." Nathan demanded, lifting the shotgun to his shoulder. "Who are you?"

As dim moonlight from the ceiling mirror cast a glow over the man's blood-covered face, he coughed and wheezed through his words. "Why ... do you care ... who I am?"

Kelly walked toward them, carrying the violin case. The elevator closed, and the motor restarted its quiet hum.

Nathan lowered the gun to his hip. "He's half dead."

She set the violin down but kept her fingers tight around the edge of the mirrors. "So he's the one who killed my father?"

"Yeah. I hope I can get some information before he dies."

The man coughed again, his breaths now gurgling as blood oozed from his nose and mouth. "Don't let ... Mictar have that mirror ... whatever you do."

"Why not? Why does he want it?"

"He needs it ... to merge the dimensions. Only interfinity ... will give him full control. Only that mirror ... can finish the job ... or stop his plan."

"Why did you want it? What would you do with it?"

"Destroy it ... so Mictar can't use it."

"Why are you trying to kill me?"

"Sacrifice is necessary ... to save billions of lives."

Nathan raised the shotgun to his shoulder again. His voice shook with rage as he cocked the hammer back. "That reason doesn't fly. I've never been in your way."

The man lifted three bloody fingers. "There are three mirrors ... one surviving Nathan ... and one yet to be born ... Only you and your mother ... have the power ... to call on Quattro ... so I ..."

"So you went to Earth Yellow with Mictar and Gordon to kill my mother before I could be born, didn't you? You took the burglar's place so you could find Francesca and murder her. And you killed Mrs. Romano."

His grin revealed a set of blood-covered teeth. "Smart boy."

"But how? If you're trying to stop Mictar, how can you use his mirrors to cross dimensions?"

The man's eyes began to roll wildly. "Kidnap one ... to get the secret ... then ..." He let out a long breath and closed his eyes.

Nathan stepped closer and focused on the man's face. It had stopped twitching, and his jaw had slackened. He extended the butt of the shotgun toward Kelly. "If you're not scared of guns, then cover me while I check him out."

"Are you kidding?" She set the mirrors down, grabbed the gun, and raised the butt to her shoulder. "My father taught me everything a son should know — basketball, spark plugs, and shotguns."

Nathan crouched and checked the man's pulse. "He's dead." Rising again, he took the gun back from Kelly. "I guess we'll leave his body for Mictar to clean up."

The elevator motor stopped. While Kelly picked up the mirrors, Nathan watched the door slide open. Clara, Daryl, and Francesca squeezed through, Daryl hustling in front as she headed for the computer screens on the worktables.

Nathan stood between Francesca and the dead attacker. "Keep her away. She shouldn't see this."

Clara set her hand at the side of Francesca's face and guided her toward Daryl, who was already busily tapping on a keyboard.

Pressing the mirrors against her side with one hand and carrying the violin case in the other, Kelly followed them, the camera still dangling at her chest. "I guess you must still be in contact with the other side."

"Hot line to the great beyond." Daryl pulled her cell phone from her belt and slid it onto the desk, making it spin slowly. "My twin told us about Nathan kicking that guy's butt. Now I need to sync her up on our mirror so we can talk face-to-face."

Nathan propped the gun on his shoulder and joined them. "Does Francesca have to play the music again?"

"No," Daryl replied, her gaze riveted on the laptop screen. "Daryl Red found a music generator that deciphers and plays the radio telescope's connecting feed. She's showing me how — Yep." She pointed at an icon in the lower left corner. "Here it is."

As she adjusted the control, the mirror above changed from

a starry sky to the mesmerizing array of colorful shapes they had seen before, each one vibrating and dancing to a cacophonous stream of musical notes played from speakers in the walls. Daryl's fingers flew from keyboard to mouse and back again. Seconds later, the notes blended into a perfect harmony of violins playing a ghostly tremolo and a French horn adding a subtle, restful flavor.

"It's Strauss's 'Blue Danube,'" Nathan said as he set the shotgun on the floor. Good thing the gun hadn't damaged the mirror. They'd be up the creek without a canoe *or* a paddle.

The shapes in the mirror broke apart and bled into each other, painting an aerial view of the telescope room floor. In the reflection, Clara seemed to be speaking, but no sound came through.

Daryl turned and waved at her likeness in the mirror above. "She's got good taste in clothes. I love that top."

Kelly smirked. "Maybe she'll let you borrow it."

Craning his neck, Nathan strained to listen. "Can anyone hear her?"

"I hear something," Francesca said. "Something about the funeral."

Daryl leaned close to the laptop screen. "Apparently Daryl Red hasn't figured out how to turn the voice volume up while the music's playing, so she's typing out Clara's words." She pointed at the advancing letters on the screen and read them out loud, pausing as she waited for whole words to appear. "You have to get back to Earth Red in time for the funeral. It's morning now, so the service is only a few hours away."

Nathan touched Francesca's shoulder. "Since Earth Yellow is catching up so fast in time, we have to get Francesca back, or her whole life will be messed up. She might never meet my father, and I'll never be born there."

Kelly set the mirrors on the desk. "Can we risk it? Your Earth Blue father said you had to be at the funeral on Earth Red. What if we get trapped on Earth Yellow or even just delayed?"

Clara looked up at the ceiling. "Maybe you should risk it. You can probably ruin one of Mictar's goals."

"What goal?" Nathan asked.

"If you time it right, you can go back to Earth Yellow and get the third mirror before Mictar does. He's sure to go after it."

"Good thought!" He spun back to Kelly. "What year did your father buy the mirror from the guy in Scotland?"

"About fifteen years ago. Not long after I was born, I think."

He stepped close to Daryl's workstation. "At the rate Earth Yellow is catching up, when will it get to fifteen years ago?"

Daryl squinted at the screen. "Impossible to tell. Sometimes it zips along, and sometimes it's just a little bit faster, but it still has about fourteen years to go. It's nineteen seventy-nine there right now."

"That raises an interesting question in my mind," Clara said. "What will happen to Francesca? I don't think she's aging here at her Earth Yellow rate, or else her body cycles would be crazy. But will she suddenly age if she goes home, or will she be younger than she's supposed to be?"

Nathan set his chin on his hand. "So if we don't take her back now, we might ruin her life. If we do, I might miss the funeral. And with either choice, I have to stop looking for my Earth Blue parents. Both choices really stink."

Kelly raised her hand. "I vote for Earth Yellow. If time is passing faster there than here, won't Earth Red kind of slow down while we get Francesca home? I mean, we'll have more time to get the job done, right?"

Nathan pointed at her. "She's brilliant!"

Still hanging on to the violin case, Kelly dipped her knee in a mock curtsy. "I humbly accept your accurate assessment of my intelligence."

Clara lifted her feet in turn. "I need some boots. The bovine manure is getting pretty deep in here."

"I'll adjust the settings," Daryl called out. "Earth Yellow coming right up!"

Kelly gazed at the ceiling. "Where will we go in Earth Yellow? Did this observatory even exist thirty years ago?"

"Great question." Nathan stood next to her and watched the mirror change. The chaotic rainbow of colors returned along with a new blend of dissonant noises. Soon, a harmony of notes emerged, and the scene above coalesced—a daytime view of a spring forest with windblown leaves plummeting to the ground, clouds racing overhead, and a squirrel scampering up a tree like a furry bullet.

He let out a low whistle. "That squirrel's had too much coffee!"

"Time's passing faster," Daryl explained. "I suppose it'll slow down for you when you get there."

Nathan searched the landscape but found no sign of civilization. "Do you think we'll come out where the observatory is going to be?"

"That's my guess." Daryl looked up at the forest. "Kind of out in the middle of nowhere, isn't it?"

"Yeah." He checked for his wallet. "At least I have money now, so maybe I can get some decent transportation back to Iowa."

"Do we stand in the middle of the room again?" Kelly asked.

Nathan hustled toward the telescope. "I'd better get the body out of the way." He grasped the corpse by the wrists and dragged him to the wall.

"Check his pockets," Clara called. "Maybe we can find a clue of some kind."

He searched the man's pants pockets and found four shotgun shells and a wallet. After rifling through the wallet, he kept a driver's license and a plastic card that was embedded with an odd set of letters and numbers. After pushing the wallet back into the man's pocket, he strode to Clara and set his findings on the desk. "If you have to leave, hide the shotgun and shells in the ladies' room downstairs, so we'll know where to find them when we get back."

Clara grabbed a rolling shotgun shell and stood it upright. "If we have to leave, you might have a hard time getting back."

"Maybe not," Daryl said. "The other Daryl might be able to get you home."

"And what if she has to hide, too?" Nathan asked.

"Stop being a worrywart. I found the security codes for all the doors. In fact, I can change them from here if I want to. Daryl Red has the codes there, too, so we can frustrate the bad guys for quite a while. They won't know the new codes."

Kelly shifted the violin case toward the cordoned-off entry door. "How did the shotgun guy get in here? It doesn't look like he blasted through."

"Maybe that door isn't secure." Daryl shifted back to her keyboard. "I'll get it locked down."

"Are you taking the mirrors?" Clara asked.

"I'll take one of them." He picked it up and tucked it under his arm. "If one of us gets caught, at least the other mirror will be safe."

Kelly reached for Francesca. "Let's go. We'll get a hot breakfast and find a place to sleep."

The girl yawned and meekly took Kelly's hand. "And a bath?"

"We'll see what we can do."

Nathan led Kelly and Francesca to the center of the room. Nodding toward the wall where the switches had been in Earth Red, he pressed the mirror against his chest. "Ready with the lights?"

Clara walked over to the switch. "Here we go!"

The trumpet fixtures on the perimeter wall flashed to life, sending white beams toward the ceiling that forked into dozens of semitranslucent shafts as they bounced from the apex. The shafts reshaped into brilliant vertical bars around the trio and again melted their surroundings.

Soon, the forest scene shaped itself around them. The racing clouds seemed to put on the brakes and slow to a reasonable speed. Instead of plunging like lead weights, green leaves began to float to the ground in meandering spirals, blown off their erratic paths by gusts of wind that chased the clouds above. The squirrel slowed as well, flicking its tail erratically as he looked on from his perch near the end of a branch.

In the distance, a bank of dark clouds spread a blanket across the sun, casting a deep shadow over the trio. Lightning flashed. The cloud-to-ground strike sent a rumbling boom across the forest and tremors under their feet. A few large raindrops pelted the leafy floor, making a crackling sound as they landed. A fresh breeze blew through Nathan's hair, cool and invigorating as it kicked up a swirl of dead leaves at his feet. They flew in a cyclonic waltz, blocking the freshness and surrounding them in a dreary blanket of decay.

He tried to peer through the flurry. He had seen this place before, the mirror's very first strange apparition back in his bedroom.

A sudden gust blew the leafy whirlwind away, clearing their view. To the right, a tri-fold mirror, twice Nathan's height and three times as wide as his arm span, stood upright, supported by four-by-four wooden posts embedded in the ground.

Shuffling through more dead leaves, the previous autumn's carpet that spring had not yet swept away, he stared at the seemingly impossible, but now familiar, reflection, an aerial view of the telescope room with Clara and Daryl waving at them from the computer desk. "Interfinity must have erected this here as their transportation dock for Earth Yellow."

While returning the wave, Kelly touched the right-hand panel. "I guess they thought of everything, didn't they?"

Holding out his palm to catch the spattering rain, Nathan squinted at the darkening sky. "Maybe, but we didn't think to bring an umbrella."

Francesca pointed toward the horizon. "Look!"

As the leaves kicked up again, Nathan bent over to follow her line of sight. A dark twisting funnel roared down from the approaching cloud bank. "It's a tornado! A big one!"

14

FINDING FRANCESCA

"It's coming toward us!" Kelly swiveled her head from side to side. "Which way to the road?"

Nathan pointed toward what appeared to be a trail, a narrow path with fewer leaves than the surrounding area. "That way!" He thrust the mirror toward her. "You take this." Scooping Francesca into his arms, he dashed along the path. As the wind whistled through the branches, leaves and twigs rained all around along with nickel-sized droplets that splashed on his hair and clothes. "Are you with me?" he called back to Kelly.

"Right behind you!"

Francesca stayed quiet, nuzzling her cheek against his neck, even as he leaped over protruding roots or a fallen tree. "We have to find a low area, a ditch or a rainwater trench!"

Kelly's hoarse voice battled the chaotic noise. "It's all flat!"

Glancing back, Nathan caught sight of the tornado again, an enormous black funnel of spinning fury. It churned through the forest like a wild monster, uprooting trees and spewing them into the sky. The deafening rumble drowned out nearly every other sound. Only the high pitch of Kelly's shouts managed to overcome the racket and find their way to his ears.

He spun around. "Give me the violin!"

Kelly sprinted toward him, reaching out the case. Without a word, he set Francesca down and took the violin, popping the latches while Kelly held up the mirror where he could see the raging demon behind them. As the tornado screamed closer, he jerked up his instrument and sawed the bow across the strings, playing a wild rendition of "Be Still My Soul."

The monstrous funnel drew so close, all he could see in the mirror was its black twisting wall as it tossed out dirt and debris. The wind blew a vicious slap that knocked Francesca to the ground. Hanging on to the mirror with both hands, Kelly straddled her and dropped to her knees to cover Francesca's shaking body while keeping the mirror in place.

With his back to the cyclone, dozens of rocks and sharp wood fragments slammed into Nathan, his body a shield for the two girls. Finally, the reflection changed, a dim forest road with a van parked near a tree.

"I need a flash of light!" he yelled.

As if in response, lightning blasted down from the sky, knifing into a nearby tree and slicing off a huge limb right over their heads. The tornado lurched forward, spreading its funnel like the deadly arms of death itself. Kelly clenched her eyes shut. Nathan bent over, waiting to be crushed or swept away.

Suddenly, all was quiet. Staying bent, he listened to the strange silence and studied the ground he stood on. His violin case now lay open on a paved road. After setting the violin inside, he looked over at Kelly.

Still holding the mirror, her wide eyes darted all around, and a smile spread across her face. "Now that's pretty cool!" She pushed a hand under Francesca's arm and helped her to her feet.

Leaving the case on the ground, Nathan stood up straight. "Cool is right, but I'd rather not go through—"

A new voice interrupted. "Okay, now I've seen everything."

Nathan pivoted. "What?"

Just across the road, a young man leaned against a commercial van, watching them with his arms folded over his long-sleeved T-shirt. "Like I said. Now I've seen everything."

He pushed away from the van revealing the lettering on the side — *Stoneman Enterprises*.

Nathan drew his head back. "Gunther?"

"In the flesh." Carrying a tire iron, Gunther frowned as he walked toward them, a set of keys jangling from a ring on his jeans belt loop. Although his hair was shorter, his face hadn't changed. His voice sharpened to a menacing tone. "For a couple of kidnappers, you sure have a lot of divine help ... or is it demonic help?"

"Kidnappers?" Nathan backed away, spreading his arms in front of Kelly and Francesca. "What are you talking about?"

"You still have her," Gunther said, stopping and pointing the tire iron at Francesca. "Now I can finally clear my name for good."

"Clear your name?"

"I didn't want to believe you kidnapped Francesca. I thought maybe someone else took all three of you."

"We didn't kidnap her. We're trying to get her home."

Gunther gave him a sarcastic smirk. "It's taken you almost a year to decide to do that? A little slow, aren't you?"

"Cool it a second," Nathan said, holding up his hands. "Just tell us what's happened since we've been gone, and I'll explain everything."

Gunther kept a firm grip on his tire iron, but his voice eased. "That day I dropped you off, I noticed a guy drive in as I was leaving, so I went back to check it out. When I saw him sneaking up toward the house with a gun, I took this tire iron and chased him. I got there just as he shot — " He glanced at Francesca. The little girl's eyes had grown a half size wider. "Anyway, I clobbered him, but he was a tough nut to crack. He fought back and got away, but I didn't chase him, 'cause I wanted to stay and help, but you two were gone, kind of vanished into thin air. I called the police, and when they showed up, they asked me where Francesca was. I had no idea a little girl even lived there, so I just told them everything I knew.

"They didn't believe me at first, and when they couldn't find her, they put me in jail for two days. When they developed the pictures in the camera Mrs. Romano had with her, they saw the three of you. Now here's the really weird part. In the picture, there was a big mirror behind you, and it showed the guy with the gun behind Mrs. Romano, but there wasn't any mirror in the room.

"Anyway, they decided to keep me locked up for a while, because it also showed me getting ready to bash the guy's head, proving I was there with you. Since they didn't have any evidence that I actually kidnapped her, and since I obviously didn't have time to dispose of three bodies, they finally let me go. They dusted for fingerprints, but I guess yours didn't match anything on file, and they showed the photo to thousands of people and put it on TV, but they came up empty."

Nathan nodded toward Kelly and Francesca. "That's because we went to another dimension. We were only gone a little while, and time moves faster here than it does there."

Gunther lowered the tire iron. "Another dimension?"

"Look," Nathan said, spreading out his arms, "I know it sounds crazy, but I told you the truth before, and you believed me, and I'm telling the truth now. Didn't we just appear out of nowhere? Where do you think we came from?"

"Well, she doesn't look even a day older. They change pretty fast at that age." Bending over, Gunther stared at Francesca. His eyes began to glisten, and his anger seemed to melt away. Suddenly, his brow scrunched low. "Wait a minute!" He turned abruptly and jogged to his van. After climbing into the back double door, he returned with a poster, unrolling it as he walked. "Here's a blowup of the photo. I noticed something ..."

"You carry around a poster of her?"

"Yeah ... well ... After searching for her for so long, she kind of grew on me." He handed one end to Nathan and stretched out the slick paper. He touched Francesca's poster image, rubbing his fingertip along her nose. Then, after rolling up the poster, he crouched in front of her, drawing close and studying her face. "She still has exactly the same scratch, after all this time."

Gunther reached out slowly and drew Francesca into his arms, his movements smooth and gentle. She returned the embrace, her eyes focusing on Nathan as she looked over Gunther's shoulder. She seemed confused yet delighted.

As Gunther pulled away and rose to his feet, he turned back to Nathan and extended his hand. "Welcome back."

Nathan shook his hand. "Great to be here."

"How'd you get here?" Kelly asked. "Or, better yet, how'd *we* get here?"

"I just drove out to a deserted road on my way to my folks' house and waited." Gunther shrugged his shoulders. "I have no idea how you got here. Like Nathan said, you just kind of appeared here out of nowhere."

Kelly scanned the forest. "Where are we, anyway?"

"Near the Iowa and Illinois border. I had just finished a class at school, and this professor-looking type came up to me in the hall. He showed me a photo—the same one we used to make the poster—and asked if I knew the two of you and Francesca. I wasn't sure I could trust him, so I said something like, 'What's it to you?'

"He told me your names. He also knew about me being in the house when it all went down, and he wanted me to help him find the three of you, something about saving your lives. He said he needed someone Nathan could trust, but this guy was sure you wouldn't trust him. So he couldn't do it himself."

"What did he look like?" Nathan asked.

Gunther made circles with his thumbs and forefingers and set them over his eyes. "He wore those owl glasses, like John Lennon wears, and he's short with kind of a round head."

Nathan looked at Kelly. "Sounds like Dr. Simon. Must be his counterpart in this dimension."

"He didn't tell me his name," Gunther continued. "He said that if I wanted to"—he drew quote marks in the air—"be of service, I should drive to a safe place and wait for you there."

"What safe place?"

"I asked the same question. He said it didn't matter where I went as long as I was there within a certain time frame that he wrote down."

Nathan raised his eyebrows. "So he knew when the three of us would arrive?"

"Well, not exactly. It was a two-hour window."

"How long did you have to wait?"

Gunther glanced at his wristwatch. "Only twenty minutes. I brought my textbooks to study, so it wasn't a problem. When I went to jail, I got fired from my delivery job, so I decided to concentrate on school. Figured it was about time I graduated."

"What about the tornado?" Kelly asked. "Didn't it affect you?"

"The radio said it was a hundred miles to the northeast. Just caught a little thunderstorm on my way over here."

"We were right in its path." Nathan said. "It nearly blew us to kingdom come." He looked over at Kelly. With her hair frizzed out and her clothes ruffled, he realized that he probably looked just as mangled. He brushed through his hair, knocking out a shower of leaves, twigs, and dirt. Kelly took his cue and combed out her own hair.

One question still bugged him. How could they possibly show up in a place that Gunther just pulled out of a hat and at exactly the time they were about to get plowed by a tornado and a tree? If they could find Simon, whatever color he was, he'd have a lot of questions to answer.

Gunther backed away, looking around as if worried about someone watching. "This dimensional stuff is too deep for me.

I'm just your driver, so if you want a ride somewhere, let's get going."

They piled into the van, Kelly and Francesca in the front and Nathan in the cargo area in the back. Nathan leaned forward, bracing himself on Kelly's headrest. Although her hair smelled of pine mixed with toadstools, it carried the aroma of safety after a storm, a good, safe sensation. "Think we should check out your house?" he asked.

Kelly shook her head. "It's hours away, and it's too risky. That's the first place they'd look for us. And, besides, we don't know how much time's left before we have to get back for the funeral."

"True." Nathan glanced at his wristwatch, but, of course, it couldn't possibly keep track of time on Earth Red. "I wish we had a cosmic clock." He pulled his phone from his pocket and looked at the screen. No signal. But what did he expect? It was 1979. "Gunther, can you take us to a telephone? I want to make a few calls to see what's going on."

"Sure thing. There's a Texaco station and a McDonald's a few miles up the road. You hungry?"

"Starved." Nathan pulled out his wallet and showed Gunther a twenty-dollar bill. "They probably won't take these new-style twenties, will they?"

"What's this?" Gunther took the bill and narrowed his eyes. "Are you into counterfeiting now?"

"Never mind." Nathan pushed his wallet back into place. "I have some older fives and ones. The McDonald's clerk probably won't look at the dates."

After eating lunch and using the restroom, Gunther, Kelly, and Francesca returned to the van while Nathan used the pay phone at the gas station. When he hung up the receiver, he motioned for Kelly.

She hopped out, and while she ran toward him, he adjusted his watch to match the time on the station's outdoor clock.

"What's the news?" she asked as she came to a stop.

Glancing over her shoulder at Gunther and Francesca, Nathan whispered. "I talked to Nikolai, Francesca's violin teacher. He and his wife raised her in our world after her mother died. I asked him if Francesca were ever found, would he take her in."

"What did he say?"

"He went nuts. He even started crying. Of course he'd take her. He and his wife were never able to have children."

Kelly looked back at the van, her face drooping sadly. "By the way, Francesca figured it all out. She knows her mother's dead. She's been crying ever since you got on the phone."

Stuffing his hands into his pockets, he stepped toward the van and looked through the front passenger window. Gunther was helping Francesca climb into the back. Even from where he stood, he could see her reddened, tear-streaked face.

Nathan took in a deep breath and let it out slowly. "Just let her cry. I know how she feels."

"How long did you cry when your parents died?"

"I don't know." As a slight tremble crossed his lips, he firmed his chin to quell it. "I haven't stopped crying yet."

"Sorry. Stupid question." She brushed her hand tenderly along his forearm. "Where does Nikolai live?"

Nathan ambled toward the van. "He's in Iowa City, but he insisted on meeting us in Davenport in an hour to save time. He gave me an address, and he's already on his way."

Walking beside him, she nodded toward the highway. "Davenport is right across the river. Gunther said we're near the border, so it shouldn't be far at all."

"Yeah, that'll help." Nathan continued his stroll toward the van. He wanted to complain about having to wait even an hour but it'd just be empty grousing. He had thought about getting

Gunther to take them straight to the observatory site. Then he could drive Francesca to Iowa City, but that would be too much of a risk. What would happen if he got caught with her, or something happened to her, and she couldn't vouch for him? He'd be in jail the rest of his life ... or worse. They'd just have to take their chances that this dimension's time was screaming along.

When Nathan opened the van door, Gunther was sitting alone in the front, reaching over the seat and caressing Francesca's head as she lay on a mat in the back. Curled in a fetal position and heaving an occasional spasm, she clutched a stuffed rabbit tightly in her arms.

"I told her about Mr. Bunn," Gunther said. "My little sister left him here months ago. Francesca climbed back there and laid down, so I sang her a lullaby. I guess she went to sleep to escape my voice."

Half closing his eyes to ward off the tears, Nathan smiled weakly. "Thanks, Gunther."

Kelly slid in first, followed by Nathan. "I found a place for Francesca," he said.

"You did?" Gunther's brow arched up, but his tone seemed less than joyful. "Where?"

"Her violin teacher in Iowa City. They're childless, so they're really excited."

Gunther started the van. "That's not too far. Little over an hour."

"He said he'd meet us in Davenport in the Galvin Fine Arts Center at St. Ambrose University."

"I know where that is." Gunther shifted the gear and twisted to see behind him as he backed out. "Fifteen minutes. Twenty, tops."

"Better take it easy, though. If anything happens and we're caught with a supposedly kidnapped girl, we'd never see the light of day, especially you. If you want, we could drop you off somewhere, then take her to Nikolai, and pick you up later."

"Don't worry about me." He shifted again and punched the accelerator. "This little girl lost her mama. I'd do anything for her."

While traveling just under the speed limit on Interstate 88 westbound, Nathan told the entire story as quickly as possible, relating every detail he could remember, finishing with the dis-arming of the shotgun-wielding murderer and their transport to the future location of Interfinity Labs, which happened to lie right in the path of the tornado. "So, now we have to try to get Francesca's life back in order. She has to eventually meet Solomon Shepherd and marry him on the twentieth of Decem-ber in nineteen eighty-six."

Gunther glanced at his rearview mirror. "So do I tell all this stuff to her violin teacher ... what was his name? Nikolai?"

"Nikolai Malenkov. I guess you'll have to. He needs to know that someone's out to kill Francesca. He can't protect her otherwise."

"True, but I could keep an eye on her, too, help her find Solomon, kind of guide their steps until they meet each other."

"You want to be her guardian angel?" Nathan asked.

"Sure. Why not?"

Francesca let out a whimper from the back but soon quieted.

Kelly lowered her voice. "Wouldn't that take too much time? I mean, you have your own life to live."

Gunther matched her low tone. "You probably noticed that I'm not exactly a normal guy. I mean, I'm a truck driver who believes this crazy story you're telling me. I might not be the best student around, but it doesn't take a genius to see that there's a higher power behind all this cross-dimensional weird-ness, so maybe this is exactly what I was meant to do." He gave his shoulders a light shrug. "I only have a semester to go. I'll find a job near Iowa City and be her invisible guardian."

Kelly gave him a peck on the cheek. "You're a special man, Gunther."

"Yeah," Nathan said. "We'll never forget you for this."

Gunther's face flushed. "Just stay away from twisters for a while. I can't be waiting for you out on wilderness roads every time you pick a fight with one."

When they arrived at the university, Gunther parked in the Galvin Center's nearly empty lot. Only an MG roadster, an old red pickup truck, and a motorcycle occupied any of the fifty or so spaces.

Nathan jumped out and searched the area for Nikolai, hoping he could find a much younger version of his mother's gentle music teacher. As he crossed the parking lot, Kelly hurried to join him. "Any sign of Nikolai?"

"Not yet. I remember seeing the Earth Red version of him driving a nice BMW, so I don't think he'd own anything like what's already parked here. I told him what the van looks like, so maybe he'll find us."

"Has it been an hour?"

"Just about. He should be here soon."

She nodded toward the building. "Won't hurt to take a look inside, will it?"

"Wait!" Nathan pointed at a light blue Volvo turning into the parking lot. "That looks more his speed."

As the Volvo pulled in next to the van, the driver rolled down the window. A thin-faced man with a full head of salt-and-pepper hair glanced around nervously before speaking in a friendly but serious tone. "Are you Nathan Shepherd?"

"Yes." Nathan bent over to address him directly. "Nikolai?"

"Yes, yes." He craned his neck, sticking his head farther out the window as he lowered his voice. "Where is Francesca?"

Nathan pointed at Gunther's vehicle. "In the van. I thought you said you were bringing your wife."

He gave a rapid nod, still speaking softly. "I was, to be sure, but I received a call immediately after yours warning me not to retrieve Francesca. It was a man, a friendly man, actually, who said I would be endangering her life." He checked his rearview mirror and glanced at the fine arts center before continuing. "I couldn't leave you waiting for me, so I sent my wife to a safe place and came alone."

"Do you think someone's watching your house?"

"I believe so, and perhaps for quite some time, but I was unaware of it until that moment. When I left my house, I became much more watchful and noticed a green pickup truck parked at the curb two blocks away. I am quite sure I saw the same vehicle later on the interstate, but it passed me, and the driver did not even offer a glance."

Nathan straightened and scanned the area, stretching his arms to make it look like he was yawning rather than conducting a search. "No sign of the truck, but I'll bet—" Although he stopped talking, he kept turning. "Don't look now, but I spotted a guy with binoculars behind a tree near that house across the street."

Nikolai stiffened, and his voice grew jittery. "Do you have a suggested course of action?"

"We need to do something they won't expect." Nathan looked at the entrance to the center—three double doors bordered by brick columns that rose to the roof. "Do you know this place?"

"I have performed here three times. It was the only destination in the city I could remember."

"I've got an idea," Nathan turned back to Nikolai. "Can you lead us to the stage?"

"Of course." Nikolai pushed his door open and got out. "It's easy to find."

Nathan collected his mirror and violin from the van and headed for the door with Nikolai, while Gunther, carrying the still sleeping Francesca, followed a few steps behind. Nathan glanced back to check on Kelly. Trailing by several yards, she shuffled along and kept a watchful eye.

As soon as they passed through the entry door, the lovely sounds of someone practicing Dvořák's magnificent cello concerto greeted their ears. Whoever the cellist was had just begun an early measure of the solo portion and hit every note with vigor and ringing clarity. It sounded like the music was coming from the other side of an open door at the end of a hallway directly in front of them.

"The stage is in there," Nikolai said, pointing at the door.

Nathan lifted the mirror. The reflection slowly altered, changing from his tired pale face to a dim room of some kind. As the image sharpened, a small stuffed rabbit came into view. He smiled, laughing under his breath. "Mr. Bunn!"

"Mr. Bunn?" Kelly jogged to catch up and looked over his shoulder. "What does it mean?"

"It means we can use my idea." He strode through the door and hurried down the stairs at the side of the seating area, then climbed up to the stage. As he passed by the cellist sitting at the middle of the raised platform, Nathan gave him a nod. "Nice touch."

The cellist, a young man with long arms and a bright smile, lifted his bow. "Thanks."

"Mind if we look around?" Nathan asked as he continued into the backstage area.

"Sure. Go ahead."

As the others caught up, Nathan scanned the paneled gray floor. "We need sheets, robes, cloaks, anything like that."

"Curtains?" Kelly asked, lifting a wad of black material.

Nathan picked up another wad, an old red curtain. "I guess they took down these old ones and replaced them."

"Perhaps they use different curtains for different events," Nikolai said.

"I think they'll work." Nathan draped the black curtain over Francesca and tucked it around Gunther's arms. "Nikolai, will you bring these back when we're done?"

He nodded. "Of course."

After setting down the violin and mirror, Nathan held out his arms, fashioning a cradle. "Okay, Kelly, up you go."

Kelly pointed at herself. "You're going to carry me?"

"Sure. You're not much bigger than Francesca. All bundled up, no one will know the difference."

She set her fists on her hips. "Thanks. Like I needed another short joke."

Nathan set one arm on Kelly's back and slid another behind her knees. With a slight grunt, he hoisted her into his arms. "You and I will go with Nikolai in his car. That way, they'll probably think I have her."

She laid her arm around Nathan's neck. "What if they don't?"

He eyed Francesca's bare feet protruding from under the curtain. "She took her shoes off," he whispered.

"Not a problem." Gunther shifted the black material and covered her feet.

"No. Leave them uncovered." Nathan cocked his head toward Nikolai. "Take Kelly's shoes and put them on Francesca."

"Ah!" Nikolai smiled as he transferred Kelly's Nike's to Francesca. "An excellent plan! I'll remove her socks as well."

After her shoes and socks came off, Kelly wiggled her toes. "I have polish on my nails, and it's cherry red."

"Let's hope he can't tell from where he is." Nathan turned toward the front of the stage. "Okay, cover Kelly and make sure her bare feet stick out, but not so much that it's obvious."

Nikolai draped the red curtain over Kelly, leaving her toes

uncovered. "I believe we are ready to go," he said. "I will get your violin and mirror."

"Curl up, Kelly," Nathan said. "Try to make yourself smaller."

He could feel her tuck her knees up and nestle her head against his chest. "Like this?" she asked, her voice muffled.

"Yeah." He pushed out a quick breath. "Good thing you're a lightweight."

Her voice sharpened. "I weigh one hundred and eight pounds!"

"Feels like one oh seven. I told you to eat more French fries." Nathan began marching toward the stage's stairway. As he passed the cellist again, he gave him another nod. "Keep up the good work."

The cellist stared at him. "Yeah. Thanks."

When they reached the door, Nathan whispered to Gunther, "Don't look at the stalker. Let's just load them up and get out of here. I'll head north. You head south. Let's meet where you picked us up."

Gunther shifted Francesca a bit higher. "Sure thing."

Nikolai jogged ahead and opened the van and car doors, allowing Gunther and Nathan to set their loads down in the back. After closing the door, Nathan extended his hand toward Nikolai. "Mind if I drive? If they're out to kill Francesca, it could get dicey."

Nikolai pulled out his keys and dropped them in Nathan's hand. "An excellent suggestion."

While Nathan started the car, Nikolai hurried around to the passenger's side and set the violin and mirror on the floorboard in front of him.

Giving Gunther a nod, Nathan eased out of the parking lot and headed for the main highway. "I'll take a direct route to see if he's following us."

Kelly spoke up from the back. "Do I have to stay hidden and miss all the action?"

"If anything happens, I'll give you a blow-by-blow." When he reached Highway 61, he turned north and punched the accelerator. "Do you see anyone behind us?"

Nikolai looked back. "I cannot tell. There are many cars, but no obvious followers."

"Maybe when we get to the interstate, we'll be able to spot a green truck. They'll have to use that route to cross the river to get to Illinois."

After a minute or two of silence, Nathan asked, "Could you help me solve a mystery?"

"Certainly, if I can."

"Remember that night at Ganz Hall in Chicago when a double murder took place?"

"Yes, of course. My wife and I played in the quartet. It was a frightening night indeed!"

"What happened? Do you know who the victims were?"

"I will tell you what I know, which isn't much. Helen and I stayed after the performance, because a young violinist from the quartet that played before ours wished to speak to us at length about Dvořák, his favorite composer. The three of us sat on stage for so long, someone turned the lights off without realizing we were still there. We thought it amusing at first and simply went on with our conversation. Soon, however, someone entered the side door and set up a floor-standing mirror. We guessed that he had not seen us, so we stayed quiet to see what his intentions were. He went out, and moments later, he and another man brought in two coffins and arranged them on tables on the opposite side of the stage.

"Since we could see bodies in the coffins, we became quite nervous and tried to remain perfectly quiet, but one of the men, a tall, pale-looking fellow, saw us. The two men became violently aggressive toward us, so we defended ourselves. Unfortunately, the only weapons we had were our violins, which did not survive the battle. After quite a skirmish, they captured us and locked us in a storage closet. It took some time, but we were able to break out. I sustained several serious cuts, as did the young musician, but my wife was unharmed. To this day, I have no idea who lay in the coffins."

Kelly piped up from the backseat. "So that's why you didn't make it back home on time."

"I was quite delayed, to be sure. We stayed overnight in the hospital and answered the authorities' questions the next day."

Nathan breathed a long "Hmmmm." Someone or something led him to believe that Dr. Malenkov and his wife were in the coffins as replacements for the Rosetta pieces. But why? To make him look for Dr. Malenkov's name in the email draft folder? But so much more was going on than just the solution to the Rosetta puzzle. Whoever this invisible sleight-of-hand magician was, he had more up his sleeve than a couple of aces.

Something green caught Nathan's attention in the rearview mirror. He tightened his grip on the steering wheel. "I see the pickup. It's a couple of hundred feet back."

Nikolai turned and looked. "He seems to be lagging. Is he really following us?"

"Let's find out." Nathan pressed the accelerator and extended his hand. "Please give me the mirror and play something on the violin."

He laid the mirror in Nathan's palm and pulled the violin from its case. "This is a strange concert venue, but I will do as you say."

Nathan set the mirror at his side. "Just watch. Explaining it would take too long."

"What shall I play?"

"Anything."

Nikolai raised the violin and began a Beethoven sonata. As they zoomed along in the right-hand lane, the pickup kept pace but stayed back, apparently satisfied to keep them in sight. After a few miles, they passed a police car hiding in a gap in the bushes at the side of the highway. As soon as the pickup zipped by, the patrol car flashed its lights, roared onto the pavement, and gave chase.

The pickup took off and rapidly closed the gap between it and Nikolai's Volvo. Nathan set the mirror on the dashboard. "That's weird. All I see is the sky, like the mirror's pointing straight up."

"I don't like the sound of that." Kelly sat upright but kept her head low. "Is it okay to be seen now?"

"Not yet." Nathan pointed ahead. "There's the bridge."

As soon as he eased up on the gas, a heavy jolt shook the car, shoving it close to the shoulder. Nathan wrenched the wheel back to the left. "The truck's ramming us!"

Kelly peeked over the backseat. "Slow down more! The cop's closing in!"

"But the bridge is dead ahead! I can't let him slam me into it!" Nathan pressed the pedal again. "We'll take our chances in Illinois!"

As he sped across the long span, the truck bumped them again, this time pushing from the left rear corner. Nathan tried to correct with one hand, but the Volvo slid toward the low concrete barrier that served as the bridge's protective railing, slowing both vehicles to a crawl. "Kelly! Help me hold the mirror!"

She thrust her body forward and lay prostrate while bracing the mirror. "Got it!"

Nathan grabbed the wheel with both hands and fought back, jerking to the left and banging the truck. "Nikolai! Keep playing!"

"I still see the sky!" Kelly shouted. "What does it mean?"

"Just hang on!" The steering wheel froze. As the passenger's side squealed against the concrete, the truck turned toward the Volvo at a ninety-degree angle and locked them in place, roaring its engine as it shoved again and again.

Kelly rocked back and forth, grabbing the wheel to keep from rolling. "He'll push us over the edge!"

"The cops are running this way," Nathan said, still fighting the wheel. "They'll never make it in time!"

Kelly latched on to Nathan's arm. "What'll we do?"

"Dust off the 'Our Father' prayer!"

Nikolai switched from Beethoven to Handel's *Messiah*. "If I die," he shouted, his bow swaying wildly, "I will die in the arms of Christ!"

"The mirror's changing!" Nathan called, still fighting with the wheel and pumping the accelerator. "I see Mr. Bunn!"

With a deafening rumble from its engine, the truck gave a final shove. The car rolled over the barrier and dove headfirst toward the Mississippi River.

Still clutching the mirror, Kelly screamed. As the plunge shoved Nathan against his seat, he laid an arm over her back, gritting his teeth. "Just ... hang ... on!"

Nikolai hugged the violin and case, closing his eyes as he prayed out loud. "Our Father, who art in heaven ..."

The water raced toward them. The car began a slow spin. Nathan reached for the door, pulled its handle, and kicked it open. The interior light flashed on. As a splash erupted in front of him, a fierce jolt rattled his bones. Then, everything fell dark.

15

TICKETS TO DISASTER

A painful thump on his backside snapped Nathan's eyes open. His vision pulsed with photonegative blackness. "Kelly! Nikolai! Where are you?"

An excited voice shot back from somewhere close. "Nathan! Where did you come from?"

Nathan stared at a stuffed rabbit in his hand. "Gunther?"

"Yes. Can't you see me?"

Nathan rubbed his eyes. Apparently he was sitting cross-legged on the back cargo floor of the delivery van. Gunther sat in the driver's seat next to Francesca, driving through light fog on a rural highway.

"Yeah. I can see you now." He looked around the dim van. Kelly lay facedown next to him, moaning. Beside her, Nikolai sat with the violin and case in his lap, leaning against the side window. His eyes were open, but he seemed in a daze.

"How'd we get here?" Nathan asked as he reached for Kelly.

"I was going to ask you that. I heard a loud bump, and you just showed up."

"I guess we got transported again." Nathan turned Kelly over. As her arms tightened, clamping the mirror against her chest, she fluttered her eyelids and winced, accentuating a bloody gash across her forehead just below her scalp. Using his thumb, he wiped away a trickle of blood oozing toward her ear. "It was just in time, too. That pickup pushed our car over the side of the bridge, and the last thing I remember was splashing into the Mississippi."

Gunther flashed a thumbs up. "That's exactly what we need. It's perfect!"

"Perfect? We're pretty beat up, especially Kelly."

"I don't mean that." Gunther looked back at the trio. "Is everyone okay?"

"I think we will be." He glanced around the cargo area. "Do you have a first aid kit?"

"You bet." Gunther touched Francesca's head. "Hey, sweetheart, can you look under your seat for a white metal box?"

While she looked, Gunther slowed the van and pulled into the grass at the side of the road. "What I meant was, they'll think Francesca's dead, so they won't try to find her anymore."

Nathan let Gunther's words sink in. He was right. Not only that, the stalker would think Nikolai and himself were dead as well, so they were in the clear. Still, Nikolai and Francesca might have to hide out somewhere; he couldn't just show up back at home and start teaching again.

Francesca handed him the first-aid kit. "Found it."

"Thank you." Gunther passed it to the back.

Nathan ripped open a sterile pad and dabbed Kelly's three-inch-long wound. He looked up at Nikolai. "Are you okay, Dr. Malenkov?"

Setting the violin and case down with shaky hands, he nodded, his eyes wide and fixed straight ahead. "It was ..." He swallowed and licked his lips. "It was very much like a nightmare I have had the last several nights. I fall toward the water, and when I near the surface I feel a great wind and see a bright light. Then, I wake up."

"I just felt a bump on my backside." Nathan gently removed the mirror from Kelly's tightened fingers. Blood stained the top edge. "Looks like she clocked herself with the mirror, but I can't tell if she hurt anything else."

A low whisper rose from Kelly's lips. "I'm just sore all over." Her eyelids fluttered again, this time staying open as she glanced around. "We survived?"

"Looks that way." He pulled out three adhesive bandages and tore open the first one. "And we're still on Earth Yellow. The Quattro mirror kept us in the same dimension, just like always."

She sat up and turned toward the front. At the sight of Francesca, she smiled, though a tremble in her lips revealed her pain. "So, our plan worked perfectly."

"Except for an unscheduled plunge into the Mississippi ... yeah, it was great."

"What about Nikolai's car?"

Nikolai finally shook himself out of his empty stare and waved his hand. "It is nothing. A big piece of metal." He smiled at Francesca. "But she is a flesh and blood treasure."

Kelly gazed through the windshield. "Where are we going now?"

Gunther pointed at the map, still attached to the sun visor. "No place in particular. I just started driving toward where we met, but now that you're all here, you can plot the course."

Nathan leaned over the seat and looked at the map. "We have to get back to the transport site. It's in the middle of no-where right now, but the Interfinity observatory is going to be there someday."

"I can get us real close," Kelly said. "I'm not sure if all the roads will be the same here, but if we find the path of the tor-nado, all we have to do is follow the damage."

Gunther set his finger near the border between Illinois and Wisconsin. "The news said the twister first touched down out in the boonies just west of Rockford. I'll start heading that way."

"Nikolai," Kelly said, turning toward him. "Why don't you ride up front with Francesca? You'll be more comfortable."

"Very well." After setting the violin in its case and snapping the lid closed, Nikolai extended his hand. "May I have the rabbit, please?"

Nathan gave it to him. "Sure. I guess Mr. Bunn belongs to Francesca now."

"For Francesca, yes, but also for me." Nikolai held the rabbit close to his chest. "I think Mr. Bunn is the only occupant of this vehicle who understands what is going on less than I do, so he will be my partner in ignorance."

Nathan grinned. "I'll explain as much as I can on the way, but we'd better get going."

After Nikolai settled into the front seat with Francesca, and Nathan and Kelly arranged themselves comfortably on the floor in the cargo area, they cruised down the road, still cutting through light fog. Nathan explained everything he could remember, asking for help from Kelly at times to fill in the gaps.

Nikolai clasped his hands together, his eyes sparkling. "I am very curious about how music seems to open the passage between the dimensions. Have you noticed any pattern? Are some pieces more effective than others?"

Nathan shifted his gaze to the van's ceiling. "Not that I can think of. I've seen classical, rock, and country do the job. But the strange thing is that the Interfinity radio telescope picked up a lot of noise from space, and Francesca was able to hear the music inside all that racket."

"Is it so strange that melodies and harmonies are inherent in creation?" Nikolai asked. "The precision and order of the cosmos comprise a multitude of symphonies, each one playing hymns in praise of their Creator's magnificence."

Nathan pondered those words for a moment. Although their meaning seemed clear enough, they also seemed elusive. Something was missing. He gazed into the maestro's deep gray eyes.

"But wouldn't that mean Vivaldi or Beethoven or Dvořák didn't actually write their music? I mean, if they just heard it in creation and pulled it out of the air, they aren't the geniuses we think they are. They're just great copycats."

"Oh, no," Nikolai said, waving his hand. "Such a conclusion is not necessary at all. If man, made in the image of God, creates a masterpiece *ex nihilo*, he celebrates the creation of God, the one who did the same when he fashioned the world."

Kelly cocked her head to the side. "*Ex nihilo?* What's that?"

"Out of nothing," Nikolai explained. "God is able to form matter where matter didn't even exist. Man also has creative power, so he can design architectural wonders, paint an abstract mosaic, and compose music out of nothing, creations that have never existed before."

"So how does the music get into space?" Nathan asked.

"I can offer only a guess, but when a man decides to reflect God's creative majesty, is it not reasonable for creation to echo man's offerings of worship?"

Nathan bobbed his head. "Yeah. I suppose so. But how could music open a dimensional door?"

"I have no idea, but here is something that might help, something my teacher taught me when I was Francesca's age back in my mother country. When a musician composes, he is a translator of the divine voice. He sets the majesty of creation into a combination of notes that has never been heard before, yet it tells a story that has been spoken by God ever since the beginning of time."

Nathan looked at his knuckles. It seemed as though a breathy kiss had brushed by. "My mother used to say something like that."

After navigating back roads strewn with debris from tornado damage, Gunther stopped in front of a large sign with red block letters that said, *Future Home of Interfinity Labs — 1986.*

"Now that's convenient," Kelly said. "It's still going to be seven years until it's built."

"Too convenient, if you ask me." Nathan jumped out of the back of the van and jogged up to the sign, a four-by-four foot square that stood a few inches higher than his head.

Kelly joined him. "What do you make of it?"

"Look." He kicked up a clump of dirt where one of the posts entered the ground. "Freshly dug."

She pushed on the sign, tilting it back an inch or two. "Not very sturdy. It couldn't have survived the tornado."

Stuffing his hands into his pockets, he gazed at the surrounding landscape. Uprooted oaks and snapped pines littered the field. Hardly a tree stood upright as far as the eye could see, a stark portrait of devastating fury. He shook off a shiver. That same fury had come within seconds of making kindling out of him and the two girls.

While Nikolai and Francesca got out and stretched their legs, Gunther trudged over the flattened grass and joined Nathan. "The sign's new all right. No way it should still be standing."

Kelly picked up a three-foot-long branch stripped of leaves and, squinting in the glare of the midday sun, touched the letters with the pointed end. "Daryl said the company used to be called StarCast. Shouldn't the sign say that instead of Interfinity?"

"You're right." Nathan touched the red paint at the bottom of the *I* in Interfinity. It was still tacky, not more than a few hours old. Obviously someone was helping them find this spot, someone who thought Interfinity was the only name they knew. Could Dr. Simon be setting up a meeting? Or maybe an ambush?

Gunther broke off a blade of grass and narrowed his eyes as he searched the devastated forest. Kelly shuffled close to Nathan and leaned her head against his shoulder. He set his feet to support the added pressure. The weight of her head felt good;

it meant she trusted him. But what a responsibility! He had to make decisions that affected two lives hanging precariously in the portent of a catastrophic dimensional collision. And if he decided wrong, who could tell how many people would suffer and die? Sacrificing himself to save others was scary enough, but could he ask Kelly to do the same? Yet what choice did they have? They had to get back to Earth Red as soon as possible.

He shielded his eyes and looked into what was left of the forest, skinny trunks broken like matchsticks, their upper halves either lying on the ground or hanging on by tufts of exposed wood fibers. Crouching, he pointed between two clusters of shrubs. "If this road is in the same place as the one back home, the mirror should be right about there, maybe a hundred yards back, if it's still standing."

Kelly crouched with him, then stood again. "I can't see it from here. I hope it didn't break."

"I'd better stay with Francesca and Nikolai," Gunther said, "in case we get some unexpected company. If you're not back in half an hour, I'll assume you crossed dimensions again."

Gesturing for Kelly to follow, Nathan headed toward the van. Francesca stood next to the passenger door, once again clutching Mr. Bunn with both arms, while Nikolai stood at her side.

After retrieving the violin, Nathan stooped in front of Francesca and stroked her dark locks. "Kelly and I have to go. You know we're leaving you in good hands, right?"

With new tears welling, Francesca nodded. "I wish you could stay."

Kelly bent over and took her hand. "We have to go back to our world. Gunther and Nikolai will make sure you're safe."

Francesca embraced Kelly. "Don't go! I love you!"

Kelly heaved a quick breath, pausing for a moment before prying Francesca's tightened fingers away. Her voice squeezed to a high pitch. "I have to go, honey. But we'll see each other again, I promise."

"You do?" Francesca's eyes flashed a glimmer of hope.

Pressing her lips together tightly, Kelly nodded.

Francesca's chin quivered, shaking loose her gathering tears and casting them to the ground. "I can't ever go home, can I?"

Closing her eyes, Kelly shook her head.

Her slender fingers trembling, Francesca lifted Kelly's hand. "Then will you pray for me?"

"Yes ... Yes, of course I'll pray for you."

Francesca blew on Kelly's knuckles, mixing her breath with a dripping tear. "Love is the breath of God," she said softly, "and prayer is the melody that makes it sing."

Kelly drew her hand back. "I'll ... I'll remember that."

Blinking away his own tears, Nathan hugged Francesca. "When your son's born, don't listen to his complaints about practicing his violin. Okay?"

She patted him on the cheek. "Don't worry, Son. I'll chain him to his music stand."

"Thanks, Mom." He gave her a wink and backed away. Now barely able to speak, he nodded at Kelly. "Let's go."

As they circled around to the driver's side, Francesca crawled to the middle of the front bench, while Nikolai sat by the door.

Gunther had already slid behind the wheel. "Don't forget this," he said, reaching the mirror through the open window.

Setting the violin down, Nathan grasped the mirror with one hand and Gunther's shoulder with the other. His tightening throat squeezed his voice higher. "You watch over them, okay?"

"Like you said, I'll be a guardian angel." After Francesca settled into her seat, Gunther pulled the belt over her lap and buckled it. "Keep in touch if you can."

"We will." After picking up the violin, Nathan handed the

mirror to Kelly, and they headed back toward the strange Interfinity sign and the ravaged field, the sun now at its zenith. Puffy white clouds streamed from the horizon and drifted across the blazing disk, giving them relief as they marched onward.

Kelly took Nathan's hand. "Do you think we'll ever come back to Earth Yellow?" she asked.

"We have to. Simon Blue's probably hanging around in Earth Yellow, so we'll have to figure out how to contact him."

He picked up the pace, stepping high over broken branches. It took only a few minutes to locate the tri-fold mirror, flat on the ground and covered with green leaves, some still clinging to fallen branches.

"The mirror side's down," Nathan said, lifting the edge. "Maybe it survived after all."

Kelly dropped to her knees and peeked underneath. "It's dirty, but I don't see any cracks."

After clearing the debris, they pulled the mirror upright and angled the three panels, balancing it until it stood on its own. Then, standing in front of the smudged glass, they stared at the image, an aerial view of the telescope room.

"Looks like Daryl Blue still has us tuned in," Nathan said, "but I can't see anyone."

"It's kind of dark. Maybe they're in trouble and had to hide." She bent forward slightly, narrowing her eyes as she studied the image. "I see a bug of some kind. Is that a fly?"

Nathan stepped closer to the mirror. "Yeah, but it's barely moving at all, like it's hovering."

"So time's still a lot slower there than here. That's a good sign."

"Maybe. But that's Earth Blue. We need it to be slower on Earth Red." Pulling up the hem of his shirt, Nathan stepped right up to the mirror. "If I have this all straight," he said, wiping the center panel with his shirt, "we'll go back to Earth Blue first, and then we'll have to catch another bus to Earth Red."

"A bus?" Kelly crossed her arms and let out a gentle huff. "More like a roller coaster."

Nathan backed away from the glass. "So do we flash a light, or do they?"

"I think we do. It looks like they don't know we're ready to come back."

"You got your key ring light?"

She pulled the keys from her pocket. "Right here."

"I hope it's enough. The lights in the telescope room really put on a show, and that thing's kind of puny."

She flicked it on and shone it in his eyes. "It's worth a try. A flashlight worked before on your mirror."

He blocked the light with his hand. "I think there's a huge difference between using Interfinity's technology and just letting Quattro do its thing. They've figured out the mechanics, you know, how to tune their computers into the right dimension, how to decode the music to bring it up on their screen, and how much light to use to send someone across." He tapped his mirror with a finger. "I think Quattro's different. It doesn't respond to a formula. It shows what's going to happen in our dimension without me doing anything, but the only way it shows other dimensions is when there's music, and it doesn't actually affect what we do unless there's a flash of light."

"But Quattro doesn't always work when we want it to."

"Right. It's kind of temperamental."

As they stood close together less than two paces in front of the mirror, Kelly guided the flashlight's pale beam over the glass, painting a dim circle in the center, barely visible in the noontime sun. They stared at it for a moment, but nothing happened.

"Not bright enough," Nathan said. "What else can we use?"

She pulled on the strap around her neck. "The camera?"

He shook his head. "The last time I took a picture of one of the mirrors, it gave me a pretty wild jolt. The same thing happened to Clara."

Kelly looked back toward the road. "Headlights from the van?"

"No way. He'd never make it through all the broken trees."

She pointed at the sun. "We already have a light, but it's hiding behind some clouds right now."

"That might work." He set down the violin and strode to the back of the mirror. Using both hands, he carefully shifted the frames to catch the sun's veiled rays. "If it peeks out from behind the clouds, it'll be like a sudden flash."

Kelly set the smaller mirror beside the violin and helped him. "I guess before the tornado hit, the trees blocked the sun. What'll keep it from transporting something accidentally after we leave?"

Nathan angled one side a few degrees closer to the other. With the sun still shielded by clouds, it was impossible to tell if he had the mirrors aligned correctly. "If we turn off the music from the Earth Blue side, I think this would become a regular mirror again, so someone would have to open it with music to go anywhere."

"I think that's as good as we're going to get it," Kelly said.

"Let's give it a try." Nathan spotted a slight movement behind one of the broken maple trees. He quickly averted his gaze back to Kelly and whispered. "I saw something."

"What?"

"I don't know. Something behind you." Still watching the tree out of the corner of his eye, he walked casually to the front side of the mirror and headed toward his violin where his own mirror lay. "We're not alone."

Kelly hugged herself and rubbed her upper arms. "Don't do this to me, Nathan. It's not funny."

"I'm not kidding." He picked up his mirror and angled it toward the maple. In the image a wavy-haired, bespectacled man peered at him from behind the tree. "You might as well come out, whoever you are. I already see you."

"An interesting paradox, indeed."

Nathan swung around. Exactly as the mirror had predicted, a man stuck his head out and looked at him through dense, circular glasses. Although his thick head of hair contrasted sharply with the man Nathan knew on Earth Red, his soft voice and hint of a British accent were unmistakable.

Nathan glanced at Kelly and slid between her and the newcomer. "Dr. Simon?"

"Yes." He walked out into the open. Wearing a leather jacket and blue jeans, he didn't fit the professorial stereotype the Earth Red image always tried to maintain. And he seemed much younger, young enough to be Simon's Earth Yellow version. "As I was saying," he continued, "this Quattro phenomenon is quite interesting. You saw me peek out at you in the reflection, yet I could have decided not to do so."

Nathan spiced his tone with a testy edge. "You could've stayed where you were to see what would happen." He stealthily set his feet, ready to fight if necessary.

"True," Simon replied, wringing his hands together nervously, "but my need to talk with you was far greater than my curiosity."

Nathan searched the newcomer for a weapon, but he seemed unarmed. He relaxed his fingers and tempered his voice. "So, what do you want?"

As Simon's face lit up, he sped through his words. "In order for us to continue our interdimensional tests, we want to try to avert a certain disaster in my dimension, that is, Earth Yellow. Of course, this is exactly what we have always wanted to do, use this technology for the good of mankind, but now you have given us a chance to succeed in our endeavors."

Kelly stepped forward. "Who is 'us'? Do you work for Mictar?"

"Not at all. There are two competing forces at work. Mictar and Dr. Gordon from Earth Blue make up one side, while my counterpart on Earth Blue and I, as well as Dr. Gordon from Earth Red, make up the other side. It has taken until now to decide how to apply our abilities, and you have given us a timely opportunity. With Quattro assisting us, our prospects are greatly enhanced."

Nathan laid a finger on his chest. "So is that why you need me?"

"Since you are the only one available who knows how to use it ..." Simon folded his hands at his waist. "Yes, that's why we need you."

"I'm the only one available? Does that mean you don't know where my father is? He knows how to use it."

"Mictar is holding your parents hostage." Simon took a breath and puffed out his chest. "If I could free them, I would."

"Why don't we concentrate on rescuing my dad? Since he knows about Quattro, he'll be glad to put it to use for the good of mankind."

"We already have that goal in mind. My Earth Blue counterpart has set a plan in motion that we hope will set the prisoners free, but it must wait until the funeral."

"So," Nathan said, crossing his arms, "what's the plan?"

Simon hid his hands behind his back and retreated a step. "If I told you, I would lose some leverage in persuading you to avert the disaster."

"But if I take time to stop it, I might not make it to the funeral on time."

"My counterpart assures me that we should make it. Time passage here in comparison to the other dimensions has been increasing of late."

Nathan flopped his arms at his sides. "So what do I have to do?"

"In both Earth Red and Earth Blue, an airliner crashed at

O'Hare airport in Chicago on this date." Simon withdrew a folded sheet of paper from his jacket pocket and handed it to Nathan. "This describes how the aircraft failed. The engine on its left wing fell off due to an improper replacement procedure, and it stripped the hydraulic system and retracted the slats, preventing the pilot from knowing what to do to properly correct its tilt. Our task is simply to prevent the crash in Earth Yellow, using Quattro in order to study how we might harness its power in the future."

Nathan scanned the article. "Why don't you just call the airline? Just say something like you got a tip that a terrorist messed up that engine, and they should check it out."

"That might work quite well, but it also might not. I am not willing to put 271 lives at risk." Simon pulled a pair of tickets from his back pocket. "I need an agent on board who will make sure the passengers survive, and I assumed the girl would want to go with you."

Nathan stared at the tickets. One bore his name, and the other spelled out Kelly's. It was as though Dr. Simon held a pair of death orders in his stubby fingers. "So," Nathan said, plucking the tickets, "you want us to fly in a doomed jet."

THE SHADOW OF DEATH

Simon shook his head. "Not at all. The airliner won't be doomed if you prevent the disaster."

"Sure, but let's just warn the pilot or something." Nathan pushed the tickets back toward Simon. "It would be crazy to fly with them!"

"Keep the tickets," Simon said, folding his hands again. "If warning the authorities is a sufficient rescue plan, then they will either repair the engine problem or conduct the passengers to another plane. If you are confident in this, and you care for the lives of your fellow human beings, why should you fear taking the flight?"

"Because ... Well, I guess ..." Nathan heaved a sigh. "Okay. You got me."

Kelly patted Nathan on the shoulder. "He wants to skip the flight, because he has to get back in time for the funeral."

Turning toward her, Nathan shook his head. "I could use that excuse, but it wouldn't be true."

"As I said," Simon continued, "you should have no fear. If you do your job wisely, you will be able to complete your mission." He turned and gestured for them to follow. "We have dawdled too long, so now we have to hurry."

As they followed his lead, Kelly swiveled her head from side to side. "I don't see a car anywhere."

Simon withdrew a small key ring and tossed it back to

Nathan. "I have been told that you are capable of riding a motorcycle."

Nathan caught the pair of silver keys. "Yeah. Pretty well."

"My counterpart dropped me off with two Hondas that I have hidden under some branches." He passed a line of broken trunks and stopped at a pile of debris that rose twice as high as his head. "Can Miss Clark ride as well?"

"Like a pro," Kelly said. "I have my own bike at home."

Nathan faced her and laid a hand on her shoulder. "Look, Kelly. You don't have to risk this. I can probably get it done by myself."

Narrowing her eyes at him, she planted a hand on her hip. "You gotta be kidding me! What're you going to do? Leave me out in the woods?" She pressed a finger into his chest. "And whose life is it, anyway? If you're going to risk yours, I'm with you all the way to the bitter end."

Nathan caught the sincerity in her eyes. Her courage was amazing. Not only that, her loyalty to him left him practically breathless. Turning back, he gave Simon a nod. "Sounds like we're in this together."

Simon pulled one of the large branches off the pile of debris. "That is acceptable, but when I mentioned the young lady, I was wondering if she would be able to ride with you, not on a motorcycle of her own. I don't have another mode of transportation for myself."

"Then I'll drive," Kelly said, "and he can take the back."

Nathan waved his hand. "Uh-uh, Sister. You might be good on a bike, but if things get ugly, I've probably got a little more experience in getaways."

"Spare me the sermon, Brother Nathan. We're not going to run into trouble between here and the airport."

Simon pulled two more branches from the pile. "I will not get involved in your lovers' quarrel, but I must insist on leaving immediately. You will ride together on the blue motorcycle, in whichever manner you decide."

"Look, Kelly," Nathan said, spreading out his hands, "I—"

"Never mind." Kelly began helping Simon clear branches. "You don't have to explain. I'll ride in the back."

Nathan grabbed a protruding limb. "Are you sure?"

"I'm sure." She jerked a huge leafy branch away and swatted it to the ground behind her.

After clearing off the bikes, Nathan loaded the violin and mirror in a saddlebag and hopped onto the blue one, while Dr. Simon climbed aboard the other, the same model, but trimmed in red. Nathan adjusted one of the rearview mirrors. "Sweet. Looks like it has plenty of horsepower."

Dr. Simon pushed a helmet over his head. While Kelly pulled an elastic band from her pocket and tied her hair back, Nathan grabbed a shiny blue helmet from the handlebar and put it on. Without a word, Kelly took hers, a sparkle-coated maroon one, slid it on, and climbed on the back, grasping the sides of her seat.

Dr. Simon started his engine, revving it a couple of times before easing his way through the mangled forest.

After starting his own bike, Nathan followed. As they headed away from the road Gunther had used to find the area, they zig-zagged to avoid branches and splintered stumps while bumping over hidden dips and swells in the otherwise flat land. Kelly let out a few oomphs, but she kept her hands tightly clutching her saddle.

Within a few minutes, they reached a hardened dirt road. Simon gave them a thumbs up and sped away on the smoother surface. Leaning forward, Nathan gave chase, quickly closing the gap before slowing to stay a few bike lengths behind.

When they finally motored onto a paved highway, Kelly

slowly wrapped her arms around Nathan's waist and laid her head on his back. "I'm sorry!" she shouted.

As the stiff headwind whistled all around, he twisted his neck and shouted back. "Sorry for what?"

"For being a brat!"

Nathan sighed and patted her hands, interlocked just under his ribcage. "You're not a brat. You're ... assertive."

"Keep treating me like a lady, Nathan. I'm not used to it, but I like it."

After traversing an interstate highway for about two hours, they arrived at Chicago's O'Hare International and pulled up to Terminal Three's passenger drop-off zone. Nathan glanced at his watch. It was 2:17. He took off his helmet and tucked it under his arm. "What time does the flight leave?"

Simon slid off his own helmet, mussing his hair into a frazzled mop. "I'm not sure of the scheduled time, but the actual runway time in your world was a minute after three." He extended the keys to the other motorcycle to Nathan. "Leave the helmets. It will lighten your load."

Nathan set his helmet on his seat and stuffed the keys into his pocket. "We'd better hurry. Getting through security might take a while."

"I have heard about your 9-11 disaster," Simon said, "but it hasn't happened here. Security is not as tight."

Kelly gave Simon a suspicious glare. "What are you going to do while we're risking our necks?"

"My counterpart will arrive soon to pick me up, but we will stay long enough to ensure that the motorcycles are not taken away. Assuming that you will successfully prevent the disaster, you may then use the bikes to go back to the observatory site. From there, you will return to Earth Blue before you journey home to Earth Red."

Nathan raised a finger. "Just one more question. If for some reason, the mirror isn't tuned to Earth Blue, is there any way for us to bring it up in the reflection?"

"Yes. You may play a certain melody on your violin." He withdrew a slim iPod from his shirt pocket along with its attached ear buds. "We have recorded on this amazing device from your world all the known compositions that open dimensional passages. If you look at the display screen you will see a note that explains where the compositions work and to what destination they will take you."

"Cool," Nathan said, reaching for it. "That'll help."

Simon pulled it back. "The music device isn't yours to keep." He dialed up a selection and handed Nathan the ear buds. "Do you recognize this?"

He plugged the buds into his ears and listened. After a few seconds, he closed his eyes and took a deep breath. "It's Waxman's 'Carmen Fantasy.'"

Simon arched his eyebrows. "Can you play it?"

"Mom loved that piece, so she played it a lot." Nathan took out the buds and gave them back to Simon. "She tried to teach me, but I never could get it right. I still have some of it in my head, but I don't know how much."

Simon wrapped the wires around the iPod. "Let's hope you don't have to test your memory."

"The way things have gone," Kelly said, hanging her helmet on the handle of Simon's motorcycle, "he'll have to test it."

Nathan detached the saddle pack from the motorcycle and held it at his side. "Let's move. The more time we have to convince them, the better."

After passing through the terminal's sliding doors with Kelly, Nathan checked the flight number on his ticket and searched the listings on a schedule monitor. "There it is. Flight 191."

After getting their boarding passes, they hurried to the security check. As his saddle pack passed through the X-ray machine,

Nathan leaned close to Kelly. "This is nothing compared to how it is now."

"Good thing. Even a mirror might be considered a weapon."

"Or a violin."

When they arrived at the gate, the passengers had lined up at the jetway door and were slowly filing in. Nathan marched straight to the check-in desk where a tall, slender young man stood typing at a computer terminal. He looked up and gave Nathan a mechanical smile. "May I help you?"

Nathan tapped his finger firmly on the counter. "Listen, this might sound really stupid, but what if someone had a bad feeling about this flight, like a premonition about an engine falling off the wing, would you check it out?"

Dropping his gaze back to his desk, the clerk scratched a note with a pencil, apparently unmoved. "Sir, that happens all the time. So many people fear flying, they have nightmares about their flights, and with the recent epidemic, more than half the passengers on any flight have had nightmares about their plane crashing."

"But aren't some of the nightmares coming true?"

"Some, yes, but we can't possibly check out every bad dream." The clerk looked up, again wearing the mechanical smile. "In any case, air travel safety hasn't changed at all, so passengers are flying at the usual rate."

"Yeah. I guess that makes sense." Backing away, Nathan gave him a friendly nod. "Thank you."

He bumped into Kelly and spun around. "I could make a ruckus and claim the engine is messed up, but they might not believe me, and then they'd probably haul me off and ask me a million questions. I'd never make it to the funeral."

"Call in a bomb threat. No one would know you did it."

"You mean use a pay phone?"

"Or a customer service phone."

He scanned the room and found a yellow phone on the wall near the gate. "Those might be traceable. As soon as they answer, they might know exactly where I am."

"Then I guess the pay phone is the only way."

He reached into his jeans pocket. "I have some change. I hope I can find the number for the airport."

"Just dial the operator or nine-one-one."

"Did they have nine-one-one thirty years ago?"

"I guess you'll find out soon enough."

He looked down the long corridor and spied a bank of six phones about a hundred paces away. Three men and one woman stood chatting at the ends of the short, silver cords.

With Kelly following, he hustled toward them, but as soon as he closed in, a forty-something woman in a business suit took one of the two open phones, and a teenager wearing a Northwestern T-shirt took the other.

He pivoted and whispered to Kelly. "We can't afford to wait. Let's get on the plane and speak to the pilot. They sometimes have the cockpit door open when passengers are boarding."

"What time is it?"

Nathan checked his watch, then a monitor to make sure. A digital clock in one corner displayed the time. "Two thirty-six. It's going to crash in about twenty-five minutes."

They quick-stepped back to the gate and took their places at the end of the line, now dwindled to about ten passengers. A gray-haired man in front of them turned around. With a tap of his cane on the floor, he broke into a nervous smile. "Another procrastinator. I know how you feel."

"Really?" Nathan said. "How do I feel?"

Although the man's bare forearm rippled with muscles, animating the tattoo of a fierce-looking dragon, his fingers trembled around the cane's hooked end. "If you're like me, you're scared as a cat in a rocking chair showroom. I had a bad dream about this flight, and I was going to skip it, but my wife said I was being silly. She said everyone's been having nightmares, and the trip was too important to cancel because of a dream."

"Why are you going to Los Angeles?" Kelly asked.

"Booksellers' convention. I'm an author, and my first book's coming out. I'm a retired cop. Lots of stories to tell, you know."

Nathan lowered his voice to a whisper. "Yeah, I guess so."

When they finally shuffled to the jet's entry door, he peered to the left. The cockpit door was already closed. Hot prickles spread across his neck, followed by a stream of sweat.

As he turned into the closer of the two aisles, a sea of faces all across the cabin seemed to rotate his way—a young woman with a pixie haircut settling a newborn in her lap, a uniformed Hispanic man pushing a military duffle bag into the overhead bin, and a little girl bouncing in her window seat, shaking her red Shirley Temple curls as she clutched her daddy's hand—each one a precious life, souls who had no idea that only a few minutes separated them from a meeting with the Almighty.

While he waited for the soldier to finish loading his duffle, Kelly grabbed his hand from behind. "It can't be more than fifteen minutes now," she said, her whisper turning hoarse. A muffled clump sounded from the front of the cabin. "And now they've closed the door to the jetway."

"I know! I know!" He nodded toward his saddle pack. "Can you pull out my violin? I have to do something to get the pilot out here."

She unzipped the bag, withdrew the violin case, and flipped open the clasps. "What are you going to play?"

"I have something special in mind." With every head now turned toward them, Nathan set his violin under his chin and raised the bow. Glancing around, he let out a nervous laugh. "A bon voyage piece, if you don't mind."

The redheaded girl clapped, and shouted, "Play 'Turkey in the Straw'!"

Her father reached for his wallet. "Do you take requests?"

Nathan tried to give them a smile, but his lips felt too frozen to move. "Sure, but let me play this one first."

As soon as the violin sounded the first note, a gruff, female voice interrupted. "What do you think you're doing?"

He twisted his neck. A flight attendant stood behind him, an angular-faced brunette who wore a chilling frown. Nathan played on. "I heard," he said, speaking so loudly everyone could hear, "that one of the passengers is scared the plane is going to crash, so I thought I'd calm him down. This piece is called 'Dance of Death' by Saint-Saëns."

"'Dance of Death?'" The attendant cleared her throat sharply. "Sir, I must ask you to stop and take your seat. You're frightening the other passengers."

"But this is such a lively piece." While Nathan continued playing, another flight attendant picked up a telephone and pressed a button, a frown souring her face.

The first attendant pulled on his arm. "Sir, I must insist—"

Nathan lowered the violin and nodded toward the front of the plane. "May I speak to the captain?"

Just as the attendant turned, the cockpit door opened. The captain, dressed in a navy blue jacket and white shirt, strode heavily toward them and halted about three rows away. "What seems to be the problem?" he asked.

The attendant pointed at Nathan. "This gentleman was—"

"Sir," Nathan interrupted. "May I have a word with you in private?"

Narrowing his eyes, the captain glanced at the attendant briefly, then nodded. "Come to the front."

After handing the violin to Kelly, Nathan followed him to the boarding area. With a sharp spin, the pilot spoke in a harsh whisper, barely moving his lips. "The comfort of my passengers will not be compromised. I cannot tolerate any action, even the playing of a violin, that might upset their confidence in the safety of this craft." As he leaned closer, his eyes seemed to pulse with rage. "Do you understand?

Nathan took a step back. "Yessir, but I had a ... a premonition, I guess you'd call it. So did another passenger." He angled his head toward the wing. "Your left engine is messed up. Something bad's going to happen to it."

The captain extended a rigid finger toward the wing. "That engine is fine. Every part of this jet is checked according to a strict schedule. I'm not about to allow mass hysteria over nightmares, Bigfoots, or Loch Ness monsters to endanger this flight." He leaned so close Nathan could feel his hot breath. "Do I make myself clear?"

Nathan steeled himself, forcing his voice to stay calm. "Yessir. But—"

"No buts, or your butt will be off this aircraft." The captain did an about-face and stormed back into the cockpit, closing the door with a loud clap.

Nathan winced at the sound. That guy meant business. But who could blame him? He'd probably heard a thousand nightmare stories by now. At least he had enough compassion not to kick him off the plane right away.

He checked the seat number on his boarding pass and headed down the aisle. When he met Kelly, he whispered, "Let's just find our seats," and continued striding toward the back.

Glancing at the row numbers as he hurried past, he tried to ignore the irritated passengers stabbing him with icicle glares. He stopped at the wing and rolled his eyes. "Wouldn't you know it? We have the emergency row!"

He folded the empty saddle pack and shoved it under the seat in front of him, while Kelly laid the violin case under the seat in front of her. As she handed him the mirror, she leaned close, her whispered voice spiked with alarm. "Are we really going to take off?"

"I have to save these people somehow," he whispered back. "If you want to leave now, it should be easy to get kicked off. Just make a scene, and I'm sure the pilot will oblige."

"I can't leave without you." She locked her arm around his. "But how do you plan to stop the crash?"

"I'm working on it. I was thinking maybe the mirror could transport us all out of here." He glanced at his watch. 2:40? It had to be later than that. Why would it suddenly slow down? He tried to get a look at the watch on the wrist of a man in the seat across the aisle, but it was too far away.

The man extended his arm and turned the watch toward him. "It is two fifty-five, Nathan, son of Solomon. Will the brief delay you caused be sufficient to bring about your desired end?"

Looking at the man's face, Nathan flinched. Gaunt and white haired, he was the image of Mictar, though he had no ponytail, and his eyes carried none of the murderer's malice. Yet, they seemed just as unearthly—dark, fiery, and piercing.

Every sound in the cabin dampened to silence, and every movement ceased. Even Kelly's rapid breathing stopped as though she had frozen in place. Nathan gave a weak reply. "Who ... who are you?"

His lips seemed to move in slow motion. "I am Patar, the one who sets free."

"How do you know my name?"

"I have been watching you," Patar continued, his voice wafting through the eerie silence. "Your defiance of my brother and his schemes is courageous and good, but you are now wandering in dangerous lands. There are other ways to prevent the ultimate conflict." He pointed a slender white finger toward the front. "You still have time to escape."

Nathan let his gaze move across the colorful array of faces, some smiling, others anxious, each one a reflection of an inner array of hopes and fears. "But what about all these people? Shouldn't I try to rescue them?"

His pale lips bent downward. "That is a question of moral duty. I cannot answer it for you."

"*Can* I rescue them? I mean, is the crash predetermined?"

He raised a single eyebrow. "When man's will is involved, who can say? Most events are predictable, yet what is predetermined will always be heaven's secret. What you see in the mirror merely reflects the ruminations of your mind—what you expect, what you long for, what you fear the most. The mirror is not a window to the future; it is a view port into what might be. Its power is quickened by your faith in what you see and how you respond to it. You might call it a reflection of your supplications."

"What do I do about this ultimate conflict you mentioned? And how do I fight your brother?"

Patar stood and took a step across the aisle. He laid a hand over Nathan's eyes.

Nathan clenched his eyes shut but couldn't move. The hand clamped down, but not tightly.

"Fear not, son of Solomon, and open your eyes. I bring you a gift that will protect you from my brother and equip you for the battles to come."

As light flashed, Nathan relaxed and opened his lids. Soothing warmth bathed his eyes, like bathwater swirling around aching muscles. After a few seconds, Patar lifted his hand and backed away. "Choose whatever path you must, but beware." His voice lowered to a snakelike whisper. "If these souls are cheated out of death, their escape will create more darkness than light. Take care not to stir darkened pools when you know neither the depth of the water nor the creatures that lurk beneath the surface." He slowly turned toward the front and settled back in his seat. "With your choice, we shall see if man's destiny is predetermined or merely predictable." Without another word, he morphed into a human-shaped cloud of thin mist and disappeared.

Suddenly, the passengers jerked back into motion. The vent shot out cool air once again, and Kelly lurched toward the aisle. Catching her breath, she leaned toward Nathan and whispered. "What just happened?"

"I'll tell you later." Nathan sank down in his seat, a queasy feeling knotting his stomach. What should he do now? Patar seemed to think he should let all these people die. How could a force of good possibly want that? Still, if Patar had the power to make time freeze, and he was Mictar's enemy, shouldn't he be trusted? And he seemed to know all about Quattro, but would a Mictar look-alike really be on the right side, or was he in this battle with his brother for how it might benefit him?

As he closed his eyes, the gaunt phantom's face hovered in his mind. Who was he? The name was familiar, but why? He searched his thoughts. Soon, his father's words drifted in. *"Patar would tell Nathan the right thing to do, but he's likely to scare him away."*

His mother's firm words echoed in reply. *"Our son will not be frightened. He will choose wisely. He has the same warrior spirit I saw in you when you were his age."*

Nathan blinked his eyes open. His heartbeat thumped like a jackhammer in his chest. He stared at his reflection in the mirror. His chin quivered, and his tense lips had turned nearly white.

Kelly looked on. With her eyebrows bent low, she glanced from the mirror to Nathan and back to the mirror again. Her voice carried softly up to his ear, a slight tremble giving away her terror. "What are you going to do?"

"I ... I don't know. I just don't know." He watched himself lick his pale lips, hoping his eyes would glow and give him some sign that the mirror would do its magic, but his pupils stayed dark. Even without it, he could probably still save the passengers, maybe scream that he saw someone tamper with the engine or act like a lunatic until they delayed the flight and checked the engine. That might work. They'd probably check it and find the problem, and then blame him and throw him in the slammer. But at least he'd save all their lives.

Maybe he could see if the mirror showed the engine falling off before it happened, but would he be able to warn anyone in time? Would they listen to him if others in the plane saw it, too? He could also play something on his violin that would bring an image to the mirror and transport them to a safe place. But would he and Kelly go alone? Would everyone on the airplane go with them? Or would it not work at all, abandoning him and Kelly to suffer in the devastating carnage?

He clenched a fist. If only he knew what to do! If only his father were around, he would just ask and—

A ground crewman's flashlight caught his eye as he waved it across the ground. The motion brought back a flood of memories, his father making the same gesture with his own flashlight as he stood on the driveway when Nathan made ready to jump from the roof. His words rang in his mind. *"I make you a solemn promise that your fall will be softened enough to prevent all injury. If you trust me, you will put aside your fears and take a step in the progress of your faith. If not, you are free to turn around and come down."*

Lifting the mirror toward the window, he adjusted the angle until he could see the wing. Everything seemed normal, just a copy of the long metal appendage and a gleam of sunlight near the tip. After a few seconds, the pavement in the reflection lurched, then moved forward. Nathan locked his arms in place. The jet in the mirror was backing up!

Kelly bent toward him and watched the image. "You look white as a ghost."

All he could manage was a timid, "We're going to take off."

She looped her arm around his again and laid her head on

his shoulder. As her fingers kneaded his arm, she spoke with a quiet whimper. "Do you have a plan yet?"

Nathan tightened every muscle, trying to keep his body from shaking. Steadying his voice, he whispered, "I have to let it happen."

Kelly paused for a moment. "But we can still escape, right?" She reached for her buckle. "We can just get up and demand that they let us leave."

He grabbed her wrist and pulled it away from her belt. "Just trust me. It's going to be all right."

"But how can you be so sure? Do you know something I don't know?"

"I think I do." He angled his finger toward the seat in front of hers. "As soon as the flight attendants check everyone, get my violin out."

She sat up straight, her arm stiff as she slid away. "Here she comes."

Nathan pushed the mirror behind him. As the brunette attendant strolled quickly down the aisle glancing at buckles, he settled back and smiled at her. When she reached their row, she slowed to a halt. Flashing a chilly stare, she took several seconds checking their seating area. Then, with a huff, she continued her march toward the back.

Using her foot, Kelly pulled the violin case along the carpet and slid it toward Nathan. He caught it with his own foot and waited for the attendant to pass by again on her way to the front. When all was clear, he pulled the case up to his lap.

Just as the mirror had predicted, the plane lurched and began a slow roll backwards. Kelly grabbed the arms of her seat, massaging them with tightened fingers.

Taking a deep breath, Nathan unlatched and opened the case as quietly as possible. After taking out the violin and bow, he laid the case on the floor and slid it back in place with his foot. Then, he retrieved the mirror and braced it on his knees.

Kelly released her stranglehold on her seat and reached for the mirror. "I'll hold it."

He adjusted the mirror to show the wing. "Keep it right there."

The plane stopped its backward maneuver, and, with a high-pitched purr, the engines came to life and propelled it forward. As the jet rumbled toward the runway, Nathan closed his eyes and prayed. A crash was inevitable. Only Quattro could save them now. But whom would it save?

He opened his eyes again. Although in reality they rolled slowly toward the main runway, the mirror showed the tarmac lines speeding past the window. Suddenly, in the midst of a huge billow of smoke, the engine flew up from the front of the wing, tumbled over the top, and hurtled back toward the tail area.

Nathan jerked his head away. It was really going to happen. The plane was doomed.

In real life, the jet turned onto the black-streaked pavement and accelerated. With each tiny jolt over the runway's grooves, Kelly flinched, shaking the mirror.

Nathan set the bow on the strings. The timing had to be perfect. If he played too soon, a frightened passenger or an angry flight attendant might snatch his violin away. If he played too late, the dimensional window might not open in time ... if it would at all.

With long, easy strokes, he began the first measure of "Amazing Grace." Years ago his mother had taught him the song, one of his first when he was barely more than a toddler, holding an eighth-size violin in his chubby hands. And as he played, quite badly, most likely, she played along and sang, her voice matching the composer's passion.

The plane jerked. Just as the nose tipped upward and the landing gear lifted off the ground, the engine flew up in front of the wing and zoomed past the window. A chorus of gasps spread across the field of seats like a gust of wind. Screams erupted. Hands latched onto armrests. A rumbling roar from the good engine on the right pounded through the cabin. The jet rattled, a bone-jarring shake that chattered teeth and jiggled loose skin on every white-knuckled passenger.

Kelly cried out, "Nathaaaan! I don't want to die! I'm not ready to die!"

He stopped playing and grabbed her hand. "Don't give up yet! Hang on! It's the only way we can survive!"

Strangling his fingers, she breathed rapid, heavy breaths. "Okay ... Get a grip, Kelly ... Get control of yourself." Her breaths eased, long and quiet, but her hand stayed latched on to his.

Nathan pulled away and continued playing, now with more passion than ever as he watched her still-terrified eyes. What could he do to help her?

As they continued their upward lift, Kelly jumped, again shaking the mirror, but she bit her lip and hung on. The camera dangled in front of her, thumping her chest with every jolt. The plane rolled slowly to the left, much more steeply than it would for a turn. Screams again broke out all around as passengers tipped to the side, reaching, grabbing, clawing to stay upright.

Kelly squeezed her eyes closed. Her face quaked as she stretched out her long, plaintive cry. "Nathan! Help me!"

Leaning against the window, Nathan swept the bow through the end of a measure, grinding his teeth. What could he do to help? What could anyone do? The mirror displayed a sea of twisted, burning wreckage and dozens of bloody, charred, and dismembered bodies. Any second now, he and Kelly would join them.

NEW PERSPECTIVES

As the jet shook even harder, more screams filled the cabin—calls to Jesus, cries for mercy, and unintelligible wails. An overhead bin popped open, spilling a duffle bag and a canvas overnighter on top of two men across the aisle. The smell of burning fuel and rubber filled the cabin.

With new panicked shouts bouncing all around, Kelly braced one hand on the seat in front of her and sang the first phrase of Nathan's tune, her voice feeble and quiet. "Amazing grace, how sweet the sound, that saved a wretch like me." Every word rattled through her chattering teeth as she hung on to the mirror. During the second phrase, a woman joined in from behind as did a man somewhere to the side.

The jet rolled to ninety degrees and flew sideways. The cabin lights flickered off, leaving only shafts of sunlight pouring through the windows. More bins flew open up and down the aisle, spilling suitcases and garment bags. Smoke billowed into the front of the cabin and spread toward them.

The mirror blazed with fire, falling ash, and death. Still playing, Nathan glanced out the window. The tip of the wing sank, a mere thirty feet from a fatal brush with the ground.

As Kelly and the others sang on, Nathan stopped playing and reached the end of his bow toward the reading light in the overhead console. Would it work? Or was the plane too crippled to deliver power to the lights? He caught a glimpse of the camera, swinging back and forth from Kelly's strap. There was no way he could reach the shutter, and the flash probably wasn't turned on. He strained to push the console button, fighting the horrible quaking of the wounded jet. Giving the bow a desperate shove, he hit the switch. In the dimness of the cabin, the light flashed on.

The mirror reflected the weak beam, splitting it into multiple shafts. Two beams pierced Nathan and Kelly, while others zipped past them. Nathan grimaced. This time, the light seemed like a flaming sword, a hot laser that sizzled through his skin and burned deep in his chest.

The mirror view, still a landscape of carnage, swelled. Wincing in pain, Kelly released it, but it stayed upright on Nathan's lap, expanding in every direction, even in depth as it seemed to absorb his legs and reach out toward Kelly's. In seconds, Nathan felt his entire body sliding into the mirror's grip. He looked back, still able to see through the window. The wingtip struck the ground, sending the jet into a wild tumble. Kelly's body flung forward, throwing her into Nathan and forcing both of them into the mirror's grasp.

Holding out his violin to keep it safe, Nathan rolled to a stop in an open field. The jet cartwheeled only a few feet above his head, and the nose section knifed into the ground about fifty yards away, digging a rut before breaking away from the fuselage. The rest of the body slammed down and smashed a hangar in a thunderous explosion of horrible thuds, cracks, and squeals as its momentum swept an avalanche of destruction across the field.

Metal tore from metal. Fire gushed into the sky in an enormous billowing cloud of orange. Heat rushed past Nathan in a rolling wave, singeing his skin and whipping his hair upright. The mirror, still in his lap, radiated warmth through his pant legs.

Kelly grabbed his arm and buried her face in his sleeve, screaming, "Nathan! They're dead! They're all dead!"

Someone jumped past them and dashed toward the wreckage, then another limped by, supported by a cane. Nathan looked around, counting. Two, three, four ... at least four other people sat or stood around in horror while two hurried into the crash zone. Grabbing the mirror and still clutching the violin, Nathan rose and staggered toward the burning wreckage. Kelly stumbled along beside him, each leg wobbly and weak.

In the midst of crackling fires and sizzling metal, sirens wailed their approach. The two men who charged ahead had stopped and now just stood and surveyed the field of hopelessness. Burning body parts lay strewn in a swath of superheated fires. No one could save them now.

One of the men dropped to his knees. Clutching his thinning gray hair with both hands, he shouted into the rising vapors. "I knew this would happen! Why didn't I stop it?"

Nathan sidestepped toward him. When he drew close, he recognized the tear-streaked face of the author they had met in the terminal building. His cane lay at his side.

"I saw the crash in my dreams!" the author continued. "I should have done something!"

The first man joined them, a short, stocky man with a full beard and weary gray eyes. "I dreamed about it, too," he whispered to Nathan. "Did you?"

Nathan glanced at the mirror, now tucked under his arm, but he couldn't feel it. All sensation had drained away. His limbs, his body, even his face and hands felt completely numb. Staring at the devastation, he could barely find strength to speak. "Yeah. I saw it. I think ..."

The man scanned the other survivors. "I think we all did."

Nathan looked back at them—a young woman in seventies-style green pants standing petrified as she watched the fires churn, a middle-aged woman in a navy blue business suit weeping as she talked to Kelly, and a young couple sitting together in a sobbing huddle. "I think I know what you mean."

The man extended his hand. "Name's John, but my friends call me Jack."

Nathan shook his hand, hot and sweaty, but carrying a pleasant grip. "I'm Nathan."

Jack wagged his head back and forth. "I suppose we should have said something. Maybe if all of us had spoken up, they might have listened."

As fire engines roared close and a helicopter beat its blades overhead, Nathan turned back to Kelly. She held the camera in her hands, the strap still around her neck as she snapped a picture of the crash scene. The flash lit up, though it didn't seem as bright as usual in the mid-afternoon sun. As she lowered the camera, her voice matched her teary, anguished eyes. "One of the survivors asked me to take some pictures for her. I hope it's okay."

Nathan glanced at a business card in her hand. "Sure. I guess it won't hurt anything, but I don't see how you're going to get the pictures to her."

She picked up the violin case and opened it, nodding toward the saddle pack at her feet. "I found them near where we landed."

Nathan methodically laid the violin and bow inside, closed the lid, and snapped the latches. He stuffed the case and mirror into the bag and snatched it up. "Let's walk. The terminal's not far." Staring hard at the airport buildings, he strode toward them, not wanting to look back as he listened to the turmoil in his wake—blaring sirens, shouting rescue workers, and sizzling fires. Every sound made him wince inside, a dissonant song of death, a "Dance Macabre" performed on the strings of demonic violins. And he hadn't been able to prevent it.

Kelly's voice seeped into the flow of sounds. "Are you all right?"

"How could I be all right?" He winced again. His words had come out harsh, like a stabbing dagger.

Her cool fingers slid into his free hand. "It's not your fault."

He grasped them gratefully. "I know." But that was all he could say. Death loomed over his mind like a shadow—dark, empty, and icy cold. And now he had to go to a funeral—his parents' funeral.

After following an access road that led them to the front of the terminal building, they found the motorcycles where they had left them, leaning on their stands with the helmets still in place. Cars had parked in every lane, halting the flow of traffic. People milled all around. Their conversations buzzed, wordless in Nathan's ears. A few uniformed men and women hurried from place to place, some barking into walkie-talkies, but Simon was nowhere in sight.

Nathan slipped on his helmet, attached the bag to one of the cycles, and dug out the keys. "Here," he said, tossing one set to Kelly. "Can't afford to wait for him."

She caught the keys and mounted the other bike. With her helmet already on and her dirty beige slacks and blue polo shirt rippling across her body in the breeze, she looked like a mosaic of misplaced pieces, a muscular choir girl mounting a wild mustang, a true hell's angel.

As he straddled the seat, he nodded at her. "We'd better not travel together. Just stay close enough behind to keep me in sight."

"Why?"

"Word's going to get out that we survived. I said something about the engine to the gate clerk, so, if they think I had anything to do with the crash, they'll try to hunt us down, but they'll be looking for two teenagers traveling together."

She gave him a thumbs up. "Got it."

He dug into his pocket and pulled out a wad of dollar bills. "For tolls," he said, stuffing them into her hand.

Tightening his grip on the handlebars, Nathan started the motorcycle and weaved through the lanes of parked vehicles. When he approached the front, he reached a row of airport security cars. Apparently they had intentionally blocked the access road to halt the flow of traffic.

Nathan eyed the officer in a driver's seat as he passed by. As if in reply, the car's siren squawked a brief note. When Kelly's bike scooted by, the officer rolled down his window and shouted over the motorcycles' rumble. "Stop! Pull over to the sidewalk!"

Giving the engine a shot of gas, Kelly raced away. Nathan roared after her, keeping watch in his rearview mirror. The blue lights on the police car flashed to life, and its siren howled as it gave chase.

Kelly slowed down. When Nathan caught up, she shouted. "Ever done any dirt biking?"

"Yeah. Why?"

"Get ready!"

As they passed a merge lane for cars entering their road from an upcoming overpass, she slowed even further. When the officer zoomed closer, she turned into the grass, spun a one-eighty, and headed into the entry curve in the wrong direction.

Nathan swung around and tore after her. As cars blared their horns and knifed out of the way, he checked his mirror, barely catching a glimpse of the patrol car skidding to a halt back on the main road.

When they reached the feeder highway, Kelly crossed the pavement and hugged the right-hand side of the road, roaring across the overpass in the wrong direction. Again, Nathan followed. When she found a narrow gap in the guard rail that lined the center of the median, she angled her motorcycle through it and kept going, this time in the same direction as the cars already speeding along. Keeping close behind, Nathan looked back. No one followed.

After cruising far enough to get out of sight of the officer, Kelly pulled into a restaurant lot and parked behind the building. She cut her engine off and slumped her shoulders.

Nathan slammed on the brakes and skidded to her side. "You okay?" he asked as he shut down his bike.

She nodded. "Just worn out. You?"

"Same." He looked around the vacant lot. The restaurant was either closed or out of business.

A wailing police car screamed past, then another. He peeked around the corner. A third cruiser came by at a much slower speed. An officer looked their way, scanning the front parking lot.

Nathan pulled back. "We'd better cut through some side roads and get out of here."

He swung his motorcycle around and headed away from the highway. They pushed their bikes up a gravel embankment and over a set of railroad tracks. Once across, they ran down the other side and onto a residential street. Now hidden from the main highway by the railroad berm, he turned back toward the airport. "If we head that way, we'll eventually get to Interstate 88. Since we were last seen heading north, they should concentrate on that side of town."

She started her engine and nodded. "I'm right behind you."

"Remember. Not too close."

She nodded again.

After meandering through the neighborhood, Nathan located a ramp to the main highway and headed west, careful to stay just under the speed limit. In his rearview mirror, he spotted Kelly merging into the right lane, falling behind a little farther every few seconds.

He zipped along, keeping an eye on her as she hung back about a half-mile or so. Letting out a sigh, he shook his head. She was an incredible combination of female charm, sharp wits, and ice-water coolness. Most girls would've scrunched into a fetal curl and cried like a baby, but even locked inside a doomed jet already falling from the sky, she never lost her head. She even sang the song! Amazing!

He glanced at a ring on his finger, a covenant band of gold his parents had given him when he turned thirteen. His father's words still rang clearly in his mind as large hands pushed the ring over his knuckle.

In some ways this is a gift for your future wife. It will remind you to cherish her even before you ever meet, to keep your body and mind pure so that on your wedding day, when you meld together into one flesh, hers will be the only skin you ever touch with intimacy. Her lips will be the first yours ever meet in tender passion and the last when one of you goes to meet our Savior. Yes, this is a gift for her, yet for you as well, for when you present yourself to her as a holy vessel, you will feel God's pleasure, for you will have no memories of past loves, no scars from romantic wounds that never fully healed, and your union will never be haunted by the ghost of a past lover who now rests in the bosom of another.

Nathan looked at Kelly, now just a smudge in his mirror. As her reflection shrank even further, he enlarged her form in his mind, giving shape to her body and imagining her without a helmet, her sunlit hair flowing in the wind behind her familiar face. He focused on her eyes, sad and lost.

He let out a heavy sigh. What about *her* scars? What about the ghosts from her past? If the two of them ever joined as one, could she forget about those phantoms? Could *he* forget them?

He sighed again and searched for her in the mirror, but she had gone beyond the reflection's edge. Twisting his neck, he looked back. There she was, still following his lead. But she was so far away ... so very far away.

18

A NEW KEY

Nathan set the motorcycle's kickstand and unzipped the saddle pack. He glanced around at the broken trees and scattered branches. No sign of Dr. Simon.

After parking her bike next to Nathan's, Kelly shuffled through the debris toward the tri-fold mirror. In the reflection, the Earth Blue scene had disappeared. Now it showed only the same mangled forest that surrounded them.

Nathan pulled his violin case from the bag and fumbled with the clasps.

Kelly grasped his hand. "Nathan, you're trembling."

He looked down at his shaking fingers. "Yeah. I guess I am." Taking a deep breath, he tried to calm his nerves. He'd never be able to play the "Carmen Fantasy" unless he relaxed. He flipped up the latches and withdrew his mother's violin. He didn't remember much of the piece, so the dimension had to open in a hurry.

As he laid the bow over the strings, Kelly gave him a firm nod. "You can do this."

Feeling more at ease, he set his feet and watched himself in the mirror. Then, after starting with a short mid-range stroke, his fingers immediately flew across the neck and ended the run with a sweet high note. After another quick mid-range stroke, he played a rapid run from the high to the low registers, then moved to a slower, sweet melody that lasted about fifteen seconds.

He paused and stared at the mirror. Nothing. Still just his own image gawking back at him, his shirt tail hanging out on one side and his dirty hair locked in a rigid windswept pose.

"I ... I can't remember any more."

She clutched the camera tightly. "You have to remember. We don't have any choice."

"I know. I know." He took in a deep breath and began again, playing the same notes, but, after a long pause, he lowered the bow. "It's no use, I—"

"Nathan!" She stared at his Quattro mirror, wide-eyed. "Look!" As she turned it toward him, she broke into a wide smile.

The reflection showed his mother, dressed in gray sweats, standing in a home studio with her violin in playing position. Next to her stood a younger version of Nathan, maybe two years his junior, also with a violin in hand. With each one looking at sheet music on a stand in front of them, his mother spoke, but no sound came forth.

Kelly gave voice to the image. "Your mother says, 'Watch my fingers, Nathan.'"

His throat clamped so tightly, he couldn't reply. He shuffled as close as possible and readied his bow again, squinting at his mother's hands. After the first note, her fingers glided along the neck, then stopped as she spoke to the boy again.

Kelly whispered, "'Now you try it.'"

Nathan played the notes again, this time with perfect precision.

His mother tucked her violin and clapped. Lifting her bow, she played the next few measures. Her fingers again seemed to caress her instrument as a gentle angel would pet a lamb. She paused and pointed her bow at the younger Nathan.

This time, the real Nathan didn't wait for a command. He played the notes flawlessly, copying his mother's tender touch.

The tri-fold mirror image slowly darkened.

"She says she's going to play the rest all the way through, so watch carefully."

Nathan set his bow again and leaned close. Sweat beaded on his forehead, and his tongue dried out. "It's so fast. I'll never be able to copy it just by watching."

"Yes, you can, Nathan. I believe in you!"

He looked up at her. "Did you say that, or did my mom?"

"I said it." Kelly bit her lip before continuing. "You're the best, Nathan. I've never met anyone like you. I know you can do this."

Nathan let his mind drift back to that day he stood with his mother, looking up at her in wonder as she played this intricate piece with blinding speed and flawless beauty. As she leaned toward him, the view seemed to envelop him, bringing her face so close that her fair skin and jet black hair loomed over him like a protective mother eagle. With a whisper, she blew on his knuckles.

Kelly's voice gave life to the whisper. "May the breath of God fill your soul with the melody of everlasting love."

Shivers ran up his arm, across his shoulders, and into his other hand. As his mother straightened and readied herself again, his fingers seemed charged with energy, begging to fly into action.

Francesca Shepherd played. Nathan Shepherd answered. Though her reflected instrument sang in silence, he channeled the sound to the same violin, feeling her energy and passion flow through his fingers as each note rang sweet and true.

As the celebration of musical zeal threaded rapid runs across the ebony fingerboard, the reflection in the tri-fold mirror altered with the same fervor. Within seconds, the telescope room in Earth Blue took shape.

Kelly's voice seemed a distant echo. "It's working!"

Francesca played the last measure with a dazzling flair. Nathan copied her movements, adding a dip of his body and an accentuated vibrato as he pushed the bow through the final note.

The moment he finished, his mother bowed toward him. Tears welling, he bowed in return, barely able to restrain the spasms in his chest as he gazed at her face, the gleaming eyes, the rose-petal cheeks, and the lovely smile as she laid a hand on his shoulder, "Well played, my dear son, an aria of strings for our heavenly Father."

The touch brought an electrified jolt, shocking him back to reality. He turned to Kelly. "Did you say that?"

Tears streaming down her cheeks, she lowered the mirror and embraced him. "I couldn't say it," she whispered as she brushed her lips across his cheek. "You must have heard her yourself." She pulled his wrist gently. "Come on. We can't wait for the sun. We'll have to use the camera."

After laying the violin in its case and packing it and his mirror in the saddle bag, he followed her to the front of the tri-fold mirror. When Kelly raised the camera to her eye, a hint of brightening crossed the storm-ravaged field. The orange ball in the sky edged under the bank of clouds and aimed its beams directly at the mirror. The polished glass bounced the rays. The middle pane directed its beam straight out while the other two mirror panels angled the light, intersecting their reflections with the central radiant shaft.

At the point the beams met, a vertical halo of brilliant colors formed, an oval-shaped rainbow that pulsed at twice the frequency of a beating heart.

Nathan jerked Kelly's hand. "Jump for the colors!"

They leaped together into the halo. The rainbow enveloped their bodies in a wash of yellow, blue, and red, altering the grass at their feet into a blaze of hues, as if a frenzied artist had brushed every color from his palette across the littered field.

In the reflection, the telescope room expanded and swarmed over them with dim shadows. The familiar perimeter walls bent around their bodies, the tour entry door on one side and the elevator on the other. Soon, everything settled, and they were once again standing under the high-arching, reflective dome.

Kelly tugged on Nathan's sleeve. "Looks like we're alone."

"You're not!" The pert female voice came from under the computer desk. Daryl emerged, carrying the shotgun with both hands.

Clara followed, wincing as she straightened slowly. "Tight squeeze under there."

"We heard someone coming," Daryl continued, "so we scooped up all our stuff, turned out the lights, and hid. We think it was Mictar. He saw the stiff and took off, so he'll probably be back soon."

"I take it you delivered Francesca?" Clara asked.

"Yeah. Sort of." Nathan lowered the saddle pack to the floor. "She's in good hands."

"Earth Red has sped up in comparison to Earth Blue, so you have to hurry." Daryl gave Nathan the shotgun, then reached into her pocket and transferred four shells to his pocket one by one.

"Let's send them home," Clara said as she backed up toward Daryl's computer. "I'll hang on to the other mirror for safekeeping."

Daryl reached for the laptop's mouse pad. "Click your heels together, Kelly-kins, and remember to say your line!"

As she picked up the saddle pack, Kelly looked down at her feet, letting the camera dangle low. "You mean, 'There's no place like home'?"

"You got it!"

"This isn't Kansas," Kelly said. "It's Illinois."

Daryl pointed at her. "You'd better say your line, or a tornado might take you back to Oz."

"Listen, Miss Hollywood, don't talk to me about tornadoes. I was just—"

"Cool it, ladies." Nathan set the shotgun against his shoulder. "I hate to be the cowardly lion, but we'd better get out of here."

As if to accentuate the point, the elevator door closed and headed down. Someone must have called it from below.

"Time for us to make tracks." Daryl waved at them. "Have a good trip."

The lights once again flashed on. As before, the image in the mirror above seemed to descend and spread out, enveloping them in its grasp. Everything around them morphed into warped shapes and intermixing colors. Seconds later, the scene cleared, revealing the telescope room once again with Clara and Daryl staring at them. If not for their different clothes and the lack of a dead man lying on the floor, it would have been impossible to tell that they had transported at all.

Clara ran forward and embraced Nathan. "We have to hurry," she said. "According to the schedule on the computer, Interfinity is showing the telescope to a tour group in ten minutes."

Daryl typed madly on the laptop's keyboard. "I'm restoring the computer to how we found it." After a final tap, the mirror above transformed into a view of the morning sky, dark blue, with hints of orange filtering in from one side.

Kelly extended the saddle pack toward Nathan. "I'll trade you. I've always wanted to ride shotgun."

"I hear voices." Daryl nodded at the tour entry door. "Over there."

"They're coming." Clara pointed at Daryl. "You hold the camera. We might have to run, and Kelly has her hands full."

While Daryl pulled the camera strap over Kelly's head, Clara punched the elevator call button. As soon as the door opened, she rushed inside and squeezed against one side wall, while Daryl flattened against the other. Nathan pushed between them, leaned the saddle pack against the back door, and turned to face Kelly, backing up as far as he could. She stepped in, but in order to fit past the doorway, she had to set the gun butt on the floor and straddle the barrel with her legs as if riding it like a witch on a broomstick.

As they squeezed together, Nathan eyed her. Now she was a gun-toting angel, a pixie with a pop. After all the references to *The Wizard of Oz*, a silly question lodged in his brain. *Are you a good witch or a bad witch?* He rolled his eyes at his own lame joke and kept it to himself. For better or for worse, Daryl was rubbing off on him.

Once everyone had cleared the door, Nathan pressed the button for the bottom level. Across the way, the tour door opened, and a tall man in a black business suit entered the telescope room. He stared right at them but disappeared from sight as the car door slid shut.

Nathan gave Clara a nudge. "That was Dr. Gordon. He saw us."

"Just what we need," she replied. "They'll probably have a guard waiting at the bottom floor."

Daryl shook her head. "Not likely. I changed the code on the door leading to the secure area. It's the only one I didn't change back."

As the motor hummed, Nathan raised his voice a notch. "My father left me a note saying we could trust the Dr. Gordon on Earth Red, so I don't think we have to worry."

"But he might be from Earth Blue," Kelly said. "Could you tell if he had a wound on his cheek?"

"I'm pretty sure he didn't." Nathan glanced briefly at the barrels again. "Just in case, get the gun ready. It should still have one shell in it."

Kelly slid the gun upward through her hands and propped it on Nathan's shoulder. As soon as the door opened, she angled it outward, ready to shoot, but no one was there.

Nathan grabbed the saddle bag and withdrew the mirror from inside. When the others had filed into the elevator's alcove, he crept toward the hall and signaled for everyone to stay back. "I'll see if the coast is clear." He held the mirror at an angle that allowed him to see the curved pathway toward the security door. No one in sight.

He shoved the mirror back into the saddle bag and hoisted it up. "I'll bet Gordon didn't sound the alarm. Let's make a break for the back door."

With Nathan leading the way, all four padded as swiftly and softly as possible. When they reached the secured door, Nathan peeked through the window. A heavyset woman stood with her back to them, vacuuming the hallway carpet at the intersection to the exit corridor.

He backed away from the door. "Clara, where's your car?"

"In the main parking lot. At least I hope it's still there."

"Kelly's Toyota is out in the woods, so we'll have to split up. They'll be looking for me, so while Kelly and I try to sneak out the back door to her car, you and Daryl can play it cool and go out the front door. Let's meet at a gas station at the main highway, but if something happens, we'll be in touch by cell phone."

Clara nodded. "An excellent plan."

"Kelly," Nathan said, touching the shotgun. "Better leave that here. It'll attract attention."

"It'll discourage pursuers."

"Okay. Have it your way." He curled his arm around the saddle bag and pushed the door open. "Let's go."

He jogged quickly toward the maid, cut around her to the right, and headed for the exit. Hearing a loud shriek, he glanced back. Kelly ran close behind, the shotgun in full view, while the maid flipped open a mobile phone and punched a button.

Nathan burst out the back door, still unbroken in Earth Red, and the two dashed down the stone path that led into the woods. As soon as her car came into sight, Kelly unlocked the doors with her key fob and tossed it to Nathan. "You drive."

He caught the keys and flung open the driver's door. While Kelly hopped into the passenger's side, he set the saddle pack in the rear seat and slid behind the steering wheel, inserting the key and cranking the engine in one motion.

Kelly sang out, "We've got company."

A guard carrying a handgun jogged toward them, too heavy and slow to catch up in time. He stopped and pointed the gun. "Stay right where you are, or I'll shoot."

Keeping her eye on the guard, Kelly reached toward Nathan. "Got more ammo?"

He dug the shotgun shells from his pocket and poured them into her lap. "Don't let him see the gun."

"I got it under control. Just be ready to peel out." As he lowered her window, Kelly broke down the twin barrels and slid a shell into the empty chamber, keeping the gun out of the guard's view.

"You're only going to scare him off, right? He's just doing his job."

"Trust me. I know what I'm doing." The moment she locked the gun in place, she propped it up on the window frame. "Floor it!"

Firmly gripping the wheel, Nathan slammed down the pedal. The tires skidded wildly in the grass, throwing two rivers of dirt behind them. A bullet cracked through the rear window and slammed into the backseat.

Kelly fired the shotgun. In the wake of a deafening boom, she rocketed backwards into Nathan's lap just as the tires finally caught hold. The car shot forward. He jerked the wheel to the right, narrowly avoiding a massive oak, then slid into a sharp turn to the left as he tried to aim the car toward the main parking lot.

When the car straightened, Kelly pushed against the glove box and slid back to her seat.

Nathan tried to look back at the guard. "Did you hit him?"

"No, but he'll probably have to change his underwear." She grabbed Nathan's arm. "Look out!"

Three guards stood at the edge of a parking lot on a rise about fifty yards away, aiming rifles with scopes. She grabbed her shotgun again. "Swing to the left so I can get a good view!"

"You gotta be kidding me! No more shooting!" He pulled the car to the right. "We'll have to take a shortcut."

She pointed straight ahead. "You're heading for a creek!"

"I see a bridge."

"It's just a footbridge!"

"Not anymore." Several loud cracks sounded from the guards. Two bullets clanked against the car's frame. Nathan zoomed onward.

The steep-banked creek dug into the landscape a mere thirty yards away. The closer they got, the narrower the footbridge seemed, just skinny slats nailed over thin plywood.

As another bullet ripped into the trunk, the Camry roared ahead. "We're too big!" Kelly screamed.

"Think thin!" He pressed the accelerator. Hitting a small incline just before the bridge, the tires leaped onto the slats and clattered ahead. The rearview mirrors slammed into the guardrails, folding the mirrors against the sides of the car. As wood splinters flew all around, the bridge sagged precariously. Seconds later, the Camry flew off the end and surfed down an embankment that led to a covered walkway in front of the main entrance.

"More people!" Kelly shouted.

"Including Clara and Daryl." Nathan laid on the horn and pumped the brakes, trying to slow down without going into a full slide, but the wet grassy slope gave barely any traction.

The crowd scattered. He jerked the wheel back and forth, avoiding a dog and a petrified old lady, until he finally spun the car and stopped on the concrete walk, leaving the rear door no more than three feet from Clara and Daryl.

"Get in!" Nathan ordered. "No use taking two cars now."

Clara threw open the door, and she and Daryl piled in, Daryl still clutching the camera. He slammed down the gas again, and, with at least a dozen people looking on, he jumped the curb, bounced into the parking lot, and zoomed away.

More rifle shots echoed behind them, but no bullets hit the car. With the shotgun barrels now pointing at the floorboard, Kelly laid her head back. "I think I'm going to be sick!"

Nathan let out a long breath, flapping his lips as he relaxed his grip on the wheel. "When my stomach catches up to me, I'll pass around the barf bags."

Kelly gave his arm a light punch. "Where'd you learn to drive like that?"

"Getting away from a kidnapper in Boston." He angled his head toward her and grinned. "But no one seemed to care. Everyone else drove the same way."

Daryl leaned forward from the backseat. "Think they'll chase us?"

Nathan glanced up at the rearview mirror. "I see Gordon Red's Lincoln, but I don't know if Gordon Blue has the same kind of car or not."

"I don't trust either one," Kelly said. "We'll have to outrun him. With the moves you have, you'll shake him for sure."

He pushed the gas again, but the engine responded with a clattering sound. "Uh-oh. That's a bad sign." As the Camry tried to climb a hill, it slowed and sputtered. "Better load up the shotgun, Kelly. You might have to discourage another pursuer."

She leaned out of the window and sat on the frame, her sneakers now barely touching her seat. "I got him in my sights," she yelled, "but he's not backing down!"

Clara patted Nathan's shoulder. "Kelly's my kind of girl."

"Can you tell who it is?" Nathan called, leaning her way. "Is it Gordon?"

"Can't tell yet! But he's closing in fast!"

Nathan yanked on Kelly's ankle. "Don't shoot! I'm pulling over! I can't outrun him." He guided the chugging car to the side and stopped, pulling the emergency brake to keep it from rolling back down. "Everyone else stay here."

He opened the door and stepped out onto the road. Kelly balanced on the window frame, her shotgun now lying on the roof, but her finger stayed poised at the trigger. "Steady there, deadeye," Nathan said, winking at her. "I think it's going to be okay."

She smiled and winked back. "I gotcha covered, hot rod."

As a warm breeze whipped their clothes, the black Town Car drove up and stopped about a hundred feet behind the Camry. Dr. Gordon emerged slowly and lifted his empty hands. "I have no weapon," he called. "Will you trust me now?"

19

A NEW DUET

Nathan leaned back against Kelly's car, trying not to show his nervousness. "It depends. I want to see the left side of your face."

"My face?" Turning his cheek, Dr. Gordon edged closer. "I take it you left some kind of wound on my Earth Blue counterpart."

"You could say that." As Gordon climbed the hill, Nathan squinted at the smooth skin on his cheek. "Looks like you're clean."

Gordon halted. "Will you call off your assassin?"

Nathan glanced up at Kelly. She had raised the shotgun and propped it under her arm. "Cut it out. He's on our side."

"I wasn't even aiming yet." She laid the gun back on the roof. "I was just watching."

Gordon finished his climb and stopped in front of Nathan. "I can't say I blame you for being cautious, but you have also thrown caution to the wind on more than one occasion."

"If you mean the highway chase, that was before I knew there were two of you. I was afraid that—"

"You were afraid," he interrupted, pointing a finger at Nathan. "I've been hearing reports about you. You've shown a lot of courage at times, but courage isn't something you can afford to switch on and off. Shooting at guards, racing down the highway like a madman, and being afraid to hear me out at the school isn't going to cut it. If you want to rescue your parents, you'd better shake that yellow stripe off your back."

Nathan scowled at him. "Wait a minute! I was—"

"Don't you dare insult Nathan!" Kelly shouted, still sitting on the window frame. "Most of the time he was protecting me, and I was the one blasting the shotgun, not him. And I didn't shoot at the guard. If I had, he'd be pushing up daisies."

"Protecting you?" Gordon shifted his finger toward her. "Dragging a girl on his adventures got Nathan Blue killed as well as Kelly Blue. So much for protection."

Tightening a fist, Nathan pushed away from the car. "And it was the other Gordon who killed them. Maybe it wasn't protecting a girl that got Nathan killed. Maybe it was trusting the wrong people."

Gordon backed away a step. "I see your point. In any case, Dr. Simon is not pleased with your—"

"Dr. Simon?" Nathan repeated. "So he *is* behind all of this?"

"Not behind it. He's trying to stop Mictar and my Blue counterpart. It wouldn't be a wise idea to upset his plans."

Nathan rolled his eyes. "Well, good old Dr. Simon might not be pleased, but I'm not exactly jumping for joy with how he's handling things. Simon Red told Mictar that he arranged my parents' deaths, so trusting him in any dimension isn't exactly the first thing I want to do."

"I understand your distrust." Dr. Gordon waved his arm toward his Lincoln. "I will drive you to the funeral site and explain what I can along the way." He popped open the trunk with his key fob. "Young lady, please deposit the shotgun in the back. You might wish to scare people half to death, but I have a different modus operandi."

While Nathan retrieved the violin and mirror from the Camry, Kelly dismounted the window frame, snatched her sweatshirt from the backseat, and lugged the shotgun toward the rear of the Lincoln, glaring at Dr. Gordon as she passed by. She muttered something under her breath, making Gordon frown.

After depositing the violin in the trunk, Nathan helped the three ladies pile into the backseat. Keeping the mirror tucked at his side, he slid into the front, his eyes focused on Dr. Gordon.

Gordon started the engine, meeting Nathan's stare with a hardened gaze of his own. "You still don't trust me, do you?"

A hint of a growl spiced Nathan's voice. "My father in Earth Blue said I should, but I'm not so sure. My real father got killed because of trusting people like you, so I'm taking a big risk."

Gordon's tone stayed calm, almost mechanical. "When weighed against the alternatives, it is not such a big risk. Going with me gets you to the funeral on time as well as the vital information you've been seeking."

Kelly spoke up from the back. "The shotgun would've pried the information from you, too."

"I assume you consider that an edgy quip." Dr. Gordon shook his head and sighed. "Young people these days have a fondness for nonsensical humor that escapes me."

Nathan winced at Dr. Gordon's remark. No sense in getting on his bad side when they needed him to explain what was going on. It was time to get to the point before he clammed up completely. He pointed at the triple-infinity emblem on Dr. Gordon's jacket. "So, what's up with all the dimensional stuff and Interfinity?"

Daryl pulled forward on Gordon's headrest. "I already told them about how you heard the music from the other dimension before you played it in ours, so you can start from there."

"Very well." Dr. Gordon settled back in his seat. "When I discovered the existence of another dimension that parallels ours, I knew right away that some people might be tempted to try to benefit from the discovery in an inappropriate manner. Whichever dimension slides into the lead, if you will, time wise, can feed information to the other—stock market rallies, sporting events, bankruptcy filings, et cetera."

"So this whole thing is a money-making scheme?" Nathan asked.

"Not at all. For my part, I hoped to avert disasters and prevent loss of life. Maybe I wouldn't be able to prevent an earthquake, but I could warn people and assist them in getting out of harm's way. Strangely, however, my Earth Blue counterpart had a profiteering mind-set. This troubled me greatly, because I had theorized that genetic duplicates would make identical decisions when presented with identical information.

"The big problems began when Mictar appeared. Long after the other Gordon and I created the twin observatories, we experimented with various dimensional transport scenarios. In one trial, after syncing with each other, we aimed our activation lights directly at the ceiling mirror, just to see what would happen if we hit the mirrors simultaneously. The beams made an intense splash of indescribable light, and when it dispersed, a man stood at the center of my observatory floor, a gaunt, white-haired man."

"Mictar?" Kelly asked.

"No. He called himself Patar, and he warned me that his brother, Mictar, had likely appeared at the same place in the other dimension." Gordon altered his voice to a snaky whisper. " 'Beware of my brother's schemes. He does not seek gold or silver, but discord and fear.' " Gordon gave a slight shrug. "Then he disappeared.

"As you have surely guessed, Mictar allied with my counterpart. His powers made it impossible for me to fight him in the open, so I decided the only way to stop his plans was to play along. Mictar gave each of the two Gordons the assignment of finding and killing you. The other Gordon succeeded on Earth Blue, while I hoped to find you in order to protect you."

Nathan clasped his hands together, trying to keep his voice calm. "What's so important about me?"

"This is where the matter becomes quite complex. When your father was called upon to recover some proprietary technology and sensitive data, stolen by a two-bit hacker, we had to take him and Dr. Simon into our tight circle of confidants. Once Solomon understood our technology, he postulated a fourth dimension that was completely different from the other three, a reality that transcended the others. He had no data to prove it. He merely claimed that common sense and logic dictated its existence."

"That's my dad. He's always the logical one."

"Yes, he has an impressive intellect, but he had another quality that intrigued me. He seemed to have an unusual insight into issues that defied empirical observation. He theorized that when we reached the point of moving from one dimension to the other, we began to alter the balance between them. In other words, the three streams of parallel events began to run askew of one another, because interference from one dimension to the other could not be exactly duplicated due to the misalignment of time."

"You mean," Nathan said, "when someone travels to another dimension, his counterpart isn't doing the same thing anymore. Both dimensions get thrown off."

"Correct. Solomon and I learned that since the dimensions no longer run in perfect parallel, the forces that separate them have been weakened. When we began the project, we had three infinities that would never intersect. Now, as they deviate from their linear path with relation to one another, they will experience random intersections that will cause havoc."

"What would those intersections look like? I mean, if it happens, what would people notice?"

"On Earth Yellow, since it is behind us in time, I would expect the people would receive some kind of signal of future events, perhaps more soothsayers and other self-proclaimed prophets providing hints of things to come, but their fortune telling would actually come true, at least for a time. Eventually, the lines would shift so far away, the events would become unpredictable."

Nathan peeked at Kelly. With her eyes sharp and gleaming, she was definitely on the same wavelength. The nightmare epidemic was a sign of interfinity's approach.

He turned back to Dr. Gordon. "What would happen here or on Earth Blue?"

"It's already happening. I believe we are experiencing weather conditions based on Earth Yellow's climate. Since Yellow is moving on the time stream far more quickly, our weather has wild swings. Only hours ago, it was probably early spring there, and we participated in their snowfall. Now it's approaching summer, and we are enjoying a much warmer afternoon, though that might not last long.

"This phenomenon prompted me to find out what you've been up to on Earth Yellow. I knew Simons Blue and Yellow had a longing to prevent some kind of disaster. It seems that the timing worked out perfectly for you to rescue the American Airlines flight."

"Not exactly. Besides Kelly and me, only six others survived."

"That's far too many. Six new puncture wounds in the infrastructure. I'm surprised events aren't worse than they already are."

"But they stayed where they belong," Nathan said. "Why would there be wounds?"

"That's a good point. Without the mirrors, I assume they couldn't have traveled across the barrier. But there has to be an explanation for the huge disturbance we're experiencing."

Kelly touched Nathan's elbow. When he looked back, she stealthily pointed at the camera, still dangling from the strap around Daryl's neck. He imagined the lens inside. Could it have sent the survivors through the dimensional fractures when Kelly took the pictures? It seemed able to launch them out of Francesca's room in Earth Yellow. Setting his focus back on Gordon, he tried to play it cool. It might be best not to let him know about the camera, at least not yet. "So, what can we do to fix them?"

"Dimensional holes are like wounds. They could heal over time, but, since we're not sure, it would be better if we could repair them quickly. Solomon studied the concepts of dark matter and energy, and he believes any dimensional break could significantly affect the infrastructure of the universe and eventually cause it to collapse, like a concrete wall punched full of holes until it falls in on itself. He called the merging 'interfinity.'

"Mictar scoffed at the idea and decided to rename the company after Solomon's theory, a joke in his mind, and a foreboding doom in ours. Your father was undaunted. He believed that your mother had some kind of gift, a way to seal the holes if she could only get the opportunity to use it. But it seems he was captured, so we must find a way to help him escape. And that brings me back to your earlier question. Mictar desires to kill you, because he believes that you possess the same abilities that your mother has. He wants Interfinity to occur, so he wants to make sure you aren't around to stop it."

Nathan set his mirror upright on his lap. So that was what Dad and Mom Blue were doing in the telescope room. Somehow her gift allowed that light to shoot out of her eyes, the same thing he saw in the younger Francesca, though weaker, probably because of her age and size. And it seemed to thrust both of them into visions of huge violins that they had to play. But however Mom Blue's vision fit into the dimensional puzzle, she wasn't strong enough to do the job by herself.

He traced the edge of the mirror with his finger. She needed his help. Somehow he, too, really did have a gift.

"How do the mirrors work?" Kelly asked.

"It is far too complex to give you the formula for the mirroring substance, but I can tell you what it does. The mirror captures light energy from the other dimensions, invisible to our eyes, of course. Yet, since the two realities are in different realms, it exists here in a scrambled state. Music, it seems, brings the light source from another dimension into harmony with ours. It is encoded by a source we have not identified."

"But my mirror seems different. It—"

"Ah! We are here." He steered the car into a cemetery entry road. "We will have to continue this conversation after the funeral. We have not yet discussed the fourth dimension thoroughly, nor how you control the Quattro mirror. After that discussion, we will embark on our mission to rescue your parents in Earth Blue."

Nathan tucked the mirror under his arm. "The other Dr. Gordon might be here, so I'm taking my mirror to the burial site."

"As you should. I have people watching for him. I will tell them that you marked his cheek." Dr. Gordon stopped his car at the side of the cemetery's grave access road behind a long line of other cars. About sixty yards ahead, a tent canopy rippled in the breeze, sheltering the grave sites. Dozens of rows of tombstones lined the gently sloping grass between their stopping point and the tent, looking like morbid sentinels of stone in horizontal battle lines, each one reciting its name and age in etched letters.

"As you probably already know," Gordon continued, "your tutor designated you as a pallbearer for each coffin, so you should go to the hearses immediately. It seems that the others are waiting for you."

"They'll wait another minute or two." Nathan jumped out and opened the back door on Clara's side. While he helped her out, Dr. Gordon opened the opposite door. He offered Kelly his hand, but she just glared at him as she got out on her own and marched around the car, her sweatshirt now covering her dirty polo. When they all gathered on the cemetery lawn, Nathan backed away. "I'll see you under the canopy."

As he turned to go, Kelly headed for the rear of the Lincoln. "Pop the trunk, Gordo; I'm getting the violin."

Nathan spun back. "I won't need it."

"We should bring everything with us." She pressed her hands into a praying position and batted her eyelids at Dr. Gordon. "*Please* pop the trunk?"

Dr. Gordon pressed a button on his key fob. "Very well. But not the shotgun." A muffled chime sounded. He pulled a cell phone from his pocket and waved at his passengers. "Go on to the grave site. I will meet you there."

Nathan jogged up the pavement toward the hearses, brushing off his dirty, smelly shirt. As he passed by the rows of tombstones, he tried to read the engravings, but he could only catch a couple of names, a Phillips and a Madison. Just hours ago, the stone slabs would have meant nothing, just marble decorations to be ignored, but now the terrified faces of the airline passengers flashed in his mind. Who could tell? Any one of these stones might be marking the grave of one of those victims. Since this was a huge cemetery in the western Chicago suburbs, that wouldn't be a stretch at all.

As he continued, he passed a bearded man kneeling at a grave site. The man held a crumpled hat against his lips as he bowed his head and stroked the marker's curved top, weeping. A surge of sympathy swept through Nathan's mind. What a portrait of grief! This miserable man poured out his heart over an empty shell he had once loved, now gone forever. Nathan wiped a tear. He would never ... never ignore a tombstone again. Each one told a story of tragedy, at least to some poor soul left behind.

As he neared the hearses, a thin man in a black suit waved

at him and opened the trailing hearse's back door, revealing a coffin. "I am Samuel Carpenter, the funeral director."

Nathan came to a stop and gazed at his reflection on the coffin's polished black surface. Nausea once again twisted his stomach. A body lay within. His mom? Dad?

"Master Shepherd," the director continued in a calm, soothing voice, "we were quite concerned about you."

Nathan kept his gaze locked on the coffin. "Yeah. The car quit working so I had to hitch a ride."

"I see. Did you try to fix the automobile yourself? Your clothes are quite disheveled."

"No." He smoothed out his shirt. "I had other problems."

The director shed his dark jacket and reached it toward Nathan. "Please borrow this, out of respect for your parents and the mourners who wish to bid them farewell."

Nathan allowed the gentleman to help him put it on. The sleeves fell past the heels of his hands, but the shoulders felt pretty good; loose, but not too loose.

The director touched the coffin with a fingertip. "This is your mother's. The other hearse carries your father." He signaled for the other men who were milling around near the graveside tent. "Your tutor selected these gentlemen from among your father's clients and your mother's orchestra friends. If you wish to renew your acquaintance with them, we can delay the proceedings further."

Nathan scanned the faces of the approaching pallbearers. None resembled Dr. Gordon. "No. It's okay. Maybe I can talk to them afterward."

"Certainly." While two dark-suited men pulled the coffin out on a gurney, the director stationed the pallbearers around the coffin, setting Nathan at the front and on his mother's body's left side. "Your tutor designated this position," Mr. Carpenter said, "the closest to the heart of your mother."

Nathan shuddered. The reality of the funeral sent a painful

jolt through every nerve, shaking his arms and weakening his knees. His mother was inside that box, her dead body, torn at the throat by an evil, sadistic murderer.

He clutched the brass handle with his left hand and laid his trembling fingertips on the coffin's smooth lid. As if emanating from the polished surface, a tingle passed through his knuckles, the same knuckles his mother would breathe on before every performance. He stared at the point of contact. His mother's words flowed into his mind as if blown there by the refreshing breeze, the lovely phrases he had heard so many times.

When I breathe on your hand, I whisper a prayer that the breath of God will fill your soul with his music, the melody of everlasting love that guided our Savior to the ultimate sacrifice. Because such love lasts forever, I know, my son, that we will be together through all eternity.

His heart raced. Tears fell across his cheeks. Then, a warm grip rested on his shoulder. "Nathan, are you all right?"

He turned to see a bald man with a large nose. "Dr. Malenkov?"

"Yes, of course. I thought you saw me earlier."

"I was looking for someone else. Are you playing something for the funeral?"

Nikolai patted him on the back. "Yes, yes. It is a great honor, yet a tragic occasion."

"What piece did you choose?"

"The Vivaldi duet, an arrangement I created that allows me to play it as a solo. Your mother's part fades away at the end while yours finishes strong."

Nathan swallowed down a tight catch in his throat. "That ... sounds great."

"You are welcome to join me. I can play your mother's part in the old arrangement."

"No. No thanks. I don't think I could handle it."

Nikolai moved his hand back to Nathan's shoulder. "I saw

your tears, so I told the director to wait a moment. Do you need a replacement?"

He shook his head. "I can make it. Thanks anyway."

"I am not a pallbearer for your father, so I will be glad to take your place there if the need arises."

Nathan averted his gaze. "I'll be all right. Thanks again."

"Very well. I will be on the other side of the coffin. I feel so blessed that I was called to this task, yet heartbroken that my daughter left the earth before I did."

The gentle musician's words jolted Nathan's memory. With all his knowledge of how his mother grew up, couldn't Nikolai help Francesca on Earth Yellow?

"Wait!" Nathan said, spinning back toward Nikolai. "How long did my mother live with you? How old was she when she met my father? Did you arrange their meeting?"

"So many questions!" Nikolai said, smiling. "Let us talk afterward. It is time to go." He walked briskly around the coffin and took his place. Then, when the director gave a hand signal, the six men lifted the casket and marched toward the burial site. As they approached, a woman standing under the canopy raised a violin and began playing Bach's "Jesu, Joy of Man's Desiring."

Nathan sighed. This lady was good, quite good, in fact. But she wasn't Mom. As she washed out a note that needed to be played with the precision of a musical surgeon, he cringed. Oh, how he longed to play with Mom! Just one more time! But it couldn't be. Never again.

He glanced over at Nikolai. Tears streamed down the old man's cheeks, following deep lines traced there by years of loving care. He, too, probably wept for lost days—future days he had hoped to play with his favorite pupil as he awaited his own passing into eternity, as well as days in the past he once shared during peaceful bedtime songs and rousing morning lessons. This sad old man had more treasured memories, perhaps a greater loss. He had lost a daughter, once given to him as the result of a tragic murder, now taken away because of a devil's wicked hand.

Nathan firmed his chin. This occasion, though solemn and tragic, deserved the best music possible. If Nikolai could do it, he could do it.

As they passed under the yellow canopy, he scanned the audience, about twenty-five or thirty men and women clad in various shades of gray and black, sitting or standing among at least eighty metal chairs, probably six rows with maybe fourteen chairs in each, divided in half by an aisle down the center. He let his face dip into a slight scowl. Why so few? Hadn't Clara let all their orchestra friends know about the funeral? Or had all the news about fast-moving blizzards scared them away? A graveyard wasn't exactly a place people wanted to go during a time of fear. Obviously parents had decided to keep their kids home. There wasn't a child in sight.

After setting his mother's coffin down on the right side of a huge display of flowers, Nathan turned toward the array of chairs. Clara, Kelly, and Daryl sat in the second row, one row in front of Dr. Gordon.

Nathan strode across the fifteen-or-so feet between the coffin and the front row and whispered, "Kelly. I need Mom's violin."

She lifted the case from her lap. "Right now?"

"When I get back with Dad's coffin."

Nathan headed to the second hearse with the other pallbearers. Only Nikolai stayed, pulling a violin case out from behind the flowers as Nathan left the canopy's shade. Another man joined the group of coffin handlers, a man who looked exactly like Dr. Gordon. Nathan spun toward the chairs. Dr. Gordon was gone. Why had he joined the pallbearers? He certainly hadn't mentioned doing that. He scanned Dr. Gordon's face, but since he walked to his left, he couldn't see if there was a cut on his left cheek.

As they closed in on the other hearse, Nathan leaned toward him. "Dr. Gordon?"

"Yes, Nathan?" He kept his face forward, not allowing Nathan to check his other side.

"You didn't say you were going to be a pallbearer."

"It was a last-minute decision. One of the other pallbearers fell ill." He finally turned and pointed at his cheek, his unmarred cheek. "I sense that you need to see this to allay your fears."

Nathan let out his breath. He wasn't Gordon Blue.

The director lined them up again around the second coffin. With the head of the casket pointing toward the canopy, he guided Nathan to the front handle on the left side. "Your tutor said you needed to be at your father's right hand. You were his stalwart helper and never failed in your efforts to come to his aid."

Wasting little time, the six men carried the coffin to the waiting mourners and placed it to the left of the floral arrangement. As they set it down, one of the men bumped a partition behind the flowers. Covered with a white sheet, the partition shook, sending the sheet rippling down the front and exposing a mirror, identical to the one in Nathan's room, complete with divider lines separating the individual squares. The reflection seemed normal, at least for now, showing only the lush flowers and the seated audience beyond them.

As the other pallbearers filed to their seats, Nathan glanced at the lower left-hand corner of the odd backdrop. A square was missing. Was this really the mirror from his room, or had someone transported it from Earth Blue?

Turning back to the mourners, he found Clara in the aisle seat of the second row. His mirror lay in her lap, angled slightly toward him, allowing the polished surface to catch his eye. Across the aisle and three rows back sat a man with a familiar bearded face. He straightened his crumpled fedora and clutched the brim against his chest.

Nathan focused on his weary eyes. It was Jack from the plane crash on Earth Yellow! He was one of the survivors! But why was he at the funeral?

Nikolai, carrying his violin, stepped in front of the flowers and guided the bow across each string as he tuned his instrument. Kelly strode forward with Nathan's violin, already removed from its case. He took it and the bow and, trying not to move his lips, whispered, "Fill the empty spot," then nodded toward the mirrored partition.

She glanced at the reflection, bobbed her head, and hustled back to Clara. As she walked, she did a double take at the bearded man.

Trying to shut off the distractions, Nathan turned to Nikolai and bowed. "If you don't mind, sir, I reconsidered your offer. I will play my part if you will play my mother's."

The old man smiled. "Nathan Shepherd, I can think of no greater honor." He bent over and, taking Nathan's bow hand, blew on his knuckles. "Music is the breath of God," he said softly. "Let us tell of his love to these mourners and give them a reason to turn their mourning into joy."

While everyone else settled in their seats, Nathan quickly rolled his jacket sleeves up two turns and began tuning the violin, keeping an eye on Kelly as she sneaked around to the back of the mirrored partition. Kneeling and slowly reaching around from behind, she set the square in the corner. It seemed to jump from her hands and lock in place as if pulled by a magnet.

A sudden gust rippled the top of the tent's canopy, a cold gust, much colder than normal for September. Nathan shivered, glad now for the director's jacket. But what could it mean? Had Earth Yellow already moved into late autumn?

As most of the onlookers tilted their heads upward, Nathan stayed focused on the mirror. Starting from the newly placed square, a wave of radiance crawled along the surface, brightening the reflection to a razor-sharp clarity. When it reached the opposite corner, the strange light pulsed once and vanished.

Kelly stayed behind the mirror, shivering as she drew her hands into her sweatshirt sleeves. When she looked up at Nathan, she pointed at the camera dangling from the strap around her neck. "It's the only light we have," she whispered.

Increasing the volume as he continued to tune his violin, he whispered back, "It'll have to do. I'm guessing Simon Blue put the mirror here, so we have to be ready to use it."

She nodded, then ducked low. Nathan glanced out at the tombstone-covered lawn. Snowflakes swirled through the breeze, already speckling the grass with patches of white. The mourners reached for cloaks and sweaters, apparently prepared for the unpredictable shifts in weather.

Nikolai set a hand on Nathan's shoulder and, seemingly unaffected by the sudden wintry blast, addressed the audience. "We wish to honor our departed loved ones—I, my cherished daughter, and Nathan, his beloved parents—with the performance of a Vivaldi duet he and his mother arranged and played together many times. As we make these violins sing, do not be alarmed if you feel the spirit of Francesca Shepherd as she bids farewell to us all."

Raising his mother's treasured instrument to his chin, Nathan shook off a chill and stepped to the elderly teacher's side. "I await your lead, Maestro."

Nikolai set the bow on the strings and, with a long vibrant stroke, played the beginning note of the duet.

Nathan closed his eyes and answered with the familiar notes of his lightning-fast response. Then, opening his eyes slightly to watch the mirror, he played on, blending in with the master's smooth, effortless tones. Soon, he would play solo. The last time he performed that part, his parents disappeared and he was left standing alone on stage, playing a solo that never ended. This time, he would watch all the players—Nikolai, Dr. Gordon, and anyone else who might spring a surprise.

As Nikolai backed away, Nathan shifted to the center, keeping his body angled enough to see the mirror. He tried to focus on the reflection, but the music had other ideas. Every phrase seemed to massage his mind, bringing back memories of his mother. The recollections soothed and stung at the same time, blessings that reminded him of the pain of love torn away before its time.

Then, images of his father mixed into his memories. As Francesca wept and trembled, Solomon laid a hand on her cheek, a tender caress that always seemed to calm her down, no matter what troubles stirred her turmoil. He held her close, kissing and nuzzling as sweet words passed between them like the same silvery notes Nathan played in their honor.

Seconds from now, Nikolai would play again, taking his mother's part at the place she had abandoned just a few days ago. As his part built to a crescendo, her final words seemed to brush by his ears. *"I will join you again when the composer commands me."*

A newcomer walked into the back of the seating area and remained standing, a tall white-haired man—was it Mictar? Patar? Dr. Gordon bent over and skulked along his row of seats, then headed toward the rear. He stood close to the gaunt man and the two spoke quietly.

Nathan glanced at Kelly, still hiding behind the flowers. She saw them, too. Could she tell them apart? Were they Gordon Red and Patar, or Gordon Blue and Mictar?

Suddenly, the mirror flashed. The reflection displayed bright, colorful shapes that quickly bled together to form a blurred figure, veiled by the floral decorations that separated the two coffins. Kelly crawled out and shoved the flowers out of the way, staying on her knees as she slid some to the side and knocked others over until the entire mirror came into view.

The image clarified, showing Francesca Shepherd standing with a violin, her bow at the ready position. On one side, a sheer curtain flapped in a gentle breeze, and on her other, a poster bed with a bare mattress sat on a carpeted floor.

Straining to keep his breathing in check, Nathan swept through the final notes of his solo. As murmurs spread across the onlookers, the reflected Francesca joined the duet, answering the composer's call. The notes rang through like carillon bells, sharp and echoing, yet as lovely as any angel could hope to create. Nikolai, his eyes wide, lowered his violin and backed away another step.

As if guided by his mother's entrancing gaze, Nathan walked slowly toward the mirror, his legs heavy. He focused on her eyes. Yes, they were looking right at him. She could see him! And now her lips moved, a quiet whisper drowned out by her thrumming melody.

Crouched at Nathan's feet, Kelly relayed Francesca's words. "Take a picture of the mirror." She leaped to her feet and aimed the camera at the mirror, backing away as she framed in the coffins at each side. When she reached the second row of seats, the camera flashed. Light spread out over Nathan and everything around him—the mirror, the coffins, and even Nikolai. A sizzling beam shot out and struck the lens, smashing it to pieces.

Kelly dropped the camera and shook her hands. "It's hot as fire!"

The mirror scene expanded. Their view of the inner room widened, spreading out to show Nathan's father standing nearby, shackles binding his ankles and wrists, though the attached chains seemed broken as they dragged freely. The floor where Francesca stood pushed outward and blended into the cemetery grass as the two dimensions merged into one. The swelling dimension looked like a soap bubble with thick, rubbery walls, yet as clear as crystal.

Francesca extended her hand and cried out, her voice now

penetrating the barrier. "Take my hand, Nathan! Pull us out of here!"

Kelly echoed the cry.

Nathan shouted, "I hear her now!"

In the image, Solomon held on to Francesca. With chains dangling, he raised a hand. "Son! Now is the time! Rescue us!"

Dr. Gordon ran up the aisle, grabbed Kelly from behind, and pressed the edge of a dagger against her throat. "Don't touch them, Nathan! If you bring them back, I'll slit her wide open!"

Several mourners jumped to their feet. With the blade already drawing a trickle of blood from Kelly's tender skin, most stood petrified. Daryl lunged, but Clara jerked her back.

Nathan's knees buckled, but he managed to hold himself up. As a gust blew a stream of snowflakes across his cheek and flapped the canopy's ceiling, he lifted a fist and rasped through his sandpaper throat. "Let her go!"

Suddenly, Jack stormed up the aisle and latched on to Gordon's wrist, pulling it away from Kelly's throat. As Gordon jerked back to fight, the dagger swiped against her shoulder and dug deeply into her sweatshirt.

Kelly let out a pitiful wail. Blood dampened her sleeve and dripped from her fingers. Jack wrestled Gordon to the grass, toppling chairs on the front row as they rolled to the side.

Mictar leaped for Kelly and wrapped an arm around her chest. Three men from the audience rushed to subdue Gordon while two others leaped toward Mictar. Twin jagged sparks shot from Mictar's palm and pierced the chests of the would-be rescuers. They fell to the ground, their bodies quivering.

The first three rescuers pulled Gordon upright. A trickle of sweat drew a purplish line down his cheek, exposing part of a bruise. Jack struggled to his feet. A bloody gash stretched across his forehead.

As cold gusts breezed through, everyone fell into a terrified hush. Hovering a hand over Kelly's eyes, Mictar spoke quietly.

"Son of Solomon, heed my warning. If you take one step toward the gifted one, I will make this girl suffer beyond all imagination."

Nathan wheeled toward the mirror. The image shifted forward another few inches and stopped. Francesca and Solomon, their bodies now filling the screen, stretched out their arms as far as they could reach. A voice again punched through the barrier. "I'm sorry for leaving you alone on stage!" Francesca cried. "We had to change places with the Blue Shepherds before it was too late! Since Mictar had killed them earlier, we used their bodies to make him think we were dead, too. Pull us home and we'll explain everything!"

Nathan clutched his jacket. "Left me on the stage?" He thrust his finger toward the other dimension and screamed at Mictar. "Are they my real parents?"

"They are," Mictar hissed. As Kelly gasped, flinching under the ghostly hand, more blood dripped from the ends of her fingers. "But I am pleased that you found them for me," he continued. "They escaped at the observatory, and now they will be mine once again."

The mirror image slowly contracted. Solomon and Francesca slid backwards, shrinking with the reflection, their hands grasping empty air. A huge gust ripped the canopy away from the stakes and sent it flying across the cemetery. Biting wind squealed through the funeral party, and heavy snow cascaded from the skies.

"Nathan!" Kelly shouted, peeking under Mictar's fingers. "Get them out! Hurry!"

Nathan laid the violin down, plunged his fist through the barrier, and grabbed his mother's hand. After punching through with his other fist, he wound his wrist in his father's chain, set his feet, and began to pull, but they didn't slide right through. With his feet slipping on the dampening grass, it was like dragging two dead bodies through thick mud.

"Don't believe me, Shepherd?" Sparks of electricity arced

from Mictar's hand, drilling pinpoint scorch marks on Kelly's forehead. She grimaced, pressing her lips tightly together.

Still pulling, Nathan looked back at his parents, snow swirling between him and the mirror. Their forearms were already through the barrier, and their heads drew so close, the crystalline dividing wall magnified every line in their frantic expressions.

Kelly cried out in a plaintive moan. "Rescue them, Nathan! I'm not worth it! I'm just a—"

"Be silent!" Mictar pressed his hand completely over her eyes. "Forever!"

Nathan gulped. What should he do? He needed time to think! He glanced at his parents, but their silent, motionless stares gave him no answers ... only more questions. Why had they suddenly frozen in place? He swiveled his head back toward Kelly. She had also stiffened into a mannequinlike pose. The mourners, with faces like stone, stared in solidified horror. Only Mictar seemed aware of the change. Although his feet stayed planted, his eyes moved, darting back and forth as if searching for a reason for the suspended animation.

Nathan turned his gaze back to the mirror. Now, although his parent's protruding limbs remained, the reflection altered to a new scene, a copy of the funeral surroundings—himself poised in front of the mirror, gripping his mother and father in the same way; Mictar standing with Kelly in his grasp, within arm's reach; and the frozen onlookers anchored in the midst of a dusting of snow.

As Nathan stared at the reflection, his eyes flashed. White beams poured forth and splashed against the glassy surface. His image in the mirror suddenly activated and jerked his parents out of the dimensional barrier. They lurched into the funeral scene and sprawled over the ground. Mictar let out a raging scream, fire sizzling under the hand he held over Kelly's eyes.

The reflection expanded and enveloped Nathan. His mind

seemed to meld with the reflection, and his vision shifted to the new point of view as if he had taken over the other Nathan's body. While his father and mother struggled to their feet, Mictar glowed with a shimmering light and vanished. Kelly collapsed in a heap, her limbs and torso limp.

As if in a surreal, slow-motion dream, Nathan's parents embraced him, but he could only fix his gaze on Kelly. With blood forming in a pool under her shoulder, her body quivered fitfully, her scorched eye sockets blankly staring straight up.

Then, her shaking ceased, as did everything else. Locked in his parents' warm arms, he stared all around, finally focusing again on the mirror. In the reflection, a tall man with white hair stared back at him, his hands folded over his waist while the other funeral scene, the one Nathan had left behind, painted a dreary backdrop.

Nathan could barely mouth the man's name. *Patar.*

"The power you call Quattro awaits your decision," Patar said.

Nathan couldn't move. Unable even to shiver, he mumbled, "My ... my decision?"

"You wanted time to decide, so you now have the luxury of seeing the results of one of your options."

Shifting his gaze toward his mother's face, Nathan took in her expression. As a tear dangled from her chin, she stared at him, more love flowing from her eyes than he had ever seen before, pure joy at once again looking upon her dear son. His father, too, seemed filled with joy, yet, with his jaw set like steel, he was ready to go to war.

Nathan looked back at Kelly. Her black eye sockets stared straight up—vacant, abandoned, forsaken. The image of her ravaged face would haunt his memory forever, the sightless countenance of a terrified girl, wandering in futility, only to suffer and die in the midst of life's greatest search, lost forever.

Patar spoke again. "It is time to decide, son of Solomon. As soon as you are returned to your point of crisis, you must act."

As Patar vanished, Nathan felt his mind moving again. He flew into the reflection and found himself where he was before, his grip locked on his parents, and Kelly in the clutches of Mictar, still alive, still struggling to hold on to that precious gift.

Nathan released his grip and lunged at Kelly. With a whip of his neck, he bashed his forehead against Mictar's nose, sending him flying backwards. As his head thudded on the ground, dark blood gushed from both nostrils.

Nathan embraced Kelly and fell to the snow-covered grass in a rolling motion, tumbling two full rotations to get away from Mictar. Then, with a leap to his feet, he helped Kelly up and dove toward the contracting dimensional bubble. As he slid across the snow, his hands penetrated the barrier once again. In the other world, his father dropped to his knees and grabbed Nathan's wrists. His father's face strained, his lips moving, but now his voice could no longer break through.

Kelly called from behind, her voice weak and shaking. "Pull, Son! Pull!"

Nathan rose to his feet and pulled with all his might. Suddenly, a hand blocked his vision, and Mictar spoke in a hideous, throaty voice. "Now, Solomon, you will watch him die."

Painful needles of light shot into Nathan's eyes. The fingers around his wrists, his father's fingers, gave way. Nathan lurched backward, knocking Mictar's hand to the side. With a violent spin, he thrust an elbow into Mictar's belly, then kicked him in the groin. Mictar's thin form staggered back, his eyes pulsing like red beacons. At least five men marched toward him, but, when he lifted his hands, new arcs of electricity shot out from his palms. Four of the men hesitated, but Jack burst toward him in a flying fury. Leaping on Mictar and wrapping his arms around his lanky frame, Jack beat him on the back with his fists.

Lugging his stocky attacker, Mictar staggered toward the mirror. The image from the other dimension was now a flat reflection, showing Solomon and Francesca staring out, hand in hand, tears streaming down their cheeks. With his arms flailing, Mictar dove headfirst into the mirror and disappeared with Jack in a splash of light.

At the point he entered the mirror, a long crack etched the glass. Spreading rapidly and branching out, the crack covered the entire surface. Like crinkling cellophane, the polished surface rippled, then crumbled, falling to the ground in sparkling shards and leaving the supporting wall standing bare.

Nathan dropped to his knees and pounded the ground with his fist, raising a splash of slushy snow. He almost had them! Just another second, and he'd have had them out of there!

Kelly laid a bloody hand on his forearm, patting him several times as if searching for something on his sleeve. "Oh, Nathan! I'm so sorry!"

He took her hand and held it against his face, shaking so hard, he smeared her blood across his cheek. "It's not ... not your fault. It's mine. I should've ..."

As police sirens wailed in the distance, several men escorted Dr. Gordon past the onlookers, two men in front, three in back, and two on each side. He glared at Nathan but said nothing.

Nathan growled at him. "What did you do with Gordon Red?"

Gordon Blue sneered. "Do you think me a fool? See to that yourself."

Clara slid her arms under Nathan's and helped him up, while Daryl hoisted Kelly to her feet. "We need to get both of you to a hospital," Clara said.

Nathan brushed off his clothes. "I'm fine. Just Kelly. She's hurt pretty bad."

Staring into space, Kelly touched the wound on her shoulder.

"I'll go, but we'd better find Gordon Red. He might need a hospital, too."

Nathan waved a hand in front of Kelly's eyes. "Can you see okay? You look kind of dazed."

She shook her head. "Everything's foggy, like it's getting dark."

"An ambulance just pulled up," Nathan said. He intertwined his fingers with hers, ignoring the streams of blood. "Let the police find Gordon. You're going to the hospital, and I'm not leaving your side."

Pulling down his sweatshirt hood, Nathan leaned his waist against the metal bedrail and pushed a bouquet of long-stemmed pink roses under Kelly's nose. "Like them?" he asked.

With her bed propped up, Kelly took a long sniff, then folded her hands over her flowery hospital gown. Draping the front of her torso loosely, the cotton covered her well enough, but it sagged at her right shoulder, exposing a large, thick bandage. "All I smell is the bacon in your cheeseburger. I'm so hungry I might just eat those flowers."

Nathan laid the roses on her bed, scrunched the top of the Burger King bag he had left on the serving table, and hid it behind his back. "What cheeseburger?"

Staring into space, her eyes framed by dozens of black scorch marks, she blinked rapidly. "What cheeseburger? The one that's whispering to the French fries in your bag. It's saying"—she cupped her hands around her mouth and deepened her voice—"'Give me to Kelly! I must be eaten by Kelly!'"

"I see. Now you're hearing voices from fast-food bags." He waved his hand slowly in front of her eyes. "Can you see any better?"

She nodded. "Quite a bit. I can recognize people, but it's like everyone's kind of ghostly."

Standing on the other side of the bed, Clara took the roses and unwound the green paper that held their stems. Pulling up the sleeves on her beige trench coat, she threaded the stems into a long-necked vase. "Your dinner will be here soon, a nice post-surgery helping of something clear and digestible."

Kelly rolled her eyes. "Baby food, right?"

"No," Nathan said, grinning. "I saw the can. It's Alpo."

"Good. Top-of-the-line dog food beats mashed peas any day, but I'll be glad to trade you half of mine for half of yours."

"No. I wouldn't think of it. I'm too much of a gentleman to deprive you of even one morsel of such a treat."

"Oh, hush, you two," Clara said. "You're about as funny as a lanced boil."

Daryl popped into the room, a lively bounce in her step. As she lowered her hood, she shook out her thick red locks. "Brrr. It's cold out there this morning. Must be January on Yellow."

"Did you get the pictures?" Nathan asked.

"Right here." She tossed a photo packet onto the bed. "They salvaged some of the film, but the camera's a goner."

Nathan picked it up. "Did you already look at them?"

Glancing away, Daryl leaned against the bed. "What kind of girl do you think I am?"

Kelly snatched the packet from Nathan. "Insatiably curious. Nosy. An incurable snoop."

Daryl turned back and smiled. "Yeah. That's all true. But I only sneaked one peek, and I couldn't really figure out what I was looking at."

After opening the top, Kelly slid the inner envelope onto her chest. "It's thin," she said. "Only a few pictures."

"Just three," Daryl replied. "The rest of the roll was pretty fried."

Kelly laid the trio of photos across the sheet and pointed at the first one. "It's blurry, but I think I see four people, so that's the first one I took. It should show the woman who asked me to take the shots, the husband and wife, and Jack in the background. Is that right?"

Nathan leaned close. "Yeah, but it looks strange, like there's some kind of glow around their outlines."

"Maybe that's the dimensional holes forming, like the ones Dr. Gordon talked about. I wonder if all six of them came across."

"You got me." He brushed his fingertip across Jack. It was a good thing he came. Who could tell what would've happened without him?

Kelly pointed at the second photo. "This should be the one I took of the wreckage. You and that author should be in it."

"We are. We're standing near a pile of twisted metal and wires, and he has the same aura, but I don't." He picked up the last photo, a shot of the funeral scene. In the mirror, his mother stood out clearly, playing her violin. The sheer drapes covering the window behind her had blown outward, exposing the sill. Two hands gripped the painted wood, as though someone was trying to climb in. His eyes glowed red, and his fingers were long and white. Nathan nodded slowly. It had to be Patar.

The sight of his mother brought a new lump to his throat. He had touched her skin, heard her voice, felt her love! So close, yet so far! And Dad! Once again he experienced his father's great strength as well as his sacrificial love. His father had let go of a rescuing grip in order to save his son's life.

His hand now trembling, he showed the photo to Kelly. "Can you see that face and those hands on the sill? It looks like the guy I told you about, Patar."

"We'll have to get an enlargement so I can see it better." She flipped the picture back to the bed and sighed. "Too many questions and not enough answers."

"I wonder when Gordon Red's coming. Maybe he'll have some answers."

"He's in the waiting room," Daryl said, motioning toward the door with her thumb. "They wouldn't let more than three visitors come in, so he's waiting for one of us to leave."

Nathan, Kelly, and Clara all stared at Daryl simultaneously.

She raised her hands and cocked her head, smiling as she backed away. "That's okay. I understand. You don't have to knock me over the head." She blew Kelly a kiss. "Thanks for the fun. I'm really just a supporting actress in this flick, but, hey, maybe there's an Oscar nomination in the wings, huh?" She winked dramatically. "Get better quick, girl. I'm ready for some more adventures."

The clacking of shoes echoed through the hallway. Seconds later, Dr. Gordon strode in, his brow furrowed and his lips turned down. He shoved his hands into his pockets and glared at Nathan. "Your actions on Earth Yellow were more far-reaching than I thought."

Nathan took a step back. "Uh ... okay. I'm glad to see you, too."

Wincing, Gordon waved his hand. "I know, I know. Politeness demands a more genteel entry, and I am thankful we all survived my counterpart's schemes, but we have pressing issues to discuss."

"Pressing issues?"

"Of course. Did you think the ramifications of your dimensional perforations were over?"

"Well, no, I uh—"

"As I explained before, our dimensions were always exactly in parallel until we began crossing from one to another. Then, our simple presence in a foreign dimension caused slight changes, triggering an unpredictable domino effect. Maybe a driver slowed down to allow me to cross a street. Maybe he arrived home four seconds later than he would have and avoided a burglar who would have killed him. Later, this same man kills a woman who would have given birth to a research scientist who would have discovered a breakthrough cure for a disease."

Nathan folded his arms across his chest. "But maybe our effects are positive in the long run. Did you think of that?"

"Naturally. That's been Dr. Simon's goal all along, to create positive effects in the dimensions that trail in time. But I wanted to begin with small changes so we could track the chain reactions. Dr. Simon had other plans. He couldn't imagine how saving over two hundred seventy lives could possibly be a bad idea. And since Earth Yellow was about to hurtle past the day of the airline crash, he didn't bother to consult me. He worked very hard to get you to the right place at the right time.

"We cannot possibly track the rescued passengers, and as you know, one has even crossed over to our dimension, and we have no idea where he is now. And it seems that others have crossed over as well. There have been a couple of reports flying about concerning long-lost plane crash victims appearing at their former homes. Who can tell how either dimension will be affected?"

Nathan pushed his hands into his sweatshirt pockets. "So maybe Francesca and Solomon won't meet. Maybe I won't even be born over there."

Kelly patted his elbow. "Don't worry about that. Gunther will make sure they get together."

"As soon as you are able, I would like to meet with both of you again to work on these matters." Dr. Gordon edged toward the door. "It seems that your most pressing concern is still finding your parents. Simon Blue helped them escape, but since he no longer had access to the observatory, he took them to Nathan Blue's bedroom so they could use that mirror to transport. Without the missing square, they had to rely on you to get them out. Simon was searching for the piece when he heard a loud pop. He returned to the room, and your parents were gone."

"Gone?"

Dr. Gordon nodded. "The mirror is intact, so we will get the final piece and see if they can be traced."

Nathan drooped his head. It was so strange. He wanted to

pump his fists and celebrate that his parents were still alive, but now, in some ways, he felt worse than ever. They were in trouble, and he wouldn't sleep a wink until he brought them home. Still, since Jack crossed the barrier with Mictar, maybe he could help Mom and Dad. Maybe they could still be rescued.

Dr. Gordon opened the door. "The two Simons are working together, and I'll join the search very soon. In the meantime"—he spread two fingers at Nathan and Kelly—"you two need to rest and get well. From the reports I've heard, you make quite a dynamic duo."

Kelly pulled Nathan's hand from his pocket and held it tight. "You better believe we do."

A hint of a grin cracked Dr. Gordon's stoic face. "But leave the shotgun at home, little lady. The world's not ready for the rebirth of Annie Oakley." He walked out and closed the door behind him.

Clara grabbed her trench coat's belt and tied it quickly. "I must catch Dr. Gordon. I forgot to consult with him about what to do with the bodies of your Earth Blue parents, then I must locate suitable lodging for us. So, I will leave the two of you alone for a while and return for Nathan, but then he and I will have to leave for the night." She raised her eyebrows. "Is that a suitable plan?"

"Sure, Clara," Nathan said. "Thanks for everything."

Kelly groped for her hand and smiled. "You're the best."

Clara's eyes glistened as she turned for the door. "I am really very impressed with you, young lady. Very much impressed."

When Clara disappeared into the hall, Kelly felt for Nathan's hand and clutched it to her chest. She took a deep breath and smiled. "I really like her."

"Yeah. Me, too." As her hands enveloped his, her fingers trembled. "Are you cold?" he asked.

Her faraway eyes each shed a tear. "I'm not cold. I'm just scared."

Nathan leaned closer and softened his voice. "Scared of what?"

"Lots of things." She slowly tightened her grip on his hand. "What if all of creation collapses? What if I never get my eyesight back? What if we can't find your parents? What if—"

He quieted her with a long, soothing, "Shhhh ..." When her hands settled and her eyes turned toward him, he continued in a hushed tone. "Those are just 'what ifs.' Everything's going to be all right."

She blinked at him. A new tremble took shape in her lips. "But if your parents die, it'll be my fault."

"Your fault? Why?"

Again, she blinked, but this time the tremor spread from her lips to her cheeks and echoed in her hands until her entire body shook. Her voice broke into a plaintive call. "Because ... because you could have rescued them, but you saved me instead."

"Of course I saved you." He set a tender hand on her cheek. As if stilled by his touch, her tremors eased and faded away. "Saving your life was more important than getting them back."

As her eyebrows arched high, her voice pitched up as well. "But why? You've been trying to rescue your parents ever since I met you."

Nathan drew his head back. "You mean ... you don't know?"

"No. That's why I'm asking."

He pulled his hands away and set them on the bedrail. "I can't tell you."

"Why not?"

He lowered his head. "You said not to use that word."

"What word?" Even as she asked her question, she drew in a halting breath. Her wounded eyes glistened. "You ... you mean ..."

He nodded.

New tremors raced across her hands as she reached out for his. "Go ahead ... and say it."

As their four hands intertwined in a soft embrace, he whispered, "I saved you, Kelly Clark, because I love you."

Again her tremors faded. "But why would you love someone like me? I'm just a—"

"A girl who's searching." Bending closer, he raised their hands and breathed on her knuckles. "Love is the true breath of God. And I'll do everything I can to show his love to you so you'll find what you're searching for."

Tears streaming, she looked at her anointed hand. "But I don't know ... what I'm searching for."

"I think I do, at least a couple of things. We'll search for them together." As a vibrant song rang through the halls, Nathan smiled. "Sounds like you have a visitor."

The door swung open, revealing a tall man with bulging eyes carrying a pizza box high on his palm. Singing something lively in an odd mix of Italian and English, he strode to the bed and laid the box on Kelly's stomach. "Extra liver and anchovies," Tony bellowed, "just the way you like it."

Kelly stared at the box, then at her father, obviously trying to hide a grimace. "But I—"

With a dramatic flip of his hand, Tony opened the box. A wave of savory aromas washed into their faces. A large pizza with extra cheese and pepperoni decorated the bottom of the box.

Tony slapped his forehead. "I can't believe they forgot the liver and anchovies!"

Kelly smiled. "Daddy," she said, new tears tracing to her chin, "you're my hero!"

His own eyes tearing up, Tony shifted from foot to foot. His voice tracked up a notch. "A hero? Because I brought you pizza?"

Kelly shook her head. "Because you love me. If you hadn't taught me to be tough, I never would have survived."

"Yeah ... well, I knew all along that you needed to learn ..."

His voice faltered. As his face reddened, he cleared his throat. "What I mean to say is ..."

Nathan turned his head but watched out of the corner of his eye.

Tony looked at the floor briefly, then gazed at her, his tears now streaming. "What I mean to say is ... I'm glad you're my daughter."

Releasing Nathan's hands, Kelly spread out her arms. Tony shuffled to the side of the bed and pulled her into a tight embrace. As they wept together, Nathan backed away from the bed, easing toward the door without a sound.

Kelly opened her eyes and peered at him over her father's shoulder, blinking through a shower of tears. The joy in her expression said it all. This embrace was one of the treasures she had been searching for.

Nathan smiled, formed an "I love you" sign with his fingers, and left the room.

ECHOES FROM THE EDGE

ETERNITY'S EDGE

BRYAN DAVIS

BESTSELLING AUTHOR OF DRAGONS IN OUR MIDST®

A STALKER

Nathan headed down the hospital hallway, his brain focused on a single thought—finding his parents. Once mutilated and dead in matching coffins, now they were alive. He had touched his father's hands through the dimensional mirror, felt the loving strength as he tried to pull him, chains still binding his wrists. He had heard his mother's voice and once again bathed in the majesty of her matchless violin.

Yet, the beautiful duet they had played at the funeral had once again become a solo. He had failed. The dimensional portal collapsed, and there was no word from Earth Blue as to whether or not his parents might still be in the bedroom where they had sought rescue from their captivity.

He sat down on a coffee-stained sofa in the waiting area and clenched his fist. His parents were real. They were alive. And now he had to move heaven and earth, maybe even three earths, to find them.

Staring into the hall, he mentally reentered Kelly's room and saw her lying on the bed, beaten and bruised from their ordeal, her shoulder lacerated and her eyes half blind. The words he spoke to her just moments ago came back to him. *We'll search for them together.* But how could she help? With all the dangers ahead, how could a blinded, wounded girl help him find his parents?

A sharp, matronly voice shook him from his meditative trance. "Ah! There you are!"

Nathan shot to his feet. Clara marched toward him, her heels clacking on the tile floor as she pushed back her wind-blown gray hair. Walking stride for stride next to the tall lady, Dr. Gordon, his face as grim as ever, stared at a cell phone.

As they entered the waiting area, Nathan nodded toward the hallway. "Tony's with Kelly. Thought I'd let them have some daddy and daughter time."

While Dr. Gordon punched his cell phone keys, apparently typing out a text message, Clara lowered her voice. "Dr. Gordon received a cryptic email from Simon Blue. Solomon and Francesca aren't there in your Earth Blue bedroom, but apparently something very unusual is going on, and we're trying to get details."

"So that's our next destination," Nathan said.

"Yes. We have already alerted my counterpart on Earth Blue. She and Daryl will be ready to pick you up at the observatory and take you to Kelly Blue's house."

"Good. Even if Mom and Dad aren't there, it's the logical place to start looking for them."

"Are you going to break the news to Kelly?"

"I guess I'll have to. She's in no shape to come with me, but convincing her of that won't be easy."

Dr. Gordon closed his phone and slid it into his pocket. Turning toward Nathan, he spoke in his usual formal manner. "There are no further details available. We should proceed to the observatory at once. With Mictar's associates gone, there should be no trouble gaining access. I have dismissed the guards, with the exception of one whom I trust, so we should not run into any unexpected company."

"Okay," Nathan said. "Let me talk to Kelly. I'll be right back."

As he walked down the hall, he wondered about Dr. Gordon's words. It was true that Mictar's goons were gone, but what about Mictar himself? He had disappeared into the mirror with Jack, one of the survivors of the plane crash, riding on top of him, but where could he have gone?

A man in scrubs caught up and passed him, pushing a lab tray stuffed with glass bottles and tubes. With lanky pale arms protruding from his short green sleeves, he kept his head low as he hurried ahead. He slowed down in front of Kelly's door, but when it opened, he resumed his pace and turned into a side corridor, his head still low.

Nathan could barely breathe. Could that have been Mictar? Would he be bold enough to come into the hospital? And why would he be so persistent in trying to get to Kelly? What value was she to him?

As Nathan neared the room, Tony came out. Bending his tall frame, he released the latch gently and walked away on tiptoes. When he spied Nathan, he jerked up and smiled, his booming voice contradicting his earlier attempts to be quiet. "Hey! What brings you back so soon?"

Nathan kept his eyes on the side hallway. No sign of the technician. "Some news for Kelly. I have to head back to the scene of the crime."

Tony shook his finger. "Better not. She was so tired, she fell asleep in mid-bite. And if she's too tired for pizza, she's too tired for company."

"You let her eat it? She's only supposed to have—"

"Hey," Tony said, laying a hand on his chest, "I didn't know about her diet until after I brought the pizza. But if you want to tell her what she should and shouldn't eat, be my guest."

"I know what you mean." Nathan glanced between the door and the other hallway. "Okay if I sneak in and leave her a note?"

He grinned, his eyes bugging out even more than usual. "Just don't get any ideas, Romeo."

Nathan returned the smile, though he chaffed at the comment. Tony was joking, of course, but sometimes he blurted out the dumbest things. He wouldn't dream of touching her inappropriately, not in a million years. His father had drilled that into his head a long time ago—never intimately touch a woman who is not your wife.

"I'll behave myself." He reached for the knob and nodded toward the other hallway. "Mind checking something out for me? I saw someone suspicious, a guy in scrubs, head that way. It looked like he was going into Kelly's room, but when you came out, he took off."

"You got it." Tony crept toward the other hall, pointing. "That way?"

"Yeah. Just a few seconds ago."

"I'm on it." When he reached the corridor, he looked back, his muscular arms flexing. "Time to take out the trash."

Nathan opened the door a crack, eased in, and closed it behind him. Walking slowly as his eyes adjusted, he quietly drew the partitioning curtain to the side and focused on Kelly's head resting on a pillow, her shoulder-length brown hair splashed across the white linen. He stopped at her bedside, unable to draw his stare away from her lovely face. Black scorch marks on her brow and cheeks and a thick bandage on her shoulder bore witness to her recent battle with Mictar. Her closed lids concealed wounded eyes, maybe the worst of all her injuries. Still, even in such a battle-torn condition, she was beautiful to behold, a true warrior wrapped in the sleeping shell of a petite, yet athletic young lady.

He searched her side table for a pen and paper. A portable radio next to a flower vase played soft music, a piano concerto—elegant, but unfamiliar. He spotted a pen and pad and pushed the radio out of the way, but it knocked against a flower vase, making a clinking noise. He cringed and swiveled toward Kelly.

Her chest heaved. Her hands clenched the side rails. She

scanned the room with glassy eyes, panting as she cried out. "Who's there?"

Nathan grasped her wrist. "It's just me," he said softly.

Her eyes locked on his, wide and terrified. "Mictar is here!"

Making a shushing sound, he lowered the bed rail and pried her fingers loose. "You were just dreaming."

"No!" She wagged her head hard. "I saw him! In the hospital!"

"Do you know where?"

She turned her head slowly toward the door. As a shaft of light split the darkness, her voice lowered to a whisper. "He's here."

A shadowy form stretched an arm into the room, then a body, movement so painstakingly deliberate, the intruder obviously didn't want anyone to hear him.

Nathan grabbed a flower vase and dumped it into a basin. Wielding it like a club, he crept toward the door, glancing between Kelly and the emerging figure. She yanked out her IV tube, swung her bare legs to the side, and dropped to the floor, blood dripping behind her.

The shadow, now fully in the room, halted. Nathan clenched his teeth. Kelly scooted to his side, holding her hospital gown closed in the back.

As the door swung shut, darkening the room, a low voice emanated from the black figure. "If it is a fight you seek, son of Solomon, I am more than capable of delivering it. In my current form, a glass vase will be a pitifully inadequate weapon. I suggest you give me what I want, and I will leave you in peace."

Nathan tightened his grip on the vase. Should he ask what he wanted? Even replying to a simple question seemed like giving in. Mictar was baiting him, and he didn't want to bite. "Just get out, Mictar. It's two against one. It only took a violin upside your head to beat you before, and you couldn't even take on Jack by yourself at the funeral."

Mictar's voice rose in a mock lament. "Alas! Poor Jack. He was a formidable foe … may he rest in peace." His tone lowered to a growl. "You can't take me by surprise this time, you fool. Your base use of that instrument proves that you have no respect for its true power. And now you have neither a violin nor a Quattro mirror to provide a coward's escape."

Nathan peered at Mictar's glowing eyes. The scarlet beacons seemed powerful and filled with malice. Yet, if he had enough power to overcome, why hadn't he attacked? Nathan set his feet and lifted the vase a bit higher. Maybe it would be okay to find out what this demon wanted. "Why are you here?"

"To finish my meal. If you will turn the girl over to me, I will consume what I merely tasted at the funeral and be on my way. But, in exchange, I will leave you with two precious gifts. I will tell you how to find your parents, and I will relieve you of that handicapped little whore."

Nathan flinched. Kelly gasped and backed away a step.

"Ah, yes," Mictar continued, his dark shape slowly expanding. "That word is profane in your ears, yet I wager that it rings true in your mind. Kelly Clark is not the paragon of virtue your father would want for your bride. She clings to you like a leech, because she is soiled by—"

"Just shut up!" Nathan shouted. "I don't want to hear it!"

The humanlike shadow swelled to twice its original size. "Oh, yes, you do. You want to know every lurid detail—who touched her and where and how many times. She is your dark shadow, and you will never find your parents while you entertain a harlot at your side."

"No!" Nathan slung the vase at Mictar. When it came within inches of his dark head, it stopped in midair. Nathan tried to reach for Kelly, but his arm locked in place. His head wouldn't even swivel. Everything in the room had frozen … except for Mictar.

The shadow continued to grow. His dark hands drew closer and closer. "I saved the last bit of my energy," Mictar said, "to perform one of my brother's favorite tricks, motor suspension of everything within my sight. Now I will take yours and the harlot's eyes, and I will need no more to fill Lucifer's engine."

A knock sounded at the door. "Nathan? Is everything okay?"

Tony's voice! Nathan tried to answer, but his jaw wouldn't move. His tongue cleaved to the roof of his mouth. A dark hand wrapped around his neck and clamped down, throttling his windpipe.

Another knock sounded, louder this time. "Nathan, the nurse says it's time for vitals."

Another hand draped his face. Sparks of electricity shot out, stinging his eyes.

"I'm coming in!" Light flashed around Mictar's hand, but Nathan still couldn't budge. Pain jolted his senses. His legs shook wildly as if he had been lifted off the floor and rattled like a baby's toy.

Suddenly, the darkness flew away. Mictar's body, a black human form with no face or clothes, zoomed past the nurse and crashed against the back wall. Tony, his arms flexed for action, charged.

Mictar jumped out of the way. Tony slammed into the wall and sprang back. He staggered for a moment, then slumped to the floor. Mictar grabbed the nurse from behind. As she kicked and screamed, he laid a fingerless hand over her eyes and pressed down. Sparks flew, and Mictar's body lightened to a dark gray, details tracing across his gaunt pale face and bony hands. His white hair appeared, slick and tied back in a ponytail. The lines of a silk shirt and denim trousers etched across the edges of his frame, completing the full-body portrait of the evil stalker.

Nathan tried to help, but his feet seemed stuck in clay. He slid one ahead, but the other stayed planted. Kelly hobbled toward the melee, not bothering to cinch her gown. She helped her father to his feet, while Mictar's body continued to clarify. The nurse sagged in his clutches, but he held on, light still pouring into his body from hers.

His legs finally loosening, Nathan stumbled ahead and thrust his arms forward. He rammed into Mictar, but, as if repelled by a force field, he bounced back and slammed against the floor. New jolts sizzled across his skin, painful, but short-lived. He looked up at the stalker's pulsing form, now complete and radiant. He dropped the nurse into a heap of limp arms and legs and kicked her body to the side.

Tony crouched as if ready to pounce again, but his movements had slowed. Wincing, he picked up an IV stand and drew it back, ready to strike.

Mictar tilted his head up and opened his mouth, but instead of speaking, he began to sing. His voice, a brilliant tenor, grew in volume, crooning a single note that seemed to thicken the air.

Covering his ears, Tony fell to his knees. Kelly stumbled back and pressed her body against the wall. A vase exploded, sending sharp bits of glass flying, and a long crack etched its way from one corner of the outer window to the other.

Fighting the piercing agony, Nathan rolled up to his knees and climbed to his feet, but the latest shock had stiffened his legs, and the noise seemed to be cracking his bones in half. He could barely move at all.

Mictar took a breath and sang again. This time, he belted out what seemed to be a tune, but it carried no real melody, just a hodgepodge of unrelated notes that further thickened the air. Red mist formed along the floor, an inch deep and swirling. As Mictar sang on, the fog rose to Nathan's shins, churning like a cauldron of blood. With the door partially open, the dense mist poured out, but it wasn't enough to keep the flood from rising.

A security guard yanked the door wide open. With a pistol drawn, he waded into the knee-high wall of red. Dr. Gordon and Clara followed, but when the sonic waves blasted across their bodies, the guard dropped his gun, and all three covered their ears, their faces wrinkling in pain.

The window shattered. Mist crawled up the wall and streamed through the jagged opening. The floor trembled. Cracking sounds popped all around. The entire room seemed to spin in a slow rotation, like the beginning of a carousel ride.

"Nathan!" Dr. Gordon shouted. "He's creating a dimensional hole! He'll take us all to his domain!"

"How can he? There's no mirror!"

"He can stretch one of the wounds that already exists."

The spin accelerated, drawing Nathan toward the window. "How do we stop him? He's electrified!"

Dr. Gordon staggered toward Nathan, fighting the centrifugal force, but he only managed two steps. "Neutralize his song!"

Nathan leaned toward the center of the room, but he kept sliding away. "How do I do that? I don't have my violin."

The outer wall collapsed. Fog rolled out and tumbled into the expanse, six stories above the ground. The floor buckled and pitched, knocking everyone to their seats. While Nathan pushed to keep from being spun out of the room, the nurse's body slid across the tile and plunged over the edge with the river of red mist.

His body too weak to fight, Nathan slipped toward the precipice. He latched on to the partitioning curtain and hung on with all his might.

Mictar took a quick breath and sang on.

The bed's side table bumped against Nathan's body. The pen fell, bounced off his shoulder, and disappeared in the fog.

Still hanging on to the curtain with one hand, he looked up at the wobbling table. The radio! With his free hand, he shook the supporting leg and caught the radio as it fell. With a quick twist, he turned the volume to maximum.

Now playing a Dvořák symphony, the radio blasted measure after measure of deep cellos and kettle drums. Trumpets blared. Cymbals crashed. Violins joined in and created a tsunami of music that swept through the room.

As if squeezed toward him, the mist swirled around Mictar's body. His song dampened. He coughed and gasped, but he managed to spew a string of obscenities before finally shouting, "You haven't seen the last of me, son of Solomon! When we meet again, I will have prepared my ultimate weapon!"

The mist covered his head and continued to coil around him until he looked like a tightly wound scarlet cocoon. The room's spin slowed, and the cocoon seemed to absorb the momentum. Mictar transformed into a red tornado and shrank as if slurped into an invisible void.

Seconds later, he vanished. Everything stopped shaking. Nathan turned off the radio and crawled up the sloping floor to where everyone else crouched. Dr. Gordon latched on to Nathan's wrist and heaved him up the rest of the way. His voice stayed calm and low. "Well done, Nathan."

Kelly threw her arms around Nathan from one side and Clara did the same from the other. "Don't ever leave me alone again," Kelly said, "not for a single minute."

Sirens wailed. An amplified voice barked from somewhere below, but Nathan paid no attention to the words. He just pulled his friends closer and enjoyed their embraces.

Tony, sitting on his haunches in front of Nathan, clenched his fist. "Now that's what I call taking out the trash!"

Carter House Girls Series
from Melody Carlson

Mix six teenage girls and one '60s fashion icon (retired, of course) in an old Victorian-era boarding home. Add boys and dating, a little high school angst, and throw in a Kate Spade bag or two ... and you've got the Carter House Girls, Melody Carlson's new chick lit series for young adults!

Mixed Bags
Book One

Softcover • ISBN: 978-0-310-71488-0

The Carter House residents arrive shortly before high school starts. With a crazy mix of personalities, pocketbooks, and problems, the girls get acquainted, sharing secrets and shoes and a variety of squabbles.

Stealing Bradford
Book Two

Softcover • ISBN: 978-0-310-71489-7

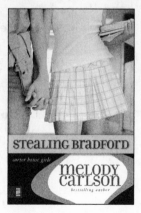

The Carter House girls are divided when two of them go after the same guy. Rhiannon and Taylor are at serious odds, and several girls get hurt before it's over.

Books 3-8 coming soon!

Pick up a copy today at your favorite bookstore!

ZONDERVAN®
.com

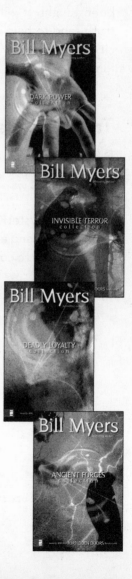

Echoes From the Edge

A New Trilogy from Bestselling Author Bryan Davis!

This fast-paced adventure fantasy trilogy starts with murder and leads teenagers Nathan and Kelly out of their once-familiar world as they struggle to find answers to the tragedy. A mysterious mirror with phantom images, a camera that takes pictures of things they can't see, and a violin that unlocks unrecognizable voices ... each enigma takes the teens further into an alternate universe where nothing is as it seems.

Eternity's Edge
Book Two

Softcover • ISBN: 978-0-310-71555-9

Nathan Shepherd thought his parents were murdered during an investigation, but it turns out his parents are alive after all! With the imminent collapse of the universe at hand, due to a state called Interfinity, Nathan sets out to find them. With Kelly at his side, he must balance his efforts between searching for his parents and saving the world. Will Nathan be reunited with his parents?

Book 2 coming October 2008!